The Sugar Merchant's Wife

The Sugar Merchant's Wife

Erica Brown

CANELO

First published in the United Kingdom in 2005 by Orion Publishing Group Ltd

This edition published in the United Kingdom in 2018 by

Canelo Digital Publishing Limited
57 Shepherds Lane
Beaconsfield, Bucks HP9 2DU
United Kingdom

A CIP catalogue record for this book is available from the British Library.

Print ISBN 978 1 78863 129 7
Ebook ISBN 978 1 78863 046 7

This book is a work of fiction. Names, characters, businesses, organizations, places and events are either the product of the author's imagination or are used fictitiously. Any resemblance to actual persons, living or dead, events or locales is entirely coincidental.

Look for more great books at www.canelo.co

Printed and bound in Great Britain by Clays Ltd, Elcograf S.p.A.

To my copy-editor Rachel for her unending patience.

Chapter One

For the rest of her life, Blanche would detest dandelions. She could cope with them in flower, glowing like bright suns in the grass, but not when they turned fluffy-white, their seeds tossed like tiny parasols on the breeze.

Dandelions grew profusely on the common opposite the Bedminster cottage that Blanche's husband had bought on a whim. His original idea had been to use it as extra quarters for the servants. However, Blanche and the children had fallen in love with its pretty rooms and twisted apple trees and given it a name – Little Paradise.

'It is not a playground,' Conrad had said.

Smiling bewitchingly, Blanche had argued that the children should have exercise in the open air.

Conrad had pointed out that they had a garden at Somerset Parade.

Blanche had convinced him that their children burned off more energy playing in the empty rooms of the cottage and running on the common opposite where sheep still grazed and the grass grew waist-high.

She won the argument, and for a while Little Paradise lived up to its name.

It was after Anne went picking dandelion clocks on the common that everything changed.

'They're just weeds,' Blanche remarked as she straightened the newly hand-painted sign that hung from the cottage gate.

Anne held her chin high and said to her mother loftily, 'I think them very fine and if I put them in a vase in my bedroom and leave them close to the window, they can fly away like fairies when the wind blows.'

Blanche laughed.

Clutching her bouquet, Anne crossed to the common to collect more.

Blanche craned her neck and smiled at the sight of Anne's straw bonnet bobbing up and down as she picked her dandelions.

Her attention was drawn to the sight of an old woman struggling along the path that dissected the common into two uneven halves – a street seller on her way home judging by the tray she carried.

'Lemonade, my dear,' Blanche heard her calling to Anne. 'Only a penny a glass. I have just enough left for a slip of a girl.'

'Damn this blasted kite!'

Blanche tore her gaze away from the woman and directed it at her son. 'Wash your mouth out, Maximillian Heinkel!'

Max pulled a face. 'It's enough to make a man swear,' he grumbled.

'You're not a man,' his mother said in a chastising manner, then wistfully to herself, 'Please stay a child for a little longer.'

Accompanied by his younger brother and sister, Max was attempting to fly a kite. The wind was less than exuberant. Like a dead bird it trailed behind them, bumping and shuddering through the grass.

'I think it's time we went home,' called Blanche.

'I bet it isn't,' said Max, who was always prepared to hold an opinion on anything.

A church clock struck four.

'I think I won the bet. Now let's see how much you owe me,' she said, holding her finger to her chin and looking as though she really was calculating a figure.

Max groaned despairingly. 'Already? We haven't got it flying properly. Couldn't we stay a little longer?'

'There's not enough breeze and there's nothing to be done about it today,' his mother called back as she shut the cottage gate.

Resigned that kite-flying was over for the day, the children obeyed, though Max dragged his feet. Blanche smiled to herself. Conrad called him defiant. She preferred to think that he was more independent than the others. He didn't get dejected as they did when given orders he had no wish to obey, but contemplative, as though he were considering how best to achieve his desire without appearing belligerent.

Tucking the kite behind his back, he came to his mother's side. She eyed him lovingly. She shouldn't have favourites, but sometimes she couldn't resist being too proud of him. She tried not to show it too much in front of Conrad. Good man that he was, he had married her knowing that she was expecting a child that wasn't his. At the time she had thought that Nelson Strong was his father, but could not tell her new husband.

Nelson had made love to her before she knew he was her half-brother. The truth of that still made her tremble. It was only when Max was born two months before he should have been, that the truth struck her and she remembered a night spent with another man...

Behind his intelligent eyes, Max's brain clearly ticked like a clock. He was already planning his next day of kite-flying. 'I'm back at school soon and the weekends are not always the best time if the weather's bad. But school breaks up in four weeks. There will be days then. What do you think, Mother?'

His adamant expression struck a chord in her heart. Blanche smoothed the dark-blond hair where sun-lightened streaks fell over his brow. 'I think that this is not the best place for flying kites. It's too close to the river. We shall take the carriage to Durdham Down when we next go kite-flying. The wind is brisker up there.'

Max brightened. 'Good.'

'I'm thirsty,' said Lucy, her youngest, slipping her hand into that of her mother. Bright blue eyes shone like moons in her baby round face.

'I'm sorry, but the pump at the cottage needs mending. You'll have to wait until you get home,' said Blanche.

'I'm not thirsty,' said Anne, addressing Lucy in a childish effort to invoke jealousy. 'I bought some lemonade from that old woman back there.'

'Can I have one, Mother?' Lucy asked, adopting the plaintive voice that usually got her what she wanted.

'Me too,' added Adeline.

Blanche sighed. After all, it was a long walk back. 'I suppose so.' She turned to where the old woman had been with her stone jug and tin cups, but she was gone. A cloud of dandelion clocks flew around in a sudden gust of breeze in the place where she'd been.

Blanche sighed. 'I'm afraid we'll have to stay thirsty.'

'Not me,' said Anne, 'I'm not thirsty at all,' and she laughed and danced along the edge of the common and most of the way home.

It was the most wonderful sound to her mother's ears, a sound she would treasure for ever. It was the last time for everything.

—

Blanche stared at the bedraggled stalks wilting in a vase on the window sill. Just days ago they'd been growing in the sleek grass in front of Little Paradise. Anne had been well. Now she was very sick and, like the flowers, was dying.

'If I lose Anne, I swear to God I will never, ever bear another child,' Blanche murmured.

Conrad was standing behind her, his hand on her shoulder. She felt him tense and knew he would take her bitter words to heart. It couldn't be helped. Anne's face was deathly white, her skin shiny with sweat and the room stunk as a result of the continual emptying of her bowels.

Conrad was a good man and Blanche had never lacked for anything, but she'd give it all now, including her own life, for her daughter to recover.

'Shall I get Mary to bring you some tea and something to eat?' asked Conrad solicitously.

Blanche shook her head. Although her mouth was dry and her stomach ached with hunger, suffering in such a little way seemed inconsequential and in a strange way, just. Such discomfort was trivial in comparison to what Anne was going through.

Blanche stroked her daughter's damp hair away from her brow. Anne had been given laudanum but she still grimaced with pain though had ceased screaming. Seeing her knees drawn up to her stomach and her body convulsing in agony had been the worse experience – so far.

'It won't be long,' the doctor said softly. 'Perhaps just before dawn.'

'We can only pray,' said Conrad. 'Her life is in God's hands now.'

Blanche kept her gaze fixed on her child. 'She's going to die,' she said, her body cold as ice. 'God is deaf.'

Her husband removed his hands from her shoulders and saw the doctor out. On his return he tried to convince her to take some refreshment and leave everything to the nurse.

Blanche allowed herself to be persuaded and swallowed a cup of tea and a morsel of food. When a church clock struck midnight, she awoke to find that she'd fallen asleep on a settee in the drawing room.

Conrad slept across from her in a chair. She didn't wake him but swiftly refreshed herself and went back to her daughter's room. The nurse had straightened the bedclothes and placed a bunch of lavender in a vase at the side of the bed. The dandelion stalks had been thrown away.

Blanche sent the nurse away. 'This is my child,' she insisted. 'I will take over now.'

The room was warm and dark by virtue of the heavy green damask curtains covering the windows. The smell of lavender filled the air, bunches of it hanging before the open windows. More lavender was scattered over the floor, the bluish-purple buds releasing their heady aroma with every soft footfall. It was said that it helped keep the 'miasma' at bay. She'd remembered it from the Reverend Strong's room when she'd been in service at Marstone Court, the Strong family's mansion outside Bristol.

The Reverend had been dying of a lung disease, the congestion building and necessitating him being turned in his bed so he could breathe. She also remembered Tom and the Reverend's good deed. He had adopted Tom, snatching him from a life on the streets, perhaps to end up dead or destitute, hung or transported to Botany Bay. Ten years had passed, yet it came back to haunt her even now.

She hoped the lavender would do more for her little one; anything she could do, she would do. The past had no bearing here. The present, and Anne having a future were all that mattered.

She'd eaten little and the sleep she'd just had was not enough to make up for the days and nights of sitting beside her child's bed. Hours of patting the fevered head with cold compresses and getting her to sip a little liquid finally took their toll. Eyelids heavy, she sank her head onto her folded arms at the side of the bed and slept deeply. Not until daybreak pierced through the curtains did she wake with a start and know immediately that death had come with the rising sun. Her child was still and terribly silent. The rasping chest and the laboured breath were gone.

She couldn't cry. That was the strangest thing about it. The fear and worry of the past few days seemed to have soaked up her tears and her voice. There was only a great emptiness inside where her heart used to be.

Even when the bedroom door opened and Conrad entered, she still sat holding her child's hand.

He touched her shoulder, a gesture meant to convey both strength and sympathy, and that he felt exactly the same. At last he managed to say, 'She is with God now.'

'God!' Blanche shook her head so vehemently that a few dark tresses fell from a swiftly disintegrating chignon. 'I don't want her to be with God. I want her to be here with me.'

Her body shook with sobs. The world would never be the same again. The laughter was gone.

-

The smell was the first sign that death stalked the mean houses around Lewins Mead where whole families shared one room.

Behind the ramshackle door of her one-roomed home in Cabot's Yard, Edith had been battling it for days.

'It's the stink that makes people sick,' she said, and took another sip of the dark, brown beer they called porter. Beer helped her forget that she was poor and hungry, that Lizzie, her youngest child was crying with pain and that her husband was away at sea and only returned to fill her belly with another baby.

Molly from downstairs poked her head round the door. 'Mrs Carter's youngest is gone. Died in the night. Not even a year old, bless 'im.'

Edith sighed. 'Not surprising in this bloody place. I lost four of mine before they were five. How many 'ave you lost?'

Molly shrugged. 'Can't remember.'

'How's the little 'un?'

Edith had heard Molly's newborn crying in the night, in terrible pain by the sound of it.

Molly shrugged again. 'I gave the mite some water to cool her down. Ain't got no milk left,' she said, and patted the flatness where her breasts should be. 'What you doin' with them flowers, Edith?' She nodded at the mean bunch of lavender hanging at the window.

'Helps keep the cholera at bay. It's good for sickness. Used to do this out at Marstone Court when I was in service for the Strong family and looking after the old Reverend Strong. Nice man he was.'

'Could afford to be nice with all that money,' Molly remarked.

'No, he was really nice. Even adopted a street urchin and treated him like a son. Tom, his name was. Tom Strong.'

Molly simpered. 'Sounds as though you were sweet on him.'

Edith felt herself blushing. 'He was 'andsome and brave. But there was nothing between us. He liked my friend Blanche best.' She sighed. 'She married someone else.'

'Do you ever see her?'

Edith paused. She'd been about to lie, but changed her mind. 'I've seen her a few times with her children and her husband. She was dressed beautiful and got out of a carriage.'

Molly picked at her teeth. 'Did yer make yerself known?'

Edith was dismissive. 'Course not! Look at me...' She indicated her patched skirt and the sack on which she'd sewed strings to make it an apron. 'What would she think? The last time she saw me I was wearing the livery of the Strong family. I looked grand as could be, just as I should for service in the household of sugar merchants. Now I looks more like I climbed out of a coal hole or a rag and bone yard.'

Molly swiped at the flies, stragglers of those that buzzed in a black cloud around the privy.

'This place stinks,' said Freddie, Edith's eldest, wrinkling his nose so that his freckles seemed to bump into each other.

Edith made a wry face and Freddie made one back.

Cocky little sod, she thought and smiled.

'Should 'ave got more of that stuff,' Freddie added.

'I knows that,' she muttered, reached up and crushed the lavender in her palm. Crushing the blooms released the perfume, she remembered.

'You ain't got enough,' Molly remarked.

'Ain't never got enough,' Edith grumbled.

Over on the bed, Lizzie was still groaning, her knees drawn up with pain towards her stomach.

Molly disappeared and most of the flies went with her.

Edith tried to quell her fear as she mopped her daughter's brow. Lizzie lay on a trestle bed made from tea chests in the corner. Her eyes were closed, her face was hot and she muttered deliriously as she heaved her thin little body from side to side.

Edith reached for the empty water pail in which she'd been dipping the cloth and swung it towards Freddie. 'Yer sister needs more water, Fred.'

For once, he didn't bother to argue. Edith guessed he was as worried as she, but they weren't the sort of family that shared emotions. Only tough people survived in their world.

Freddie bolted off to the cast-iron pump that was set in a stone arch just across the alley. When he got back, the bucket was only half full.

'Well, that ain't much,' she said, her red knuckles resting on her hips.

'It's them,' he exclaimed, water sloshing from the bucket as he slammed it down on the floor. 'Beannie and 'is mates. They're looking for a roller. Wanted me to come along with 'em.'

Edith eyed him accusingly. 'Freddie Beasley, you ain't mixing with bad company again, are you?'

Freddie wiped the snot from his nose. 'Course not. Said I 'ad more important things to do, so they pushed me about and called me a sissy.'

'Little sods! Don't they know yer sister's ill?'

Freddie picked up a stick of firewood, bent down and prodded it into a mouse hole causing plaster the size of a dinner plate to fall to the floor. 'Said 'is little brother died last week, and Ernie said, "So what? My father died yesterday." And Tim said that he'd lost three sisters and that was more than anybody!'

Edith barely stopped mopping Lizzie's brow. 'Comes to something when kids are counting up their dead as though it was a bloody game. So who are they going to roll?' She hoped it was the landlord. She didn't like him at all. He'd told every woman in the lane that they could work off their rent if they wanted to. One or two had, then found he still charged them the same rent anyway. But she was disappointed.

'The doctor,' Freddie said, as half his stick disappeared into the mouse hole and another piece of plaster crashed to the floor.

Edith left what she was doing and grabbed his shoulder. 'There's a doctor round 'ere? You never told me that before.'

Freddie's eyes shone like beacons in his dirty face. 'He comes round nosing into other people's business, that's what Beannie said.'

Edith flew to the window. Across the alley, where jutting upper storeys dimmed any light that chanced to get through, three children squatted around a stream of water that ran out from the wall of one of the hovels before disappearing into a barrel-vaulted culvert. The culvert was small and old. Water had long ago washed away the mortar that had held it together. Some of its bricks had fallen from its roof and the children were using these to damn the flow of water, which was gradually spreading across the dusty ground.

Edith poked her head out of the window as the sound of footsteps echoed from the alley that led to Cabot's Yard. The man was in the early years of middle age, was soberly dressed and carried a black leather valise. Edith watched as he sauntered slowly along, thoughtfully eyeing the slit of sky above the narrow lane. From there he glanced to the water pump, the privy and to where the three urchins were playing with the dirty water.

The children's heads bunched together as they tittered like sparrows amongst themselves. The moment he averted his gaze, they were on him fast. He looked astounded, coming to a standstill as they pressed around him like dancers, their grubby hands in the pockets of his coat and waistcoat as they demanded pennies.

'A farthing'll do, mister.'

'Ha'penny'll be better.'

The smallest urchin sidled around the back of the man, his quick little eyes darting between his two friends who were pressed up close to their victim.

Thinking to do so might make her look respectable, Edith whipped off her apron before opening the front door. 'This way, doctor!'

Three filthy, pox-marked faces threw her hateful glares as she strode across the road. 'I think you've been looking for me,' she said, taking the man's arm and hustling him towards her own front door.

When attacked by the urchins he'd looked astounded. Manhandled by Edith he looked terrified. 'Madam, I—'

'I'm not a tart! Don't you go thinking that. I've just done you a good turn. Now let's see that you've still got your watch,' she said, throwing a meaningful glance at the three rapscallions who brooded in the shadows across the lane.

'Ah!' he said, as he took on her meaning. He fumbled in the pockets of his waistcoat and sighing, withdrew a silver chain complete with its watch.

'Good.'

Safe in her own house, she set him down in a chair, put the kettle on the hob, and asked, 'Is that right yer a doctor?'

'Yes,' he said, his eyelids flickering as he took in the desperation of his surroundings.

'So what you doing round 'ere then?'

'I'm interested in cholera.'

Freddie stopped stirring the mice up and turned to stare at their visitor.

'You'll find plenty of it in Lewins Mead,' said Edith, her voice filled with worry.

Lizzie started to scream.

'My daughter's sick,' she said quickly, judging it the right time to invoke some gratitude in the man. 'Could you help her? I haven't got any money...'

Without speaking, he went to where Lizzie was bathed in sweat and the cloying stink of sickness. His eyes filled with pity as he bent over the bed, hesitantly at first, then more quickly as his interest grew. 'How long has she been like this?' he asked.

'Since yesterday.'

Edith brushed her own sweaty hair away from her brow. Her head felt hot. Was she getting sick too?

'Has she eaten?' he asked.

'No.'

'Has she drunk anything?'

Edith pointed to the bucket. 'Just water – gallons of it.'

'It's to be expected. She's very dehydrated.' The doctor glanced at the bucket, his eyes narrowing with the intensity of his frown. 'I suppose you got this from the pump opposite.'

'Yes.'

'Boil your water. Thoroughly cook all food. Don't leave it out for flies to walk over it. Keep everything covered. And you must get your water from one of the pumps close to St Augustine's Quay.'

Edith spread her hands lamely. 'What difference will that make? It's all water, ain't it?'

The doctor shook his head. 'No. The water down on the quay comes from Jacob's Well, an underground spring on St Michael's Hill. It's pure and uncontaminated.'

'Will Lizzie live?' Edith asked, her face pinched with worry.

There's a chance if you follow my instructions. You must replace the fluid she's lost, but *only* use water from St Augustine's Quay and boil it, to be on the safe side.'

She turned to tell Freddie to go to St Augustine's Quay for water, but only his stick remained on the floor – much to the relief of the mice no doubt. Her son and her wooden pail had both disappeared.

The doctor stood. 'I have to go now.'

Concerned for his safety, she said, 'I'll come with you.'

She walked with him as far as St Augustine's Quay where they both watched as Freddie filled his pail from the Quay Pipe. It was more crowded around the quay, which made Edith feel strangely vulnerable, awkward and ragged. She began to turn back. 'You'll be safe now,' she said.

'Many thanks for your kind attention,' he said, tipping his hat.

'Don't do that,' she said, looking embarrassed, and left him there, perplexed but resigned to her behaviour. She couldn't possibly tell him that quality gentlemen only tipped their hats to trollops and she certainly wasn't one of those.

The traffic that circled St Augustine's Bridge came to a standstill, giving her plenty of time to cross. There were wagons, gigs, landaus and growlers, men pushing barrows and huge shire horses pulling brewery drays. If a horse hadn't lifted its tail and deposited its droppings only inches from her feet, she wouldn't have noticed the occupant of the grand carriage that had come to a sudden stop beside her.

'Blanche!' She said it without thinking of the consequences. Suddenly she wanted to speak to her old friend, no matter how ragged she looked and how grand Blanche was. 'Blanche,' she called again.

Her old friend stared straight ahead, her expression unsmiling and her lips pressed tightly together.

'Blanche,' she cried more frantically and waved both arms.

Her cry was lost in the noise of the city, the shouts of costermongers, steam hammers and hooves and wheels as the traffic moved forward.

'Stuck-up cow,' she yelled once she'd crossed to the quay.

'Were you shoutin' to somebody in that posh carriage?' asked Freddie. 'Did you know them?'

'Yeah, in another place and another time,' said Edith and grimaced. 'Used to be a friend.' She shrugged. 'Water under the bridge.'

Chapter Two

'Never go back. Someone told me that once,' said Tom Strong as he tipped molasses into a warmed tot of West Indian rum. His brow furrowed with sudden concern. 'I have to say that my instincts tell me I shouldn't.'

'Never mind instincts, Tom,' said Nelson Strong, his cousin by adoption. 'What about reality? What about business in an expanding *empire* — I mean the *family* as well as the country?'

'That's reality too,' said Tom, nodding towards the door of the inn, which opened frequently to expose a view of the quay where ships loaded and unloaded cargoes from all over the world. It was sleeting with rain, but the misty wetness did nothing to diminish the city's potential or Tom's enthusiasm. 'Boston bustles with the youthful vitality of a stripling son out to prove himself. Why should I want to go back to the old country?'

Nelson sprawled back rakishly against the broad width of a New England settle, a blond wave of hair skimming his high, pale forehead. 'America may need to prove itself, but you do not, Tom. You've done well. I've heard your praises sung by every merchant from Charleston to New York, and in Boston...' He waved his hand like a triumphant banner. 'You're an important man here, but what about Bristol? Your family misses you.'

Tom's eyes darted back to Nelson's face. 'I'm not really a Strong like you are, Nelson. We're at two ends of a spectrum. You're Sir Emmanuel's son and heir to a sugar fortune. I was born on the streets and my mother was a whore.'

Nelson laughed. 'At least she did what she did to stay alive. There are many women of high birth who do it purely for pleasure.

Uncle Jeb adopted you and accepted you as his son. That's good enough for me.'

Tom shook his head. Nelson sometimes exasperated him with his simplistic view of life. Tom took things more seriously. 'I have a shipping company to run. I owe it to my father-in-law. He's become bitter enough since my wife died without me upping anchor and sailing away.' He let his gaze drift around the quayside coffee house where a cup of best Brazilian cost just a few cents and the steam from boiled blue crabs loitered temptingly among the rafters. This had indeed seemed like home before Margaret had died. He'd convinced himself that the feeling of loneliness would become less painful with the passing of time and that his father-in-law still needed him.

Nelson persisted. 'Will you at least let me tell you our plans?'

Tom swallowed a mouthful of sugared rum, which warmed his throat and made his head swim. 'If you must.'

Nelson sprinkled a little opiate on his coffee before he continued. 'I still have my bad habits,' he said on seeing a hint of disapproval on Tom's face.

Tom managed a weak smile. He didn't approve, but it was Nelson's problem, not his.

Nelson took a sip of coffee and a deep breath. 'We want to modernize the fleet. The days of sailing ships are fast drawing to a close. Steamships take only half the time to get to Barbados and are not at the mercy of wind and tide. We need someone who knows about shipping to oversee the changeover, and before you ask why not me, I know little about ships.' He grinned suddenly. 'Come to that, I know precious little about sugar cane except that it grows from the ground in hot climates.' His sudden burst of laughter attracted curious looks. 'Though I certainly know how to spend the wealth it generates.'

'An expensive habit,' Tom remarked, as Nelson took another sip of the heady brew.

Nelson shrugged and sighed heavily. 'Can't seem to do without it nowadays.' He laughed again, but without mirth, his amusement freezing to a smile. 'It's being a married man. It drives some men to drink – like my father. In my case,' he shrugged, 'I don't touch alcohol. Father drinks enough for us both! Opium helps me cope with marriage to a wealthy heiress with breasts like pancakes and a belly like unbaked bread. In my head,' he added after taking another sip, 'I am surrounded by bare brown breasts and hips that sway like a ship on the sea. I can't be hung for merely thinking adultery, Tom. So I shall go on sinning, at least in my mind.'

Tom suppressed the urge to comment that Nelson had not changed. Instead he remarked, 'So your father is not too well?'

Nelson shook his head. 'Brandy, rum and port have done their share of harm to his body. I'm not sure what he's got in his mind.' He frowned as he leaned forward, the vagueness slipping from his eyes as he fought to concentrate on what he was trying to say. 'I fancy,' he said at last, 'that father feels he is running out of time and that his fortune should run out with him. His extravagance has got worse since my stepmother died. First he wasted money on understandable things – women, horses, drink and enormous gambling debts. But now...' He shook his head helplessly. 'One trip to that place at Brighton built by John Nash, and that was it. Apparently he's also seen some book compiled by Napoleon about his stay in Egypt. There are pictures of tomb paintings, strange statuary and all manner of grave goods depicted in it. Since then, Marstone Court has been full of brick layers, stonemasons, carpenters and decorators, leaving sphinxes and hawk-headed gods in their wake.'

Tom grinned at the image. 'A shrine to wealth and importance and perhaps the hope of immortality.'

'Given half the chance, I'm sure he'd have his sarcophagus placed in the knave at Bristol Cathedral.'

Tom laughed. 'And all shall come to worship...'

'The god Mammon,' grumbled Nelson, then added, 'I'm sorry about your wife, Tom.'

'Thank you.'

'I suppose you miss her?'

Tom paused and looked intently into Nelson's eyes, as if he could read every thought flickering through his mind. 'I admit to missing her, but don't say there's no point me staying here. Don't ask whether I'm lonely or do I have another woman. The answer to each question is no.'

'It's been a long time, Tom. I know things happened that you'd prefer to forget – like Uncle Jeb's ship the *Miriam Strong* going up in flames and the captain being killed. If it's any consolation, I heard the fellow who did it, Reuben Trout, was found with his head smashed in.'

Tom pretended to be surprised. 'Is that so?'

'Apparently he was set about by unknown assailants. The police didn't pursue the matter. You know what it's like around the docks – tough men one and all and no one knows anything. Quite frankly, from what I remember at the time, whoever killed him deserved a medal.'

Tom's expression was implacable. Inside he felt an enormous sense of relief. Nelson could not know it, but he'd finally resolved one of the reasons Tom had never gone back to England.

As Nelson rattled on, Tom returned to the memory of that night ten years ago… Reuben Trout, a nasty piece of work, had killed a known prostitute named Sally Ward whom Tom had befriended and helped. Trout was also suspected of arson aboard the *Miriam Strong*, the Reverend Strong's charitable training ship for young orphans. It was well known in the dockside taverns and fighting parlours that Tom had been searching for him, bent on revenge, the night he was killed although Tom knew who was really responsible… He was glad to hear that the case was closed.

Nelson's voice brought him down to earth. 'Tom, are you listening to me?'

'I'm sorry. What was that you were saying?'

'There's been a lot of cholera in Bristol of late. You knew we lost George and Arthur?'

Tom nodded, remembering Nelson's two young half-brothers. 'Horatia wrote to me.'

Nelson smiled. 'My sister writes to you regularly?'

'Less frequently during my marriage. Her letters have increased of late, especially with regard to the proposed shipping venture.'

Nelson smiled. 'I'm not surprised. She still cares for you.'

Tom sidestepped the comment and all that it implied. 'So there's been a lot of cholera?'

'An outbreak almost every year for the past ten or more. Lots of people have died. You probably knew some of them and would be saddened at their plight.'

'Would I, indeed?'

'The city's been hit very badly. It's the children dying that affects people the most. Some women fade into a kind of melancholic decline that leads to their death, or at least to them being interred in an asylum. Blanche Heinkel has been very low, so I hear.'

Tom could hear his heart beating above the silence. A vision of dark hair, grey eyes and coffee-coloured complexion danced into his mind.

'They say she's a changed woman. She hardly ventures out except to brood in a funny little cottage that Conrad owns. He's worried about her and will go to any length to cure her.' Nelson shrugged. 'And if all else fails…' He swigged back the last of the opium.

Tom felt the colour draining from his face. It was Blanche who had haunted his dreams even as he lay in bed beside his wife. He noticed that Nelson's eyes were beginning to swim in his head and his speech was sounding slurred.

'You loved her, didn't you, Tom? I love her too,' whined Nelson, his head slowly sinking onto the table.

Tom resisted the urge to say that he'd no business loving her, certainly not as a lover, but the past was past and Nelson's eyes were flickering shut.

'I have a meeting to attend,' Tom said, rising from his seat.

'Think about it,' Nelson managed to say.

Tom slipped the owner a few dollars to get Nelson back to his hotel. He thought it unlikely they would meet again, unless something unforeseen occurred.

Alistair Carew was a ruddy-faced man in his sixties with a shock of white hair and a well-developed paunch. He was leaning against a very fine fireplace in the room where he directed the business of the shipping company he'd built from nothing. His roots were in Scotland, but he was every inch an American with an enormous appetite for food, drink and spending money.

His nephew, Arbroath McKenny, his sister's boy, was also in the room. Arbroath and Alistair were incredibly alike. Arbroath's hair was dark, but a fledgling paunch pushed at the buttons of his waistcoat.

'Dreadful weather,' said Tom, shaking the rain from his coat before passing it to the butler who swiftly vanished.

'And more rain to come, so I hear,' said Arbroath.

Alistair took a puff of his cigar and said nothing.

Arbroath's presence alone was enough for Tom to sense that serious discussions had occurred in his absence. Alistair's silence, and the fact that he didn't look Tom straight in the eye, confirmed it.

Tom stood with his legs slightly apart, his hands clasped behind his back, ready to deal with whatever might come. He was purposely terse. 'So! This is a serious matter.'

Arbroath looked surprised. 'How do you know that?'

'In this weather, it has to be serious, especially where you're concerned, Arbroath. I thought you preferred the more clement weather of Georgia?'

Arbroath visibly coloured, though he thrust out his chin as though willing to take a blow on it if need be.

Alistair cleared his throat before Tom and Arbroath could trade more insults. 'Gentlemen.'

Tom looked at his face. There were dark rings beneath his eyes that hadn't been there a few months ago. He'd also lost a little weight, not from around his waistline where less would have made him look healthier, but from his face. He looked sad and almost as though he was melting away. Losing his daughter Margaret had changed him.

'I have decided to hand over my share of the company to Arbroath.'

Tom felt his temper rising, but kept his voice steady. 'You mean the controlling share?'

Alistair nodded. 'That is correct.'

'Including Margaret's share?'

Embarrassed, Alistair looked away. 'I wish to keep control within the family.'

'It doesn't make sense to leave it in the control of outsiders,' said Arbroath.

Tom felt empty and angry that he should be dismissed so carelessly. He also wanted to flatten Arbroath's smug expression. Not only had he lost his wife, but now his livelihood.

Alistair tucked his thumbs in the armholes of his waistcoat. 'Bearing in mind that you do own a number of shares, there's no reason why you can't stay a company executive and, of course, you will still own the *Demerara Queen*.'

'Of course I will,' said Tom through clenched teeth. 'She's my ship.'

'I'm sorry, Tom,' said Alistair, his voice as worn-out as his health. 'I don't want the responsibility of it any more.' He sank into his chair, his head in his hands. 'My pride in the business died with my daughter. Cruel as it may sound, I really do not want anything more to do with you. You were Margaret's husband and it upsets me to be reminded of her passing. I'm sorry, Tom. Everything is left to the family.'

'But we had plans,' Tom protested. 'New routes, new cargoes and new steamships.'

Arbroath looked suitably smug. 'I intend running the business in the way it's always been run. Our fortune was made using sailing ships and that is the way it will stay.'

Tom was flabbergasted. 'With no regard for progress?'

'If you mean steamships, certainly not. It's far too risky.'

Tom shook his head.

'Let's not part as bad friends,' said Arbroath.

'What makes you think we're parting company?'

Arbroath showed no sign of embarrassment. 'We wouldn't get on, Tom. You know it, and so do I. Come. Will you shake my hand?'

Tom stared at the proffered hand, the neatly clipped and incredibly clean fingernails, and the lily-white skin that had hardly tied a bootlace, let alone pulled on a rope. He felt the greatest repugnance for Arbroath, but only pity for his father-in-law.

'So it's finally come,' he said without taking Arbroath's hand, his angry gaze fixed on Alistair.

'Perhaps if there had been a child...' Alistair began.

He sounded pitiful and Tom suddenly found himself hating him. He never had before. He'd tolerated him as a business associate, though never as a friend. All the same, he'd considered him an honourable man. That particular illusion was now shattered.

Tom held his head high as he made for the door. 'Goodbye, Alistair.'

The slammed door curtailed their farewells. There's nothing more to say, thought Tom as he headed for his carriage. He'd been squeezed out as the result of an old man's grief and a younger man's ambition. Boston had suddenly lost its appeal. Old friends and an older city beckoned. For the first time in years he wanted to return to England.

Chapter Three

'My wife used to be a warm and wonderful woman. Now she is distant. Sometimes she wanders the rooms of the cottage where she took the children on the last day our daughter enjoyed good health. I fear following her there because she reacts so angrily if I do. My eldest son has followed her and told me this. He says she also sits in the window seat and stares across at the common where our daughter picked flowers that day.' Conrad Heinkel rested his elbows on his knees and buried his face in his hands. 'I don't know what to do,' he said to the doctor who'd been recommended to him as knowledgeable in the matter of melancholia. He'd described his wife's behaviour in great detail and now awaited an answer.

Dr Walters had a large head and gaunt features. His jowls settled against his collar like slabs of mutton on a plate. He reminded Conrad of an elderly bloodhound he'd once owned. He would have mentioned the fact if the occasion had not been so serious.

The doctor took a deep breath as medical men are inclined to do after a period of deep thought. 'Before matters get much worse, I think I should admit her to the institution for observation.'

Conrad shook his head. 'I can't allow that.'

Dr Walters sighed. Not all husbands were as tolerant as Conrad Heinkel, in fact, some were keen to act even when their wives' conditions were far less than serious. 'Your main concern seems to be her wandering the streets and spending time at this cottage, the last place she visited with your daughter.'

Conrad nodded. 'That is correct, though she only wanders the streets to get to the cottage. Sometimes she takes the pony and trap.' The doctor interlaced his fingers thoughtfully and paced the room.

'Might I suggest you stop her from visiting the cottage by locking her in a secure room and not let her out until she comes to her senses?'

Conrad was astonished. 'I can't possibly do that! She's not mad, just ill.'

The doctor tutted and shook his head. 'You may have to. The alternatives are too terrible to contemplate.'

'And what are those alternatives?'

Dr Walters pursed his lips and chose his words carefully. 'Your first option is to let things go on as they are and chance her staying the same or that a miracle occurs. However, if left untreated, it is just as likely that she will slip further into melancholy until she reaches a point where life has no attraction for her. If things are left to get to that stage, there is a chance she will do the unspeakable – and take her own life.'

'God, no!' Conrad exclaimed, shaking his head. 'And the second alternative?'

'If you give her into my care, I will treat her with all the latest techniques available and, of course, she will be in the company of other such poor souls. I am of the opinion that the sight of such unfortunates can be very beneficial.'

Conrad looked at him in shock. 'Are you saying that she would be incarcerated with the insane?'

The doctor's lips spread in a condescending smile. 'I am a great believer in shock treatment. It could make her realize just how lucky she is that she still has three children and a very comfortable life.'

'The lowest of men and the meanest of hovels would be better than that,' Conrad managed, his face red with indignation.

'Quite so,' said the doctor, sensing his big fee for a newly incarcerated patient was not forthcoming. 'Now let me see,' he went on, throwing his head back, his gaze directed towards the ceiling. 'There could be a third alternative. I understand your daughter died from cholera?'

Conrad nodded. 'Yes.'

'Focusing your wife's mind on the source of her sadness might help. I met a doctor lately who has some new-fangled ideas on how to combat cholera. He's caught it twice himself, so I believe. The illness may have addled his brain or his ideas on defeating it may be very sound, but everything's worth a try, don't you think?'

Conrad had a terrible urge to shake the man to death if he didn't get to the point. 'I trust he succeeds. But how would this benefit my wife?'

'He's giving a talk somewhere and asking for support from people of influence and the Corporation in particular, and I have to say you may find the subject matter rather dull. He's going to be talking about the building of a new sewerage system and disinfecting those areas of the city where the disease is most prevalent. Perhaps news of such progressive ideas might lift your wife's spirits.'

Conrad eyed him with renewed interest. 'Who is this man?'

Dr Walters reached for his hat. 'Can't quite recall the name, but I will get it to you.'

Conrad felt better as he escorted the doctor back through the Heinkel Sugar Refinery. With renewed confidence, he proudly pointed out items of interest. His business had been built up in the short time since he had come to this country from Germany and he was now a leading light in the Guild of Master Sugar Bakers, most of whom were also German. Clouds of steam rose from the boiling pans in the char house. The men feeding the hopper that tipped charcoal into the filter beds were naked to the waist, their flesh red and gleaming with sweat. The air was hot and sticky with sweetness.

'Damned hot,' said the doctor, wiping his brow with his handkerchief. 'Do let me know as soon as possible what your intentions are regarding your wife. Space at the asylum is limited.'

Conrad pursed his lips and nodded at the beer boys who crouched in a line, waiting for the order to fetch liquid refreshment for the sweating labourers. 'I have already decided. I would like to find out more about this doctor and his plans,' he said.

'If that is your wish, I will send you the details.'

'Thank you.'

For a while after the doctor had left, Conrad stared at the wall, unable to accept that putting his wife away would cure anything. She didn't rant and rave as a lunatic; she was merely withdrawn. In time, he told himself, she would stop getting up at the crack of dawn, stop spending afternoons at Little Paradise and return to being the woman he'd married. Getting her to attend a meeting and listen to what these people had to say might be the first step to her recovery. At least, that's what he hoped. Falling to his knees in the privacy of his office, he prayed to God for help – 'For her sake more than for mine.' Then he got up, blew his nose and tried to concentrate on his business.

–

A blind beggar sat against the railings outside the offices of Septimus Monk, the most powerful lawyer in the city. He sat very still and although the tin cup before him held few coins, he made no attempt to beg for more.

Inside, Horatia Strong rested her back against a tasselled cushion in a velvet-covered chair and lost no time in getting straight to the point. 'I want you to ensure that my name is not linked with this venture, that you set up this company on my behalf and that no one, not even my family, knows of my involvement. Is that clear?'

Septimus Monk eyed her warily.

She guessed what he was thinking. 'You expected one of my brothers, I presume.'

'I do not usually deal with the kind of businesses women are involved in. I only deal with large corporate matters of an international nature. I do not deal with shops, stables or rented properties unless the latter are very large concerns – and certainly not drapers and haberdashers.' His disdain was obvious.

Horatia never moved a muscle. 'I would not have come to you unless my business was of an international nature and large enough to satisfy the vanity and pay the vast commission of a man like you.'

Monk raised his eyebrows. Her directness surprised him, just as she'd intended. He'd stood proxy for many businessmen in his time. Their reasons for secrecy had never mattered to him. All that concerned him was whether the scheme was shrewdly thought out and that the remuneration would be worth the risk.

'I see,' he said and rested his elbows on his desk as he studied the straight-backed woman sitting across from him.

'I made enquiries about you before making an appointment to see you, Mr Monk. I needed to know whether your abilities were up to my standard.'

He tried hard to control his expression, but Horatia was quick to see the mix of surprise and fear that entered his eyes.

He cleared his throat. 'Then you must know from those enquiries that my word is my bond. I will respect your anonymity.'

'I don't want your word. I want your written pledge.' Her words were clipped, her expression unreadable.

Monk looked surprised. Few men had ever asked for his assurances in writing and fewer still, she guessed, had made enquiries into his personal life and background. He was the bastard son of a duke and had been doted on by his mother. His personal life could put him in jail if he wasn't careful, and Septimus Monk was very careful, although the way he dressed went some way to advertising his sexual predilections. Few men wore such flamboyant waistcoats, had hair falling in waves over their collar or smelt like a late-blooming peony.

He recovered quickly. 'Of course. I will have my clerk prepare it immediately.'

He rang a bell. The door was opened by a dark-eyed youth with pouting lips who received his instructions silently then threw Horatia a piercing, almost jealous look before he left.

'You are clear on my brief?'

Monk nodded. 'I am to set up a company and purchase the ship *Matilda* from bankruptcy, equip her ready for sail complete with crew and master. I will hold shares by proxy to your account. I am also to obtain letters of credit both here and in Nova Scotia.'

Horatia's expression remained unaltered as she handed him the document. 'This is the full list of companies who will be supplying goods for the outgoing trip and contacts with regard for her return cargoes.'

The crisp parchment crackled like burning kindling as she passed the list across.

Monk took it, his eyes scanning for the slightest flaw likely to end in loss rather than gain. The ship was 602 tons and would take coal and railway sleepers to Halifax, Nova Scotia, and bring back guano, an extremely valuable fertilizer replenished year after year by thousands of seabirds.

Although his expression was unchanged, Horatia knew exactly what he was thinking. 'As you can see, Mr Monk, no Chinese porcelain or pretty cottons, but guano. Bird shit. Muck makes money, and that muck makes things grow. The population of this country is growing and needs feeding. In order for corn and cabbages to grow more quickly, they too need feeding. I hear the results of guano are so outstanding that the price is expected to hit the roof – for exactly the reasons I mention.'

Septimus Monk sat back in his chair. It occurred to him as odd that she wasn't married. Any normal man was sure to be attracted to her – not him, of course. 'A very commendable plan, Miss Strong.'

'For a woman?'

'That's not what I meant.' He laughed a little too self-consciously.

Horatia was not fooled. The thought had obviously entered his head.

'I have no bias towards gender when it comes to business, Miss Strong.'

'No bias towards gender in any regard, surely, Mr Monk?'

Monk smiled and their eyes met in something approaching understanding. 'I have to admit to some surprise that such an eligible lady as yourself has not yet married.'

She smiled back. 'Why haven't *you* married, Mr Monk?'

He shook his head and pretended to study the folio sitting on his desk. 'It does not suit my disposition, Miss Strong.'

'Neither does it suit mine, Mr Monk. Indeed, a man would have to be very exceptional.'

'There's always someone,' Monk countered. 'Under the right circumstances.'

It was brief but for a second her expression softened. 'I suppose so. In the meantime, please ensure that my business interests are looked after without any regard to my sex or my matrimonial status.'

He bowed his head. 'I will.'

'I know I can trust you,' she said as they parted.

'You can count on me,' he replied.

Horatia's skirts rustled as she rose and made for the door. 'I know. I checked.'

After she'd gone, his clerk, Alexander, threw him a petulant glare. 'That's a hard bitch if ever I saw one,' he said, his voice jagged with jealousy.

Monk cupped the boy's face with both hands and smiled. 'That, my dear boy, is a woman after my own heart. An admirable example of her gender, my boy.'

Then his look hardened and his fist swung, fetching Alexander a heavy slap across his face that made it glow red and sent him crashing into a bookcase. Legal folios and documents fell from the open shelves and nestled around the boy's ankles.

Monk waved a finger at him. 'That lady is a client. You will not call any of my clients names – is that clear?'

The clerk stared at him wide-eyed, as blood trickled from the corner of his mouth. He touched it, felt its warmth, then looked at his bloodied fingers with amazement.

'Now fetch me a fresh quill,' Monk's expression softened along with his voice. 'There's a good boy.'

–

A heavy downpour pounded on the coach roof all the way back to Marstone Court. Horatia sat staring at the rain, though not really seeing it. Her blood was racing with excitement. She could imagine her father and grandfather feeling just as she was now when

29

they were on the verge of making their fortunes. She'd inherited a good deal of that fortune, but making money for oneself was far more satisfying than having it given to you. Business was like a drug, something she couldn't possibly live without. Not for her contenting herself with soirées, balls and weekends at country houses, filling her stomach with food and her head with gossip. At thirty-three she was unmarried and would be downright bored if her mother hadn't left her a substantial sum that family advisers had invested on her behalf. With that she had consistently dabbled in business ventures that had, for the most part, been undetected by any member of her family. She had made very good profits, though not enough to satisfy her ego. It was like a hunger. She had to be better than the men of the family. She had to be better than all men when it came to business. There was no husband, no child in her life and she doubted there ever would be. The only man she had ever loved had left Bristol ten years ago. She sincerely hoped he would come back. Nelson had gone to Boston to ask him if he would but his return was doubtful. He had married money and even though his wife had died, she didn't feel it likely that he would accept Nelson's offer. But she could hope, and in the meantime she would feed the hunger of achievement that drove her.

Chapter Four

Blanche showed little interest when Conrad told her about the meeting.

'I am told that Doctor Budd has been studying cholera for some years,' he said.

'I can't really see why you wish me to come,' she said, her hands clasped tightly in her lap.

'Think of the lives that might be saved.'

'But not Anne's. It's too late for Anne.'

He sighed. 'What about Max, Adeline and Lucy? Shouldn't we think about keeping them safe?'

Blanche clenched her jaw and said nothing. There was a wound in her heart where a child used to be. All her attention was directed at that wound, the rest of her heart left to its own devices.

Conrad made his excuses to leave for the refinery. 'I have problems there. Transferring sugar to barges is an expensive business.' He sounded disappointed.

Blanche heard the hurt in his voice and felt a slight fluttering in her chest. She hadn't meant to wound him, but she couldn't help it. 'Where did you hear of this meeting?' she asked in a feeble attempt to make amends, though her tone was sharp and lacked warmth.

Conrad stopped by the door. 'I think it was an alderman,' he lied, not daring to mention Dr Walters just in case she had heard of him and knew what kind of doctor he was. 'I'll leave you to think about it. You don't have to go,' he added, fearing by her silence that she was yet again retreating into herself.

After he'd left, she sat staring out of the window, thinking of Anne. *You have to go on living. You have three other children to think of.*

'I know,' she said, half thinking that Conrad was still in the room. But the voice she had heard was inside her head, one she hadn't heard for a long while. After all these years, her mother's voice had come back to her.

She had no time to relapse into a depression. Max, Adeline and Lucy barged into the room, their faces bright with excitement.

'The children wanted to know if you were accompanying us to see the trains at Temple Meads Station,' explained the nurse.

At first she held back, the melancholy that was her daily companion threatening to enfold her back into its clutches. It was Max who persuaded her to go.

'If you don't go, then I won't either,' he said adamantly as though he were the indulgent adult and she the child. The look on his face almost took Blanche's breath away. He looked so like his father.

'We want you with us, Mother,' Adeline added.

Lucy slipped her hand into Blanche's just as she had on the day when Anne had last been with them. 'Please?' she said plaintively.

Blanche closed her eyes and forced herself out from the dark place within. Conrad was right. Her mother was right. She still had three children. They deserved her attention. 'Then I shall come.'

Temple Meads Railway Station was warm, sooty and full of steam. The air shuddered with the sound of porters shouting, whistles blowing and steam engines, the boiling steam squealing from valves and chuffing from funnels. Round-eyed and open-mouthed, the children drank in the world around them.

Blanche found herself infected by their excitement. She heard herself laughing when Max got too close to an engine and ended up with a coal-smeared face, and when the children waved at an engine driver and he waved back. The sound was like a favourite note long forgotten and took her by surprise. Had it really been that long since she'd laughed? Her melancholia was still there, like a lead weight inside, yet it seemed smaller than it had been, as if being eroded by something stronger. Something had changed. The prospect of the meeting tonight had a lot to do with it. So did her mother's phantom voice echoing Conrad's wise words.

Getting the children back in the carriage resulted in sullen looks and half-hearted protests. They went back via St Augustine's Bridge because the children's nurse wanted to buy some lace from a street seller she'd seen there a few days before.

As usual, the centre of Bristol was a beehive of activity. Barrels, sacks and tea chests swung from the nets of waterside cranes, unloading from ship to shore or vice versa. Traffic flowed in all directions over the bridge, around the quays, bustling through to where they wanted to be.

The children opted to look at the ships whilst their nurse perused the bundles of lace. Blanche got out to take a little air, though the city heaved with the heat and smell of summer and recent rain steamed from the pavements.

She looked around her at the ships unloading cargoes of wine and barrels of sugar, the buildings crowding the quay and beyond the spires of the city's many churches. Her mind went back to when she'd first arrived in Bristol from Barbados when she'd been naive enough to think that the Strong family would accept her as one of their own. Instead her fate was to be nurse to the children of Sir Emmanuel Strong. Her destiny had been to love one man and marry another.

There was noise all around, but her thoughts were unhindered until an argument erupted just a few feet behind her.

'Don't you hit my boy, you bloody swine!'

Suddenly the years fell away. That voice! She spun round immediately, thinking it couldn't be, but hoping that it was indeed the voice she so fondly remembered.

A boy with thin arms and dirty knees was trying to fill his pail from the Quay Pipe. A man was trying to stop him, and a woman was beating at the man's head and yelling at the top of her voice.

Ragged and haggard though the woman was, Blanche still recognized her old friend. 'Edith! Edith Clements. Is that you?'

The man, who'd been attempting to ward off her blows, let his arms fall on seeing Blanche and doffed his cap. Edith froze and her mouth dropped open. The boy rubbed his head and looked too.

Aware that her wealth and status stood out among the more humble appearances of most of the quayside, Blanche tried not to appear overbearing or officious. She kept her voice steady. 'What's going on here?' she asked.

'This bloke won't let us have fresh water,' said the boy and wiped his nose on his sleeve.

Edith stood speechless, her hands wandering up and down her shoddy clothes in a futile attempt to hide them from view. Blanche felt for her.

She reached into her velvet purse and handed the man a shilling. 'They shall have their water. Now go away. I wish to speak to my friend.'

The man obeyed.

Blanche stopped herself from saying that Edith looked well because it just wasn't true. Her dress was of rough wool, patched in places and threadbare at the elbows, greasy on the hips and ragged around the hem. Her face was less rosy than she remembered, and she had dried sores at the corners of her mouth. Blanche also refrained from looking her up and down.

'It's so good to see you again.'

Edith half curtseyed. 'Blanche, I mean, ma'am – Mrs Heinkel.'

Her solicitude took Blanche by surprise. 'Oh, come on, Edith. I'm still Blanche. We're old friends. Remember?'

'Shall I take this on 'ome, Ma?' asked the boy, one shoulder lower than the other by dint of the weight of the water in his pail.

Edith nodded self-consciously, her gaze fluttering between Blanche and the boy. 'Yes. Clear off home!' She waved him away.

Freddie went just a few steps then stopped, curious to know what was going on.

There was an awkward moment between them, broken eventually by Blanche. 'Your son?' she asked.

Edith nodded. 'Yeah. That's Freddie. I have four children,' she added with undoubted pride.

'So have I,' said Blanche, then paused as she remembered. 'No. I used to have four. One died. That's besides Conrad's children, of course. But they've both married. One lives in London and one in Hamburg.'

Edith seemed to come alive suddenly. 'Only one? I've lost four kids over the years, two to typhus and two to cholera. But I've still got Freddie here, then there's Lizzie, Billy and Polly, though our Lizzie ain't so good.' She shrugged. 'What can you expect living where I do?'

Edith's matter-of-fact manner took Blanche aback. There was no sign at all of regret, bitterness or recrimination, just an acceptance that life was hard and only temporary. Not surprising really, she thought on remembering the home Edith had once taken her to.

'Do you still live in the Pithay?'

Edith shook her head. 'No. Cabot's Yard. It's just off Lewins Mead, not that there's much difference between that and the Pithay.'

'And you have no water there?'

'Oh yes.'

'So why are you filling your pail here?'

'The doctor said that our water was no good and to get it from here. Must say it's working. Our Lizzie seems a lot better. There's a lot dead of cholera round Lewins Mead, but don't look like our Lizzie's going to join them, thanks to the doctor. He reckons she'll pull through.'

Something clicked inside Blanche's head. Was this the same man her husband was talking about?

'This doctor, what was his name?'

Edith frowned and sucked in her top lip as she racked her brain. 'Somethink like a flower.' Her face brightened. 'Budd. Doctor Budd. There, I knew it was something to do with a flower!'

Blanche raised her hand to her forehead. The coincidence made her reel. She had lost one child, but Edith had lost many. 'Take this,' she said, rummaging again in her purse and handing her old friend five shillings.

Edith eyed the coins as though they might burn a hole in her palm. At the same time she was almost licking her lips at the thought of what she could buy.

35

Blanche wondered when Edith had last had some food and what she'd eaten. Precious little, she decided on hearing a loud rumble from Edith's stomach above the traffic noise.

Freddie interrupted. 'Are you coming, Ma?' he shouted.

'I can't take it,' said Edith, thrusting the coins back at Blanche.

Blanche shook her head and tucked her hands behind her back. 'You must, for old times' sake. We have to meet again,' she added, but Edith had turned towards her son, the coins still in her hand.

Before disappearing into one of the alleys that led from the quay to Lewins Mead, she stopped and looked over her shoulder. Her expression was tense, almost sorrowful. 'You're a fine lady now, Blanche. Go back to you fine house and your clean water. Leave the likes of us alone.'

It hurt to know that the last words were meant as a warning, but Blanche understood. Edith was ashamed of her appearance. Her world was dark and filled with dirt and disease. But although they were divided by wealth and status, they were united by grief. Edith might not allow it to show, but it was there. Blanche knew it was.

By the time Conrad got home that evening, Blanche was dressed ready to go to the meeting. He was surprised, but also pleased.

'Do you have the details?' she asked.

Conrad nodded. 'Yes. Why this change of heart? Much as I am glad to see it,' he added hastily.

Blanche checked her appearance in the mantel above the fireplace. There was a new brightness in her eyes and a determined look to her chin. She attempted to explain how she felt to Conrad via her own resolute reflection.

'Until recently, it was as if I was the only woman in the world to have lost a child, then I met someone today who's lost many children to disease. My loss seemed so small compared to hers. What's more, there's precious little the likes of her can do about it.' She turned to face him, her eyes flashing in direct competition with the diamonds sparkling in her ears. 'But we can do something, Conrad. In fact, we *must* do something. It's up to us.'

'My dear!' Conrad seemed as though he were about to burst with happiness.

Blanche was pleased to see it. He'd coped with her depression since the death of their daughter and deserved to be happy.

He took hold of her by the shoulders, his blue eyes twinkling. 'I knew you would get well in your own good time. I knew it regardless...'

On seeing a raised eyebrow, he stopped abruptly. Her quizzical look remained, urging him to continue, but of course he couldn't.

Blanche's tone was clipped. 'I haven't been ill, Conrad. I've been grieving. Time, they say, is the only cure. In my case I needed something extra.'

Conrad spluttered excuses. 'That's what I meant,' he said, colouring slightly and praying she never found out that he'd consulted Dr Walters. He attempted to return to the subject. 'Who was this person? Anyone I know?'

'You may remember her. Her name was Edith. I used to work with her at Marstone Court. She used to be sweet on Captain Strong.'

His smile wavered at the mention of Tom Strong, but he quickly recovered. This was not the right time to point out Blanche's own past relationship with his friend Tom Strong – prior to their marriage, of course. All the same, he'd never found it easy to mention his name, perhaps never would until jealousy was tempered by old age. 'Poor woman,' he remarked.

'Yes,' said Blanche, still eyeing him as if he were withholding something from her, but less accusingly as she warmed to her subject. 'And it's the poor who suffer most, isn't it? I have to do something about it, Conrad. I have to make recompense for thinking that my loss was greater than anyone else's.' She touched his hand. 'Thanks to you I'm in a position to do that.'

–

The meeting was being held at the Red Lodge, a place of high rafters where pigeons roosted and wide floorboards creaked under foot.

'There are lots of people here,' Blanche said to Conrad as she eyed the well-dressed crowd. 'Far more than I thought there would be.'

Silk rustled, bonnets and top hats bobbed in welcome. The air was filled with whiffs of cologne, lavender water, rose water and mothballs.

He patted her hand reassuringly and gushed like a schoolboy, still over the moon that she'd decided to come. 'They are all very interested, though I am afraid some are here purely out of self-interest. The doctor's plans have found favour in the city, which means lucrative contracts once the sewerage scheme is approved.'

Six people sat on chairs placed on a raised platform at one end of the room. Once the auditorium was fully seated, a whiskered man with a chequered waistcoat and a monocle winking at one eye rose to his feet. His introduction was brief. Then Dr Budd rose to his feet and Blanche found herself regarding him with a mix of admiration and sympathy. It could not have been easy to challenge current medical thinking. Neither could it have been easy to get the city Corporation on board if Conrad's comments about the aldermen were anything to go by.

Blanche listened spellbound to what Dr Budd had to say. He first told of a visit he had made to one of the most deprived parts of the city, describing the smell of a communal privy and the abode of a man, his wife and their six children.

'Most of the floor is taken up with two large beds in which all the family sleep,' explained Dr Budd. 'The room in which they live is underground and has only one small window. Despite being indoors, the bad aromas of the privy persist. The following conversation has been recorded in my official report, copies of which I have had printed at a price of tuppence each for those who are interested.'

He waved his notes at a small pile of pamphlets set before a pale, dark-haired woman with a care-worn face, presumably his wife. He proceeded to read from the pamphlet and his description of the degradation and bad smells was so vivid that some ladies held handkerchiefs to their noses. One or two fainted.

'There you are!' shouted a middle-aged man with a thrusting lower lip and the look of a medical or clerical man. ''Tis the smell, the miasma! Just as I've always said it was!'

'And I too have said it,' shouted another man, his clothing and haughty manner much the same as his colleague.

'So say all us doctors of medicine!' shouted a third. 'Begone with your quackish ideas, Doctor Budd, back to Devonshire or France, or wherever else you purport to come from!'

A babble of noise erupted. Those who'd come to listen looked on questioningly as other loud voices joined the fray.

'The miasmas the problem!' someone else repeated.

'A stink,' shouted someone else. 'Call it what it is.'

'The stink is the problem. But would there be no disease if there were no stink? Is that what the learned physicians are saying?' Everyone and anyone seemed to join in, pertinent points seeming to get through despite the rumblings of dissent from one side or the other.

'If the dock officials did their job right, we wouldn't have this stink,' shouted an equally pompous man.

'He's an alderman,' said Conrad as if that explained everything.

Blanche craned her neck so she could see better. 'I'm astounded that people can be so hostile to new ideas,' she said with disbelief.

They both looked to where another man, his features sharp as a weasel, leapt to his feet and pointed his finger like a spear at the latter gentleman's face. 'It is not the fault of the dock officials, of which I count myself a good and worthy member! If the Corporation had diverted the sewers when they built the Floating Harbour, it wouldn't be filling up with filth!'

''Tis for you to pay to have it done, and by God you will,' shouted the alderman.

'We shall leave the courts to decide that!' the dock official shouted back.

'They have been arguing about this for years,' Conrad explained to Blanche, 'and still nothing is done. The Floating Harbour has become an open sewer.'

As they spoke, all hell broke lose. The alderman, his face red with anger, waved his walking stick at the dock official, who proceeded to push his way through the rows of chairs, his eyes bulging and his fists ready for action.

Chairs scraped, top hats flew and ladies screamed with alarm as able-bodied men intervened before the alderman and the dock official came to blows. The noise continued.

Blanche was exasperated. 'This is terrible. Nothing will be achieved if they go on like this.' She turned to Conrad but his chair was empty and people were on their feet all around her. Where was he?

She got to her feet. Men of all shapes and sizes surrounded her. This meeting by which she had set such store was disintegrating into a rabble – and such finely dressed people too. 'Never judge a man by his clothes,' she muttered to herself.

The sound of a hammer hitting a copper gong echoed around the room.

'Silence for prayer,' boomed a commanding voice.

Raised voices dropped an octave then two, then more and then silence. No one, no matter how great and good, was going to interrupt a call to prayer.

Men who had lost their tempers and raised their fists, now swept their hands over tousled hair, picked up their hats and bowed their heads.

Conrad, head and shoulders above most men, stood on the platform, his great head and broad body towering over everyone. Clasping his hands in prayer, his voice boomed around the room. 'Ladies and gentlemen. Shall we pray to God that we will eventually come to agreement on this grave subject?'

At the sound of his voice the last murmur of dissension disappeared and heads bowed in prayer.

Blanche smiled down into her clasped hands. Her husband's behaviour surprised her at times.

After intoning a prayer for good judgement and wise counsel, Conrad rested both hands on the lectern and spoke as though he were delivering a sermon. His voice was stern and strong, just as it was on Sundays when he was sure of his God and intent on sharing his deeply held beliefs with others.

'Two years ago my wife and I lost a dearly beloved daughter. Much as I love my God and believe that he does most things for a reason, my faith was severely tested when my daughter died. My wife and I would have liked Anne to be with us a little longer. Faithful to the memory of my child, I came here seeking to know what progress is being made with regard to defeating this disease. Old ideas have not worked. What have we to lose in opening up our minds – and our purses – to new ideas? Please, for the sake of my daughter and all those whom we have loved and lost, listen to what is being proposed. From what I have gathered previous to attending this meeting, interim measures will be used to combat the disease such as disinfecting those areas with a history of bad cholera outbreaks. In the meantime, plans will be finalized for a large sewerage project that will improve our lives and make Bristol a place to be proud of.'

'How do we know our city really is that bad?' someone asked.

A city alderman stood up, his square chin hard as iron and his thick fists clinging to his coat lapels. 'Ladies and gentlemen. I am not one for long speeches, but perhaps I can enlighten you on the situation. In eighteen forty-five a commission investigated this very carefully and came to the conclusion that Bristol had the third highest death rate in the country. Only Manchester and Liverpool were worse, and in these cities there was the added factor of poverty on a scale unknown in Bristol. The conclusion must be drawn that Bristol is as bad as, or worse than, any other city in terms of environment and health.'

'Then we should be mightily ashamed!'

The room erupted with noise at the unheralded interruption.

This time there was no fear of a fight ensuing. The voice was that of a woman, one that Blanche recognized as yet another voice from the past. Disbelieving her ears, she looked round. Horatia Strong! For a split second their eyes met and the years rolled away.

She still had the same overbearing presence Blanche remembered from her days at Marstone Court and she was still beautiful – like an icicle caught in a ray of sunlight.

The strength of her presence, her stature and her status, caused everyone to turn and wonder. There she was, standing there in the midst of the crowd like an actress about to take an encore, a queen waiting to accept the homage of her courtiers.

'Something should be done and will be done,' Horatia stated as though she'd already drawn the plans herself. Her voice was as clear as a bell. 'And before either the dock officials or the Corporation plead poverty and lack of funds, then I – Horatia Strong – will finance the initial efforts. I have lost a number of my family to this deadly scourge. This city was built on sugar – a lot of it grown on the Strong plantations in Barbados. Let sugar make the air sweeter for us to breathe!'

A hush fell over the throng, then others, some in the hope of entering Horatia's social circle, also pledged their assistance.

Blanche could hardly believe what she was hearing.

Still standing at the lectern, Conrad looked consternated, though pleased that someone was voicing a positive view he'd hoped others would express.

Blanche turned her head from Horatia and looked at her hands, which were presently enclosed in gloves of soft purple leather. She fingered the handle of her parasol thoughtfully as she tried to come to terms with Horatia actually echoing her own thoughts. It wasn't that she exactly hated Horatia, but they were very different women and there would always be a bone of contention between them – if you could call him that. They'd both loved Tom Strong; perhaps they still did.

On Conrad's return she roused herself from her thoughts and smiled at him.

'I was surprised to see Miss Strong here,' he said. 'I am sure her presence will greatly influence support for this project.'

Irritated that Horatia should have a central role, albeit as a financial benefactor, Blanche couldn't bring herself to believe it was her only motive. She knew Horatia of old.

'I remember being told before leaving Barbados that the Strong family only care about sugar. Perhaps that's not entirely true,' she said.

Conrad looked at her questioningly. 'Are you not being a little unfair, my dear, in view of your position in the Strong household when you first arrived here?'

Blanche stiffened. Although she now felt committed to helping Dr Budd, she bristled at the thought of Horatia and the Strong family being involved – perhaps for their own ends.

'Sugar can be used for a lot of things,' she said at last.

'Yes. That is so,' said Conrad, frowning as he sought to grasp her meaning. 'The money it generates, like sugar, can be used in many pies.'

Blanche held her parasol handle with both hands, far more tightly than she needed to. 'Yes. So what pie is Horatia baking?'

Conrad's face clouded over. 'You are pre-judging her.'

Blanche shook her head. 'I don't think so.'

'She has lost members of her own family to this dreadful disease,' Conrad said, his voice low and his tone disbelieving.

Blanche remembered the day George and Arthur – half-brothers to herself and Horatia – had been buried. The news had come to her via a groom who worked at Marstone Court and was courting one of her scullery maids. She'd cried that day and a high wind had rattled the doors and windows and sent leaves flying high into the sky. A vision of the boys, whom she had known all too briefly, running through the parkland clinging to the string of a home-made kite would stay with her always.

Horatia, of course, had never indulged in such antics. To Blanche she would always be the haughty doyenne of a family without a heart. Horatia certainly didn't have one.

'That wouldn't concern Horatia overmuch. George and Arthur were half-brothers. She never liked them when I knew her, never had much to do with them in fact if she could possibly help it.'

'Now, now,' he said, his voice quiet against her ear as he patted her arm in an effort to calm the anger he saw in her eyes. 'You must be charitable, my dear.'

Blanche shook her head. 'I'm sorry. I find it hard. This was supposed to have been a way forward from our loss. The fact that some are here angling for business has spoiled things.'

Conrad looked concerned. 'You don't know that for sure... please... Blanche...'

'I'm sorry.' She smiled at other women, all chattering excitedly at the presence of Horatia Strong. She sighed. 'Perhaps you're right.' She reached up and smoothed the furrow in her husband's brow. 'Don't worry, Conrad. Whatever happens, I am determined to play some part in this, for Edith's sake as well as for Anne's.'

His frown disappeared and he patted her hand. She was glad to see him smile and his face relax. He'd worried about her long enough.

'I'm sorry,' she said again.

'Pah! You have nothing to be sorry for. Put the woman from your mind. Forget the past. The future beckons and belongs to our children.'

Blanche smiled. He was right and made her feel better. Marrying him had never been a matter of passion, more to do with a steadfast relationship in an uncertain world. When past slights or present problems surfaced in her life, he was always there to smooth them over.

Her renewed spirits might have remained if Horatia hadn't spotted her.

'Oh no,' she said to Conrad. 'She's coming this way.'

Horatia was smiling and holding her head high. A dark blue feather curved from her bonnet to her face, its tip ending at the corner of her mouth.

Blanche had no wish to speak to her. She took her husband's arm and whispered, 'Can we go now?'

'Face your demons,' he whispered back.

'A good description,' Blanche muttered.

He disentangled himself from her arm. 'If you'll just give me a moment to speak to the good doctor and Alderman Wright... I'm sure you can cope,' he added.

Reluctantly, she agreed.

Horatia smelt of violets. A bunch of them were pinned to her pelisse. They looked real and fresh, and the colour of her bonnet matched her eyes. Her smile was surprisingly warm, perhaps even triumphant. Blanche couldn't think why. Horatia was still a spinster. Tom was long gone.

'Well, Mrs Heinkel! It's been a long time since I saw you last, and to think, at one time I saw you every day when you were wiping the bottoms of my brothers and sisters.'

It was exactly the sort of statement Blanche had expected. Conrad would never have believed it.

Blanche pursed her lips and gripped her parasol handle, making believe it was Horatia's neck. It went some way to giving her strength. 'I think this is hardly the time and place for sarcasm. I was sorry to hear those poor little souls whom I took care of so well are no longer with us.'

A flicker of regret softened Horatia's features. 'Ah, yes. Of course. And I was sorry also to hear you lost your daughter.'

Although taken by surprise that Horatia knew of Anne's death, Blanche didn't show it when she thanked her.

Horatia never had been a sentimental person and it was no surprise when her punctured expression passed and the veiled sarcasm returned, though the question was totally unexpected. 'And your son – Max, isn't it? He is well, I hope?'

Something about Horatia's smile reminded Blanche of a cat about to pounce on a bird.

Somehow she kept her voice even. 'He is quite well.'

Horatia returned the smiling acknowledgements of others attending the meeting as she continued. 'You must bring him out to Marstone Court. I'm sure Father would be pleased to see him.' She leaned closer so no one else could hear what she said next. 'After all, my dear, he is a member of the family, even though he was born in embarrassing circumstances…'

Blanche felt her face reddening with anger. This was Horatia in her true colours, uttering comments meant to wound, needing to be superior no matter whose company she was in.

Blanche gritted her teeth as she replied, her jaw aching with the effort of keeping her voice low so no one else could hear. 'He is *my* son! He is nothing to do with the Strongs.'

'Sshh!' said Horatia, raising her finger to her lips. 'You wouldn't want the whole city to know that Max was not fathered by your husband but by your Nelson, your half-brother, my brother.' She suppressed a sudden laugh, her eyes darting about in mock fear that someone might be listening to their conversation. 'What's so funny is that my father has taken it in his head to turn one of our reception rooms into an Egyptian temple. From what I understand it was quite normal for the Egyptian pharaohs to lie with their sisters. Just like you and Nelson, my dear.'

If only Horatia knew the truth about Max's birth! Blanche would dearly have loved to slap her half-sister's face but she couldn't risk it. The room was packed. Her son's future could be ruined by wicked gossip. Her heart raced, but she kept her voice calm. 'My son attends Clifton College as a day pupil, but if I have to I will send him away to board rather than have the Strong family interfere in his life. My children and my marriage are important to me. Of course, you wouldn't understand that being a spinster.'

Horatia winced as the barb hit home, but Blanche's satisfaction was short-lived. The cat-like expression returned to her half-sister's eyes. 'I thought you might have been very happy to visit us at Marstone Court and meet up with old friends. We expect Captain Strong to be with us again within the next few weeks. I thought you would have jumped at the chance of seeing him again. He's lost his wife. I think he's lonely. But never mind. I'm there to provide consolation.'

Blanche stayed silent. Her mouth was too dry to say anything. Tom was coming back. The temptation to visit Marstone Court was suddenly very attractive. She remembered times beneath the trees, her feet and dress wet with dew after running through the grass, the Strong children chasing a kite – Rupert, Caroline, poor little George and Arthur. But for Max's sake, and for Conrad's, she couldn't.

'I shall send you an invitation,' Horatia said. The width of her smile stretched the bonnet ribbon running under her chin. 'After all, we have such a lot in common.'

'Like this project?' said Blanche. 'Although I can't help getting the impression you and I are supporting it for different reasons.'

Horatia's eyes took on a strange look. 'You are content to be a wife and mother, Mrs Heinkel. I am not. I am more like my father than my brothers are. I have his drive, his ambition—'

'And his ruthlessness.'

The smile returned. 'But much more so. I will allow no one and nothing to get in my way. No one at all.'

For some obscure reason, Blanche wasn't convinced that business success was the only thing Horatia cared about. Her comments regarding Tom betrayed her feelings, much as she might deny them if pressed. At present there was nothing else in her life except outshining her brothers. Tom's return might result in a different story.

'Did she upset you?' Conrad asked after Horatia had gone and he'd returned from his discussions.

'No more than she ever did.'

'I take it she did not mention her reasons for being here.'

Blanche shook her head. 'No. But she didn't need to. She may be a woman, but she's first and foremost a Strong. Her interests are purely mercenary.'

Conrad shook his head disapprovingly.

Blanche smiled. 'I know. I'm not being very charitable. Perhaps you're right,' she said, slipping her arm through his.

She decided it would be unwise to tell him that Horatia did indeed have one particular weakness like any other woman. If she did then she would also have to tell him that Tom Strong was coming back to England after ten years away. Let sleeping dogs lie, she told herself. Conrad was happy that she was something like her former self. Better to stay silent than see a new worry surface in his eyes.

Chapter Five

Lines born of age and experience creased Tom's eyes as he surveyed the city scene, smelt the mix of soot and sweetness, and tasted its odd grittiness that only a draught of water could swill from his tongue.

It was midday and the sun was attempting to penetrate the haze that clung to the skyline of churches, factories and refineries. The quay was a bustle of movement and noise. Brawny men bent into the capstans on St Augustine's Quay, close to the culvert that brought fresh water from Jacob's Well to where ships tied up to disgorge their cargoes of sugar, rum, tobacco, molasses and chocolate.

His attention was drawn to a bunch of labourers who were using rope and tackle in front of the old tavern where he'd drank with Sally Ward and first met Blanche, who had just arrived from Barbados. He found himself remembering how she'd looked that day – but not her clothes, except her hat, which had become very bedraggled on the journey to Marstone Court. No. It was her eyes he remembered most of all. They were dark grey and shone like polished pewter in her coffee-coloured face. He wondered how much she'd changed. With a pang of regret he saw that things along the quay were changing before his very eyes. Grunting and shouting, the workmen were manhandling a weather worn wooden carving from its place above the door and onto the cobbles. It was a sculpture of a half-naked American Indian Princess, the Noble Savage after which the tavern was named. Tom eyed the faded paint that still clung to the scarred wood and wondered at the reason for its fall from grace and spot above the tavern door.

'What are you doing with that noble lady?' he asked.

One of the labourers doffed his hat. 'They people in the Christian Morality League says it's not right to show bare breasts – even wooden ones.'

Tom fancied he saw a cheeky gleam in the man's eyes. It seemed grossly unfair that the Noble Savage was being discarded. Likely her own people wouldn't regard her bare breasts as offensive, he thought, remembering America. She was beautiful in a primitive and innocent way. Surely she deserved better, an Indian princess in need of rescuing by a knight in shining armour.

Tom scratched the nape of his neck with the silver tip of his walking cane. He'd never been a knight, and was never likely to be, but he found himself offering to buy her. 'I for one do not disapprove of her lack of clothes. I want her for myself. Let's say two sovereigns, shall we?'

The labourers looked up at him from beneath battered hats, their eyes twinkling in the dirt of their faces, nudging each other and grinning.

Tom fetched two sovereigns from his pocket. 'Is that enough?'

Questioning glances were exchanged.

'We can't leave it 'ere,' one of them blurted. 'And we was told to take it away and burn it.' There was a crafty look in his eyes, which swivelled to look at his colleagues before returning to Tom. 'That 'uld keep a fire in the grate goin' fer weeks that 'uld!'

Tom waited for the others to react before fetching out another sovereign. 'So let's say three sovereigns.'

'We 'as to put it somewur,' said another man, who had just one good eye, the other seemingly sewn shut and something yellow and viscous seeping from its corner.

'You're a rogue,' said Tom as he fetched out another coin.

The man pretended to take umbrage. 'Now just you look 'ere—'

Tom swiftly raised his cane. 'No! You look!'

The man grimaced, his one healthy eye worriedly eyeing the point of the walking stick that was presently stabbed against his shoulder.

'Five sovereigns,' said Tom. 'More than enough for you to hire a horse and cart and show a good profit.'

Thoughts of money replaced those of violence. A crooked smile lifted the man's mouth. 'Thank you, sir. Thank you kindly.'

The others conceded once their leader had agreed terms.

The man with the viscous eye doffed his hat solicitously. 'Now whereabouts do you wants it?'

'I'll tell you,' said Tom, pleased with what he'd achieved, though he couldn't for the moment think where the hell he would eventually put her.

He gave them instructions to take the carving out to Marstone Court – specifically with instructions for the footman there to deal with its unloading and location in the rambling mansion. He imagined the footman's face and hoped it was Duncan, if he was still there, but it didn't matter if it was not. In his experience, the footmen at Marstone Court adopted more airs and graces than the Strong family itself.

'You're a gent, sir,' said the man with one eye, doffing his hat again and again.

'Stop!'

Tom turned at the sound of his first mate's voice. Jim Storm Cloud, a Red Indian from America who had accompanied Tom on many a voyage, was shouting at someone who had dared to fill a pail from the quayside water pipe.

'Get off with you! That water's for the ships, not for the likes of you!'

The young boy went sprawling, but quickly righted himself, grabbed his pail and swung it against the first mate's legs. 'I wants it fer me sister,' he shouted defiantly, the loudness of his voice and the prospect of violence drawing a crowd. 'She's got to 'ave it! She's got to!'

'Now, now,' said Tom, reaching for the boy. 'What's—'

Thinking he'd attracted another assailant, the boy swung the wooden pail hard into Tom's knees. There was a cracking sound and an exclamation from the crowd. Tom grimaced.

'Ragged little ruffian,' someone shouted.

Recovering swiftly, Tom caught the boy by both shoulders, meaning to threaten the lad with a good thrashing. He found himself completely disarmed by sunken eyes that were bright despite the hunger etched on his face.

Jim Storm Cloud grabbed the pail, swung it by its handle and smashed it against a cast-iron capstan where it broke into smithereens.

'My pail! My pail!' The boy looked as if he would burst into tears. 'Oh no!' His bottom lip quivered as he fought to hold back the tears.

'This water is for ships,' said Jim.

Tom shook his head. 'The Quay Pipe is free to any man.' He bent down so that his face was level with that of the boy. Keeping his voice soft and his gaze steady. 'Why this particular water, young fella?'

The boy's freckles seemed to take on a life of their own as his face crumpled with concern. 'My sister got the cholera. The doctor said that if she had water from 'ere, she would live and she did, and he said that if we all drank this water, then none of us would get sick.'

Tom laid his hand on the boy's shoulder. 'Where do you live, son?' The boy wiped his snotty nose on the back of what little was left of his sleeve. 'Cabot's Yard in Lewins Mead.'

Tom stopped smiling. A host of emotions sparked in his eyes. 'That's close to Cock and Bottle Lane.'

The boy nodded.

'What sort of place is it?' asked Jim Storm Cloud on seeing Tom's expression.

'A very old place.'

'It stinks,' said the boy.

Tom smiled. 'True.' The boy smelt too, mostly of poverty rather than outright filth. Thin, knobbly wrists poked like knotted sticks from a grey jersey that looked as though it had been cut down from something larger. His knees were scabbed, the crusts standing proud of dirt and hard skin.

'What's your name?' Tom asked.

'Freddie Beasley of Cabot's Yard,' the boy said proudly, his thumbs braced in what remained of his coat pockets.

'Then, Freddie Beasley of Cabot's Yard, you shall have your water.'

'How can I 'ave it now?' cried the boy, his face puckered with concern. 'That bloke there's broke me bucket!'

'He'll get you another,' said Tom straightening. 'Won't you, Jim?'

Jim Storm Cloud looked consternated, his brows beetling close together and his chin jutting out in an attempt to swallow his objection as he fetched another pail.

Tom reached into his pocket. 'Here's five shillings to give to your mother so she can replace the broken pail.'

Freddie snatched it warily, then wiped his nostrils on the sleeve of his shirt.

When Jim came back, the boy eyed him with interest. 'You bin burnt?' he asked, his face creased with puzzlement. 'You're ever so red.'

Jim's jaw dropped. First came a sharp grunt that started deep in his chest like a strong cough, then he was laughing, bellowing like a bull and stamping his feet so that the dusty ground rose in clouds around his feet.

Tom laughed. 'Jim is a Red Indian. He's from America.'

Before Jim's laughter had died away, a high-stepping Hackney with brightly jingling harness and pulling a smartly turned-out gig, trotted along the quay, workmen scattering in its path.

'Horses ain't allowed 'long 'ere,' somebody shouted.

Ignoring this, the driver, a young man of good looks and obvious wealth, tossed the reins and half a crown to a small boy and sprang from the gig onto the slippery cobbles. 'Captain Tom!'

Tom was amazed. If he hadn't known better, he would have said that Nelson Strong was younger in England than he was in America. But he knew it wasn't Nelson. Nelson was sailing from Boston to Barbados to while away a week or two looking over the plantation, though looking over a few dark-skinned beauties might be nearer the truth. Tom overcame his confusion, adopting a calmly pleasant expression as he swiftly calculated the only person it could be.

'Don't you recognize me, Tom?'

A slow smile spread over Tom's features. 'I've a suspicion I do, though the fellow I'm thinking of was no more than four feet high when I last saw him.'

The young man gripped Tom's shoulders with his hands. 'Then stop looking at me as though you've seen a ghost! I know I look like my brother – but he is a trifle older than me,' he said with obvious relish.

'Rupert?' He could hardly believe it. Rupert had been just a boy when he'd left Bristol.

Smartly dressed in well-tailored clothes, Rupert beamed. 'I'm no longer imprisoned in a nursery at the top of the house, being taught by a governess, or packed off to the school that came after that.' His cheeks turned pink. 'Captain... Tom... I'm so pleased to see you. You can't imagine how excited we all were to receive Nelson's letter...'

It was Tom's turn to clap his hands to Rupert's shoulders, shaking him with good humour as though Rupert were still the boy of good disposition with a liking for the sea. 'Your timing is admirable. How did you know I'd be here?'

Rupert beamed proudly. 'News travels fast in Bristol when one of her old sons is expected – one of her more successful old sons, should I say? Nelson told us all about your shipping line in Boston and that your brother-in-law now runs it. I'm sorry about your wife,' he added more soberly.

'That's all in the past now. I'm back in Bristol and there's another shipping line to build into an empire. There's so much I want to know, especially about the steamships.'

'Have you seen them yet?'

Tom shook his head. 'No. I was also wondering about your father. How is he?'

'Unchanged in some ways, though still the same in others. Of course, you know my mother died some years ago.'

Tom nodded. 'I'm sorry.'

Rupert shrugged. He didn't say that he didn't care, but Tom got the impression that he did not miss her and could understand why. Lady Verity had not been the most loving of mothers.

'Everyone is looking forward to seeing you again,' Rupert said once he'd regained his smile and dragged his gaze from the ship. 'Let's be off. Marstone Court awaits us.'

'My ma used to work there!' Tousled and not smelling too good, the urchin with the bucket forced himself in between them. 'She told me about that place with the grass, the trees and the big 'ouse an all. She used to work there looking after an old gentleman with dribble down 'is chin and a wheelchair. And she 'ad a friend there too. She was foreign and dark and 'er mother was a slave in the Sugar Islands!'

Both men looked down at him.

'Scallywag,' said Rupert with obvious amusement.

Tom barely heard him. He was too busy studying the boy's face. He noted the hazel eyes, the freckles and rounded features. His curiosity was aroused.

'What was your mother's name, boy?'

'Edith,' said Freddie, his eyes shining brightly in his dirty face.

There was only one servant of that name that Tom remembered. 'You're Edith's son? Edith Clements?'

The boy blinked up at him. 'S'pose I am,' he said looking a little unsure. 'Only she married me dad so ain't called Clements now.'

'I remember Edith,' said Rupert. 'She was very friendly with Blanche, our nanny, who married Conrad Heinkel. Did you know that, Tom?'

'Did she?' Of course he knew, just as he knew that Blanche was Rupert's half-sister, although Rupert did not.

As the memories flooded back, Tom eyed the buildings that ringed the harbour. For a fleeting moment, he half expected to see Blanche running along the quay, her dark skin shining, her eyes as deep as pewter and bright as silver, and her hair streaming out behind.

'Give Edith my best regards,' said Tom, having regained his self-control. Tapping the boy on the shoulder with his stick, he added, 'Tell her Captain Tom Strong sends his best.'

Face flushed with pleasure, Freddie's mouth hung open like a fish on a hook before he managed to say, 'That I will, sir! That I will!'

Freddie didn't know many people of quality, in fact, he didn't know any at all, and this was the first who'd ever spoken to him as though he mattered.

Tom looked down at the boy who was watching and listening with unrestrained interest. 'Go on, boy. Take your water.'

Freddie set the pail Jim Storm Cloud had given him beneath the filler pipe and used both hands to turn the stout, iron cock.

Rupert continued. 'I'll get your luggage sent on,' he said, his hand already raised to summon a brawny body to carry out the task.

Tom swung his walking stick over his shoulder and looked to where the labourers were wrestling the Noble Savage into an upright position in order to make loading her easier on their muscles. 'I trust no one will mind, but I'm taking a lady with me.'

Surprised and aware of Tom's reputation, Rupert raised his eyebrows. 'Do I know her?'

Tom grinned and patted Rupert's chest. 'Not intimately. She's old, half naked and weighs a ton.'

Rupert's puzzled gaze followed that of Tom. 'My word,' he said, bursting into laughter. 'What are you going to do with that?'

'It's a present.'

'Who to?'

'Horatia. Someone silent and wooden is ideal company for a woman who likes the sound of her own voice.'

–

The inn that used to be called the Noble Savage still did a good trade and not all of it legal. The dark tavern catered for many tastes. Beer and strong spirits were served on the ground floor. The upstairs rooms could be hired by the day, the night or the hour.

Silas Osborne rubbed at his bristled chin. He was down to his last ten shillings, but quite suddenly was less worried about it than he had been. His ship had just come in – metaphorically and in actuality. Needing fresh air, he'd just opened the window of the small room he'd rented. It was on the second floor and had sloping ceilings, a bed and the most frugal of furnishings. Many before him had slept between the stinking sheets, which were changed rarely and of indeterminate colour. Even though the air outside was tinged with the smoke of a busy city, it was far preferable to that of the room.

He would have taken just a few gulps and closed the window again if the sight of the men taking down the wooden Indian hadn't drawn his attention. A slow smile crossed his face. 'Well, I'll be blowed. If it ain't Tom Strong. Now what would 'e be wantin' with a scruffy ole bit of wooden injun?'

He watched thoughtfully as Tom Strong returned to his ship, a sleek, low-bellied West Indiaman, probably one of the last of her type to be made. Steam was taking over now, and rightly so. Silas would burn the lot if he had his way.

His attention was drawn to a man with hawk-like features, standing on deck, legs braced and hands clasped behind his back. His arms were bare and, like his face, red as clay. Glossy black hair, plaited and tied with something colourful, reached almost to his waist.

Silas Osborne was fascinated. The man reminded him of the lump of carved wood that had just been removed from the front of the inn, only he was male and much more colourful. But his attention kept returning to Tom Strong. Someone he knew very well was always saying that he wanted to know the minute he returned, that he had an old score to settle and he'd pay well for information.

Silas fingered a boil beneath his chin, digging it until it bled, and still he was thinking. *How much did Stoke want to pay? Ten, twenty, thirty sovereigns?* He gritted his teeth as he tried to work it out. His calculations were interrupted suddenly.

'Are you going to pay me now?' said a muffled voice from behind him on the bed.

Silas sneered but didn't look round. 'Did we agree a price?'

'A sovereign! I did all you wanted me to. I'm worth it, ain't I?' Her voice was a plaintive blend of demand and fear.

'Y-e-s,' the man said slowly. 'Though not so much as that man down there,' he murmured to himself.

Scratching the fleas from his chest and feeling in a far better mood than earlier when he'd awoken with a hangover, he turned back from the window. The prospect of money – a lot of money – energized his sagging body and made him reconsider his intentions.

The whore he'd picked up last night was struggling from the bed, her linen undergarments stuffed against her groin in an effort to soak up the blood flow he'd caused.

'Where the bloody hell do you think you're going?'

She froze, her eyes wide with fear above the white cotton. 'I'm going now – when you pay me that is…'

His smile was cruelly confident. Better times and better whores were on their way. In the meantime he'd continue playing at being the cat to the trollop's mouse.

'I 'aven't finished with you yet, 'ave I? And when I do, I'll pay you even more, won't I?'

'You sounds as though you got plenty of money. You didn't just now.'

His smile turned grim. She was braver than he'd given her credit for. Leaning over her, he braced his arms either side of her shoulders, his palms flat on the lumpy mattress.

'Enough for you fer now, and soon, once I've seen that old rogue Stoke, who calls 'imself Councillor Cuthbert now, I'll 'ave plenty!'

Chapter Six

Bootless, his legs thin and his clothes patched, Freddie Beasley ran determinedly, avoiding the street gangs who attempted to gain his attention, tempting him with claims that a pie man was close by.

'Drop 'im and he drops his tray, and we picks up his pies!' they shouted. 'Come on, Freddie!'

The thought of a fresh pie – even one that had fallen into the dirt and got stepped on in the skirmish – was enough to set his mouth watering, but he wouldn't be distracted. Not today.

Today he wanted to make his mother happy. He was sure his news would do that.

Freddie thought about things more than he talked about them. He kept his feelings to himself. He'd lost four brothers and sisters last year and the anguish of watching them die had remained with him for ages afterwards. He'd never showed his sadness, of course, not when his mother was around. Whilst his father, Deke Beasley, was away at sea, he was the man of the house. That's what his mother said. His father never said much on the matter, but then he spent most of the time drunk when he was home. On the whole, Freddie liked his father better when he wasn't there.

Following his brothers' deaths, there'd been respite for a while. Mother, his sisters and he had succumbed to no more than the usual coughs and wheezing chests of a winter spent in houses not fit for pigs. Icy weather meant frosted patterns on the inside of the window panes, the chimney filling the room with smoke from a smouldering fire, and icicles hanging from the pump in the yard, their only source of fresh water.

His mother was bending over a washtub when he arrived back, water sloshing from the pail. A wide smile divided his face.

After putting down the pail, he stood to attention before the tub and gave his mother a snappy salute. 'Captain Strong sends 'is regards,' he said as though he were six feet tall rather than a little less than four.

Edith's mouth dropped open and her cheeks went redder than they did when she was blowing at a coal fire. 'Captain Strong? You've seen Captain Strong?'

'He sends his best regards.'

'You little beggar! You're lying!'

'No I ain't!' Freddie grinned. 'Besides his regards, he sent you this.'

Edith's eyes and mouth were as round as the coins she held in the palm of her hand. She shook her head in disbelief. First, Blanche and now, Tom. It seemed too good to be true, but she couldn't help being doubtful. Hopelessness had become a way of life. She grabbed Freddie's ear. 'How did you know it was him?'

'Ow! Let me go, Ma.'

Edith let go his ear then rubbed it affectionately. 'Was it really him? Was it really?'

Freddie's grin brightened their grim surroundings. 'I told 'im you used to work at 'is place, and that you 'ad a friend from the Sugar Islands.'

'Blanche,' said Edith, her voice wistful. She sank slowly down onto her one and only three-legged stool. 'Well, fancy that. After all these years; first I sees Blanche, and then you sees Captain Strong.' She shook her head, her eyes dreamy.

They had a good supper that night. Freddie went out for a ham bone and two loaves of bread. They ate silently and quickly like starving rabbits, their jaws chomping at the best food they'd had for days. Edith sent Freddie out around the pub for two bottles of beer, enough for all of them to have a sip.

After they'd eaten and drunk their fill, Edith put the leftover coins into a tin tea caddy she kept hidden behind the plaster. The family were sworn to secrecy about the hiding place. If Deke found out where it was when he got home – whenever that was – it would all go on beer.

They settled down in front of the fire, the kindling and coal sending sparks flying up the chimney. They were warmer and better fed than they'd been for ages.

Freddie's face glowed in the light of the fire. 'You liked it out at that Marstone Court, didn't you, Ma?'

Edith smiled. 'Too right I did. At least I used to know where me next meal was coming from.'

Sensing she was about to recount her tales of Marstone Court, the children gathered round on bended knees, their faces upturned and expectant.

'Lovely days,' Edith murmured as she remembered.

'Was that before you met me dad?' Freddie asked.

He knew it was, but mention of his father always did the trick. She'd start talking about the old days, better than any story they'd ever been told.

'It most certainly was. There was no Deke Beasley in them days, him with his wicked words and his cheeky grin. It was downhill all the way once he came on the scene,' she said vehemently. Eyeing their faces, her voice softened. 'But there, if I hadn't met him, there wouldn't have been you lot.'

She ruffled their hair and laughed at their grimy faces. And there wouldn't have been any of the others who'd only had a few years of life before meeting their maker, she thought and sighed. That was the trouble with Deke Beasley; he was vigorous and she was fertile. Nine months to the day after he came home from sea, there'd been another mouth to feed. It had happened every year since she married him.

'So tell us about you and Blanche,' Freddie demanded.

'You do keep on, Freddie Beasley,' she said with pretend annoyance, then grinned and hugged him close. 'Blanche used to run like the wind. I remember her running with kites around the big park at Marstone Court. There were red deer in that park, and sheep and rabbits and lots and lots of birds. And sometimes we'd go on picnics beneath the trees and sometimes we'd go into Bristol and go aboard a ship that taught destitute boys about seamanship. It was called the *Miriam Strong*.'

Freddie's mouth dropped open. 'I'd have liked that,' he said.

Edith grimaced. 'You're a chip off the old block, you are.'

Freddie grinned and shook his head. 'No, I'm not.'

Edith weighed him up in an effort to evaluate just how much of the father was in the son. 'No. I don't think you are,' she agreed finally.

That night she turned over on the bed shared by the whole family and closed her eyes. Within minutes she was at Marstone Court, running with the children, chasing Blanche and a high-flying kite, a sweet dream that only lasted till dawn.

When morning came, Lizzie managed to get out of bed for the first time since she'd been taken ill. Smoothing the damp hair away from her child's hot forehead, Edith felt hopeful. 'I'll make you some soup. Would you like that?' she asked with her customary exuberance.

Lizzie smiled weakly and mumbled that she would. Edith felt her heart leap in her chest.

'I've got money,' Edith added. 'Oyster soup, I think.'

Edith ignored the fact that her daughter's skin was still clammy and there were dark circles beneath her eyes. It would go. She was sure of it. Anyway, she had to have hope. Everyone living in Lewins Mead had to have hope; there was sod all else to live on!

After swinging her legs out of bed and tucking the meagre bedding around her daughter's thin little body, she shouted for her son.

'Freddie! Get along and get me a pound of oysters and mussels.'

'Get us some too,' shouted a thin voice from down in the basement. Edith bit her lip. Molly McBean and her brood had less than they did. She was always asking Edith for leftover food or clothes that Edith had given up trying to mend. What were rags to Edith were Sunday best to Molly McBean. Molly herself had a hunched back and protruding teeth. Her poor little mites were bandy-legged and their hair was full of lice.

She'd calculated that the money from Tom and Blanche would last them for a fortnight at least, but not if she shared it with Molly. Mentally she tossed the coins from one hand to another, counting them as they went. She could tell Molly to cadge her daily bread from elsewhere, but she didn't have the heart.

Sliding her tongue to one side of her mouth, Edith dug out her money tin from the hollow behind the flaking plaster, and prised open the rusty lid. For a moment she eyed the few coins possessively before sighing and letting them drop into Freddie's outstretched hand. 'Oh well...' she sighed resignedly. Goodness knows where their next meal would come from once it was spent, but at least they'd eat well while it lasted.

As a trio of servants removed the custards, cakes and cheese from the dining table, Horatia turned away from the french doors. 'Tom! You are wicked!'

She was referring to the wooden statue that was presently being unloaded from a wagon and trying not to laugh.

Tom grinned through the smoke of his cigarillo. 'I couldn't resist. Call it a coming home present.'

She flashed her eyes and looked at him in mock displeasure. 'Rupert told me what you said.'

Tom groaned. 'The scoundrel! Never trust a man in a chequered waistcoat.'

Horatia gurgled with laughter. 'But I forgive you.'

Her breasts swelled against her tight, turquoise bodice and her eyes sparkled. More than anyone else at Marstone Court, Horatia Strong was glad Tom was home.

Sir Emmanuel Strong was slumped in a chair, his waistcoat straining over his paunch. 'Will someone fill my bloody glass?' he demanded, banging his whisky tumbler on the table at the side of his chair.

Out of sight of her father, Horatia threw Tom an exasperated look.

Tom shook his head just as secretively and raised a finger to his lips. *It's no trouble. Let's keep the peace.* He took the decanter from the sideboard and refilled it. Nelson was right. Sir Emmanuel drank far more than he used to.

After a swig of whisky, the old man eyed Tom speculatively, his eyes bloodshot in an overblown face. 'My daughter pretends to be a blushing maiden, but we are not fooled, are we, Tom?'

'Father!' Horatia sounded genuinely offended, though she smiled, her gaze fixed on Tom.

'I don't mean physically, my dear,' said her father, his words slurred with drink. 'I have every faith in your chastity. You know its value and, as in business, will hold out for the best deal.'

Tom was amazed both by the statement and Horatia's composure. Apart from a tension around her mouth, her expression was unchanged. What was she thinking?

'I mean business, Tom,' chuckled Emmanuel. 'My daughter pretends that she's the same as any other spinster; socializing, soirées and seducing likely husbands with a fluttering of eyelashes and a glimpse of bare bosom. But she's not. I know she's not.' He grinned at Horatia as if she'd been trying to hide her true self and he had found her out. 'She's like a spider in a web. She has my brain, Tom, trapped in a female body. I'm not sure whose brains my surviving sons have got, but I know damn well they're not as shrewd as she is.'

Horatia spoke loudly over her father's head and directly to Tom. 'He's going mad. I'm sure of it. Another year or so and we'll have to think of having him put away.' It seemed meant in fun, but Tom wasn't sure. It never paid to be too sure with Horatia.

Emmanuel shook a finger at his daughter. 'It wouldn't be in your favour to commit me to an asylum, my dear. Not until I do what I have to do. The old dog's not finished yet!' He turned to Tom. 'I'm rewriting my will, Tom. A powerful thing a will.' His eyes sparkled. 'I'll be head of this family to the bitter end – the very end – or woe betide them all. Now. Let's hear about this company you built up. Started from nothing, so I hear.'

'Not exactly from nothing. The company was in a mess when I first encountered it. I identified the weaknesses, sought new vessels and new markets. Initially there were just three ships and few cargoes. There are now fifteen ships and many routes have been gained from those less open to progress and too slow to adapt.'

'And you married the owner's daughter. A very shrewd move. I'd have done the same myself.' Emmanuel's eyes shone almost as brightly as they had ten years before, but he was eyeing Tom differently now, almost as though he were seeing a reflection of himself.

'Margaret, my wife died, as you know. Once she was gone and control of the business passed to a family member with no interest in progress or expansion, there seemed to be no point in staying. Steamships are the future, and Nelson came along with a timely plan to use steamships on the West Indian Trade. The time had come for me to leave, so I took the *Demerara Queen* in settlement of my portion of the business and came here—'

'You came home,' said Horatia, who had so far listened in silence.

Emmanuel's face shone with admiration. 'I'm sorry about your wife and losing control of the business, Tom, but everything happens for a reason, and do you know who I thought of when I heard about your success?'

Tom shook his head. 'No, sir.'

There was a loud slapping noise as Emmanuel's palm hit the chair arm. 'I thought of my grandfather!' he exclaimed. 'Like you, he made the first Strong fortune from nothing. On arrival in Barbados he hacked fields from forest and planted cane with his bare hands and a few indentured servants. Later on he bought a few shiploads of slaves from Africa. Everything grew from that.'

With a loud slurp, he took a swig of whisky before sinking back into his chair. 'Yes, you're just like my grandfather, so much, in fact, that I could almost believe you are a full family member and not just an urchin my brother picked up from the street. Indeed,' he said, his eyes shining, 'a true family member! Admirable, Tom. Admirable.' He raised his glass for Tom to refill, which he did.

Tom poured himself a glass of port and a sherry for Horatia. 'My life in America is all behind me now.'

'Letting you go is their loss and our gain,' said Horatia, her fingers trailing across his and her grey silk dress rustling as she twisted to face him. 'Adopting progressive practices and inventions before anyone else is the way forward, especially steamships. You know that as well as we do.'

In the past Horatia had not always been Tom's favourite person, but he was certainly warming to her. It was obvious that she was truly interested and fully understood the facts. He found himself addressing her with his ideas rather than her father.

'Do you realize how much time will be saved on a trip between Bristol and Barbados? Do you know that you can double, even treble the amount of trips you do in a year?'

Horatia shook her head, her eyes betraying that she was hanging on every word he uttered.

Emmanuel interrupted, his glass empty again. 'Only thing is, can we get the cane to grow fast enough for that many trips?'

'I understand what you mean, sir,' said Tom. 'Eight sailings a year can easily be turned into sixteen, perhaps even more, with the power of steam. As I see it, you have two options. First, you endeavour to gain other markets. In effect, the steamship company will stand alone and not be merely an appendage of Strong Sugar. Tax advantages need to be considered. The second option is that Strong Sugar endeavours to increase its yield of sugar with the help of applied fertilizers; I hear the guano from Nova Scotia is particularly beneficial to crop growth.'

'Fill my glass!' said Emmanuel, struggling to his feet. 'See?' he exclaimed loudly to his daughter, not noticing her surprised expression. 'Didn't I tell you that my brother Jeb did a good job of bringing up this young man? You're a credit to the family, Tom. A credit indeed. Why, what you're suggesting is almost like a new triangular trade; goods out of Bristol – perhaps iron or coal – to

Nova Scotia, then guano from there to Barbados – sell it to growers on the other islands if we can – then sugar and rum back here. It's a capital idea. Why has no one thought of it before?'

Overcome with excitement, Emmanuel let the empty glass fall to the carpet, tottered slightly, and reached for Tom's arm. 'I wish you were my son, Tom. I'd feel I was leaving the Strong inheritance in capable hands. As it is…'

Embarrassed by Emmanuel's uncharacteristic sentimentality, Tom said, 'You have your sons, Nelson and Rupert.'

Emmanuel waved the idea aside. 'Let's not talk of them. Let's discuss our plans and capabilities. Let's also talk of my mortality. Leaving my interests and wealth in capable hands helps me cope with the thought of eternity. Come, I want to show you my epitaph, my Egyptian room. You must see my Egyptian room.' Emmanuel steered Tom towards the west corridor.

Tom threw Horatia a pleading look. Was she coming too? She shook her head. He fancied she suddenly had something else on her mind, wondered what it could be.

Duncan and another footman stood either side of a pair of double doors, which were flung open at their approach.

Tom felt the head footman's eyes follow him and saw the jealousy simmering there. As he passed through the door, closely following the stumbling figure of Sir Emmanuel Strong, a shiver ran down his back, as though a knife were embedded between his shoulder blades.

The doors closed. The sound of their footsteps echoed over the marble floor and walls, the room's colours turned mellow by simple tallow candles held in iron sconces cast in the Egyptian style.

Although the room was cold, Duncan's look had been colder. As a man, he was arrogant. As a servant who coveted above his station, he erred towards dangerous. Duncan adored Horatia. My return is not welcome, thought Tom.

The situation was quite extraordinary. It wasn't unknown for servants to have a crush on their employers, but it was amazing that Duncan's feelings for Horatia had lasted so long.

Tom shrugged it off. Emmanuel's enthusiasm for his latest building project was too powerful to ignore. 'This is my Egyptian room,' he said, spreading his arms and staggering as he twirled around like a child's wayward top.

'It's like a temple,' said Tom, surprised by its coldness and slightly intimidated by the procession of figures forming a frieze around the walls.

'Not a temple, Tom, it's a tomb,' said Emmanuel, his voice echoing in the stillness.

Tom fingered the stone sarcophagus that dominated the room. It was heavy and solid, at variance with the stick-like furniture raided from the tombs of dead kings and now standing in the corners of what had once been a morning room. No natural daylight was evident.

'There are no windows,' Tom observed.

'I had them bricked up. The pharaohs built their tombs without windows.'

Tom eyed the old man thoughtfully. Was he comparing his own wealth and power with a pharaoh? It occurred to him that perhaps Horatia had heard similar comments, had formed her own conclusions and really was considering having her father put away.

Emmanuel rested his hands on the stone tomb and peered into its depths. 'It's quite comfortable. I've had a pillow and mattress placed in the bottom. I take a nap in here now and again.'

To Tom's amazement, Emmanuel began clambering over the stone ledge.

'Sir,' he exclaimed, grabbing his arm. 'Surely you've no wish to occupy your grave until you have to?'

With one leg posed awkwardly over the lip, and standing on tiptoe, Emmanuel grinned. 'Why not? I'm going to spend eternity in here. Might as well get used to it.'

Genuinely concerned for the old man's welfare, Tom tried again. 'It's freezing in here. Let us go back to the drawing room and have a glass or two of Madeira to warm us up.' He said it with a smile like people do when they're trying to jolly along someone older and senile, or someone young and wilful.

Emmanuel shook his head, his thinning hair wafting around his head like scraps of broken cloud. 'Promise me, Tom, that if I should die in this stone coffin, you allow no one to get me out, put me in a wooden coffin and bury me in the family mausoleum. There are two wives buried out there and a few children. I don't want to disturb them, and they probably don't want to disturb me. I believe that the only way I am going to attain everlasting peace is to remain here. Will you promise me that after I die, I remain in this coffin and am never buried out there? Do you promise me that, Tom?'

Strangely enough, it didn't seem an unreasonable demand and, with a bit of luck, he might not be around when it happened. Tom nodded. 'If that's what you want.'

Emmanuel smiled. 'I knew I could count on you, Tom. You always did stand up for what was right.'

'Blame your brother for that. After all, he was a clergyman.'

Tom assumed a relaxed expression, as Emmanuel thoughtfully traced his tongue slowly along his bottom lip.

'My brother was a good man. He used to make God sound as if he were a beloved grandfather or a favourite uncle. He did well by you, Tom. You're a good man too, but you've also got greatness in you.'

'If you say so, Sir.'

'My sons haven't got greatness. They're good enough, but not ambitious or shrewd. Now, Horatia on the other hand...' He laughed. Tom thought he also looked proud.

'She's a fine woman,' Tom said.

Emmanuel nodded knowingly. 'And will make someone a fine wife.'

Tom laughed. 'But only a fine husband who doesn't mind an independent spirit and a devious nature.'

'You, Tom,' said Emmanuel, his right index finger jabbing at Tom's shoulder. 'You! Horatia would not tolerate a lesser man.'

'The choice is hers,' said Tom, wondering if Horatia was aware that her father was laying the ground for a union between them.

'It's yours too. I'd approve, Tom, and I'd make it worth your while.'

Preferring to take it as a joke, Tom shook his head and laughed. I've only just got back to Bristol, Sir. Give me time to catch my breath.'

'She'll make you rich, Tom.'

'Better still if she can make me happy.'

'Let's see,' said Emmanuel. 'Let's see.'

He sank down into the stone coffin. Tom stood for a while, thinking on what the old man had said. His thoughts were finally interrupted by the sound of deep snoring from within the tomb. Emmanuel slept, but not yet for eternity.

Chapter Seven

With the aid of his stick, Cuthbert Stoke, who now called himself Sydney Cuthbert, limped across the room to the window. Lips pursed and nostrils flared, he watched as Silas Osborne whistled his way down George Street.

And so he should, thought Stoke, still bristling with the news Silas had brought and the price he'd demanded for it.

Stoke had come up in the world since his days of pimping and promoting bare knuckle bouts in and around the city. He was respectable now, a man with a fine household and legitimate businesses including city centre properties and slaughterhouses.

His house in George Street had five floors, the basement area housing the kitchen, scullery and laundry room, the top floor being the servants' quarters. He also had a son who was of such fine character that he'd never questioned his father's reasons for changing the family name. Gilmour was as innocent as his mother had been.

The door opening followed a polite knock. 'I saw a rather despicable character leave the house. Who was he?'

At the sound of his son's voice, Stoke stopped clenching his jaw and forced his grimace to become a smile.

'Gilmour, my boy.'

Gilmour had a homely look about him and a sensitive manner not inherited from his father. He looked concerned. 'Did he upset you? You look a little down.'

Stoke shook his head. 'He did not upset me. He merely reminded me of someone who did.'

'Oh dear. I'm so sorry.'

'No need to be.'

Stoke eyed his round-faced, pink-cheeked son with amazement. He'd never quite come to terms with Gilmour's cherubic looks and genteel demeanour, which was totally at odds with his own. He was so like his mother; a homely and respectable lady whom Stoke had left in the country whilst he'd gone to seek his fortune in the city.

Stoke squeezed a smile and tapped his leg. 'The same man who threw me across a room causing my leg to shatter.'

He didn't mention that this man, Tom Strong, also threw a fight, which caused him to lose a great deal of money. He'd never told Gilmour the more sordid details of his past life, only that he'd had an accident, which necessitated him using a cane.

'Is it hurting at present, Father?'

Stoke grimaced and rubbed tellingly at his thigh. 'A little, son, but it will get better soon.'

And not with medicines or a warm poultice, he thought, as a plan for revenge formed in his mind. Rumours had abounded that Captain Tom Strong had murdered Reuben Trout on the night he was found with his head caved in. Ten years had gone by and due to lack of witnesses, the matter was forgotten. There's the rub, thought Stoke, as his son poured him a measure of brandy. Persuade Silas Osborne to be a witness and you'll have the best revenge a man can have. Tom Strong would swing from the gallows, and good riddance too!

'Here's to my leg getting better,' he said with sudden cheerfulness and downed his brandy in one big gulp.

-

The sight of the great steamship filled Tom's heart with joy. There were three being built. The one they were looking at was closest to completion.

'She has an iron skeleton, which means her holds are unobstructed with cross-trusses,' the engineer explained.

Tom nodded. 'She has excellent lines considering she's made of iron.'

'I knew you'd like her,' said Horatia and squeezed his arm. Her eyes were bright with excitement. 'You can name her if you like.'

Tom looked to her father for approval. 'Sir?'

Emmanuel smiled despite the cigar clenched in his teeth. 'Certainly, Tom. Name her.'

Tom eyed the ship's strong lines. One name above all others came immediately to mind. 'A lot of men will depend on her strength. Her name should reflect that.'

Emmanuel nodded. 'A good sentiment for a good ship.'

'And she deserves a good name,' Horatia interrupted, a hopeful look on her face, one hand on her bosom as if her heart were racing. 'Come along, Tom. What will you name her?' She sounded breathless.

Tom addressed Sir Emmanuel. 'I don't have to decide now, do I?'

'Of course not.'

'In that case I will think about it.'

Horatia persisted. 'Will you name it after a lady?'

Tom smiled warmly at her. 'I think I shall consider all the lovely ladies I have ever known and decide which is the most appropriate.'

Horatia laughed and took his arm as they made their way to the engineer's office. His answer both puzzled and pleased her. He'd named no one, but had smiled as if one were uppermost in his mind.

The engineer doffed his hat and asked them to wait inside whilst he oversaw the launch of a ship around which a crowd of shipwrights swarmed, the vessel held upright by tautly strained ropes. 'I do apologize, gentlemen – lady,' he said.

Tom noted that this ship too was steam-powered, though smaller than the ones commissioned by Emmanuel Strong. Its name was *Mathilda*. 'May we watch?'

'You are most welcome.'

Sir Emmanuel asked if the owners were present so that he could congratulate them. The engineer answered that they were not and that an unnamed company owned the ship and was managed through a Bristol solicitor.

'Probably a foreigner,' he added. 'They sometimes prefer to be anonymous. Being foreign can be an obstacle to obtaining British trade.'

It took close to half an hour, but eventually the steamship slid into the water. Everyone cheered, including the Strong party. Horatia cheered the loudest and her face shone with excitement.

Tom leaned close to her and shouted above the din. 'You cheer as if this ship belonged to Strong Sugar.'

'It's good practice for when ours are launched.'

Tom suddenly became aware that someone else was watching the launch with an amused expression on his face. The man was tall, refined and dressed in a way that invoked suspicion.

'Popinjay,' Sir Emmanuel muttered on noticing the same figure. 'That's the lawyer, I suppose. Septimus Monk. A shrewd mind, but not the sort you'd want to share a room with – if you get my meaning,' he said to Tom, tapping the side of his nose.

Monk looked in their direction, doffed his hat and, smiling, bowed slightly. Tom returned his acknowledgement. Sir Emmanuel ignored him. It struck Tom that Monk seemed transfixed by Horatia, odd in the circumstances if his reputation was to be believed.

The moment they were back in the carriage, Emmanuel got out his hip flask. 'To steamships, Tom! And to another generation of Strong expansion,' he added, raising his flask to Tom and Horatia in turn.

Tom took a swift sip. Horatia did the same. 'Today is special,' she said in response to Tom's surprised expression and proceeded to light up a cigarillo. Tom did the same and they shared the same match, his hand cupping hers.

'I don't know that I approve of women smoking. It's not healthy,' said Emmanuel as he took out another cigar. Tom and Horatia exchanged amused looks.

The old bridge at Ashton was closed for repairs so they followed a detour that would take them into the city and back out again. Tom asked if they could stop at his ship so he could check with

Jim that everything was alright. The carriage waited as Tom went aboard the *Demerara Queen* where Jim Storm Cloud was sitting on a barrel. To Tom's surprise, Edith's boy Freddie was sitting at his feet, arms hugging his knees. Jim stopped telling one of his many stories of life on the prairies, looked up and got to his feet. 'Captain.'

Freddie got up too. 'My ma nearly had a fit when I told her I'd seen you.'

Tom laughed. 'Did she now!' He turned to Jim. 'Soon, we'll have a fleet again, though they'll be steam not sail. But the old girl still has a part to play,' he said slapping at the helm. 'Down to Spain, perhaps for oranges, or Oporto for the Croft Company.'

Freddie went on. 'She said it was funny, me seeing you and her seeing her friend Blanche on the same day. After all this time... that's what she said.'

The mention of Blanche stopped Tom in his tracks. 'What else did your mother say?'

Freddie shrugged. 'Only that she saw her friend, Blanche. That's all she said. Oh, and that she looked sad 'cos her little girl died from the cholera.'

Blanche had never been far from Tom's thoughts since his return to Bristol. Now his heart went out to her. It had occurred to him to visit her at home, but she was a married woman. He could hardly ask Conrad how she was – not in any great depth. Besides he didn't want word of a visit to Mrs Heinkel getting back to Horatia. Perhaps if he saw Edith first he could get some idea of Blanche's situation. Edith and Blanche had been great friends.

'For old times' sake, I think I must visit your mother,' he said, smiling down at Freddie. 'Will you take me to her?'

Freddie beamed so widely it looked as though his face might split in half. 'Course I will.'

Tom made his excuses to Emmanuel and Horatia. 'I'm taking this young lad back to his parents. He's been making a nuisance of himself to my first mate,' he lied.

'That's not what—' Freddie began.

Below the window and out of the sight of the carriage occupants, Tom's hand clapped swiftly over Freddie's mouth.

Horatia protested. 'Tom? I'll come with you.'

Emmanuel patted her hand and bid her sit back down. He winked at Tom. 'I don't think you'd feel comfortable with the sort of people Tom's off to see. We'll see you later, Tom.'

'My apologies to you both.'

He had the sense to throw Horatia a kiss, poor compensation for not keeping her company, but greatly appreciated judging by her instant blush. She'd been clinging to him ever since he'd got back from America, talking business mostly, but becoming more intimate each time they were alone. He put her out of his mind for the moment and followed Freddie Beasley to Cabot's Yard.

Blanche decided she owed Edith a great debt. If she hadn't bumped into her that day, she would never have been persuaded to attend Dr Budd's meeting.

'Edith and her family are almost destitute,' she said to Conrad. 'I'm going to take her some food.'

Conrad was delighted to see his wife so full of her old spirit but also told her that it was wildly reckless to venture into the most deprived part of the city. He insisted that John, their coachman, should go with her. Clothes the children had grown out of were piled in the trap along with a tin of biscuits, two pounds of cheese, a side of smoked bacon and a large pork pie. She'd also taken three blankets from the housekeeper's cupboard, much to Mrs Henderson's disgust.

The sky was bright with silver-white clouds that became yellow and grey as they passed over factory chimneys. The day turned darker once they'd crossed the Drawbridge and entered Lewins Mead. Blanche gazed down at the dark water where rats slid from sloping banks and fed as they squirmed among the rubbish. She wrinkled her nose. The smell was terrible. Even the horse needed greater urging to go forward through the piles of rubbish left to rot in the narrow alleys. The coachman clicked his tongue and used a flick of the whip.

Looking up, she saw a woman hanging from a window on one side of the street passing something to a neighbour on the other. The sky was just a ribbon between the two roofs. The place was dark, dank and smelled of decay.

The coachman slowed the horse and asked if she could tell him the exact address.

'Cabot's Yard. It has to be down here,' she said.

'Down there,' shouted a match seller who had heard her. She felt obliged to buy a bundle of matches tied with string. She also felt obliged to hand over far more than their true price. 'For your trouble,' she said, and the match seller thanked her profusely.

'Good job we only brought the trap, Mrs Heinkel,' said John, as the alley narrowed. 'The carriage would never have got through.'

Blanche sighed. 'It's a shame. I could have piled so much more into the carriage.'

John grinned to himself. Mrs Heinkel made him feel warm. She was a good person and hadn't once considered that she might be putting herself in danger. Lewins Mead was worse than the Pithay and that was putting it mildly. He took one hand off the reins and felt for the loaded pistol the master had insisted he take with him. 'But you are not to tell your mistress,' Conrad had added.

'This is it!'

Blanche jumped down before John had time to pull the horse to a halt.

'Here,' she said, pointing to the name etched into the wall of a ramshackle building – Cabot's Yard. Another narrow alley, too narrow even for the trap, led to it.

Duty-bound though nervous, John passed a shilling to the most honest looking person he could see. 'Look after the rig well, boy, and there'll be another shilling when I get back.'

The boy grinned. John winced. The gap in the boy's front teeth was big enough to drive a train through. John took the goods from the back of the trap and followed his mistress, his eyes darting from side to side and his bravery bolstered by the slap of the pistol against his hip.

Cabot's Yard looked deserted. The air smelled of dirt and tufts of grass grew from unkempt drains and mouldy window sills. At number five someone had made the effort to scrub their front step and paint it white. Blanche naturally assumed that this must be Edith's home and rapped smartly at the door.

Her heart raced as she imagined what Edith would say on seeing her again and how much she'd appreciate the things she'd brought her. Bumping into Edith had played a part in lifting her from her depression. She couldn't possibly just forget her.

She had the sudden feeling that someone had peered at her from the small, square window to the side of the door. When she looked, however, she fancied they'd darted away, not wishing to be seen. Undaunted, she rapped again.

'Looks like no one's at home, madam,' said John from behind the pile of clothes and food. 'Should we try another day?'

Blanche said nothing but stepped back and looked at the upstairs window. Suddenly it opened and a woman's head popped out. 'What do you want?'

I've come to see Edith. I don't know her married name, but she used to be called Edith Clements.'

'Beasley. Edith Beasley.' The woman wiped her nose on a dirty shawl that hung from her shoulders, then squinted at John's bundle. 'What you got there, then?'

'It's for Edith. There's clothes and food. Can I leave it here with you?'

The woman's face brightened. 'Course you can. Leave it outside me front door.'

Presuming that the door in front of her was Edith's, Blanche searched for another door but was unsuccessful. 'Where exactly is your door?' she asked.

'It's round the back,' the woman said quickly. 'But it don't matter. Leave it there and I'll be right round.' She disappeared.

'Leave it there, John.' Blanche indicated a dip in the cobbles at the side of the door.

John looked worried. 'Don't you think it might be better to take it away and bring it back again?'

Blanche was adamant. 'We have to trust people. Leave it. Anyway, Edith doesn't look like the only one in need of food and clothes around here.'

He did as ordered then helped her back into the trap.

'And don't look back,' she warned him as he took the reins, an anxious look on his face. 'Whoever takes it is welcome. There's plenty more where that came from.'

John had been about to glance over his shoulder, but managed to restrain himself in time.

They'd gone only twenty yards or so when the alley twisted to the right and Cabot's Yard was gone from view.

'I hope you know your way out of here, John,' said Blanche, as they rounded the crumbling walls of what had once been St Augustine's Priory.

'So do I, madam,' he muttered, thought of the pistol, and hoped his aim was as good as it had been in his army days.

–

'Fanny Arkwright, don't you dare!'

Fanny, who lived in a room above Edith's, had just been in the act of reaching for the bundle of clothes and food, when Edith opened her door and pounced on her.

'So why didn't you answer the door if you wants it?' Fanny demanded petulantly, disappointed at being found out.

'I got me reasons and they ain't none of your business!'

Edith wrested the clothes and food from her neighbour's grasp, her glower enough to burn the currants in a bun.

Fanny spat on the ground and stamped her foot. 'You should give me some. I was gonna look after it for you.'

'I bet you were!' Edith slammed the door.

'Why didn't you answer the door, Ma?' asked Lizzie, who was still thin but looking better every day.

Edith sighed and rumpled her daughter's hair. 'Me and Blanche used to live in luxury. How can I let her see me living in a dump like this?'

The other children gathered, their eyes wide with wonder as they ran their hands over the thick woollen blankets and took their pick of the clothes Blanche had left.

'Will we ever live in luxury, Ma?' they asked.

Edith could hardly tell them the truth – that they would live and die in a place like this because people like them had to know their place and stick in it. She chose to lie. 'We won't ever have a mansion, but one day we might have a little cottage with roses round the door and an apple tree in the corner of the garden.'

'Will we, Ma?'

The questions finished the moment the food came out. The kids dribbled. Edith found her own mouth was watering. It was hard, but she had to ration things out and thought she always would. Living frugally became a habit that was hard to break.

'Bread and cheese now, then a few biscuits, but that bacon can be hung up.' She hung it on an iron hook set into a beam, then watched her children, their faces bright with excitement as they shared out the food and turned over the clothes. Would life always be like this? A struggle for existence from one day to the next?

'Are you alright, Ma?' Lizzie asked.

Edith rubbed at her eyes. 'Just crying with happiness 'cos I can't wait to see our Freddie's face when he sees all this.'

Suddenly the door burst open and Freddie rushed in. 'Look who I've brought,' he shouted excitedly, as a tall figure ducked into the doorway behind him.

Edith almost dropped the piece of pie she'd cut for herself. 'Captain Tom!'

Tom smiled as he took off his hat. 'Hello, Edith.'

'That's two visitors we've had today,' cried an excited Lizzie. 'The other visitor left us food and clothes and blankets and she was dressed in blue and was very beautiful. Ma said it was her friend Blanche.'

'Blanche was here?' Tom could hardly believe his timing.

'She's only just left,' said Lizzie. 'Ma wouldn't open the door 'cos we don't live in a palace.'

He knew where Blanche lived, knew he could find her alone if he so wished, but the fact that he'd missed her by a few minutes seemed unfair. It was as if he'd been about to reach out and touch her, and fate had snatched her away. It made him think and act irresponsibly, and no doubt later he would regret it.

'Which way did she go?'

'That way,' said the boy who had held the horse. He'd been drawn to the doorway, his nose twitching in response to the smell that had wafted out into the yard. 'She's wearing a blue bonnet with feathers in lots of different blues.'

Tom paused before he left. 'Edith, I will see you again. The *Demerara Queen* is still berthed on St Augustine's Quay. Come and see me there.'

He didn't wait for an answer.

Edith was left gawping after him. She stamped her foot. 'I didn't even get a chance to thank him!'

She sighed. More pressingly, the money was fast running out. It would have lasted much longer if she hadn't helped poor Molly out. The fact was she could do with a little more, and although she was proud, her children and bread on the table came first.

'When shall we visit the captain?' Freddie asked impatiently.

'Dressed like this?' Edith waved her work worn hands at her patched and faded clothes.

'It's only St Augustine's Quay,' said Freddie.

Edith sucked in her bottom lip and thought about it. St Augustine's Quay wasn't far and perhaps she wouldn't feel out of place.

'All right,' she said. 'We'll do that.'

Just then, an almighty shriek sounded and Molly McBean appeared, her dirty nails digging into her cheeks and her peg-like teeth trembling in her open mouth. 'My baby! My baby's dead,' she wailed.

Edith sighed. 'Tomorrow. We'll go tomorrow,' she said to Freddie, and went off with Molly to see what could be done.

Blanche sat quietly, as they left Lewins Mead behind and re-crossed St Augustine's Bridge and bore south towards St Mary Redcliffe.

She'd so wanted to help Edith and tell her about getting involved in the fight against disease and was disappointed at not seeing her. Reacquainting herself with an old friend who had also lost children to cholera would have meant so much to her.

The old wound in her heart threatened to open up again. If she allowed it to happen, the old melancholy would return, but for now it couldn't be helped.

'I shall be going out again when we get back, John. I shall need the trap,' said Blanche.

'Do you wish me to come, madam?'

'No. If my husband asks, tell him I'm gone to Little Paradise.'

John nodded in understanding. Everyone in the house understood and sympathized with her need to be alone. Little Paradise was her refuge.

The cottage was empty of furniture, but was clean and pretty. In one of the bedrooms, tiny violets were hand-painted all over the wall. Someone had loved the place as much as she did, at least, that was what she liked to think.

—

Tom had never taken much notice of women's fashions before, but he certainly did so now. Ahead of him was the bonnet described by the boy. At present the pony and trap was caught in traffic, but once the area around St Augustine's Bridge was left behind, it would speed away.

He remembered that Blanche lived with her husband at Somerset Parade, and clambered into a cab, intending to follow her there, despite his earlier misgivings about visiting her at home.

He stuck his head out of the window at frequent intervals, saw the pony and trap ahead and knew they were going in the right direction.

The mansard roofs of Somerset Parade threw ink-black shadows over the riverbanks at their rear. The smell of flowers and scythed grass obliterated the smell of the river and the mix of smoke from the sugar refinery, the chocolate factory, the shot tower and the glass kilns. The blue sky was gone and it was raining.

He directed the cabbie to stop at the end of the street of fine town and mews houses.

'Wait here,' he said and got out. He walked just a few paces then stopped. The evening had turned gloomy – more like November than June. The sycamores and beech trees dripped moisture. Shivering, he turned his coat collar up against the relentless drizzle as it trickled down his neck and dropped from the end of his nose.

He suddenly felt a fool. What was he achieving by standing here? Was he going to knock on her door? He wanted to, but it wouldn't be right. The best thing he could do was to go home.

As he turned to leave, he saw the horse's ears prick at a muted sound. The pony and trap came back out of Somerset Parade and turned left, heading towards Redcliffe Church. Blanche was driving and she was alone.

Without regard now for how seemly it might be, he urged the cabbie to follow.

They followed the trap down over Redcliffe Hill and across the bridge. It was within walking distance, and though they had crossed 'The Cut', the fine houses of Redcliffe were still in view. But this was Bedminster. 'The Cut' was a man made stretch of water that took the river's tide. Once it was crossed, grim colliers' cottages, dwarfed by winding wheels, scarred what had once been farmland on the left of the road. On the right-hand side, nothing had changed. The old common, the fields and the copses gathered protectively around the last of pretty cottages where farm labourers and boatmen used to dwell.

Blanche turned into Apple Tree Lane at the bottom of the hill. By the time Tom had arrived, the horse was already resting on three legs, its head beginning to droop until it became aware of another horse entering the lane. Pricking its ears and raising its head, it let out a long neigh.

'Stop here,' Tom ordered the driver. 'And wait.'

There were no lights on in the house. He had presumed she was visiting someone, but if this was so, why were there no candles or oil lamps lit?

On entering the garden, he saw that the door had been left slightly ajar and was swinging on its hinges. The gap it left, leaking out a little of the dark mysteriousness of whatever was within, beckoned him. It creaked on its hinges as he pushed it open.

He entered, smelt her and felt his blood thundering into his head. This was madness. It should have been easy to leave, but he found it wasn't. He'd never sleep tonight if he didn't see her now.

—

The moment Blanche entered the cottage she knew that something had changed. Little Paradise had been her sanctuary since Anne's death, the place she had come to gaze across at the common and imagine her daughter picking dandelion clocks. This evening she had no wish to do that. Her heart felt lighter and her mind seemed filled with other things, not least knowing Edith's situation and the more positive aspect of fighting what had caused Anne's death.

There was a noise.

The sound of creaking joinery was not unusual in the old cottage, but there was something different about this. She couldn't recollect hearing such regular rhythm before.

Footsteps! It could only be footsteps.

Although her spirits were higher than they'd been for a long time, she still valued her right to privacy. Conrad knew very well that she liked to be alone here.

Her eyes flashed angrily as she shouted at the door. 'Honestly, Conrad, you could have left me to my own healing for a little while longer.'

The door opened slowly. The years rolled away.

Dark hair, blue eyes; exactly the strong face she remembered, mostly in her dreams.

He straightened with a casual grace that belied his height and firm build.

It was ridiculous, but for a moment she found it hard to say his name. It had remained unspoken for so long. At last it came. 'Tom.'

He smiled as though he'd never left, as though the years had never intervened. 'I followed you.'

Blanche gasped and shook her head. 'You shouldn't be here, Tom.'

Her gaze dropped to his hands as they played over his hat. They were tanned, she remembered they'd always been tanned.

'I've come to run a shipping company.' He smiled as though something had amused him. 'Steamships. That's why I came back to Bristol.'

'I see.'

'I also wanted to see you. I needed to know how you were. I understand you lost a child.'

She nodded, her mouth opening and shutting soundlessly.

Tom took two steps closer, then a third and a fourth. She counted them. Why would she do that? Vaguely, she realized it might be linked with the way she'd counted her strides as she ran along the Barbadian beach of her youth. Perhaps his presence was a bridge between her more recent past and further back.

He looked almost boyish when he began to explain, though a few grey hairs gleamed at his temples.

'Nelson persuaded me to come back – a business venture – I wasn't going to but... there was nothing left for me in Boston. My wife died and my in-laws preferred to dispense with my services.'

He kept fiddling with his hat, looking down at it as if searching for the right words to say.

'And you followed me.'

He nodded. 'I couldn't resist.'

'You shouldn't have.'

He tilted his head to one side, so boyish again. 'Why?'

Reasons seemed suddenly hard to find. 'Because it isn't right.'

She turned away and raised her hands to her face. Her palms were cool against the heat of her cheeks. Her blood was rushing; her heart was racing. She felt like a girl again. No! Of course it wasn't right.

'I'm sorry. I came here as an old friend. I went to your house in Somerset Parade and saw you driving your trap. I wondered where you were going.'

Blanche sank down onto the window seat and turned her face to the scene outside the window. 'I like to come here alone. I sit and look at the common and imagine my daughter playing there before she died.'

'I'm sorry. I shouldn't have come.' Head bowed he made for the door.

'No! No need.'

Her exclamation was spontaneous. She looked at him, remembering what had been between them and feeling again the old passion. Her protectiveness of Little Paradise seemed less important than it had been. It was almost, she thought, as though Tom had broken a spell that had kept her tied to this place.

'Tell me about your life in America,' she said.

He sat beside her on the stone seat and told her about Margaret, Boston, the Indians and the Clipper ships with their tall masts and acres of sail. He told her about coming home and his plans for expanding the Strong family interests into steamships.

'You always were ambitious.'

Tom looked surprised. 'Was I?'

She smiled in that smooth, soft way of hers that made him want to kiss her. 'You just didn't know it. You're too strong a man to be otherwise. It runs in the family.'

'But I'm not a Strong. You know that. In fact, I haven't a clue who my father is.'

Blanche touched his hand. 'Whoever he was, I think he'd be proud of you.'

'Now tell me what you've been up to,' he said.

She didn't hesitate but told him about the family, her household and her keenness to get involved with helping people like Edith.

'The city Corporation are looking into ways of improving the sewerage and water supply in the city so that cholera never strikes again. I went to a meeting about it.'

Tom laughed as he shook his head. 'I'm amazed. You and all those stuffy old men talking about sewage!'

Blanche frowned at him. 'You're being condescending.'

Tom adopted a sheepish look. 'I'm sorry. I didn't mean to be.'

'Besides, I wasn't the only woman there. Horatia was there too, though I don't think for the same reason. I hear she has her eyes on the contracts that such projects produce. She's quite a formidable woman.'

Now it was Tom who frowned. 'Yes. She is.'

An awkward silence seemed to fall between them. Blanche got up, found her legs were weak and almost sat down beside him again. It was tempting to do so, but she was aware of where it might lead.

'We shouldn't be here alone. I think I should go.'

Tom got up too. 'Of course.' He followed her down the stairs. At the bottom he offered her his hand. 'It's good to see you again, Mrs Heinkel.'

'Blanche,' she said taking his hand. 'I was always Blanche to you and always will be. Nothing has changed.'

The hand that held hers was warm.

'Nothing?'

No, she thought, looking up into his face, nothing at all. Excitement, warmth, anticipation; they were all there, just as in the time preceding her marriage to Conrad.

'Welcome home,' she said, and felt her eyes misting with tears. 'I've lost a child and gained a friend.'

He nodded. 'Regained a friend.'

He held both her hands and kissed her forehead. She did not object. This was about comfort and the warmth between friends – at least, that was what she told herself. Deep down she knew it wasn't true.

A sudden shaft of brightness pierced the mauves and greys of the leaden sky, brightening the room and making her face glow.

She heard Tom's intake of breath. 'Blanche!'

She did not protest when he cradled her head against his shoulder. It was what she needed. All the pent-up emotion of the past years spilled out. Deep sobs racked her body.

He held her close, one hand in the small of her back. 'Blanche! My darling Blanche!'

She reminded herself that she had children, but it was no good. She could not dismiss her feelings that easily, but she had to, she just had to.

'No,' she said, breaking away.

He stood against the window, his profile dark against the gathering dusk. 'Will you still come here? Will you come here to see me?'

She looked at him and remembered how it had been when she'd first come to England from Barbados, expecting to be accepted as a member of the Strong family, and ending up as nurse to those who turned out to be her half-brothers and sisters.

Tom too had not really belonged, but had risen above it all, so much so that Horatia had fallen in love with him. It was only natural that they should have been attracted to each other. After Tom had gone to sea and Blanche had married the kind and generous Conrad Heinkel, who had badly wanted a new mother for his children, she'd assumed her feelings for Tom Strong were well behind her. But they were still there, flirting with her mind and her heart.

'You seem uncertain.'

'I'm married, Tom. I have three children. I come here with them sometimes.'

'But mostly you come by yourself?'

She nodded.

'Then I will come here when you are alone.'

Blanche shook her head. She didn't like the way she was feeling. The way her body had reacted to his touch had unsettled her, and she didn't like him assuming that nothing had changed between them – though it hadn't. She knew it hadn't. All the same, her confusion spilled out in sudden anger.

'You can't come back here after all these years as though you've never been gone and expect to take up where you left off. It isn't right, and I won't be taken for granted.'

'I wouldn't do that.' He returned no anger. His voice was even.

'We can't do this, Tom. We have different lives.'

Tom shook his head. 'We each have only one life. Despite my marriage you were never far from my thoughts. We're meant for each other, you and I. You know it just as well as I do but what we do about it is up to us as individuals. Don't ask me to dissuade you or promise not to come here again. I can't promise any such thing. If you're here I will come. The day you're no longer here and the door is closed against me, I will leave you in peace.'

It seemed so sensible, an open-ended bargain. She could make a decision about it when the occasion arose. 'And that's your promise?'

He nodded. 'It is.'

Chapter Eight

Edith caught glimpses of herself in the panes of a chandler's window as she dashed along the road with young Freddie clinging to her flapping skirt. She'd pinned her unruly locks into a tight bun at the nape of her neck, though a few curls had already escaped, straggly and wildly curling across her face. Her dress was newly laundered and used to be dark blue. It was slate grey now after years of washing, and there were patches sewn beneath the arms where the material had rotted as a consequence of sweat and hard work. Sadly, it was the best she had, one of only two she owned. God, but there were times she wished she were still in service to the Strong family at Marstone Court. At least she'd been decently dressed and fed, and they'd had plenty of soap and water – enough to take a wash every day if she pleased.

Freddie ran alongside, a wooden pail bouncing against his grubby knees. Every so often she glimpsed him looking up at her, his mouth hanging open.

Edith marched on, heart pounding like a pair of bellows. 'That bloody Molly McBean,' she muttered, her overlarge shoes slapping against the cobbles like a sprightly carthorse. Yesterday she'd wanted to follow Tom and thank him for the money, and it wouldn't have hurt to ask for a little more. She wasn't proud. She had children to feed. But Molly had come, shrieking on about how her little one was ill and what should she do. Molly was the reason that Tom's money hadn't gone as far as it should. Edith felt sorry for her neighbour who had the misfortune to live in the cellar. Worse place in any house was a cellar. Black mould grew out from the plaster and fungus sprouted like sturdy shelves in the corners.

Much as she'd tried to revive it, the baby was dead; another little soul taken long before it should be and left wrapped up in rags on a shelf in front of the window. Sad, thought Edith, but there, that was Lewins Mead for you. Death was like a dockside tart – hanging around on every street corner – only with a wider choice of clientele.

They erupted from the side alley and into the wide thoroughfare that was Broad Quay, near St Augustine's Quay. Masts and spars pierced the morning mix of sunlight and mist, which made them seem as sparse as poplars, black and stripped of their leaves.

Freddie's little legs hurried faster as he pointed excitedly. 'That one.'

Edith came to a halt, looked then stepped on the gangplank of a sizeable ship and went aboard.

'Ahoy there!' She giggled at the expression, but it seemed appropriate. She'd heard sailors shout that all along the quay. 'Anyone there?' Craning her neck, she peered over the deck for any sign of movement.

'I am.'

Edith almost jumped out of her wits. There he was, big as life before her, yet she hadn't seen him. The thought unnerved her, and the sight of him unnerved her further. He was big, broadshouldered and bare-armed; his hair was like a black cloud hanging down his back.

Freddie recognized Jim Storm Cloud and sucked in his breath. 'That's the first mate and his skin's that colour because he's an injun from America! He told me to bugger off at first but we're best mates now. He tells me stories.'

'Does he now?' muttered Edith, her gaze fixed on the mountainous man coming towards her. The slanting rays of the morning sun lengthened his shadow, making him seem larger than he actually was – and that was quite large enough.

Freddie had told her all about him, but the sight of him still left her speechless.

Once she'd regained control of her tongue, which in the interim had cleaved to the roof of her mouth, she stated why she was there, her hand resting on her hip and her chin held high.

'I've come to see Captain Tom. I'm an old friend of his.' She said it loudly – enough to frighten him and give her the courage she needed to carry on. 'I want to thank him for a favour he did me – a respectable favour I might add, just in case you was thinking anything else.'

Stony-faced, Jim Storm Cloud looked her up and down.

Sensing his disbelief, Edith rolled up her sleeves as though she had every intention of giving as good as she got should he fancy his chances of throwing her off the ship. With a determined clatter of her sloppy shoes, she thrust her nose as close to his as she was able; it barely reached his chin.

'I *am* an old friend.' She was almost tempted to stamp her foot, but remembered how loose and worn-out her shoes were. They were all she had and she couldn't risk losing them in the dirty water that eddied around the mooring.

Jim Storm Cloud seemed unimpressed by her threatening stance. 'Well, you won't find him here!'

Edith cocked her head like an angry old hen. 'So where will I find him?'

'None of your business.'

His mouth snapped shut just inches from her face.

'No need to snap me nose off! And anyway, it is my business. I *am* an old friend, I just told you that, you foreign git! What's the matter with you? Got jam in yer ears?'

Storm Cloud looked dumbstruck for a moment, as though it suddenly came to him that she might – just might – be telling the truth.

'And I am Freddie's mother,' she said suddenly.

The Red Indian leaned on the ship's rail and eyed St Augustine's Quay as though he was thinking about buying it for a knock-down price. He looked at her and she looked back, fascinated by his gleaming skin, his imposing height and the fact that his muscles bulged like potatoes beneath his skin.

Sharp eyes shone from within a face that looked as though weather from every four corners of the globe had beaten it around at some time or another. After thinking about it, he looked round and said, 'I think we've agreed that Tom Strong is a good man.'

'The best! Will you thank him for me? That money he gave me was the difference between life and death for the likes of us.' Her confidence waned as she wondered what her and Freddie must look like – scruffy, dirty, threadbare, poor. She felt mortified when he looked her up and down.

'I think he will want me to give you this,' he said, and handed her a few shillings.

She started to protest.

He held up his hand. 'You are an old friend. What are friends for? Captain Strong would approve. His friends are my friends.'

Edith clutched the coins to her chest. 'That's really kind of you.'

He shrugged and, for the first time, his granite face broke into a smile.

Suddenly, she felt like a young girl again. She didn't know this man, but she liked the way he talked and his sentiments about Tom Strong were good enough to consider him a friend.

'What about the water, Ma?'

'Oh, ah! I forgot.' Edith sighed. 'Silly cow, ain't I?'

Together they went to the Quay Pipe. Edith felt Storm Cloud's eyes on them. Pushing fiercely at the pipe handle, she told herself not to be a silly goose. She was a married woman with a houseful of children and shouldn't be thinking such thoughts. Brooding on children took her thoughts to Deke Beasley, her husband. Like Jim Storm Cloud, he was a seafaring man – but that was where all similarities ended. Soon he'd be home and her poor but happy little world would be turned upside-down.

Freddie placed the pail beneath the waterspout. Caught up with her thoughts, Edith could barely find the strength to turn the stiff iron bar that operated the ancient standpipe.

'Let me, Ma.'

Edith moved aside. Freddie grunted with effort, his ragged sleeves falling back to reveal his scrawny little arms.

Storm Cloud saw the thin arms and muttered under his breath. No child should be that thin, though he'd seen enough of his own people like that, dying from disease and starvation at the coming of the white man. He'd been one of the lucky ones, taken in by Tom's father-in-law, educated then given a job on a ship. Although he'd been willing to thrash Freddie when they'd first met, he now found himself admiring the little rascal.

Edith gave the stiff tap another good tug, hunching her shoulders and putting her back into it. The old ironwork, blighted by age, stayed stiffly shut.

Storm Cloud pushed them both gently aside. 'I will do that for you.'

Taking hold of the handle with hands made tough by years before the mast, he gave one good tug and water gushed from the pipe, filling the pail and spilling onto the dirty ground.

Once he'd turned the pipe off, he handed the pail to Freddie. 'There you are, son.'

Freddie took the pail. Edith thanked him.

Jim screwed up one eye as though there was more to Edith's relationship with Tom than she was admitting to. He eyed her, eyed Freddie, and then eyed her again.

'We were just friends,' she said hotly once she'd cottoned on to what he was most likely thinking.

He grinned, his bright eyes twinkling wickedly. 'Just a thought, ma'am, just a thought. No offence intended, and I hope none taken.'

'I don't suppose so,' said Edith with a haughty sniff. She was taken aback by what he said next.

'So you knew the captain before he was married?'

Caught unawares, though disinclined to show surprise, Edith stumbled to speak. 'Course I did. Before he left Bristol, that was.'

Hurt pride made her cocky, which was silly because her and Tom had never had that sort of relationship. It was Blanche he'd loved, which had irked Horatia Strong something chronic. Still, she had to admit to being surprised that Tom had married.

Although he'd never shown her anything but friendliness, somehow she couldn't help feeling betrayed, though Lord knows, she knew where his heart lay.

'A good man. The best of captains.'

'Yes,' said Edith, her gaze fixed on his noble face, aware that her mouth was hanging open, but unable to do anything about it. For once she couldn't think of a single thing to say.

Jim Storm Cloud nodded, his look a mix of intent and sullen abandonment. She guessed he was not a man for showing his feelings overmuch. He turned abruptly away. Their meeting was at an end.

Edith's romantic memories of Tom became completely and abruptly drowned in reality. Tom's love and affection had been for Blanche. Any fool could have seen that. And that, Edith Beasley, is what you are, she said to herself. A fool! Nothing but a bloody fool!

That Jim Storm Cloud's got a lovely voice and would make two of my Deke, she thought then. She blushed and shook herself, though the vision of him stayed firmly in her head.

'Come on,' she said to Freddie, who was struggling single-handedly with the bucket. 'Let me give you a hand.'

Water slopped from the pail on their way back to Cabot's Yard, but Edith hardly noticed. She was poor, hungry and worn out with childbearing, looking far older than her thirty-two years. Nothing in her world would ever change unless something quite wonderful happened.

Chapter Nine

'Your pieces of silver,' said Stoke as he tossed a bag of coins over the door of the sleek landau in which he was travelling.

The bag landed in a puddle at the feet of Silas Osborne.

Stoke was pleased. Everything was going as planned. He'd have his revenge on Tom Strong for throwing him across that bar, breaking his leg, and for throwing that fight, which had almost made him bankrupt. He'd had to keep a low profile for a while after. It was during that time that he'd left brothel-keeping behind and bought old, run-down properties in a less fashionable part of the city where rats were as numerous as people.

Grim-faced, Osborne bent slowly to retrieve the bag. There was a sneer on his face as he straightened. He had not relished having to stoop for what he regarded as well-earned cash, and it showed. He squinted and tilted his head to one side. 'No need to be so sharp, Stoke. We goes back a long way, you and me. Almost friends, you might say, and who knows when you'll be wantin' me services again?' Stoke snorted as though he'd just been subjected to a particularly obnoxious odour.

'I do not wish to be reminded of that particular fact. I just hope you'll remember to appear in court when you're called as a witness.'

'Won't you have to get the bobbies to look at things again, Stoke? After all, it was a long time ago. They don't like looking into old cases when they got so many new ones to deal with.'

'Leave that to me, Osborne. Just make sure you're around to bear witness or you'll be the one in prison.'

'Don't threaten me, Stoke,' said Osborne, leaning closer. 'Just you make sure I gets the other half of my money, or I'll be bearing witness against *you*.'

Stoke grimaced and wrinkled his nose. Osborne stunk. 'You're a pig of the highest order, Osborne, and very bad for business along the docks, so I hear. How many trollops have you beaten up this week?'

Osborne scowled. 'I seem to remember that you didn't exactly have a light touch.'

'I demanded discipline. I didn't beat them senseless purely for the pleasure of it.' Stoke jabbed his coachman in the back with a silver topped cane. 'Drive on, Magnus.'

Magnus barely had time to let off the brake when Osborne's thick hands slapped heavily onto the carriage door, dragging it slowly to a hesitant walk.

Osborne's eyes reddened beneath his bushy black brows. 'Too fine to pass the time of day with yer old friends then, Stoke? So bloody fine that you arrange to pay me what's due in the street for carrying out yer dirty work, not invite me to yer house in Clifton? 'Fraid I might upset yer fine-feathered friends?'

Stoke flinched. Few people – those who knew that is – dared to remind him of his past. He was a gentleman nowadays and thought he deserved to be treated as such.

'How dare you!' he growled, the brim of his hat falling with his frown.

Before Osborne could move, there was a sound of crunching bone as the silver-topped cane slammed down on his hoary knuckles.

Most men would have yelled, whipped their hands away and blown and sucked on their injured parts until they were bearable, but not Osborne. The brute barely flinched, though the blow must have hurt.

Urged on by the coachman, the carriage moved forward. With a bellow of rage, Osborne flung himself at the carriage, his body thudding against its side.

Stoke's mouth dropped open as Osborne gripped the carriage door with his brawny fingers and brought it to a lurching stop. The horses neighed and tossed their heads, sawing their mouths against the bite of the bit.

Osborne's flaccid lips spread over a mouthful of decaying teeth, and his chill, blue eyes were mere pinpricks in his narrowed gaze. 'No matter yer fine clothes, Cuthbert Stoke, you'll always be a snake, a cur, a turd from the gutter!'

'Drive on,' Stoke shouted. Beads of sweat broke out on his forehead and ran down his nose.

'Turd!' snarled Osborne as, with one almighty tug, he wrenched the carriage door off its hinges.

'Drive! Drive! Drive!' shouted Stoke, his voice high with hysteria.

'Turd!' shouted Osborne again and sent the door flying through the air.

The coachman whipped the horses on. 'Do you want to go back and deal with him, sir?' he asked over his shoulder, his voice trembling with terror and his brown face turning alarmingly white.

'I haven't got time for that, you bloody fool!' Stoke shrieked. 'I'm an important man. I have a meeting to attend and I must be there. Now drive on. Drive on!'

To his coachman's surprise, Stoke leapt forward, grabbed the whip and cracked it fiercely across the backs of the matching Flemish roans.

'Faster! Faster! I must not be late for the meeting.'

It was only a half-truth. Even if he hadn't been going to an important meeting, he would never have dared rebuke Silas Osborne. The man was an animal, a giant of a man with a temper to match. Stoke realized too late that he'd pushed him too far.

A few minutes later, a liveried footman ushered him into the presence of Sir Stanley Moorditch, a noted judge and epicurean. It was rumoured, amongst other things, that he had special furniture made to take his enormous bulk. Stoke could believe it. The man was a monster.

Much to his satisfaction, Stoke was shown into the library. A triumphant expression came over his face as he gazed around him at the book-filled shelves lining the walls. This was exactly the room he'd wanted to be in.

'What can I do for you, Mr Cuthbert?' Sir Stanley asked once both were sitting comfortably with glasses of port.

'I want a murderer arrested.'

'Really? Any particular murderer in mind, or are you not particularly choosy?'

Stoke smiled dutifully at the judge's joke. He'd heard similar many times before. 'It happened ten years ago...'

Stoke outlined the case of Reuben Trout, how the man had been found in a stable with his head smashed in, and that it was common knowledge that Captain Tom Strong had vowed to kill him.

Sir Stanley indicated that he'd taken in the facts with a series of nods. 'And you say this happened ten years ago?'

'That is correct.'

The judge hissed through his teeth. 'Well, it's not unknown for closed cases to be re-opened, but tell me, I'm curious, why do you want this?'

Stoke smiled. 'The murderer has only lately returned to the city. Let us just say that as a respectable citizen I wish to see justice done.'

Moorditch shook his head. 'I cannot see such a thing happening. There would need to be very good evidence. Rumour that Captain Strong actually did the deed is not enough.'

'A new witness has come forward.' He did not mention that the witness was also the man that had brought him the news of Tom's return, and that he was being paid to commit perjury.

'Oh? And why didn't he come forward at the time?'

The lie rolled smoothly off Stoke's tongue. 'He was a soldier and had to join his regiment immediately. He didn't think his evidence would matter that much.'

'Ah!'

Sir Stanley pondered on the matter, his brow furrowed as he took a sip of port.

Stoke guessed what was going through his mind; no one wanted to upset the Strong family if they could possibly avoid it. They were rich, they were powerful and, pulling the right strings, Tom could easily get away with it. Well, I have strings I can pull too, he thought.

Just as he'd supposed, the judge was not amenable to the idea. 'But surely, we are talking about the life of a gentleman and the death of scoundrel. And it all happened a long time ago. I mean, does it really matter now?'

'It does to me.'

Sir Stanley smiled affably and got to his feet, his drained port glass signalling that the meeting was at an end.

'Your sense of public duty is most commendable, my dear Mr Cuthbert, but I really cannot see the point of raking over cold ashes.' His plump hand landed on Stoke's shoulder. 'Let bygones be bygones. That's what I say. What say you, my dear chap?'

Stoke rose slowly to his feet. His expression left Moorditch in no doubt that he had no intention of doing that. 'Are you still a collector, Sir Stanley?'

The question took Moorditch off guard, just as Stoke had intended. The colour drained from his face.

Stoke walked slowly around the room, his fingers trailing over the leather-bound volumes. Finally, he curled them over one particular book and jerked it from its place.

'I...' The blood rushed to the judge's face. His eyes became black dots in a sea of obesity and redness.

Stoke's smile was thin and cold. With one swift movement the book fell from the shelf. What looked to be loose leaves fluttered out like broken wings and lay scattered over the floor.

Stoke picked up a few and fanned them in his hand like playing cards. 'I see you are a connoisseur of new inventions, Sir Stanley.'

He waved three photographs before Moorditch's frightened eyes.

'The camera. A wonderful new invention. And these, Sir Stanley, are photographs taken by such a camera. Dirty photographs of little girls without their clothes on.'

Moorditch's tongue flicked nervously over his lips before he blurted. 'They're only pictures, just like paintings are only pictures.'

Stoke's laugh was as thin as his smile. 'Yes, yes, of course they are. Number twenty-four, Cherry Tree Alley. An apt name, don't you think for a "cherry house" where those with money can pluck the youngest fruit? Some of these poor little girls have been sold into the house by their kinfolk. Others come by way of the workhouse. Aren't you a governor of one of the city's workhouses, Sir Stanley?'

Moorditch raised an arm and gave a small cry, as Stoke slapped his cheeks with the cards.

'The likes of you bend the law to suit themselves. The circumstances of these girls don't matter to you. They are there purely for your pleasure and you can afford such delicate, unblemished fruit. You can afford to buy anything you like.'

The sweat that had broken out on the judge's face now dripped off his chin.

Sensing victory, Stoke patted Moorditch's shoulder in the same condescending manner as Sir Stanley had patted his. 'As a judge, do you not agree that the guilty should be brought to justice?'

'Please. You won't tell anyone…'

'Do you not agree?' Stoke repeated.

Moorditch shook his head vehemently. 'Yes. Yes, of course. It will take time, but it can be done.'

Stoke flicked his finger over Sir Stanley's plum-coloured nose. 'I don't mind you taking a little time, just enough for me to savour the triumph to come.'

'I'll have to talk to the chief constable.'

Stoke raised his eyebrows. 'And?'

'A meeting will have to be arranged between the witness and the police.'

Stoke smiled. 'He'll be there. Rest assured, Sir Stanley, he'll be there.'

Septimus Monk almost bowed, as Horatia swept into the room dressed in a cream gown trimmed with coffee-coloured lace, the cuffs and collar fastened with pearl buttons. She wore an off-the-face hat with a lace veil at the front and coffee-coloured ribbons trailing at the back. Her earrings matched her outfit and were highlighted in gold. She looked feminine, but at the same time superbly efficient.

Monk indicated his desk with a flourish of his hand. 'I've spread it out ready for you.'

Horatia barely acknowledged him but went straight to the desk. Bending slightly from her corseted waist, she studied the city map. Monk had weighted it down at each corner with two inkwells, a paperweight and a polished cannonball that he usually kept on the mantelpiece.

'Have you the proposed route of the sewers?'

'I have it here.'

He placed a sheet of paper headed 'Bristol Corporation' beside her left hand. She studied it quickly, her eyes darting between the properties affected by the proposed sewer route and the map. Her fingers found the location of each street listed.

'Have you traced the owners?'

'I have indeed.'

'And you have offered on my behalf?'

'Yes.'

'There are sixteen properties here that interest me. How many are willing to sell?'

'Ten.'

Horatia straightened. 'Only ten?'

'Yes.'

'Have you offered enough?'

Monk cleared his throat. 'The money isn't the problem. Two of the properties have only just recently changed hands to a landlord who already owns four properties of the six. I fear we have a competitor. Whoever this man is, he knows the route of the sewer and is out to make himself a fortune.'

Horatia was most put out. 'How terribly vulgar! What times we live in. It appears some people will do anything for money.'

Monk thought he'd covered his smile but Horatia's eyes were quick to see it.

'Never mind smiling! I want you to purchase these ten properties forthwith. How much do you think you can get them for?'

'Two thousand pounds?'

'Two hundred pounds each.' Horatia frowned before coming to a decision. 'Buy them! Go to three if you have to, but buy them.'

'I will indeed.'

'And find out the name of our competitor. I'd like to know with whom I am competing.'

'Very well, Miss Strong.'

She paused by the door. 'You don't think this man is in sugar, do you?'

He shook his head. 'I really don't know.'

Horatia's breasts heaved with her sigh. 'He must be. Anyone who can afford that amount of money has either to be in sugar or crime. For peace of mind, I will presume the former.'

—

Blanche liked having breakfast with her children. Both she and Conrad saw as much of them as they could, unlike those households where the children were only seen at teatime.

Conrad was talking about the new sewerage proposals and his part in them.

'There will be difficulties with the owners of some of the properties immediately in the path of the sewers. You have to hear these people to believe them, my dear. Suddenly, properties bought for fifty pounds are worth five hundred. There are some people in this city who will make a lot of money from these sewers, mark my words.'

Blanche had been a little distracted since meeting Tom at Little Paradise and was only half listening, which is why things started going wrong.

'I didn't want any more porridge,' said Max, as Blanche pushed the dish she'd just filled for Lucy, in front of him.

'Sorry, Max.'

'And I don't like salt!' Lucy wailed, her tongue slapping around her lips as she tried to dislodge the porridge from her tongue.

Exasperated, Blanche threw her arms in the air. 'Lucy!' she shouted.

'Are you feeling alright, my dear?' asked Conrad.

'Yes! Yes!' Banishing thoughts of Tom Strong from her mind, she handed the bowl to Martha, Lucy's nurse. 'She wants sugar, Martha.'

'I think we have plenty,' said Conrad with a wry smile. 'It would be a fine household indeed if a sugar refiner does not have any sugar, don't you think?'

It was a joke and Blanche laughed just as Conrad expected her to, though she had been laughing a lot more lately.

Conrad spooned three spoonfuls into his milkless tea and eyed her quizzically. 'Have you been listening to what I have been saying?'

She sat bolt upright. 'Yes. Of course. You were talking about the sewers.'

She'd heard that much and no more. Her thoughts kept drifting to Tom.

'Oh dear,' said Conrad looking remorseful. 'They are not a fitting subject for the breakfast table. I do apologize.'

'No need to.'

His eyes did not leave her. 'You seem to have something on your mind, my dear.'

'Edith,' Blanche blurted, grabbing the first excuse that popped into her head. 'I keep thinking about Edith and her children living in that dreadful place. I do hope she got the things I left for her. She seems to have so little and the stench around that place!'

'She should not be living there. Why does she not move?'

'I don't think she has any choice. Her husband's away at sea. I doubt whether she gets much money from him even when he is home.' Blanche shook her head and poked with her fork at the kipper on her plate. 'I don't know what else I can do for her. From what I remember she wouldn't take charity unless she earned it. Edith was always proud like that. She used to make up tales about her family that made them sound more wonderful than they actually were.' Blanche lowered her eyes. 'Poor Edith.'

Conrad got up from his chair and kissed the top of her head. 'We will do our best. That is all we can do. Now I must go,' he said, glancing at the silver watch he took from his waistcoat. 'Magistrates must set a good example and arrive at court on time.'

Conrad had been a magistrate for several years now, serving five days in every month and took great pride in doing so.

'I trust those in the dock will appreciate your punctuality,' said Blanche.

Conrad patted each child on the head and laughed as he made for the door. 'I think they would prefer that I did not come at all.'

Chapter Ten

Molly McBean came knocking at Edith's door, blubbering like a baby, her eyes red and sore.

'It's me baby,' she wailed as she sank to the ground, her bony knees poking through the rips in her skirt.

Closing the door behind her to keep the smell out, Edith patted Molly's skinny arm. 'I know, me love! Poor little mite's dead. She was dead three days ago, me love. Remember? I did tell you so, and there ain't nothing you can do now but bury her.'

'I can't,' she wailed, her mouth a red cavern of sore gums and blackened stumps. 'There's nowhere to bury her. There's no room in the graveyards.'

Exasperated, Edith threw back her head. 'God above! I've heard of there being no room at the inn for a newborn baby, but never no room in the graveyard for a dead one!'

'What shall I do?' wailed Molly. 'Poor little mite's beginning to smell. I got to get the poor thing buried.'

There was little time for sentimentality in Lewins Mead. Molly, who was a bit slow anyway, was too distraught to think straight.

Edith noted the vacant eyes, the drooping mouth. It never failed to amaze her that men actually paid for Molly's services, but thankfully they did. How else would the poor woman put bread on the table?

Edith sighed. It was up to her to sort this out. 'We'll get her buried. You see if we don't,' she promised.

During the long months of a hot summer, cholera had claimed the lives of thousands of people in the city. More had gone to typhoid and myriad other diseases common to a seaport, not to mention the deaths in childbirth and from gangrenous infections, starvation and old age (fifty and above). Summer always brought more disease and there were just as many bodies to bury as there would be after a freezing winter. Space was at a premium. Gravediggers had been ordered to open up old graves in order to bury the fresh bodies, which meant that as many as six bodies were being interred in one grave.

'I've no money for burial,' Molly wailed, her face puckered with crying and a stream of dribble hanging from her bottom lip.

Edith eyed Molly's poor clothes and the pasty white faces of what children she had left, their eyes sunk deep into their sockets and the sores of impending starvation circling their lips.

Edith sighed and considered what she could do to help, though she had precious little in her own house. At last she said, 'I've got a penny or two. We'll try St James' Barton. There's bound to be space for a little 'un among all them great big graves.'

Molly brightened, her square jaw returning to its usual jutting defiance, though God knows, it was a last-ditch stand. 'We'll show 'em all!' she cried, punching the air with a bony fist, each knuckle crowned with a single wart.

Edith searched for her last shilling left from those Jim Storm Cloud had given her and picked up a wooden shovel. Molly went to fetch the baby. When she came back, it was wrapped in what looked like an old shirt, stained yellow and smelling of piddle.

'What happened to the newspaper you had her wrapped in?'

'Needed it for the fire. Didn't 'ave any kindling.'

No surprise, thought Edith. Molly never had very much of anything.

Rays from the setting sun made the cobbles shine like polished oranges. A solid block of sunlight fell between buildings at the end of the alley reminding Edith of a gate. And I shouldn't be going out through it, she thought to herself, though couldn't for the life of her explain why.

It didn't take long to get to the churchyard of St James's Barton, which was large, encompassing as it did the site of an old abbey.

The shadow of the square tower fell over them like a black cloak, stretching right across the road. A lantern, housed in a wrought-iron holder, hung above the entrance. Below it in the shadows, something moved.

'There's someone at the gate,' Edith whispered to Molly.

'Damn 'em to hell, the lot of 'em,' Molly muttered under her breath. 'I just knew we should 'ave waited till it was dark.'

Edith eyed the two men standing close together. Beyond them the tombstones rolled away like sentinels, though some were lopsided and looked as if they were about to lie down with the dead.

'So what we gonna do?'

The question was as much for herself as for Molly, who only shrugged and looked perplexed.

Typical, thought Edith. Plenty of boasting about what she would do, but no doing. She just wasn't able to cope with the situation.

'Let me 'ave that 'ere.'

Molly passed her the rudely wrapped bundle. As she did so, a small, bare foot fell out. Edith shuddered and did her best to wrap it up again.

'Didn't you 'ave a better winding sheet that this, Moll?'

Edith sighed. 'Right,' she muttered determinedly and purposely poked herself in the eye. By the time she got to the graveyard gate, her right eye was watering and a real tear was running down her cheek.

The men looked up when they heard her coming.

'My baby,' she wailed, holding the bundle out in front of her. 'She's dead, poor mite. Dead, and all I've ever had to love in the world.'

'Is that so?'

Edith ignored the tart response. 'You have to let me bury her.'

'Go away. We're full up.'

Edith was not deterred. 'She's only two years old, and so small. She wouldn't take up much room, honest she wouldn't.'

'Clear off,' said the other man. Just to emphasize the point he ran a wooden stave along the bars. 'You'll get this if you come near 'ere.'

Edith thrust the baby towards them at arm's length. 'But my baby? The cholera got her...'

At the mention of the dreaded word, both men sprang back from the gate. This was exactly what Edith had hoped they would do. If they left the gate then they could climb over and get the child buried.

Unfortunately, they didn't go away. One of the men darted into a dark corner next to where a flying buttress was rooted into the ground and came out carrying something. 'Now get out of yur,' he shouted, levelling an aged flintlock at her chest. 'Go on! Go, or I'll open fire.'

Edith nudged Molly. ''Ere. You 'ave her now.' She passed the baby back to Molly.

'Well, that's that,' said Molly, as they walked away, the baby tucked like a parcel beneath her arm.

'No, it isn't.'

Edith was adamant. The poor babe hadn't had much of a start in life being born to a mother like Molly. She at least deserved a decent burial.

Molly sniffed and wiped her nose with the back of her hand. 'Well, they ain't gonna let us in that gate, are they? P'raps I should just chuck 'er in the river!'

Edith was appalled. 'I didn't get much religion when I was at home, but I do knows right from wrong,' she said, and rolled up her sleeves. 'There's a tree up against that back wall behind the church. We could climb up it and—'

Molly shook her head. 'No! I don't do climbing, Edie!'

Edith eyed her accusingly. Hardly the ideal mother, she thought to herself, or wife for that matter. Molly looked grotesque. Her hair was fine, wispy and grey. Her eyes were bloodshot and those teeth that weren't missing were black in places and yellow in others. Edith frowned. Molly's man – she wasn't sure whether they'd ever actually married – had been a big, bluff character when they'd first arrived in Cabot's Yard. Now he was a mere shadow of his former self, though still managed to knock out a new baby every now and again, despite Molly's dreary appearance. And every so often she had to go out and earn some money by the same method. There was half a chance that the baby might not even have been his.

Dwelling on Molly, her husband and her morals would do nothing to help the situation. Edith forced herself to concentrate on the tree behind the church as the sun began to disappear into the darkness. It looked ideal for climbing. She could do it. She was pretty certain she could do it.

Her glance settled on the sad little bundle Molly still carried beneath her arm.

'I'll climb over,' she said. 'But we'll have to wait until the sun's gone down.'

Thank God that doctor came along, she thought. Lizzie was the only case of cholera in Lewins Mead to recover. She felt obliged to help Molly bury her dead little mite.

Soon the darkness was complete, briefly lifted here and there by a candle-lit window or the odd brazier hanging over a posh front gate.

For a brief moment, Edith was tempted to try the front gate of the graveyard again, trusting that the men guarding it might have gone home or be sheltering somewhere. The idea was short-lived. She decided to play safe. Feeling their way through the darkness, Molly with her dead baby under her arm and Edith with a wooden shovel, they made their way along the perimeter wall of the churchyard to the tree.

'Give 'er 'ere,' said Edith after taking off her worn-out shoes.

Molly passed her the baby. Gently, Edith tied her shawl around the child and herself so that the bundle was close against her body. With the child fastened to her, she began to feel her way up the sloping trunk of the tree.

Despite the rain, the bark was rough and cracked. She poked her naked toes into footholds as she climbed higher and higher, not seeing anything but using instinct to feel her way. At last she was high enough.

From far below, Molly shouted, 'Are you there yet?'

'Shut up,' Edith hissed. 'Do you want to get us caught and up before the beak?'

Carefully she edged from the tree, swinging one foot across the branch to the jagged stones that formed the top of the wall. One of the branches drooped over it and almost touched the ground. Edith clambered down it, her bare toes seeking footholds until she judged it safe to jump.

The grass was wet and slippery as she landed, cooling her feet and soaking her skirt.

'Damn,' she muttered, realizing she'd left the shovel behind. Easing the baby and shawl round in front of her, she felt for soft, recently disturbed earth. There was plenty. Almost all the graves had been disturbed this summer in a bid to bury the swiftly decomposing corpses.

Amidst the smell of grass recently freshened by rain, she began to dig with her bare hands. At one point her fingers touched something hard and slimy, another body probably, but she swallowed her revulsion. She couldn't afford to be fussy. The city's graveyards were fit to bursting and the dead child deserved a proper burial. And the others in 'ere won't mind, she told herself.

Feeling round the soft earth, she judged the hole was deep enough and placed the poor little body on top of whoever was put in last. Just as quickly as she'd dug the hole, she filled it in.

Although she couldn't see her handiwork, Edith stayed crouching, face downwards. These were terrible times unless you had money to buy yourself a decent plot. Almost as bad, no plot meant no service, no saying of pretty words on behalf of the departed. It had been an awful summer.

'Well, I'm going to say a few words fer you,' she whispered close to the ground, and clasped her hands together.

For a moment she could think of nothing. Her mother had never said prayers except a few explicitly brazen oaths when she'd been on the gin. Then she remembered Blanche, the nursery at Marstone Court and the lullabies she'd sung to the Strong children when they were young.

Squeezing her eyes tightly shut, she forced herself to remember.

Birds going home, off to bed,
And so should you my sleepyhead,
Jesus watching, don't you cry.
And I'll sing you a lullaby.

Poor little mite can't cry, Edith thought sadly, but I hope she heard me singing.

Perhaps it was the lullaby or the fact that Tom Strong was back in Bristol that made her linger and think about Blanche. She had no regrets about not opening the door to her. 'How could I?' she'd said to Molly. 'There's the likes of me turning a penny in me hand, trying to decide whether to spend it on bread today, or scrape the mould off the stale loaf and save the penny for tomorrow. And there's her, looking all grand and smelling sweet and married to that big German bloke who owns the refinery. Look at me. I'm dirty, scruffy and always big-bellied.'

As she had many times before, she cursed herself for marrying Deke Beasley, a merchant seaman, a lout and a liar who'd spun her tales of foreign lands and tended to believe in his own lies. Every time he'd come home, she'd fallen again – both for his lies and another baby.

The rain plastered her hair to her head and washed the dirt from her face. She found herself enjoying being wet, her bare toes tickled by the wet grass and almost forgot the reason she was there and that she'd meant to be swift.

Too late, she realized she'd lingered too long. The light of a lantern pierced the darkness and two shadows took solid form and lumbered towards her.

'Stay where you are!'

'Not likely,' she muttered and swung one leg back up onto the drooping branch of the tree, which partially split and dried by the summer heat, cracked beneath her weight. She fell backwards and the branch fell on top of her.

'Gotcha!' shouted one of the men.

'Stop still and we'll let you up,' the other growled.

The fall had winded her. She was wet through and although she had plenty of fight left in her, the branch was too heavy to lift. If she couldn't use strength, she'd have to use guile. Lie still and let them raise the branch, then bolt for it, she decided.

'Let me out,' she said, as plaintively as she knew how. Feigning weakness, she lay as still as some of those resting beneath the tombstones around her.

One on each side, the two men began to raise the branch.

Edith sprang halfway to her feet, meaning to run, but stumbling. Something was pinning her to the ground. For one terrifying moment, she imagined a hand had risen from the grave beneath her and was holding her fast.

'Let me go!' she shouted, her voice rising to a scream.

As she rose and fell again, the truth became apparent. One of the men was standing on the hem of her dress.

Big hands grabbed her. 'No you don't!'

She fell to her knees, hands held as if in prayer. 'Please let me go. I've got children at 'ome.'

'Then what's you doing in a churchyard at this time of night? Can't be up to any good, can you? Off to the pokey with you.'

Edith twisted her arms and her body and kicked out, though her bare feet were unlikely to inflict much pain on this hardened pair.

'But I ain't done nothing,' she shouted, struggling all the way to the gate.

The men held on. 'We'll let the beak decide that after we've taken a look around.'

Edith was terrified.

Chapter Eleven

'I have a surprise visitor for you in the drawing room,' said Conrad, who still spoke English with the careful precision of a man to whom it is a second language although he'd lived in England for years.

'I was going out,' Blanche said without looking up from buttoning the youngest child into his coat. She didn't want him to see her face in case he guessed from her expression that she was off to Little Paradise. He'd be disappointed, thinking the melancholia was taking over again. But she could hardly tell him the truth.

Visiting the cottage had never made her feel guilty in the days when she'd wanted to be alone. But things had changed. She was going there purely in the hope of seeing Tom again. For some reason she just knew he'd come there today.

She sensed Conrad's hesitation, a silent moment before he gathered up his courage, pasted a bright expression on his face and attempted to jolly her out of the mood he perceived her to be in.

'Our visitor is a man you have already met, but I am sure you will want to see him again,' he said brightly.

She looked up at him. His eyes were twinkling as though this man he was talking about was as welcome as a Christmas present. Suddenly a thought crossed her mind. Tom! He had to be talking about Tom.

Conrad had not mentioned knowing that Tom was back and she had not asked him. But perhaps today he was trying to surprise her. She threw him a questioning look. 'Someone I've already met?'

His face brightened at her sudden show of interest. 'A fine figure of a man. A credit to this city.'

'Perhaps I should meet him then,' she said, hiding her disquiet with a smile and the business of getting her children ready for their walk.

'Commendable, my dear! Very commendable!' Conrad looked as though he might burst with happiness. 'You look very fine in that dress,' he added. 'It is much better than black.'

It touched her to think he'd noticed. She'd been dressed in mourning for such a long time. Today she wore yellow, a colour that suited her complexion and made her feel happy.

'It was time,' she said, as if the reason for wearing yellow instead of black was purely due to time and nothing whatsoever to do with the lightening of her heart.

The children fidgeted and chattered like magpies, as she checked that hats and coats were warm enough.

'I'm baking,' said Max, his face as Conrad's could be at times.

'Better than being cold,' said Blanche. 'Just because the sun's shining, doesn't mean you can't get a chill.'

Max groaned.

Blanche relented and took the coat off again. Perhaps she did overdress them at times, but she couldn't help it. Such ministrations were a leftover from when she'd first come to England from Barbados and decided she'd never be warm again.

Conrad stood patiently, his hand poised on the door handle watching as his wife fastened the top button on Adeline's pelisse. 'Let Martha take over,' said Conrad, obviously impatient. 'That is why we have a nursemaid, yes?'

Blanche followed him out of the nursery, trying not to appear nervous. It must be Tom. Who else could it be? The fact that he was back must appear a complete surprise. In her mind she rehearsed what she would say. *How nice to see you again. It's been so long.*

Heart racing, she entered the drawing room, a light, airy place of pale green and white muslin curtains that ballooned into the room on the breeze blowing up from the river. With Conrad's agreement, she had not followed the fashion for dark wallpapers and heavy furniture now being adopted by notable families. She preferred the original clean colours of the Regency, just as she had favoured the empire-line dresses she'd first brought over from Barbados. Although she now wore a crinoline, she tended to dispense with heavy frills and velvet trims. Her taste was still plain, and she usually preferred lighter colours like soft lemons, greens and blues, which suited her coppery coloured skin and the dark hair that curled in wild wisps around her face. Although ten years older, she was just a little thicker around the middle, had lost her youthful coltishness, but was not quite voluptuous.

A man of intense expression and sober dress sat in an armchair close to the window. He sprang to his feet and inclined his head in an oddly continental fashion.

Blanche recognized the young doctor who had waxed lyrical on the plagues and pestilence that so racked the city.

'Doctor Budd!' Blanche smiled warmly, unsure whether she felt disappointed or relieved. She glanced accusingly at Conrad. 'I do apologize for keeping you waiting.' Her smile faded slightly. 'It's been a while since we entertained visitors. I haven't been able to… cope… not since… '

Budd interrupted. 'I understand, Mrs Heinkel. I understand perfectly.'

She asked him if he would like tea, which Conrad ordered before Blanche had a chance to.

'To what do we owe this visit, Doctor Budd?' she asked, and found herself smiling, something she hadn't done very often in a long while.

The doctor looked at Conrad.

'You may continue, Doctor Budd. You have my permission to relay everything we have discussed to my wife. My wife and I have no secrets from each other.'

Blanche nodded her head in agreement and forced a swift, 'Yes.'

'It's regarding the drains, Mrs Heinkel.'

Blanche raised her eyebrows. 'Drains? I thought that as a doctor, you were more concerned with medicine, Doctor Budd.'

'Ah! But I'm also concerned with prevention, Mrs Heinkel. And that is the subject your husband and I have been discussing in great detail.'

Conrad looked sheepish, as she gave him a quizzical look. He'd mentioned nothing, but she could hardly blame him for that. Remembering how engrossed she'd been in Dr Budd's talk and Horatia's slights after they'd left the meeting, he'd probably tried to tell her, but she hadn't noticed.

Committed to his subject, Doctor Budd carried on. 'The drains of this city are as archaic as the water supply. They are too close to each other and at certain times of the year, when the river is high and the rain is heavy, the cesspits burst out and seep into the water pipes, some of which, I might point out, were installed long before the time of Elizabeth the First. Thus bodily waste is being redirected into the city's water supply, and so, dear lady,' he went on, 'cholera strikes and many loved ones are taken.'

They were momentarily interrupted as Doris, the maid, entered with the tea tray. Doris had been with the Heinkel family for a long time and cared deeply what happened to them.

'Everything all right, ma'am?' she asked, her eyes flitting between Blanche and the doctor.

'Thank you, yes,' murmured Blanche.

'You may go now, Doris,' said Conrad, gently cupping her elbow and steering her out of the door.

Normally, Blanche would have exchanged a swift smile with her husband. Doris and her over-protective ways had always been a matter of shared amusement. But Blanche was too absorbed in Dr Budd's plans for the city.

Conrad took charge of the teapot and asked the doctor whether he wished for milk and sugar.

Budd looked amused that Conrad was so capable at pouring tea, women's work in most households and never touched by man.

Blanche saw his look and explained. 'My husband does not divide work in terms of male and female, but rather in terms of whether someone is strong enough or capable enough to do the job.' As Conrad blushed, she laughed before explaining how one of the housemaids had been flabbergasted when he took a heavily laden coal-scuttle from her grasp and heaved it upstairs.

'I told her that God gave men muscles so that they might more easily take the burden,' said Conrad.

'According to my husband, God has a hand in most things. So what do you propose to do?' she asked, directing her question at Dr Budd and waving away the tea offered her by her husband.

The doctor's voice boomed around the room. 'I intend to rectify the matter, Mrs Heinkel. Rectify the matter!'

He sprang to his feet, his teacup rattling in its saucer, energy and enthusiasm shining in his eyes.

'During my lifetime, I have had the misfortune to have been smitten with that dreadful disease we know as cholera. In fact, this malaise figured in my life even before that time. My father before me made a study of the disease, even to analysing what smells were in the air before it gathered its deadly harvest.'

'May God have mercy,' Conrad muttered.

'Not now, Conrad,' said Blanche before he could erupt into prayer. She fixed her gaze on Dr Budd's face. 'Please go on.'

He cleared his throat again, his fist clenched politely before his mouth and his nose twitching above his curled fingers.

'I have visited the more malodorous parts of this city, filthy hovels where families live six to a room – sometimes more. I have seen them gather their water from supplies contaminated by the close proximity of blocked and overflowing privies and cess-pits.'

'And these places stink of the disease, I think?' sand Conrad.

'Yes.'

Blanche immediately thought of Edith. 'Please. Continue.'

Dr Budd slapped his hands on his knees. 'Well, my dear lady,' he said, his eyes sparkling and his face bright with exuberance, 'as I said in my lecture, I have come to the conclusion that the smell, or miasma as some of my colleagues call it, has nothing to do with the disease although the problem is at its worse when the smell is present. That smell or miasma is present mostly during the summer months when the water supply is low, too low for the water to take away the human and other effluent produced in these inner city slums. Consequently it is left to fester and something unseen in the cesspits crosses over into the fresh water.'

'Something? What do you mean by something, Doctor?' Blanche asked.

He shook his head. 'I do not know as yet. Whatever causes the sickness is not visible to the naked eye. I only wish it were.' He shrugged. 'I will leave it to others to search out and discover its true cause.' He glanced appreciatively at Conrad. 'I trust to the enlightened of this city's society and the Corporation to help prevent this disease, and I believe that new sewers will help. As you know, Herr Heinkel, plans have been drawn up.'

It was strange hearing Conrad being addressed with a German prefix, but Blanche reminded herself that Dr Budd had spent a great deal of time on the Continent.

She frowned as a thought occurred to her. 'But we are high above the city and our spring water comes from beneath the rocks of the Avon Gorge. It cannot have been contaminated by city sewers, so why did my child die?'

Dr Budd seemed nonplussed for a moment. He rubbed at his forehead, frowning thoughtfully before slapping his hands on his knees. 'Can you guarantee that she never drank or ate anything on a trip to the city, to church, to her father's factory, or bought something from a street vendor?'

Conrad said, 'My wife is right. There are no sewers close by except our own, and they are new and drain straight into the river.'

Their conversation drifted away, the words seeming no more than the buzz of bees in a summer garden. One thing above all others dominated her thoughts: Could the lemonade Anne drank prior to her death have been made from polluted water?

Blanche stiffened and her voice trembled. 'Anne bought lemonade from a street seller that day at Little Paradise. She was dispensing it from an earthenware jug. My other children stayed thirsty until they returned home. I never saw the woman again.'

The thought that she might have had some part in her daughter's death appalled her. Clapping her hand to the lace collar of her dress, she fiddled with the pearl brooch that fastened it together. 'I can't believe it,' she murmured.

Conrad reached for her hand. 'Do not blame yourself, my dear. You were not to know. No one was to know.'

She took deep breaths – one after another in quick succession, and closed her eyes. This was terrible. Finally, she said, 'But how do you know this for sure? Have you seen a definite benefit from drinking water from one source rather than another?'

The doctor nodded. 'I have, ma'am. And I'm sure the water is not only responsible for cholera. I think contaminated water causes other sicknesses too. If I may tell you a story… if you wish, of course… I have after all, taken up so much of your time already…'

'Please go on,' Blanche interrupted. She wanted to hear! Of course she wanted to hear.

The doctor cleared his throat. 'One day I just happened to come across a woman with a sick child in a place called Cabot's Yard. I advised her to fetch water from the spring that runs from Jacob's Well and down to St Augustine's Quay and also to boil all food, all water that she used for washing. She did that. Her child recovered, a rare occurrence indeed. The hovel she lived in was terribly overcrowded.'

He hadn't said her name, but Blanche just knew it was Edith. An odd feeling churned in her stomach.

'If we can control the water supply, then we can control the disease,' she heard the doctor say. 'New drainage and, in the interim, my great project of having women enter these dark places with disinfectant and good advice, will help us to beat this terrible disease. The women will have to be intelligent and of good character, of course.'

'And this is where myself and other merchants of this city come in. We will help with funding,' said Conrad.

Blance leaned earnestly forward. 'You say you require intelligent women to carry out these tasks?'

'Yes, possibly with some nursing experience, or having been in charge of the women's section of schools, institutions, those sorts of things... it would be their job to oversee the disinfecting of courtyards and, ultimately, locking off communal water supplies when the situation dictates... but only those water supplies in areas that are known to have a high incidence of cholera. These women would also have to give advice to the people who live in these places, some of whom are less than genteel.'

Blanche felt a pang of remorse, not just about Anne's death but also about meeting Tom and wanting to meet him again. The bitter truth about Anne's death had brought her down to earth with an almighty bang.

'I want to take part in this.' Her voice rang with commitment and her eyes shone with intent. This was her penitence and she would throw herself into it with all the energy she possessed. 'I would like to take a more vigorous part in your project. I'm quite capable of sprinkling disinfectant around and I'm sure I can supervise turning off the pipes.'

'My dear,' Conrad began, his benevolent expression turning to concern, 'those are not good places to be—'

'Certainly not for those living there,' she exclaimed resolutely. 'The heart of this city is falling down. The houses are not fit for pigs, yet women and children are forced to live there, unable to afford anything better.' She touched her husband's hand. 'I need to do this, Conrad,' she said more softly. 'I need to have a new purpose in life.'

'Yes,' he said, his expression betraying his undying affection. 'Of course you do.'

Chapter Twelve

Edith had bitten her nails to the quick worrying about her children. They'd been alone for three days. Today, at long last, she was finally going up before the magistrates, unsure of what to say and stinking of prison.

The courtroom was crowded, though from where she was, poised on the steps leading up from the cells, she could only hear the sound of tramping feet, as one after the other, each felon was swiftly dealt with.

For the length of the stairwell, bodies stinking of sweat, drink and bad breath pressed against her. Fleas and lice hopped from one body to another. Where there was room to do so, people scratched or popped the parasites between finger and thumb.

'Always the same down thur even though they does it out with carbolic,' said a fella no older than fourteen. 'But you'll get used to it.'

'No, I bloody well won't,' Edith responded. 'I'm innocent and I'm gettin' out of yur!'

'Only if they gives you chance to speak,' said a thin woman in front of her. 'Meself, I'm gonna scream the place down. That'll get the magistrate's attention.'

Edith had been confident that she'd get out of this. From the start she'd entertained the hope that Molly would come to tell the truth. So far she hadn't. Hope finally died.

'Well, I'm goin' to speak,' Edith said defiantly. At the same time she studied the woman's face. She had a nose like a piece of jagged rock, almost as if God had stuck it on her face as an afterthought and an ill-conceived one at that. Edith couldn't take her eyes off it.

'The beak won't like that,' the woman said and sniffed a petulant dewdrop hanging from her right nostril. 'Only chance though. Otherwise all he'll do is listen to the charge and lock me up in clink.'

The woman passed further up the stairwell towards the cream oblong of ceiling, all they could see of the courtroom above.

'Next case!'

At the command, the line of miscreants was pushed up the stairs until the next case spilled out then was pulled into the courtroom by the guard at the top. 'Big Nose' proved to be next.

'Mary Jane Fletcher. Stealing a feather hat from Betsy Booker, milliner, Castle Street.'

Name and crime had barely finished mention before the woman began her screaming.

Uproar broke out. There were shouts from the court officials, screams from the woman and scuffles as those representing the law tried to get her under control.

At last a measured voice pronounced, 'It seems that this woman is in no fit state to undergo a prison sentence. One month in the lunatic asylum under the supervision of people used to dealing with such outbursts may serve you better, Mary Jane Fletcher.'

His words chilled Edith to the bone. For a brief moment she had entertained the idea of taking Mary Jane's advice and making a racket in the hope of gaining her freedom. Following this outcome, she rapidly changed her mind.

There was something else that made her reconsider. The voice of the magistrate was familiar and she racked her brain to remember where she'd heard it before.

'Next!'

Bundled up the stairs like a pile of old clothes, she was eventually spewed out into the oak-panelled courtroom like a pot of old stew. At first she blinked in the sudden brightness. The courtroom windows looked out over Corn Street and stretched from floor to ceiling. She could see the rain pattering on the copper pillars — called 'nails' — outside the Corn Exchange. Despite the weather a corn merchant was paying his dues to another – 'on the nail'. She wished she were out there too.

'Edith Jane Beasley. Desecration of a cemetery – possible infanticide.'

'Only possible?' asked the magistrate, raising one fair eyebrow over a bright blue eye.

Edith barely heard what they said. Her gaze was fixed on the magistrate. She knew immediately who he was. Before the clerk could say another word, she shouted, 'No, Mr Heinkel. Not me. You know me. Your wife knows me. I would never do that.'

Conrad Heinkel's head jerked up at the mention of his name and that of his wife. Edith congratulated herself for recognizing him in time and took the opportunity to continue.

'The child weren't mine. It was Molly's babby! She lives in the cellar below me and she was supposed to wait on the other side of the wall. Told me she couldn't afford burial, what with there bein' a shortage of plots an' that because of the cholera and suchlike. Had to 'elp her. Would 'ave felt guilty not helpin' seein' as my little girl was cured, thanks to God and that Doctor Budd.'

Conrad Heinkel looked amazed. 'Doctor Budd cured your child?'

Edith smiled at him broadly, nodded at an usher and winked at the gallery. She felt like an actress on the stage.

'Just the water, the doctor said. Go down and fill yer pail from the pipe down on the quay. And I knowed where that was, just past the drawbridge. So my little girl was saved and Molly's weren't. And anyway, I wouldn't have got caught if I hadn't stopped and said a prayer over the poor little thing. In fact, it was a lullaby Blanche, your wife, taught me.'

Before anyone could stop her, Edith sang the same lullaby she'd sung over the damp grave.

–

As the last note died away, the court fell into silence, though it wasn't long before a rising hum began from those waiting below on the stairwell. *What was going on?*

Now it was Conrad who looked disconcerted. Edith guessed he had recognized the tune. He'd surely heard Blanche sing it to his own children.

With thudding heart, she waited as he considered the matter, willing him to set her free. She blurted, 'Let me go 'ome to my children, sir. Please let me go 'ome. They've been without me for three days now and I've lost enough of them to cholera, and them in Lewins Mead all alone.'

Her outburst seemed to speed up his decision.

'Have you an income?' he asked.

'Only when me old man's 'ome,' she replied. 'If he don't drink it away before I can get me hands on it.'

He scribbled something on the paper in front of him. 'Then it's time you had an income of your own. Perhaps that will be enough to keep you out of trouble. I declare you are bonded to my wife's good offices. She has told me something of your misfortune. I believe a practical approach is needed here. My wife needs help in the house and you need honest work. I think my decision will suit you both. Case dismissed.'

He leaned over his high table, as Edith walked swiftly past him, heading for the exit. 'Make arrangements to report to my wife in the morning. Here is the address.'

Edith was ecstatic. It didn't matter that she'd only be a maid in her old friend's household. Bad things made good, she thought to herself. She did not realize that as a religious man, Conrad Heinkel would normally have given her a prison term for desecrating a churchyard, but she had mentioned her child, his wife and Dr Budd in the same breath. He had felt obliged to show mercy – for his wife's sake rather than for hers.

–

What remained of its ancient plaster clung to the walls of the shabby house like large cowpats, ugly and in imminent danger of falling off.

Situated in a stinking alley between Lewins Mead and Christmas Steps, the house was old, dark and looked as if it had been thrown into the gap between the buildings either side of it.

A huge beam divided it halfway up, so large it seemed the ground floor was buckling beneath its weight. Carvings of crosses, initials and a blessing written in Latin betrayed the fact that this noble beam had been purloined from the abbey that had once stood here. All that was left of St Augustine's was an ornate gateway and a colonnaded courtyard, hemmed in by the miserable hovels of a less holy time.

Two men took it in turns to hammer on the door of the house with fists the size of sledgehammers, the noise echoing around their dismal surroundings and attracting the attention of pale faces behind ill-fitting windows and ramshackle doors.

Taking a breather, one of the men stood back and shouted, 'Open up in there.'

His colleague looked over his shoulder to where the property's owner, the man they knew as Sydney Cuthbert, stood watching, his son by his side.

Stoke didn't usually attend the eviction of non-paying tenants. All physical aspects of his property business were left to his henchmen, but this particular exercise was for the benefit of his son. He badly wanted Gilmour to become like himself, to focus on business and not let compassion colour his judgement. He blamed himself for having left the boy's mother to bring him up, but he'd had no choice. Children and wives were an encumbrance to a young man out to make his way in the world.

Stoke nodded his approval to the big-fisted man. 'Get on with it.'

The banging resumed, but the door was stout, ancient and made of oak. Like the beam above, it might also have once formed part of the abbey.

Gilmour grimaced. He didn't like this sort of thing at all. Much as he'd appreciated the learning he'd received thanks to his father's wealth, he would never stop missing his mother. Sometimes he actually felt bitter towards her that she'd died only eight years before. They had lived quietly together, neither of them having much contact with his father. After she had died and been buried in St Anne's Churchyard at Oldland Common, a small village on the outskirts of the city, he'd spent some years in boarding school. Once that was finished with, he'd had no choice but to live with his father.

Stoke was proud of having a son and congratulated himself on not having had close correspondence with the boy until he was well past babyhood and childhood, and of an age when a father could be proud. A son gave purpose to the wealth and status he'd achieved. Gilmour was a spur to his plans and, with a growing awareness of his own mortality, Stoke was grooming him to take over when he was gone.

'Let the poor woman alone,' someone shouted from an upstairs window. 'She's been sick.'

'And she's a widow,' someone else shouted.

Stoke's weasel-like eyes darted upwards, scouring each window for the defiant expression that would soon turn to fear when he told them they were evicted too.

'None of my concern,' he shouted back. 'I don't put a roof over your head fer nothing. I expect to be paid!'

His voice echoed between the gabled roofs and crumbling walls.

'There, son,' he said, tapping Gilmour's chest, as the two men continued to hammer on the door. 'Respect, that's what you want from them. Treat them firm and they'll give you it. Now, Bill and Casey know what's got to be done. I'm leaving you here to oversee matters.'

'But I don't… ' Gilmour began, stammering slightly.

'Pull yourself together,' said his father through clenched teeth. 'Respect. Earn their respect.' His grimace turned to a smile as he patted his son's shoulder. 'Don't let me down, son. Make me proud of you.'

Gilmour's heart pounded and he felt sick. When would his father ever understand that he took after his mother and was not like him at all? Swallowing nervously, he stood rooted to the spot, listening as the sound of his father's carriage clattered away from the street at the end of the alley.

Casey, one of his father's henchmen, turned away from the door and bent to take up a sledgehammer, the sort road menders used for breaking stones. 'We'll soon be getting that door down now,' he said in a lilting Irish accent as he spat on one meaty palm then on the other.

Gilmour wasn't so sure. The pale faces that had retreated behind their broken windows and doors reappeared. He could see them gazing out like pale ghosts from the dark interiors. Their murmurings of disapproval resumed, rumbling like wagon wheels through the alley.

The truth was, he was not at all comfortable carrying out his father's wishes. It wasn't in his nature to oversee the eviction of a sick woman – and a widow at that. How could his father do such a thing? He answered his own question. Easily. That was the way his father was. His mother, no more than a girl of fourteen at the time, had always regretted marrying him. He sensed by her nervous hand-wringing and the reddening of her cheeks that she'd had no choice, that she'd already been with child. Perhaps his father had forced himself on her. Then, after tiring of being a married man, he had set out alone to make his fortune in the city.

Thinking of his mother made him angry. His father had not treated her right. He would not, in fact, he *could* not do his bidding. He made an instant decision to make things right – for his mother's sake as much as for his own.

'Wait a moment,' he shouted to the two men as they raised their sledgehammers, ready to reduce the old oak door into splinters. 'How much rent does she owe?'

The two men looked at each other, as Gilmour rummaged in the inside pocket of his fine, grey frock coat.

Bill, a red-haired man with a freckled face and a lopsided grin, shook his head. 'We can't do that. The old man – begging yer pardon, yer father – would have our guts fer garters.'

Gilmour was surprised at the strength of his resolve. His voice was strong. 'How much?'

They exchanged a swift look then shook their heads. 'No.'

Gilmour became aware that people had come out of their houses, curious as to what would happen next. Those within earshot had heard him offer to pay the woman's rent.

'Go on,' one of them said. 'Mrs Parker's got three kids and no husband. Wouldn't hurt fer someone to pay her rent, would it?'

Gilmour sensed that Casey and Bill actually enjoyed their work. Their eyes glowed at the slightest hint of violence and confrontation. He found them obnoxious. Sometimes, he thought the same thing about his father. How could they possibly enjoy throwing someone out onto the street with nowhere else to go but the workhouse?

'You can't do this,' Gilmour shouted and attempted to drag them away from the door.

Casey pushed him gently, but firmly back. 'We've got work to do.'

Gilmour found himself among the crowd that had gathered. Although mindful of the size of the men and the force of the sledgehammers, many were shouting obscenities and catcalls of derision.

Gilmour found their anger contagious. 'You'll be damned for this,' he shouted.

A cry of delight arose from the crowd as the two men were drenched by the contents of a chamber pot poured from an upstairs window.

Someone shouted, 'And very wet,' and was accompanied by catcalls and hoots of derision.

Dripping piss from their noses and turds on their shoulders, the two men shook themselves, their expressions ripe with disgust at the stink and the stuff that covered them.

'Shit!'

''Tis that all right,' said a thin-faced man at an upstairs window, a pewter chamber pot hanging from his hand. 'I ain't emptied it all day.'

The crowd laughed.

'Damn this,' said Casey, shaking himself like a huge, angry bear. 'I'll get you, you bastard,' he shouted, waving his fist at the man hanging out of the window. No one took his threat seriously. Everyone laughed.

Gilmour decided that the time was right to take advantage of the situation. He asked again, 'How much did she owe?'

Dejected, the wind knocked completely out of his sails, Bill said, 'Eight shillings and sixpence.'

'Here's ten shillings, but don't tell my father that I paid it. I'll say nothing about this incident if you don't. Do I have your agreement?'

Of course he did.

He watched them as they left the alley and he revelled in the pats on the back and the gratitude of the people around him.

Mrs Parker thanked him personally once she was sure the coast was clear.

'You're a saint,' she said, her eyes brimming with tears and a clutch of children clinging to her skirts.

He almost blushed. 'Hardly.' But he liked the feeling.

Helping others had made him feel good. He felt less than good when he thought of his father. He made himself a promise that he would do what he could to rectify his father's excesses, to put right the things he did wrong – but secretly. To do otherwise would be dangerous.

–

The first of the steamships was nearing completion. Metal rang against metal, as brawny men, their bodies stinking and slimy with sweat, hammered the last of the rivets into place.

'She'll do you proud,' said the architect, who gazed at his creation as a father to a newborn son.

Tom agreed. 'And plenty of room for goods to Nova Scotia and guano to the West Indies – and sugar cane high as pine trees!'

'Guano from Nova Scotia's becoming a popular cargo,' said the architect, his dreamy eyes fixed on the ship. 'The *Mathilda* went straight there after her launch, though I hear she's bringing her cargo back here. Apparently landowners and gentlemen farmers pay a great deal of money for the stuff. Bird shit, isn't it?'

Tom nodded. 'Yes.'

There was something unnerving about what the architect had said. Plans for shipping guano to the West Indies and improving sugar production had been kept secret. No one outside the family was supposed to know about supplying the Strong plantation with guano thus stealing a march on other owners and selling on the surplus to coffee growers in South America. But someone had beaten them to it, though for the home market, not abroad.

Another carriage clattered into the shipyard and stopped next to the light chaise Tom had driven himself. He smiled. Horatia never seemed to be far behind him nowadays.

The architect hardly seemed to notice her arrival, his gaze flitting absent-mindedly between the ship and his drawings. 'I do apologize,' he said finally, a pencil jammed between his teeth. 'There's something I have to attend to.'

Off he went, the plans still unfurled in front of him and flapping like a sail against his knees.

'Have you thought of a name for her?' Horatia asked after their initial greeting.

'Yes.'

'Are you going to tell me what it is?'

'No.'

She shrugged as though she didn't care – which was far from the truth. 'Have it your own way.'

'You'll know when she's launched. It won't be long now.'

'I look forward to it. Shall we take a closer look?'

He offered her his arm. She took it.

'I wasn't expecting you,' Tom said. 'Have you been shopping?'

'No. I had some business matters to attend to.'

'I hear you've an interest in sewage contracts. Hardly a business for a lady.'

Her look of surprise was swiftly transfigured by a tight smile. 'What makes you think I would be interested in such a disgusting venture?'

'I must admit to some surprise.'

Horatia had always been very good at hiding her true feelings. Nothing had changed. Her expression was calm, almost cold, yet he knew he could not take what she said as being the whole truth.

'Whatever made you think I would be?'

He shrugged. 'An off-chance remark from someone who saw you at a meeting regarding the matter.'

The words triggered an instant reaction in his mind. The look, the feel and the smell of Blanche made his body tense with excitement. He only hoped that Horatia did not notice.

'I take it you are referring to the meeting with regard to fighting the cholera epidemics this city sometimes suffers from. Would it surprise you to know that I have a social conscience? Many people have died from disease in my own family. Cholera kills many more poor people than it does rich. I think it only appropriate that the money that first made this city great, namely from sugar, is used to tackle the problem.'

Tom raised his eyebrows. 'Most commendable!' This was indeed a first. He'd never known Horatia even to *notice* the poor, let alone help them.

They stopped beneath the bows of the ship.

'She'll certainly be a credit to the Strong Sugar Company,' Horatia remarked, shading her eyes with her gloved hand as she took in the ship's strength and size.

'Strong Shipping Line I think we decided on,' said Tom. 'She won't just be carrying sugar. Far from it, though it appears someone has stolen our thunder.'

'Really?'

There was something about the way she said it that made him look at her. She had sounded off-hand, even amused. Her expression confirmed it. She was smiling in a self-satisfied way that made his toes curl with concern.

'What have you been up to, Horatia?'

The blue of her hat echoed that of her eyes. If she'd worn a grey hat instead, they would have reflected that too. Horatia's eyes, like the woman herself, changed to suit the circumstances.

'What did you say when I first arrived?'

Tom shrugged as he remembered. 'I said I wasn't expecting you and had you been shopping.'

'Shopping!' She said it contemptuously. 'Surely you, of all people, know me better than that. I'm my father's daughter. My true joy is gained from the cut and thrust of business, the challenge of achieving something more worthwhile than choosing a new hat!'

Tom couldn't bring himself to speak. In the past he'd thought he discerned a chilly resolve in those eyes. Now he saw resentment, even anger. She was the one who'd inherited the Strong family's business acumen. Unfortunately she'd been born a woman and nothing in this day and age could change that – unless she was clever enough to change things herself.

'I understand,' he said, and truly felt for her. 'You're a formidable woman, Horatia. Your brothers can't hold a torch to you.'

'I'm glad you think so, Tom. You're the only person I can really trust, so I will tell you all about it, so long as you promise to tell no one.'

'No one,' he said.

Afterwards he was surprised he had agreed so quickly, but as the story came out, as she told him how she'd engaged the lawyer, Septimus Monk, to act on her behalf, of purchasing the *Mathilda* out of bankruptcy, Tom was deeply impressed. Emmanuel, Nelson and himself had envisaged a shipping company that would operate in a supporting role to sugar. Horatia had identified a new market in her own country. The population was exploding. Why risk travelling a triangular route when back and forth between Nova Scotia and Bristol would reap greater rewards?

'This doesn't mean that Strong Shipping will not make money,' said Horatia with absolute conviction. 'It's just that *my* shipping company will make more.'

Tom's brain was reeling. Luckily Horatia had enough of a private fortune to follow her dream. He wondered how many women of lesser means wished they could play more than a supporting role to their menfolk.

'You promise you won't tell what I've done?'

'You're not setting up in competition, so why should I? However, there is one question I would like answered.'

'What is it?'

'The name of your shipping company?'

She smiled secretively. 'I thought about a name for a while. I wanted it to reflect my likes and dislikes and things that have amused me. I decided on Charles King.'

Seeing Tom's puzzled look, Horatia explained. 'As you know, I greatly disliked father's second wife, Verity. A memory that amuses me still was that she was always posting rewards when her lap dog went missing. She never found out that the man who continuously claimed the reward stole the dog on numerous occasions, then shared the money with his sister who worked at the house. Edith, I think her name was. I once saw him handing over the dog to Edith behind the laundry room.' She laughed. 'It was a King Charles spaniel. You see? Charles King!'

Chapter Thirteen

Horatia had not disclosed *all* her true feelings to Tom, but she was angry. Not about being found out regarding her shipping company, or even that she had attended the meeting regarding the plans for dealing with cholera. No member of the Strong family had known she was at that meeting. The only people she had spoken to there who knew Tom were Conrad and Blanche Heinkel. If she had a chance of buying property in the path of the new sewer complex, she would do so. But it was also jealousy that made her want to confront Blanche. She wanted her to stay away from Tom.

A square-shouldered woman who demanded to know her name and business before allowing her entry, opened the door of the imposing house in Somerset Parade.

With an imperious flourish of a green-gloved hand, Horatia swept her to one side. 'Tell your mistress that Horatia Strong wishes to speak with her.'

The door was left gaping, as the woman followed, like a terrier about to snap at her heels.

'Horatia who?' she demanded, as though she were far more than a housekeeper.

This was impossible! Horatia spun round. Servants did not demand anything of their mistress at Marstone Court. 'Strong,' she said, her eyes blazing. 'Tell her Horatia Strong is here and she demands to be seen immediately.'

Mrs Henderson turned on her heels, her nostrils pinched and her lips pursed. She didn't hold with hoity-toity sorts like Horatia Strong. Wouldn't work for the likes of her.

Horatia started to pace the hall, then stopped when she noticed the scruffy little woman sitting on one of a pair of hall chairs. Horatia eyed the woman surreptitiously, vaguely aware that she knew her. But dressed like that? She looked like a beggar. Horatia turned away rather than acknowledge such a shabby creature.

Mrs Henderson returned looking as pinched and put out as when she'd left. 'This way, Miss Strong,' she said, her mouth snapping shut once she'd said it.

Adopting a look of utter disdain, Horatia followed.

The room she was shown into was like a breath of fresh air. It was green and white and for some odd reason seemed to lift her spirits. She almost felt as though she could float.

Like the room, Blanche had an air of spring about her. She was dressed in a silver-grey day dress with a ruched bodice and mother-of-pearl buttons. Single pearls adorned her ears. Her eyes and skin glowed with health. Horatia suddenly felt overdressed and gaudy rather than naturally attractive.

They didn't shake hands.

'Miss Strong.' Blanche nodded curtly.

Horatia, equally curtly, 'Mrs Heinkel.'

'Would you like tea?'

'No. What I came here to say won't take long.'

Both women spoke with clipped consonants. The air in the room turned frosty.

Horatia had not come to be nice and it began to show. 'You've done very well for yourself considering the circumstances of your birth – child of a mulatto mother and brought to this country as a servant. My father's bastard child.'

Blanche felt herself turning hot, but swallowed her anger. These insults were designed to unnerve her. What was it Horatia really wanted?

'Get to the point, Miss Strong. Why are you here?'

'How's Max?'

Blanche felt her temper rising. 'Why do you want to know?'

Horatia wandered the room, eyeing the ornaments, touching the silky wallpaper and the golden gleam of a walnut writing desk.

'I have a right to know, do I not? After all, he is my nephew.' She stopped and turned. There was no doubting the threat in her eyes and her voice.

Blanche kept her temper. 'What is this all about? Why are you bringing all this up now?'

Horatia's voice simmered with anger. 'Because you have forgotten how precarious your position is. You were lucky enough to marry a respectable man and become a respectable woman. May I suggest you stay that way and refrain from bringing shame on yourself and your family.'

Aware that Edith was outside waiting to see her, Blanche kept her voice down. 'May I suggest you leave – right now!'

Horatia smiled coldly. 'I will, but first a warning – stay away from Tom. And keep your nose out of my business.'

Blanche's mouth dropped open. 'What makes you think—'

'I just know you've seen him. Remember, you have a lot to lose. Stay away from him. Stay away!'

Horatia's voice seemed to echo around the room for some time after she'd left.

Blanche stood in front of the open window in an effort to cool herself before seeing Edith. Horatia had known that she'd seen Tom. But how? Blanche herself had told no one and she trusted that Tom hadn't either. But she'd known. Blanche had already made her own mind up not to see Tom any more, but hadn't been able to bring herself to tell Horatia that. Unknowingly, Horatia had given her another reason why she shouldn't see Tom any more. No breath of scandal must affect her family, especially Max. So far as the world was concerned, Max was Conrad's legitimate son. Conrad himself knew otherwise, but he didn't know the full truth. Blanche had never dared tell him. His feelings for Max might change if she did.

Once she felt presentable, she summoned her next visitor into the room.

Blanche felt her heart lurch with pity, as her old friend shuffled across the deep pile of a Turkish rug. She was dressed in a plain brown dress and the brim of her bonnet was dented and faded with age.

It wasn't easy, but Blanche kept smiling, though found herself feeling almost ashamed of the striking contrast between the smartness of her own dress and Edith's shabbiness.

'Madam,' said Edith, and dropped a little curtsey.

Blanche felt tears springing to her eyes. This was her friend, the first female friend she'd made on arriving in Bristol from Barbados. Round in face and body, Edith had seemed to bounce through life, rarely glum and always telling stories about the exploits of her family – most of whom made their living less than legally.

Now there were dark lines and puffiness beneath Edith's eyes. Her face was thinner and her roundness was less pronounced; what fat remained seemed to sag as if tired of hanging onto her bones.

Overcome by emotion, Blanche sprang to her feet. 'Edith! It's so wonderful to see you again.'

Despite the fact that Edith smelt of mould and dirt, she hugged her close.

Edith was like a block of wood, too terrified to move. 'Madam?'

Blanche was wise enough to realise how awkward she must be feeling and let her go.

'I'm sorry,' she said, laughing nervously. 'I'm supposed to be the mistress of this house, yet I've never quite got used to treating servants as anything but friends, especially the kind and helpful ones.'

Edith seemed dumbstruck, her head turning almost full circle as she took in the damask drapes, the fringed chenille tablecloths set on half a dozen occasional tables, the pictures, the clocks and the upholstered chairs with their tasselled cushions.

'I've just had it decorated,' Blanche said, and felt foolish. It sounded as though she were making excuses for her lifestyle and that Edith was a society friend visiting, not merely a servant and felon.

Edith shrugged and bit her lip. 'I ain't seen nothing so nice as this in a long time.'

As she turned, Blanche glimpsed Edith's feet. She was wearing odd boots tied together with string. They looked as if they were made of paper. She'd heard of their existence, but had never seen them before. Edith had been shuffling either to stop them from falling off or trying to save them wearing out too quickly.

And we used to be friends…

Blanche resisted the urge to hustle her upstairs to the bathroom where she could strip, wash and replace her clothes with some of Blanche's own cast-offs. But I mustn't hurt her pride, she decided. An idea suddenly occurred to her. When Edith left the house, she would take clothes that Blanche would insist were a uniform fit for a housemaid to wear. She would also give her more children's clothes that her own brood had outgrown.

Blanche reached for the tasselled braid hanging at the side of the fireplace. 'We'll have tea together. You can tell me all about what's been happening to you since we last saw each other.'

Edith looked at her round-eyed like a frightened rabbit. 'I just can't…' she began to stammer as she backed jerkily towards the door.

Blanche took a firm grip on her old friend's arm and guided her into a chair. 'Of course you can. Besides, I've already ordered it. Mrs Henderson is waiting for me to ring for her to bring it in.'

Pressing her hands on her shoulders, Blanche got her to sit down in a velveteen chair next to a copper-topped table.

Overcome with emotion, Blanche turned away. It was terribly important that Edith didn't see her expression. Edith wouldn't stand for pity. Rough she might be, but she had her pride. It was possible that she might get angry, perhaps storm out and end up in court again. Next time it might not be Conrad on the bench.

Edith looked up nervously, as Mrs Henderson, stiffly crisp in her dark blue dress and starched white apron, crossed the room and set tea, muffins, butter and jam on the table.

Blanche watched Edith's eyes follow the food, her bottom lip sagging as her mouth began to water.

'P'raps a muffin or two,' said Edith, her eyes never leaving the plate.

'Yes,' said Blanche with a light laugh, as though they had tea together every day at this time and were both dressed in silks and wearing little muslin gloves to protect the softness of their hands. Not likely with Edith's, Blanche noticed. Her nails were broken, her fingers grimed with dirt and rough with work.

Edith had always been the one with the appetite when they'd been in service together.

'Eat as much as you like,' said Blanche, pouring tea from a Wedgwood pot into bone china cups. 'Now, tell me what you've been doing with yourself. How many children did you say you had?'

Edith grabbed a muffin, ate it speedily, and then grabbed another. As she bit into the third, a trickle of butter ran over her chin, was wiped off on the back of her hand, which in turn was licked off by a greedy tongue.

Between mouthfuls of muffin and tea, Edith talked about her husband – Able Seaman Deke Beasley – her children – those still alive and those she'd lost.

'As I think I told you, I lost a daughter to cholera last year,' said Blanche, and was surprised at the strength in her voice. It bore no trace of grief, no quavering at the accompanying thoughts. 'Cholera has to be beaten,' she added and thought of one of her husband's Sunday sermons; she sounded just the same.

Edith turned suddenly chirpy. 'Never mind. Got some children left, ain't you?'

'Yes. I have three. One boy and two girls.'

'And there's always 'ope,' said Edith, her tired eyes suddenly shining above her haggard cheekbones. 'My little girl got saved by some doctor fella that I saved from being rolled – you know – robbed,' she added on seeing the questioning look on Blanche's face.

'Doctor Budd. Yes, my husband told me.' Blanche felt humbled. Edith had lost far more children than she had, yet was still grateful to those who cared. 'A good man,' she said.

'One of the best. Glad to count him amongst me friends.'

Blanche smiled, but it diminished as a thought occurred to her. 'My husband also said you were arrested for desecrating a graveyard.'

Although halfway through a muffin, Edith paused, her eyes downcast as she put it back on the plate with those not yet touched.

Her voice was suddenly very small. 'Molly McBean's little 'un had died. She didn't 'ave any money to bury her, and there don't seem to be any room anywhere at the moment to bury anyone without a bought and paid for plot. All this cholera and smallpox, there's too many bodies and not enough earth.'

Blanche couldn't think of a single word to say. Not until this moment had it occurred to her that she was totally out of touch with common people, people who worked hard for a living or were poor and needy like Edith. Things hadn't always been that way.

She was well aware that she couldn't help everyone, but she wanted to do something for Edith, to improve her lot so that she didn't smell and could regain some of the old exuberance Blanche remembered.

When she asked about her family, her mother and brothers, Edith was very matter of fact.

'Dead,' she said flatly between mouthfuls of muffins.

'I'm sorry.'

Edith went on eating.

Blanche continued to look at her over the edge of her teacup. Gone was the old Edith who told tall stories about her family's achievements that were, in the main, outright lies invented by a fertile imagination. The new Edith looked beaten, ground down by altered circumstances.

What can I say next? thought Blanche. Edith wasn't making it easy. At last she said, 'Are you looking forward to working here?'

It seemed trite, but was all she could think of.

Edith nodded and muttered a reply through a shower of crumbs. 'I've already ordered two pound of pork bones and a sack of pinky potatoes fer a stew this week.'

'Pinky?' Blanche had never heard the word before.

Edith enlightened her. 'A bit past their best, but all right for a stew.'

Making an immediate decision, Blanche got to her feet and took a few coins from the velvet purse hanging from her belt.

'Here's a little advance on your wages.' She handed Edith two shillings – a sizeable portion from a wage of eight shillings a week, but a fortune to someone like Edith, who, she suspected, had nothing even when her husband came home.

Edith stopped eating, her eyes wide and moistening by the minute. 'That's... that's... very kind... ' She sniffed back a threatening sob, swallowing both her pride and whatever food was still in her mouth. 'But I ain't earned it,' she said and tried to thrust it back into Blanche's hand.

Blanche closed her fingers over Edith's. 'No. You must take it. You have children. You need it.'

Both women looked into each other's eyes, each too full of emotion to say anything. Their look said it all; this was old friendship and the gladness of two friends reunited.

'Do you remember when I first came to Bristol?' said Blanche. 'You befriended me when I was at my lowest. Now our positions are reversed. I promise I will be a friend to you, just as you were to me when I needed one.'

Edith thought about it, then nodded and tucked the money into her cleavage. She also left with a brown paper parcel beneath her arm containing a decent work dress, underwear and various items of children's clothing.

Blanche watched her leave from the second-floor drawing-room window. The poplars at the end of the garden were throwing long shadows across the lawn. Edith's disappearing figure looked lonely and drab, the colour of her dress blending with the earth.

Blanche leaned her head against the coldness of the window. She stayed there until the side door from the kitchen garden slammed shut and Edith was gone.

'I need air,' she said to Mrs Henderson after the children had tea. 'I'm going for a walk.'

Lacing on a pair of walking shoes, she headed for Little Paradise. By the time she got there, the first scents of evening were rising from the honeysuckle and bees buzzed around spears of pink lupins and purple larkspur.

After bolting the door, she made her way upstairs and sat in the window seat, her gaze roaming the common. In the past she'd searched for a vision of her daughter as she remembered her that day. Today was different, though she wasn't really seeing the waving grasses and rabbits bounding from burrow to burrow either. Horatia's threat had chilled her to the bone. What was she hoping to gain by it? What was there to prove? Tom, she thought. It all boils down to Tom. Horatia had been livid that they'd met again, two old flames that she couldn't seem to extinguish.

The leaves of the apple trees rustled suddenly and caught her attention. The sound of hoofbeats preceded a figure on a horse. She knew it was Tom. Horatia's warning rang in her ears.

She dropped to her knees, her head and her arms resting on the window seat so she couldn't be seen.

The sound of hooves ceased, replaced by footsteps coming up the path. The bolted front door rattled. She closed her eyes and prayed he wouldn't call her name. Hearing his voice would weaken her resolve. Protecting her children was more important than anything, but her love for him after all these years was still strong.

'Blanche?'

She closed her eyes. The way he called her name made the room spin. In an effort to block out the sound of his voice, she buried her head in her arms and covered her ears with her fists, though not tightly enough. She still heard him say something. It sounded like, 'Never mind. I understand.'

She remembered their agreement when he'd been last here. If ever she no longer wished to see him, he would understand and not pursue her, though he would still love her.

His footsteps retreated then stopped. Her curiosity got the better of her. Slowly and carefully she raised her head and saw him bent over a rose bush. She ducked as he straightened. Footsteps again, first to the front door, then down the path. Although her heart was beating with longing, she forced herself to stay down. Not until she was sure he was gone did she pop back up and look out of the window.

The garden was empty. Butterflies fluttered over the long grass beneath the apple trees and wasps buzzed among the slowly forming fruit.

Blanche heaved a sigh of relief. Once her heart had ceased racing and she'd confronted her feeling of loss, she went down to the front door and pulled back the bolt. The moment she'd done it she realized that he'd known she was here. The key was in the lock outside.

Her suspicion was confirmed. She swung the door open and saw the single red rose lying on the doorstep. Scrawled on the flagstone beside the rose with the aid of a chalky pebble were the words, 'I understand.'

Chapter Fourteen

The carriage blinds were down, a brass-bound travelling chest was strapped to the transom and the coachman had been told not to spare the horses.

Iron-shod hooves struck sparks on the cobbles, as the coach turned into Trenchard Street, a narrow and unsuitable route to the Gloucester Road, but the only one in existence. It rolled and creaked, as it swept wide of the acute left-hand turn into Steep Street. The street certainly lived up to its name. Haunches bursting with muscle, mouths lathered and nostrils snorting, the horses climbed the cruel incline.

Inside the carriage, Sir Stanley Moorditch tried to steady himself against the green leather upholstery. He'd considered what Stoke had told him to do, but opted out at the last minute and decided to leave the city. What could a man like Sydney Cuthbert do?

Unfortunately, Moorditch hadn't reckoned on his coachman or Stoke's network of informers, one of whom was the judge's own butler.

The coachman, flustered at being dragged from his dinner, wanted to get to their destination at Upper Wick as quickly as possible. They would be staying overnight prior to journeying on to Gloucester, and he was looking forward to the dinner he would get there. Because he was annoyed and his stomach was rumbling, he pushed the horses too hard. Their quarters slipped, their hooves flailed out in all directions as they lost their grip. The carriage swerved outwards then slewed inwards. The coachman tried to correct their swing, but it was too late. The carriage hit an iron bollard placed on the corner to prevent buildings being hit in the same fashion.

In one swift moment of bad judgement, all Sir Stanley Moorditch's plans for escape came to a swift end. There was a smashing of wood against metal, then a sickening crunch as the wheel folded and the carriage settled on its springs as the axle hit the road.

Great commotion followed. Women leaned out of doors, children peered from windows and men spilled out from pubs like flotsam on the tide.

The coachman made his apologies to his master who clambered out of the carriage, his immense bulk sticking in the narrow doorway before he popped out like a cork from a bottle.

Moorditch was not in a forgiving mood. To the surprise then amusement of the onlookers, he began beating the man about the head. 'How do I get to Upper Wick now, you fool? Do you realize how important it is? You idiot! You bastard son of a low-born mother!'

'Perhaps I can help you travel to your destination.'

Much to the coachman's delight, Moorditch, his face red and glistening with sweat, stopped beating him.

'My word, but that's very kind of you, sir,' he said, his angry expression replaced by one of gratitude. Unable to turn his head by virtue of his huge girth, he continued to gush words of gratitude – until he was finally face to face with the man who had made the offer.

'Cuthbert!'

Stoke smiled like a man who has only just understood a joke and is not impressed. 'Sir Stanley.'

Moorditch blustered, 'Look, Mr Cuthbert, I was just going—'

Stoke's expression turned grim. 'You are going to where you should be, and I am taking you there.' He gestured with his cane for Magnus to bring his carriage. 'Take Sir Stanley's luggage back to his house once the wheel's repaired,' he ordered. 'I'll make sure he's inside his own door before you get there.'

The coachman did not argue. With luck, Cook would still have plenty enough supper left in the pot and half a gallon of beer to swill it down.

Moorditch had as much trouble squeezing into the other carriage as he had getting out of his own. Standing on his stiff leg, Stoke slammed his foot against the judge's rump and rammed him in.

The second carriage rolled away, and men stepped forward to help repair the broken wheel of the first. One of them fetched axle grease from a carriage works at the back of a pub. As he came back out, someone leaning against the wall grabbed his arm.

'Did I hear right? Sir Stanley? Would that be Moorditch? And Cuthbert?'

'Aye, that's right,' returned the man. 'Both gentlemen, though I think one of them is not quite the gentleman he makes himself out to be.'

The blind beggar who had hold of his arm smiled. 'I don't think either of them are if the rumours I've heard are true.'

He entrusted the facts to memory for Septimus Monk – if and when they were needed.

–

The rose and Tom's sentiment stayed in Blanche's mind. Her heart ached for him but was overruled by her head. In order to remove temptation, there must be no opportunity for her to be alone with him. Little Paradise had to go, and the best way to do this was for someone to be living there permanently.

'I have a wonderful idea,' she said to Conrad.

'And what is that, my dear?'

'I want Edith in my household and she wants to be here. She gets on with the other staff very well, but it's such a long walk from here to Lewins Mead.'

'Do we have a spare bed?' asked Conrad as he helped himself to kedgeree from one of the serving dishes on the sideboard.

Blanche shook her head. 'That wouldn't be any good. She has four children. I thought we might install her at Little Paradise. Wasn't that your original idea anyway?'

Conrad sat down and tucked a napkin beneath his chin. 'It was indeed – until you and the children took it over.'

'So you agree?' asked Blanche, her face upturned to his, her eyes full of pleading.

Conrad munched thoughtfully on his breakfast and finally said, 'I think it a very good idea. Have you told her yet?'

Blanche gasped with delight. 'No. But I will. I'm taking her to the hospital with me today. I'll tell her then.'

Conrad stopped chewing and looked concerned. 'Why are you going to the hospital?'

'Nothing to do with the children or me,' she said with an amused smile, her hand stroking his. 'Doctor Budd thinks it would be a good idea for me to get some experience of disease and poor people before I get too involved with his project.'

'That sounds very sensible.'

'Yes,' she replied. 'I think it is.'

Conrad did not know it, but she was referring to both the doctor's plans and her own. Edith and her brood living at Little Paradise would be a barrier between her and Tom. Once again she'd be safe within her marriage and beyond his reach.

–

Edith chatted all the way to the hospital. Her old exuberance was fast returning, but although she was better dressed, she was still a bit smelly. It will improve greatly once she has somewhere decent to live, Blanche decided.

The hospital, dedicated to St Peter, dated from 1492 and was supported by huge black beams carved into the most beautiful and beguiling of shapes. The doors were low and the windows small and lopsided. There was a dispensary on the right of the entrance. Dr Budd and others shared an office on the left. Beyond that was an operating room, the implements laid out in regimented rows on a cotton-covered table.

Blanche avoided looking too closely into that room. The thought of saws, pincers, forceps and scalpels was too terrible for her to cope with. She'd fully expected that, at the request of Dr Budd, other ladies would be attending this very important meeting. The last person she'd expected to see amongst them was Horatia Strong.

Blanche eyed her disdainfully – a look she'd never mastered before coming to Bristol and marrying a man of means. Now she found it easy to do, though rarely did. But today was different. Horatia was here, and Horatia always brought out the worse in her.

They greeted each other stiffly, Horatia looking grand as a duchess and Blanche as fresh as a daisy.

Blanche thought Horatia looked as if she were going shopping for a fashionable hat or a new silk gown. Horatia thought Blanche looked as though she were better suited to being a flower seller or dancer.

Horatia smiled. 'How are the family?' Her smile was as false as a tin leg.

Blanche sensed the menacing undertone. 'Very well.'

'And so they should be! They are your first priority, are they not?'

'Always,' Blanche answered.

Horatia looked smug. 'What a good little wife you are!'

Rivalries were put to one side rather than forgotten as Dr Budd showed them around.

The hospital was rudimentary, the plaster peeling from the walls, the window panes cracked and the frames ill-fitting.

None of the women said a word. They were all dressed in their finest clothes, their hair curled, their complexions and hands unblemished by disease or hard work. They were like birds of paradise in the musty gloom of St Peter's Hospital. They also looked frightened. Were they up to it? Could women from their particular background have any effect at all on how people lived?

Their silence made Dr Budd nervous and it worried him. He felt a need to explain. 'The patients here are much poorer than at

Brandon Hill where I have my other hospital. The poor are left to fend for themselves to a great extent. Indeed, in some quarters they are held responsible for the disease.' He sighed. 'I suppose in a way they are.'

Horatia looked as though she were going to be sick and was holding a lace-edged handkerchief to her nose.

It pleased Blanche to see her reaction. However, she felt obliged to comment. 'How despicable to condemn people just because they are poor.'

Horatia's recovery was swift. Her eyes darted in Blanche's direction. 'Then it must be improved,' she said. 'As I have said, the Strong family are more than willing to donate a reasonable sum, and I am willing and able to give my services.'

Titters of admiration broke out among the other women. Where Horatia led, they would follow, simply because she was a Strong.

Blanche refused to be outdone. 'My husband, Conrad Heinkel owns the largest sugar refinery in the city. We will be more than willing to contribute too and I have already promised my services to Doctor Budd.'

Sensing the air of competitiveness between Blanche and Horatia, the other women joined in. By the time they'd finished, the doctor's expression reflected the abundance of pledges he'd received.

'I can't thank you all enough, but I am sure the citizens of this city will bless your names for ever,' he intoned, his face alight with enthusiastic rapture. 'You two ladies, especially,' he said for their ears alone. 'This would not have been possible without you. I thank you both from the bottom of my heart.'

After they'd accepted his thanks, he went off to thank the other women just as profusely. Horatia and Blanche stood alone.

Blanche was puzzled by Horatia's presence and her curiosity overcame her dislike. 'Why are you here? You're not known for carrying out good works in the city.'

The scent of violets filled the air as Horatia dabbed her kerchief at her nostrils 'It becomes a woman to do good works. Men like it, don't you think? Especially...' She paused for effect, her lips parted, her white teeth shining like pearls. 'Especially sea-going men.'

'That's absurd!'

Horatia raised her eyebrows. 'Is it?'

No, thought Blanche. It isn't absurd. Tom likes intelligent women, but he also likes them to have a compassionate side. What better way to impress him than helping with Dr Budd's project? And then it struck her. Horatia would use whatever it took to win Captain Tom Strong.

–

Satisfied she'd made a favourable impression at the hospital, Horatia left for another important appointment. Perhaps as a residual response to the charitable start to her day, she dropped a coin into the blind beggar's tin cup before entering the office of Septimus Monk.

Monk was suitably solicitous and offered her a chair.

'I have managed to procure five of the ten properties you wished to purchase.' He was wise enough to realize that being only half successful wouldn't please her.

He was right.

Her face froze. Her eyes were like glass. 'Who will not sell?'

'A man named Sydney Cuthbert. You know him?'

'An upstart.'

'A wealthy, and dare I say it, conniving upstart.'

'Can he be bought?'

'At too extortionate a price to be worth your while, especially when he knows he can get a good return on his investment when the Corporation push the new sewer through.'

Silence as Septimus waited for her next question, which he was sure would come. There were few men who would utter it let alone a woman. But Horatia? She was something different.

'What do we know about him?'

Septimus smiled. 'You mean, can we threaten him with details of his life that he'd prefer to keep secret?'

'That's exactly what I mean.'

When Septimus smiled, the corners of his eyes turned upwards in a strangely Oriental fashion. His lashes were sooty black, too black, thought Horatia, to be natural.

'In a strange way, my dear lady, Cuthbert and your good self have much in common. Neither of you are afraid of being – shall we say – unorthodox in your approach to business. You are both aware that information is everything. The difference between you is that you use an agent to carry out the more unsavoury aspects of commerce, whereas Mr Cuthbert prefers a more hands-on approach.'

'In short, Mr Monk?'

Resting his elbows on the desk, he steepled his fingers and peered at her over the top of them. 'In short, Miss Strong, he leaves himself open to all sorts of problems. Where there is intrigue, skulduggery and blackmail, there are witnesses. One moment and I will give you an example.' He rose from his chair, went to the window and gave three short raps on the pane. A few minutes later, the door opened and in walked the blind beggar, seemingly finding his way in as if he knew it very well indeed.

'Bedbug.   Relate to this lady the scene regarding a man named Sydney Cuthbert, a carriage and a judge named Sir Stanley Moorditch.'

Horatia frowned at Monk. The man's name was off-putting enough, but how, she wondered, could a blind man be a witness to anything?

Monk read her meaning, 'Bedbug is blind, dear lady, but he is not deaf. Neither is he a fool. Luckily for us everyone thinks he is, and thus are less than discreet in his company. In fact, his hearing is more acute than normal people because of his blindness, and his mind is shrewd.'

Horatia nodded. 'Then let us hear what he has to say.'

Chapter Fifteen

Conrad was frowning over a plan of the city when Blanche entered his study, a pleasant room with glass doors that led out into the garden.

'I came to ask if you'd changed your mind,' she said.

He jerked his head up and looked at her. She could tell from his expression that he hadn't a clue what she was talking about.

'The steam engines,' said Blanche. I'm taking the children to see the steam engines at Temple Meads Station. I know you said you were too busy earlier, but I thought you might have finished your work and be free to come with us now.'

Conrad sighed. Although his frown lessened, lines of worry were still discernible. 'I am very sorry, my dear. I cannot. The city aldermen are worried. We are having trouble buying the properties that need to be demolished in order to build the sewers. Speculators have got wind of our plans. The price of the project is soaring. I am studying the plans again in the hope of seeing a way around the problem and saving money.'

'How greedy people can be.' Blanche shook her head sadly. 'Have they no idea how many lives will be saved?'

Conrad shrugged. 'They do not care, my dear. Their priorities are not the same as yours and mine.' He looked up at her and patted her hand. 'Do you mind very much going alone?'

'Of course not. I'll take Edith with me. I didn't get round to telling her about moving into Little Paradise at the hospital. I thought I'd tell her today. I've also gathered up all the clothes that the children have grown out of, plus some of my own.'

'And mine?' he asked apprehensively, his eyebrows almost disappearing into his hairline.

'I wouldn't dare.' She smiled at him, her eyes shining and the blue of her bonnet and dress complimenting her complexion.

Conrad clasped her hand suddenly. 'I am sorry for being such an old fool.'

'You're not.' She laughed lightly, unsure of where this was leading.

'I am sorry for not having the energy to go with you.'

Blanche looked concerned. You've just said you have work to do. I won't be alone.'

With a swaying of her voluminous skirt, she turned to leave, but Conrad still held her hand as if afraid to let go.

The concern on his face had intensified. 'You do not regret marrying me, do you, Blanche? After all, you are so much younger than me...'

The question surprised her. Conrad was some twenty years older than she was. He was also one of the kindest men she'd ever met.

Cupping his face in her hands, she gazed into his face. 'How could I regret marrying a man like you? You are the most considerate of husbands, the kindest of fathers.'

'You have everything you want?' he asked.

She tried not to frown but to keep smiling, to speak lightly. 'Why do you ask?'

'I know that Captain Strong is back, Blanche.'

She prayed her emotion did not show on her face. Conrad didn't deserve it. Tom's presence had infiltrated Little Paradise, her relationship with Edith and even the cholera project through the interference and jealousy of Horatia Strong. His name had not been mentioned at Somerset Parade – until now.

'But what difference does that make to us? He's part of my past, not of my present. You're my husband.'

-

Once she'd left Somerset Parade with Edith and the children, she forced herself to forget Tom, Conrad's concern and what a bitch Horatia had been, in particular her comments about Max. A more pressing and exciting matter would take her mind off things.

'I've something to show you,' she said to Edith.

Instead of going straight to Temple Meads Station, Blanche had the coachman take them to Little Paradise.

Edith gazed with interest at the passing scene as the children told her all about the cottage.

'Bedminster used to be no more than a village,' said Blanche. 'Some bits of it are still quite old.'

But not many, she thought sadly once they'd crossed the river. Brick-built buildings were gradually spilling into the fields, squeezing out mortar-faced labourers' cottages. Here and there small lanes radiated off the main road, and apple trees hung ripe with fruit over dry stone walls.

The lane near the cottage was too narrow for the carriage. Blanche descended and Edith and the children tumbled out behind her.

Max whooped with joy and pushed his cap to the back of his golden hair as he ran through the grass. His sisters ran after him, shouting and laughing and holding their skirts way above their knees.

'I love this place,' said Blanche. Sunlight shining through the trees dappled her pale blue dress with spangles of light.

'What do you want another house for?' asked Edith as she followed Blanche down the garden path to the front door, which was half hidden beneath the tumbling wildness of a late flowering honeysuckle. 'You can only live in one at a time.'

'I'm not going to live in it. You are.'

'Me?'

Edith was astounded. Her mouth hung open and she was blinking furiously as though someone had just awoken her.

Blanche retrieved a six-inch iron key from a hook beside the door. 'See? It has a proper key, not that it's needed. People are very honest around here. It also has a large downstairs room, two bedrooms up above and a privy at the end of the back garden.'

The old hinges creaked and Edith gasped as the door swung open. Spellbound, she stepped into the cottage and attempted to take everything in.

A spider dashed into a crack in the flagstones and a pitter-pattering sounded from upstairs. The fireplace had a high grate with a hob at each side, an iron hook and a small spit hanging over it, a bread oven to one side. The windows were small, and there was a door at the back of the house and another set into the wall. 'This one leads upstairs,' said Blanche as she pulled it open.

Too astounded to comment, Edith followed her up the stairs. The wood was dry and groaned beneath their feet.

A panelled wall of painted pine divided the upper floor into two rooms, both flooded with daylight. There were two windows in each room, one looking over the front garden, and one at the back, both set tightly into the eaves.

Face bright with excitement, Blanche stood in the middle of the front room, her arms outstretched. 'Well? What do you think of it?'

Edith moved slowly around the room, touched the panelling, looked out of the front window and saw the new spire of St Mary Redcliffe rising above the trees. She turned and gazed out of the rear window. The privy was just visible beyond a tangle of fruit bushes. Blanche watched her, wanting to hug her, but she knew that despite Edith's poverty, she was proud. It didn't do to rush things.

'Well,' Edith exclaimed, a sudden stubbornness setting her chin, 'Could be nice an' cosy if a person 'ad a mind to make it so, I suppose... Lot of cleaning to be done, mind you... I mean... just look at it.' She swept her finger along the slate window ledge, and then held it up for Blanche to inspect.

'Yes. You'll have to give it a good clean,' Blanche agreed.

The sound of the children's laughter drifted up from the garden. Blanche couldn't hold in her excitement any longer. 'So what do you think?'

Edith shook her head. 'I don't take charity. You should know that.'

'No, no, no! You've got it all wrong. My husband bought this cottage for use as servants' quarters.' Blanche adopted her most pleading expression. 'You are one of our servants, but there's no room at the main house for you *and* your family. It makes sense for you to live here. I *need* you to help me, Edith.'

'Well...' Edith began.

Blanche attempted again to reassure her. 'You won't have to walk all that way from Lewins Mead any more, or leave your children with neighbours.'

Edith clapped her hands to her face. 'Oh, my word!' Her eyes shone like glass before she stiffened and pursed her lips. 'I'm quite 'appy where I am, thank you very much. I knows my place!'

Blanche grabbed her arm as she turned to flounce off back down the stairs. 'This is your place, Edith. You're part of my household now. Conrad owns this cottage, and you won't get it for free. You'll have to pay rent. And the garden will have to be tidied, the fruit bushes and apple trees looked after properly. And we'll want some of that fruit for pies. Cook would make good use of it all. Perhaps vegetables can be grown.'

Edith's pride was stiff as calico corsets, but mention of paying rent seemed to soften her stance.

Just a little more persuading, thought Blanche. 'There's another reason,' she said turning her back and looking out of the window. 'This was the place I last saw my daughter Anne playing. For a while it was my refuge. I came here alone and sat for hours on end just staring out of the window. I used to imagine I would see her come across that common opposite. You know how I felt, Edith. You've lost children too. But my mourning is over. I want the cottage to echo with children's laughter again. That's why I want you to have it.'

She turned back from the front window and the sound of her children enjoying themselves. 'And yours would love it.'

Mention of their mutual loss tipped the balance as Blanche hoped it would. Edith squealed and threw both hands to her mouth. 'They'll like it a lot,' she squeaked through her fingers, which were swiftly wet with tears. 'They'll like it ever such a lot.'

As they left Little Paradise, Blanche handed Edith the key. 'I think you should lock it,' she said.

Edith glowed, finally hanging the key back on the nail and sighing contentedly. 'My own little cottage,' she said. 'When can I move in?'

'Whenever you like.'

'As soon as I can! I'll start packing the minute I get home.' Blanche laughed and clapped her hands, though she couldn't imagine Edith having much to pack.

'Now can we go to see the trains?' said Max.

Blanche couldn't resist giving Edith a hug. 'Then that's settled. Max is right. Let's be off now and see the trains.'

Edith was silent as they drove to Temple Meads Station. Like a bottle of ginger beer, she contained her excitement until they arrived at their destination when it finally bubbled over, just as Blanche knew it would.

'Little Paradise it will certainly be by the time I've finished with it. I ain't got much, but I'll get more in time. Now let me think,' she said, counting each item on her fingers, 'I've got a bed. I've got a chair. And I can fix the wobbly leg on me table – and maybe Freddie and my Lizzie could make taffy apples in the summer and sell them down in King Street when the nobs are coming out of the Royal! And p'raps we can raise rabbits.'

The children heard her and squealed with delight at the thought of keeping rabbits, their upturned faces bright with enthusiasm. Blanche didn't have the heart to tell them that Edith wouldn't be keeping rabbits as pets, but putting them in pies.

Edith's face glowed as she listed all her hopes for the lovely little cottage, and Blanche glowed too. Giving to people in need was one of the most satisfying discoveries she'd made since marrying Conrad.

'Rich men take much from those around them,' he'd said to her. 'It is only right and proper that we give something back.'

The children had been given little flags by their nanny to wave at the steam engines as they left the station. The engine drivers, big men with thick whiskers and faces reddened by the heat of the firebox, always waved back.

The station was a hive of activity. Passengers departed and arrived, and men in uniform heaved luggage, blew whistles and waved little green flags of their own.

The children waved when they waved and Max expressed a wish for a whistle just like theirs. While her children watched the trains, Blanche touched Edith's arm. 'Tomorrow we'll look through the attic for furniture and get Mrs Henderson to see what spare bedding and curtains we have.'

'I'm so happy,' said Edith, her eyes misty and her voice shaking with emotion.

Further conversation was momentarily drowned in a loud cheer as a coal black steam engine slowly crawled forward. Steam hissed from beneath its belly and smoke chugged from its stack.

'It's gone,' wailed Max, as it disappeared in a cloud of smoke and steam.

'Can we go to the doll's hospital today?' asked Lucy, whose interest had disappeared along with the train.

'No! We're going visiting,' said Blanche. Out of the hearing of the children, she told Edith of the food parcel, the blankets and clothes she'd packed before leaving. 'They're in the back of the carriage,' she said, 'and there's such a lot, you'll need it delivered.'

The colour drained from Edith's face. Blanche guessed at the reason but decided that there was no longer any point in sparing Edith's feelings. 'Look, Edith, I've seen where you live. It doesn't matter. You're still my friend.'

Edith's expression remained unchanged.

Blanche tried again, this time bearing in mind the old Edith who tried to make herself and her family seem better than they actually were.

'You've fallen on hard times, Edith, but I know you've been used to better. Goodness, you looked after Marstone Court as if it were your own.'

'Ah!' said Edith, her face seeming to brighten. 'But our Lizzie 'as been sick, you know. And bearing in mind that you lost your Annie, so you wouldn't want to lose any more by bringing them to Cabot's Yard, would you?'

Brought up sharply by Edith's less than tactful reminder of Anne's death, Blanche instantly reconsidered. Much as she wanted to convince Edith that her dire circumstances didn't matter, that they were still friends, she had no wish to expose her children to infection unnecessarily. She remained tactful.

'Perhaps we should go to the doll's hospital first. The children can stay there while we deliver the parcels.'

'Oh, no,' Max protested.

'They do have toy soldiers,' Blanche reminded him, and he gave in, albeit reluctantly.

'That might be better,' said Edith. 'I mean,' she said with a sudden grin and in a low voice so the children couldn't hear, 'it ain't no worse than that bloody awful place in Cock and Bottle Alley where me ma used to live and them dogs me brother pinched for the rewards Lady Verity offered.'

'And your mother feeding them chopped-up rats,' said Blanche in an equally low voice.

The woman who ran the doll's hospital was plump, wore a brightly coloured dress and a mop cap from which corkscrew curls, white and stiff as waxed rope, crowded around her face.

'This place smells funny,' said Max, wrinkling his nose at the smell of linseed oil, cat's' pee and cabbage water.

Blanche pretended she hadn't heard and smiled sweetly at the beaming proprietor.

'Mrs Winter, I know it may be something of an imposition, but can I ask you to take care of my children for half an hour? I have an errand to run that is of the utmost importance. They may purchase a toy each to the value of two shillings.'

At the prospect of entertaining customers with money, Mrs Winter's cheeks grew rounder as her smile grew wider.

'Course I will, Mrs Heinkel. Anything to oblige a lady such as yourself,' she said, dropping a deep curtsey. ''Tis no imposition at all,' she repeated. 'I only wish all me customers acted like the ladies and gentlemen they're supposed to be. But there, I knows a real lady when I sees one.'

Blanche could tell that Edith was bubbling with barely contained laughter, but she managed to keep a straight face herself.

The children were already entranced by the dolls, the lead soldiers, the automatons and a dapple-grey rocking horse with flared nostrils, a long mane and a docked tail.

It didn't take long to get to Lewins Mead.

First they bundled up John with blankets, clothes and food. What remained they tucked beneath their arms.

'I know you said Freddie loved plum jam. I got Cook to put in a big jar in that trunk back there. And there's cake, half a ham, a loaf of sugar and three pats of butter plus one of Cook's wonderful loaves,' said Blanche, as they went into Cabot's Yard.

People in doorways stared as they struggled by.

'Be careful you don't trip,' shouted Blanche, seeing that the blankets were obscuring Edith's view.

But Edith didn't slow her pace, though goodness knows, she couldn't possibly see where she was going.

Despite the weight of her crinoline, Blanche ran almost as fast as ten years before, when bare legged, with the wind in her hair, she had counted her paces along the beach in Barbados where she had grown up.

Edith was not so sure-footed as she seemed, however. Tripping on the rough and broken surface of the alley, she fell forward, and so did the blankets she carried.

'Edith!' cried Blanche, running to her side, as curious faces appeared at pint-sized windows. Through a small door to her right, a host of what looked like grubby dwarves appeared, paused then dashed towards them.

'Ma! Ma!'

Suddenly Blanche knew the extent of Edith's pride. These grubby, ill-dressed urchins were Edith's children.

The biggest was a boy with a filthy face, his hair dark and matted, and his eyes blue pools in the freckled filth of his face. She recognized him as the boy she'd seen Edith with on St Augustine's Quay. A girl ran close behind him, her eyes big and dark, and her frame too thin for her height. Two smaller children, a boy and a girl, followed behind, shyly curious as they eyed Blanche, who now felt truly out of place with her fine dress. Their faces were pinched and pale. The boy helped his mother to her feet and the others gathered up the blankets.

Blanche checked the urge to wrinkle her nose at the smells of the alley and the dirty children. Cabot's Yard was *worse* than Cock and Bottle Alley. She'd left John with the carriage at the end of the alley, and couldn't wait to get back to it.

'I've got lots of lovely things for you,' she said to the children and smiled broadly – which helped keep her from wrinkling her nose.

The children remained wary, as their mother brushed down her dress and looked more dejected than Blanche could ever remember.

'What you got this time then?' asked Freddie, his wariness shunned by a forced look of aggression.

Blanche kept smiling. 'There's bread and jam and butter and lots of other food in this parcel,' she said, indicating the one she carried beneath her right arm, 'and there's nice new clothes in this one,' she said gesturing to the other.

Without a word of warning, the boy snatched both parcels and darted for the door he'd come out of.

'Freddie! Thank Mrs Heinkel right now!'

Freddie stopped, glowered at his mother then thought better of it. 'Thank you,' he said lamely and disappeared.

Edith sighed as her remaining children gathered around her. 'You'd better come inside,' she said to Blanche.

Blanche ducked through the low doorway, sure that the smell inside would be dreadful bearing in mind the amount of people living here. To her surprise she detected the faint smell of lavender.

The room was dark, the muted glow of the fire throwing shadows over the wall and doing just as much to give light as the single, small window, with it's blemished glass that disfigured the scene outside. Her eyes followed her nose to the bunch of lavender hanging before it.

There was a double bed against one wall, a single chair, a table and a three-legged stool. An iron pot hung over a primitive fire grate. Her heart filled with pity for her old friend. This was all Edith had in the world. Judging by the size of the bed, Edith slept sitting upright in the chair.

Edith pointed at the bunch of lavender. 'I hung it there to stop the smells — that's what they reckons spreads the cholera, though I ain't so sure now, not since that Doctor Budd came wanderin' through 'ere and said to me about the water. My Freddie, bless his heart, went down and got it from the quay. That was when 'e met Captain Tom. Fancy that! On that day and right there on the quay, there 'e was as large as life…'

Blanche laughed and shook her head in disbelief. 'Goodness! It seems you knew Tom was back in Bristol before I did.'

'Freddie heard Marstone Court and the Strong family mentioned, and told the captain that his ma used to work there.' She beamed as if she would burst with happiness, her face swiftly turning pink. 'That's when he told Freddie to say that Captain Tom Strong sends his compliments.'

Blanche had heard all this before, but could see that Edith took great pleasure in the retelling. 'And you received them well, I see. Your face is as red as rhubarb.'

Sensing it was time to leave, she stepped out into the dirty alley.

Edith followed. 'I'll walk with you. Ain't safe for a lady like you to be alone in a place like this.'

'It can't be that bad,' said Blanche, but didn't really mean it. Of course it was bad. The drains were bad, the water was bad and the housing was appalling. It was kinder not to agree.

The smells, the heat and the flies were truly dreadful in Cabot's Yard.

Edith didn't seem to notice at first, then saw Blanche's expression and said with a nervous laugh, 'Damn flies like the stink, don't they? Hope things smell a bit sweeter in my new cottage.'

'I'm sure they will,' said Blanche.

Chapter Sixteen

Tom hadn't meant to peer at papers that did not concern him, but he was looking for bills of lading in order to judge the size of sugar business the new steamship company could expect. It wasn't like Horatia to leave personal paperwork in an unlocked drawer, but he had distracted her attention the night before. Following a few glasses of wine at dinner, candlelight and his mellow mood, she'd become a different woman. Everything he said seemed to be what she wanted to hear. She'd touched him intimately, her breasts heaving expectantly against the tight bodice of her low-cut dress. He'd resisted temptation – this time.

The documents were deeds of properties in the city centre. He didn't know for sure, but was pretty certain that they lay in the path of the proposed new sewer. 'The sly little minx,' he murmured and smiled. She would never admit to this.

The letter with the documents specifically asked that she return the paperwork today. It was ten o'clock in the morning and he'd already decided to take a look at the progress in the shipyard. Needling Horatia about her secret dealings might hold him up a little, but he couldn't resist.

There was a large green leather winged chair immediately behind the door of the library, unseen when the door was opened. Tom took a seat and waited.

Horatia came breezing in, dressed in green velvet and pulling on her gloves. She went straight to the desk and took out the deeds, just as Tom had guessed she would.

'Off into town?' he asked.

Horatia was like a startled rabbit. Although amused, he controlled the urge to laugh.

'Yes,' she said, tucking the papers into a wallet that she stuffed beneath her arm.

'So am I,' he said getting up out of the chair. 'Can I drop you off anywhere?'

He knew damn well that she wasn't going to admit to an appointment at her solicitors because then he would ask her why she was going there and he was sure she wouldn't want to divulge the reason.

'Yes,' she said. 'I'm going to... the hospital. It's to do with disinfecting some areas of the city.'

'Then I shall take you there,' said Tom. 'I admire your courage. Not many fine ladies would dare venture into the parts of the city Doctor Budd wishes to cleanse.'

'I feel it's my duty,' said Horatia, flushing slightly at Tom's praise.

Tom offered her his arm. 'Then I am pleased to escort you.'

He knew she'd get a cab from the hospital straight to the offices of Septimus Monk if he didn't escort her directly into the keeping of Doctor Budd.

'Come, my dear,' he said once they arrived at St Peter's Hospital, taking hold of her elbow and guiding her forcefully into the dark interior. He sensed her unwillingness, though she smiled tightly, as if her teeth might fall out if she didn't.

The other women were already there – including Blanche. At the sight of her, Tom raised his hat and their eyes locked as they do when secrets are shared.

'Ladies,' he said. 'I take my hat off to all of you. You are braver than many men I have met. If this city is ever free of disease, it is entirely down to you.'

His statement was well received and Horatia's demeanour changed instantly. Not willing to appear less courageous than the other women – especially Blanche – the true purpose of her trip to Bristol was put aside, at least for now.

'Tom, you are such a dear man for escorting me here,' she said, reaching up and kissing him lightly on the lips. Tom saw Blanche lower her eyes. She wouldn't be jealous, he couldn't countenance that, but she might be a little hurt. Old wounds are always difficult to heal if left unattended for a long time.

'And don't forget your promise, will you?' Horatia added, clutching both Tom's hands in hers. 'You will collect me later, won't you, my darling? Then we can enjoy the drive back to Marstone Court. Just the two of us.'

Her term of endearment was so brazen, so full of innuendo, that even Dr Budd, who had just appeared, went a little pink in the gills.

Tom departed nodding an acknowledgement to Edith, and leaving every woman there with a gleam in her eyes.

Blanche was surprised. Although Horatia had paid lip service to cleaning up the city, Blanche had never expected her to get seriously involved. Well, she's certainly going to get her hands dirty, she decided. 'Come along, ladies. We have work to do,' she said.

Although Blanche had expected Horatia to be frosty, she was surprised to find her otherwise, as though she were trying to live up to Tom's praise for their bravery.

A team of coachmen, including John, set them down close to Lewins Mead with their jars of disinfectant. As they walked into the narrower streets, where the coach could not go, the daylight turned to dusk in the middle of the day. This was the heart of Lewins Mead. Other carriages carrying other women had stopped next to alleys just as mean as these, all armed with disinfectant and good advice.

'How quaint,' Horatia remarked on entering the more amenable though ancient alleys of the old city. 'So atmospheric. It reminds one of times gone by when men wore hose and women were called damsels.'

Her nose wrinkled and her overtures to times past vanished as they approached Lewins Mead. Ramshackle privies hung from the backs of houses between St John's Bridge and Quay Head, the resulting effluent falling directly into the River Frome. The stench was at its worse here. Steam rose from the seething mess of household rubbish, human excreta, waste from the glassworks and the skinless body of what looked like a dead dog, but might just as well have been a stillborn child. The steam smelt poisonous, similar to that rising from the new coal-burning coke boilers at the gasworks.

At the sight of three ladies, two of whom were far too well dressed to belong to Cabot's Yard, heads bobbed at windows. Care-worn women and ragged children appeared in dark doorways, sunken eyes full of curiosity, mouths open like starving nestlings waiting to be fed. Belligerent voices bawled in the blackness behind them, demanding to know what was going on or to shut the bloody door.

'That's where we get our water,' said Edith, pointing to the well.

It was of the old-fashioned type, water drawn up by means of a bucket and covered with a slate slab that had to be dragged back when water was needed. At present it was pulled to one side, the mouth of the well exposed.

'It's bloody heavy,' said Edith, noticing Blanche's worried frown.

Horatia's attention was drawn elsewhere. She pointed. 'What's that?'

Standing in the corner like a sentry box was the privy, a three-sided affair with a three-quarter door.

'The privy,' said Edith picking up a stone. 'See?' The stone hit its target and a host of bluebottles buzzed upwards in an angry mass.

Horatia turned white.

Blanche asked Edith why her children weren't there.

'They're down with Molly,' said Edith. 'I thought we could get on better with things with them out of the way, though they kind of keep an eye on her rather than the other way round.'

'Is that why you haven't moved to Little Paradise yet?'

Edith screwed up her face. 'She's none too bright and needs looking after and she cries when I says about moving. But I've had a thought about how to persuade her. It's just a case of waiting till the time is right.'

Blanche was disappointed. Since Edith had come to work for her, she'd made sure she never went home without 'surplus' food from the kitchen, and items of clothes and footwear that her own children had outgrown. She'd wanted to see how they were.

As Edith and Blanche went about their task with all the energy of Christian crusaders, determined to dispel the enemy, Horatia turned to stone.

Although she willed her legs to move, they wouldn't. Her stomach churned with revulsion, the bile rising like a swallowed slug. At Marstone Court, the smell of poverty had been hidden beneath the uniforms of housemaids, chambermaids, scullery maids and all other manner of the lower orders. Never had she witnessed at first-hand the raw reality of life for people like Edith.

Holding her hand against the velvet trim and glass buttons of her bodice did nothing to stop her heart palpitating or her nose from wrinkling. The stench was terrible; rotting refuse, urine and the ever-present stink of sewers and mouldy buildings mixed with the sickly sweetness of rats with which the poor seemed to share their lodgings.

'Retching will only add to our work,' Blanche said to her on noticing her pallor.

'I will do my best not to,' Horatia hissed through clenched teeth.

'Then perhaps you'll stop wasting time and get on with what you've come here to do.' She pointed to the disinfectant Horatia had set down. 'Pour it down and around the privy.'

Horatia stiffened her spine. She was being challenged.

You're going to be sick. You're not really the sort of woman Tom described. Deep down you're just a very rich woman, as stupid and narrow-minded as others of your class.

Horatia told herself she was made of sterner stuff, picked up the disinfectant and started for the privy. A small child ran into it ahead of her and slammed the door. Relieved at the unexpected respite, Horatia eyed the three-sided structure. The sides, like the door, were built of wooden slats and flies buzzed in and out of the knotholes.

'My God,' she exclaimed, 'it looks like a coffin.'

'In some ways it is,' said Blanche, 'or weren't you really listening to what Doctor Budd had to say?'

It's her revenge for what I said about Max, thought Horatia indignantly and threw Blanche an icy stare.

Blanche glared back at her. Convinced that Horatia had her own reasons for supporting Dr Budd's project, she couldn't bring herself to sympathize. Horatia's heart – and certainly her stomach – were not in it. She was here to impress Tom. That's none of your concern, said the voice of reason inside her head. Easier said than done. Tom was like an itch she couldn't ignore. No matter that she shouldn't scratch it, she couldn't help it. It was there, hidden from the view of others, noticeable only to her.

The privy door suddenly banged open and a child ran out and disappeared beneath a narrow arch.

Horatia stood there staring at the privy as she attempted to steel her stomach before doing what had to be done. Few people knew she had a delicate stomach. It was not something a woman of substance was ever likely to admit to and she certainly had no intention of admitting it to Blanche.

'Horatia!' Blanche jerked her head towards the privy. 'Are you going to help, or are you just here to gawp?'

Horatia stiffened her shoulders and headed for the recently vacated privy. The stink was awful but she gritted her teeth, praying her stomach wouldn't let her down and shame her in front of Blanche.

'Oh my God!' Reeling back, she let the flagon of disinfectant fall. Some was spilt, but it didn't break.

Blanche stormed over. 'What a useless woman you are, Horatia Strong!'

Horatia bit her tongue. It would have been so easy to lose her temper, but she wouldn't. Neither would she admit the weakness of her stomach. The moment was strained and oddly silent, but full of activity, as Blanche swooped on the disinfectant, muttering how pointless it was that Horatia was there.

The moment was strangely opportune. In the brief moment of enforced silence, Horatia recognized something of herself in Blanche. Resilience, strength, steadfastness and determination;

they were all there. But why the surprise? she asked herself. After all, she is your half-sister.

Blissfully ignorant of their hostile emotions, it was Edith who saved the day. 'Let me do that,' she said, easing Horatia aside. 'I've got a stronger stomach than a lady like you, Miss Horatia.'

Defeated by her stomach and relieved that someone else had offered to do the job, Horatia stepped back.

But she was far from happy. I've been defeated by a privy, she thought grimly, and I wanted to prove myself. Now what do I do?

Angry and perplexed, she tried to regain her self-esteem, to think carefully about what she was trying to achieve and whether there were different skills she could bring to the project. Backing out now was not an option. The fact that she intended making money from buying and selling properties along the proposed sewer route was beside the point. Proving to Tom that there was a softer side to her nature was just as important. Surely there's something I'm good at besides business, she thought?

Just then, she caught sight of an old man, who was looking up at her, his eyes watery blue in a creased face. The stubble on his chin was silver and his trousers were tied with string just below the knees.

He spat on the ground before leaning grandly on a long staff he carried. 'What you doin' thur?' he asked.

Although he was poorly dressed, he had an air of authority, resting on his staff as though it were a royal banner.

Horatia was strangely glad he'd asked her the question rather than anyone else. This was something she felt able to do and did so, explaining it to him in great detail. He looked at her baffled, his toothless mouth gaping.

Edith intervened. 'We're making it smell sweeter, Jack,' she shouted close to his ear. And to Horatia, 'He's deaf.' And back to Jack. 'Deaf as a bloody post, ain't you, Jack?'

He nodded vigorously, his lips drawing back in a toothless grin.

'He's not very bright either,' Edith added.

'Like this place,' said Horatia, looking and feeling thoroughly fed up.

Blanche heard her. 'You didn't have to come.'

Horatia scowled. 'Yes I bloody well did.'

Blanche looked surprised. Because she's never heard me swear before, thought Horatia then changed her mind. Blanche wanted her to give up. She wanted her to retch at the sight of all this squalor and to declare herself beaten. But I've surprised her, thought Horatia, and, for the first time that day, felt incredibly self-satisfied.

Although Cabot's Yard was always dingy, it was still possible to tell when clouds hid the sun. A grey gloom settled at the same time as raindrops the size of pennies plopped onto the grimy ground and quickly formed puddles. In no time at all skirts were sodden and feathers in hats were drooping and dripping onto soaked shoulders.

'We need to go indoors,' said Blanche, pushing wet strands of hair away from her face.

Reluctantly, Edith opened her own front door. Blanche and Horatia followed.

'It ain't much,' said Edith on seeing Horatia's shocked expression. 'But at least it's dry,' she added defensively.

'This fire is just enough to take away the chill,' said Blanche. Purposely, she made for the fire, determined that Edith shouldn't feel embarrassed about her home, and ready to confront Horatia if she showed further repugnance.

'Better than being soaked to the skin,' said Horatia as she lifted her drenched skirt over the threshold.

Blanche contained her surprise. She was happy enough that Edith's pride would not be affronted. The room was small and their skirts took up as much room as Edith's table. Sitting this close to her half-sister, Blanche noted Horatia's clear skin, the scent of her dress and her earrings – tear-shaped pearls set in gold. Horatia held herself very stiffly, as though her backbone were made of iron. Perhaps due to the back boards Blanche had seen in the nursery at Marstone Court all those years ago. Horatia's other half-brothers and sister had been strapped to them – wooden paddles that fitted across the back and under the arms – for an hour at a time, a device meant to help them sit straight.

Droplets of water scattered, as Horatia shook her hat, sizzling as they landed on the dying fire. Scrutinizing the place that Edith called home, her gaze finally fixed on the bed that Edith shared with her children.

Flexing her fingers before the meagre heat of the fire, Blanche watched for Horatia's reaction, ready to meet any sign of disdain. Comfortable within their own worlds, rich people blamed the poor for being poor. It never occurred to them that they might be trapped in their world — just as to some extent they too were trapped, though with the rigours of class and society structure rather than the urgent need to keep a roof over their heads and a meal on the table.

'Are your children upstairs?' Horatia suddenly asked Edith.

Blanche threw her a desultory glare, which went unnoticed. Horatia thought that Edith lived in more than one room.

Edith, bless her heart, didn't seem to understand her meaning. 'Well, actually, Miss Horatia, as I told Bla— Mrs Heinkel, they're downstairs with Molly, though I told them before they went, that they ain't to drink the water down there.' She looked proudly at Blanche. 'Freddie still fetches water from the Quay Pipe only – St John's if he's feeling tired after working as a beer boy in the char room. They're under strict instructions not to drink anything Molly gives them.'

Blanche beamed at her approvingly. 'Very good, Edith. You've really taken Doctor Budd's advice.'

Edith, with her pink face and her round body, her plain dress and her plain speaking, knew and understood what was at stake here. The poor could be educated to improve their health; Edith proved that. And soon, Edith's lot would improve even more.

Her heart felt it would burst with joy as she said to Horatia, 'Edith is moving to a cottage called Little Paradise shortly.'

'It has a garden with trees,' Edith added brightly.

'And not before time.' Horatia's gaze strayed to the rain trickling through the ill-fitting windows and collecting in puddles on the sills. 'Do you actually pay rent for this place?'

Edith was busying herself straightening the sparse bedding and hanging washed pots from the beams. 'Well, it certainly ain't free,' she said over her shoulder as she stretched to hang an iron pot on a nail positioned a little higher than the rest. 'I pays a shilling a week to Mrs Green. She collects it for Mr Cuthbert, the owner, though sometimes his son, Mr Gilmour Cuthbert comes round to collect it.'

Horatia's disdainful look disappeared. Suddenly she was standing close to Edith, her face full of interest. 'Cuthbert? Isn't he a city alderman?'

Edith shrugged. 'Don't know.'

'Does he ever come round himself?'

'Once or twice, but not usually.'

'Does he own many properties around here?'

'A lot, though they're not all rented for shillings. Some are rented for pounds, lots of pounds. But then,' she winked salaciously, 'they're the ones that's earning it – if you know what I means. I think Mrs Green runs one of them. She's a bawd, you know. Still, don't worry me none. I'm going to live in Little Paradise. Ain't that a pretty name?'

'Yes,' said Horatia in an absent-minded fashion. 'It is.'

'Very pretty,' said Blanche, who had listened with interest to their conversation, intrigued by the sudden fire in Horatia's eyes at the mention of Stanley Cuthbert.

'I'm going to grow potatoes, cabbages, peas and catmint in the garden at Little Paradise,' said Edith. She went on to recount her other plans, including rabbits, chickens and a watercress bed.

Blanche considered reminding her that it was only a garden and not a five-acre field, but didn't have the heart. It didn't hurt to have dreams, only when they didn't come true.

'It's still raining,' she said instead, eyeing the desolate scene outside.

Islands of rubble, mostly moss and bits of slate fallen from rickety roofs, dotted the rising water. Inches deep, it lapped at slime-covered doorsteps, slurping and gurgling around choked drains and clay gutters.

Her gaze was drawn to something long and dark creeping across the surface of the water. At first she thought it was a fat eel writhing with the swirling flood before realizing that a brown stain was seeping from beneath the privy, snaking across the yard and into the gullies, *down into the well*.

Visible proof of how cholera stalked its victims.

'Look,' she shouted, opening the casement so she could see better. 'Do you see it?' she asked the other women, her voice barely above a whisper.

'Oh my God! Is that what I think it is?' said Horatia and turned away. 'Disgusting.'

Blanche continued to watch. Although the water level remained the same, and would as long as it rained, she could see it disappearing through cracks in the cobbles and the loose earth around the base of the well. The brown stain eddied and whirled with the rainwater, finding the same channels.

Dwellers of Cabot's Yard had disappeared with the rain. Blanche stayed looking out, dejected because all their work – in the form of disinfectant – had been swilled away with the rain. Heavy and unrelenting, it formed a thick curtain, obscuring her view across the yard, splashing upwards in short sharp bursts as it hit the ground.

At first she thought the wind had caught the rain, forming the downpour into thicker shapes that swept towards her. Then suddenly she counted three shapes rising up from the cellar entrance halfway across the yard. The three children ran through the pouring rain in bare feet, their hair plastered to their heads and their clothes to their bodies.

Horatia cried out as they dashed straight into the house and the luxuriant width of her crinoline dress.

'I'm in a mad house,' she muttered as she attempted to shake the dampness from her skirt.

'You will be, talking to yourself like that,' Blanche remarked with amusement.

The two girls who had come in flattened themselves against the wall and stared at their well-dressed visitors. Their house was suddenly much too crowded, mostly by the width of Horatia's crinoline.

Freddie went straight to his mother. 'Molly's place is flooded,' he shouted as he hopped from one foot to the other. 'Her skirt's up round her ears and she's floating.'

'And she's wet up to 'er bum!' added one of the girls, easing away from the wall so she could be better seen and heard.

'And she said that the *Lizzie Brady* is in,' cried the youngest.

Blanche saw Edith pale at the last comment, before a more stoical look came to her face and she headed straight for the door. 'Bloody Molly McBean!'

The children followed.

'Do you think it's time we left?' Horatia asked Blanche. 'I don't wish to appear uncharitable towards this Molly woman, but I have no intention of getting any wetter than I already am.'

Bundling her skirt into a manageable bunch in front of her, Blanche settled herself on one of the two stools that Edith possessed. 'No. I have to stay to see if I can do anything.' Frowning, she added quietly, 'We've achieved precious little otherwise today. The rain's washed all the disinfectant away.'

'But isn't that a good thing?' said Horatia. 'Doesn't that mean the rain's done the job for us?'

Blanche shook her head. 'You saw the contents of the privy seeping across the yard. There'll be another outbreak of cholera in no time – mark my words.'

Horatia frowned. 'What a shameful waste of time.'

Blanche was surprised at the obvious concern on Horatia's face. She'd never considered her a sympathetic character. Today had certainly been a turning point for both of them.

Edith returned complete with Molly and her brood, all of them rushing into the room like a flock of soggy hens and soaked chicks.

'It's two foot high down there and stinks rotten,' said Edith, her skirts hitched up around her plump knees, and her paper boots waterlogged and breaking into pieces.

Molly, a sodden shawl covering her hump, was holding onto Edith's arm. From eldest to youngest, her children did the same, each one hanging onto the arm of the elder sibling and down to the youngest.

She was wailing loudly. 'Wass I goin' to do? Wass I goin' to do?'

'Give me a minute to think and I'll tell you,' said Edith, patting Molly's wrinkled hand. Grinning reassuringly at Blanche, she said, 'She'll be all right in a minute.'

The reassurance was obviously not enough.

'Wass I goin' to do?' Molly continued, her children joining in and wailing as loudly as she, their voices needle sharp on the nerves.

Blanche automatically thought of the size of Marstone Court and looked expectantly at Horatia.

Horatia seemed dumbstruck, her gaze fixed on the strange creature with the curved back and the oversize mop cap, the frill of which flopped on her shoulders.

No, Marstone Court and the Strong family were not ready for the likes of the McBeans.

Blanche bit her lip and considered the next, and more likely option. What would Conrad say if she took them in?

Edith hugged her neighbour close, Molly's capped hat barely reaching her chin. 'Never you mind, Molly. You can stay yur until they gets your place dried out.'

Judging by the expression on Edith's face, offering charity had not been easy. Molly had scooted off and left Edith to face the beak. But Molly had looked after the children in her absence.

Blanche was amazed by their values. The bed was big enough for husband; wife and children top to tail, but it would be a bit of a squash to fit in Molly and her brood.

During a brief break in the wailing, Edith suggested the best option of all. 'It's goin' to be ages before Molly's place is half decent to live in. If she takes over this place, could I move into my cottage today?'

Both Blanche and Horatia visibly relaxed and exchanged swift and thankful glances. Neither had been willing to visualize the McBean family taking up residence in either one of the most desirous properties in Bristol.

'I don't see why not,' said Blanche with undisguised enthusiasm.

'Wonderful idea,' echoed Horatia.

Molly's wailing continued, though not quite so resonant as before. Her eyes skitted from one woman to another as she digested the information and waited for the arrangement to be confirmed.

Edith lifted the limp frill of Molly's cap so she could look straight into her face. 'There you are, Moll. It's all settled.'

The wailing stopped abruptly. 'Bist thee sure?'

'Course I am.'

'Thees ain't 'avin I on?'

'Why should I? I'm moving into my new cottage,' said Edith in as superior a manner as any duchess. 'Should 'ave done it days ago.'

'But what about me things?' said Molly, a hopeful look in her eyes. 'It's all floating about in a sea of mucky water downstairs. I ain't got a stick left, I ain't.'

Blanche frowned. Molly was right. If Edith took her things, the place would be bare. Poor Molly and her family couldn't be expected to sleep on the floor.

'Well, let me see,' she began, holding her hand against her head, which was beginning to ache. There were too many things to think about.

The problem was taken out of her hands.

'Can we get on with this?' said Horatia. Determined to get things moving, she turned round swiftly, the width of her skirt sending a small McBean flying towards the bed. She pointed at Molly. 'This woman can take over here, and we can move you to Little Paradise, Edith. Now, I shall pay for a carter and arrange for some items to be donated from Marstone Court. I'm sure we have plenty of furniture in store that we're never likely to use,' she announced.

Blanche wanted to tell her not to interfere, that Edith and these people were her concern, but the truth was that Horatia had made a decision while she'd still been thinking about it.

Horatia pulled on her soaking gloves, pushing her fingers into the sticky leather and wriggling them for room. She turned to Edith. 'The rain seems to have stopped. Can you leave now?'

'Oh yes!' Edith cried, and nudged Molly. 'I'm moving into a cottage with a garden, and once I'm settled in, you can come and see me, if you like.'

'What about when Deke— ?' Molly began.

The dig Edith gave her this time almost bent her double.

Edith gave no one the opportunity to ask her anything else. 'Freddie! Grab that kettle. Lizzie, pick up that pot. Your kettle and pots will be fine,' she said to Molly.

The tiny room became a frenzy of activity as Edith gave directions. Bits and pieces of belongings were picked up, tucked beneath arms or thrown into a blanket whose four corners were immediately tied together to form unwieldy bundles.

Horatia and Blanche exchanged looks as they themselves were bundled around the tiny room.

'This would have been best left until tomorrow, Edith. It'll take until then to get you some furniture,' said Blanche.

'I can manage,' Edith said brightly. 'I'll make do with whatever bits of furniture you and Miss Horatia give me.'

As they both squeezed out of the door, Edith leaned close and whispered into Blanche's ear. 'I don't want that old bed anyway. It's full of bugs and fleas, but Molly won't mind. She's used to it.'

Skirts sodden, their bonnets soggy and their feet wet, Blanche, Horatia and Edith, the children following behind, hurried through the huddle of streets, courtyards and alleys as best they could, puffing and panting due to the weight of their skirts.

John had been ordered to wait in Lewins Mead with the carriage. In the streets around Cabot's Yard there was barely room for a handcart to pass, never mind a carriage, as Blanche had noted on her first visit there.

Progress was slow. Besides being loaded with Edith's multitude of pots, pans and the blankets Blanche had donated, their way was pitted with holes now turned to puddles. They picked their way gingerly as water dripped from jutting first floors and muddied eddies swirled into cavernous openings in lead-lined gutters.

Horatia, in her element when giving orders, chivvied everyone along. Like her father, she was not easily frightened by anything or anyone, but the alleys around Lewins Mead were alien to her experience. Ramshackle houses loomed over the narrow walkways. Weeds grew around rotting doorposts. Rubbish, thrown from upstairs windows without regard for passers-by, was heaped at street corners awaiting collection, which might happen within days, perhaps weeks, or not at all.

Blanche stopped to pick up Edith's youngest who had landed face down in a puddle and was wailing for all she was worth.

Street pedlars turned curious eyes in their direction, amazed that ladies of obvious wealth were walking on foot through the oldest and poorest part of the city.

Horatia seemed oblivious to the questioning looks, her only concession to daintiness being the way she held her skirt hem as clear from the mucky ground as was possible.

Blanche was as brave as Horatia, but more wary. She'd been to the Pithay where Edith used to live. Lewins Mead was just as rundown and equally dangerous. So far they'd been lucky. Pray God, she thought, that our luck continues.

Horatia saw their way was blocked before Blanche did. 'Don't be frightened,' she murmured.

'Looks like trouble,' Edith muttered at Horatia's side.

Ahead of them, two rough-looking types with square chins and hard eyes filled the wide sweep of a Norman archway, an ancient entry point to the old city wall called St John's Arch, now crumbling and grey with the grime of centuries. They wore untailored jackets and trousers that covered their bodies without any regard whatsoever for shape, length or flexibility. Their boots were of the cheapest kind, neither left nor right but made to fit either foot.

Horatia decided to give no quarter. 'Out of the way, my good men. We need to come through there.'

The biggest of the men sneered at his companion, wiped his nose with the back of his hand and said, 'Well, I ain't lettin' 'e through, not till 'e tells me what 'e's want round yur.'

At the sound of the thickly accented voice, Blanche stopped shaking the wetness from the little girl's skirt and caught up with

Horatia and Edith. The children gathered round their mother's skirt.

The biggest man's eyes travelled to Blanche and then back again to Horatia. 'I asked thee a question,' he said, his accent unchanged. 'What bist doin' 'ere?'

Faced with intimidation, Horatia adopted her most imperious accent. 'Goodness, what sort of language is that? Can you not speak English, my good man?'

Blanche tensed. Couldn't Horatia see that these were brutes, the sort who'd hit a woman without giving it a second thought?

The man went red in the face. His companion sneered and grabbed his arm. 'Steady now, steady. All the likes of 'er needs is a warning.'

The other man looked dubious. 'That ain't up to you, George. That's up to Jake.'

'We—ll...' said George as he rubbed his bristled chin.

'Yur right, John. It is up to Jake!'

George doubled under the force of a rabbit punch applied sharply to the small of the back, then the perpetrator pushed between the two men.

This was obviously Jake. His head, upper torso and arms were of normal size, but his legs were uncommonly short, the result perhaps of some accident that had stunted their growth.

'Stand easy, lads,' he said in a strong Welsh accent to the two bigger men and rubbed his hands together. 'Now let's see what we got yur.'

He had penetrating eyes and a clever face, disfigured down one side by a long scar that stretched from his eye to the side of his mouth. It had the effect of causing both to droop so that his smile was a sneer. A silver beard ending in a sharp point made his face seem longer than it actually was.

'We're letting you go, my dears,' he said. 'But like that Robin Hood, there's a fee to be paid.'

Although her legs shook, Blanche found her voice. 'What sort of fee?'

Jake grinned and licked his lips with a long tongue. Blanche shuddered. Everything about him seemed oversized – except his legs.

He scratched at his beard. 'Every coin you've got in yur purse, and every ring you' ve got on yur finger.'

Horatia was furious. 'Well, you're not having my belongings, you filthy, ugly little man!' Her voice rang out like the crack of doom.

Blanche found herself admiring Horatia's bravery.

'A woman should be able to traverse this city unmolested,' Horatia went on, her voice still ringing like an alarm bell, its resonance ricocheting off the squat buildings that crowded around them. Do you know who I am?'

As she turned her head this way and that, the purple feather that trailed from her hat lashed from side to side like the tail of an angry cat. She sounded as if someone had stepped on her tail.

Jake said, 'Do I know who you are?' He shook his head and smiled. 'No. I do not. And do I care who you are?' He shook his head again. 'No. I do not.'

Horatia showed no fear, sure in the power of her own presence, the unfailing belief that she had been born superior to the likes of Jake, John and George. She had every faith it would save her now.

Clutching her purse and the satchel she'd kept close to her side all day, she exclaimed, 'You'll have nothing from me!'

The men's ugly featured faces turned uglier. Blanche felt her stomach lurch as though it were trying to escape all by itself. Fuelled by the fear or what could happen next, she undid the strings of her purse. 'Here,' she said, opening it wide as she offered it, 'there are six sovereigns in here. Take them! Take them and leave us alone.'

Horatia stayed her hand. 'No, Blanche! You mustn't give in.' Too late, George snatched it from Blanche's hands.

Fast for a woman encumbered with tight corsets and a huge crinoline, Horatia grabbed the dangling purse strings and tugged it for all she was worth, her heels slipping on the cobbles as a tug of war ensued.

'Let them have it,' shouted Blanche, her arms around Horatia's waist.

Seeing two against one, the small man leapt through the air, kicking at their skirts as he too grabbed the purse.

Freddie launched himself at the third man's legs, clinging and kicking at his unprotected shins.

People began to appear on the empty street, drawn by the woman's cries. Perhaps alarmed that they'd acquired an audience, the thieves tugged harder.

'Will any of you help us?' Blanche shouted at the onlookers.

The curious now became the cowardly and melted into the shadows, lacking either the courage or the conviction to get involved. There would be no rescue from that direction.

Edith threw herself on the man who was pulling at Freddie's hair and raining blows upon his head. Freddie clung like a limpet to the man's legs while his mother scrabbled at his face with her blunt, thick fingers.

'Leave my boy alone, you stinking swine!'

Horatia's stubbornness was contagious. Blanche was now as determined to hold onto the purse as she was, though a few moments ago she would have urged caution and fleeing rather than fighting.

In seconds she'd changed her mind again. Out of the corner of her eye she saw a flash of Steel as the small man Jake drew a knife. Her blood ran cold.

Terrified, she shouted at Horatia to let go.

'No!' Horatia held on.

Yet she must have seen it, thought Blanche. Impetuously, and perhaps regretful for her lack of sympathy from the onlookers in Cabot's Yard, she hurled herself between Horatia and the small man. There was a flash of steel, then the sound of a knife ripping through her skirt. The short man raised his arm again. He came at Horatia from another angle. Again, Blanche attempted to hurl herself between the knife and Horatia, aware that she was putting herself in danger, but determined the thieves would not succeed.

Things happened so fast, actions and figures blurring like the details of a dream just before waking. One moment she was pushing herself forward; the next she was falling backwards, tugged from behind by something or someone she could not see. It didn't help that her hat had fallen over her eyes, though she was aware that Edith's girls were beside her.

'Cor! Look at that!' cried the eldest.

Blanche pushed her hat back from her face and once her vision was unimpaired by the soggy brim and the decorative bunch of cherries at the crown, which she'd thought so splendid that morning, her mouth dropped open.

It would not have surprised her to see Horatia lying flat out on the ground, blood oozing from her bodice and her face pale as death. What she saw instead both delighted and amazed her.

Tom Strong was swinging Jake around by his legs, using the weight and momentum of the swinging body to hit the bigger men off their feet, finally throwing the short man and sending them all tumbling like skittles.

Another man Blanche did not recognize accompanied him. His face was weather-beaten and his hair was long and black.

Edith beamed as she rubbed the top of her son's head, which seemed none the worse for having tufts pulled out of it. 'That's Jim Storm Cloud.'

As Jake attempted to rise, Storm Cloud's fist landed in his face and sent him back down. Before the two bigger men had a chance to get up, Tom grabbed both their heads and banged them soundly together. Bringing his face down level with theirs, he said, 'If I ever catch you within ten feet of these ladies again, I'll tear your heads from your bodies!'

It was debatable as to whether they understood. Their eyes were unfocused; blood and spittle drooled from their mouths.

Blood pouring from a wound where his head had hit the uneven cobbles, Jake shook his fist at Tom and Jim Storm Cloud. 'I'll get you bleeders!' he shouted. 'I'll kill you, I swears I will!'

Before he knew it, Storm Cloud was towering over him, his hair blowing around him like a dark cloak. 'With your bare hands? A knife? A pistol? I will meet your challenge no matter what your weapon.' Storm Cloud drew his finger down the front of his chest, his sharp eyes fixed on the other man's face. 'And I will split you in two.'

Taking discretion as the better part of valour, Jake's courage evaporated. He scampered off behind his long-legged friends, who had already departed, leaving behind a low murmur of admiration rippling through the gathering crowd.

Edith nudged Blanche sharply in the ribs. 'That Jim Storm Cloud ain't aff 'andsome!' she said, swaying slightly like a bashful child.

Blanche tutted. 'And you a married woman, Edith Beasley! Shame on you!'

Edith slid her eyes sidelong to Tom and then back to Blanche. The implication was obvious.

Blanche felt her face grow hot, and knew she was blushing. 'If you were Horatia's servant, she'd dismiss you for impertinence.'

Edith smirked. 'She wouldn't notice.' She dug Blanche in the ribs again and winked.

Blanche looked to where a flushed Horatia was gazing into Tom's eyes.

'Tom! You came to my rescue. How wonderful!'

'No it wasn't bloody wonderful,' snarled Tom looking at them as if they were naughty children needing their bottoms smacked. 'If I hadn't decided to call in on Jim, there's no telling what might have happened. And don't mention about taking a cab home,' he said to Horatia as she opened her mouth to speak. 'I'll take you to see Monk, then it's off home.'

She clammed up immediately.

'I live here,' Edith piped up. 'Or at least, I used to,' she added after glancing at Jim Storm Cloud. She wouldn't want him to see where she lived. 'But I'm moving to a cottage called Little Paradise,' she added, brightening. 'That's where we were off to when them louts stood in our way.'

Tom's eyes flickered. Blanche knew he had recognized the name of the cottage.

Horatia found her voice. 'We were here with disinfectant on behalf of Doctor Budd in an attempt to keep cholera at bay. Unfortunately, there was a terrific rainstorm. The drains burst and Edith offered the place she lives in to her friend. Blanche and I decided to help her move. John was supposed to be waiting for us with the carriage, although I think we may have taken a wrong turn. But we had to help Edith.'

'Very commendable.'

Blanche was dumbstruck. She joined Edith collecting the bits and pieces that had fallen out of the blankets. She didn't want to see the look on Tom's face, or hear Horatia outlining what needed doing in the city and the part she was playing in its improvement.

Charity had never been Horatia's bedfellow. And neither had Tom Strong. But perhaps that was about to change...

–

It rained on the journey to Little Paradise, but by the time they got there it had cleared. As a sly sun peered from behind a cloud, the whitewashed walls of the cottage were bathed in brightness. A rainbow arched across the sky, one end seemingly growing from a spot on the roof just right of the chimney.

Whooping with glee, the children ran towards the house. Blanche and Edith followed. John came behind carrying the bulk of their baggage.

Tom had gone with Horatia, who insisted she had a business appointment. Blanche wanted to believe her, but found she couldn't. I'm not jealous, she decided, and threw herself into making Edith and her family as comfortable as she could.

Edith's hand trembled as Blanche handed her the key. She looked at it with moist eyes and dry lips. 'A new home,' she said, choking with emotion. 'I have never had a key before, or a garden, or a front gate.'

Too full of emotion to speak, Blanche waved her hand at the door, a simple action meant to encourage Edith to go ahead and put the key in the lock. Putting it into words was impossible.

Freddie lost patience. 'Go on, ma. I'm bleedin' freezin'!'

Edith tapped him round the ear. 'Less of that language!'

He smiled as he rubbed at his ear. It hadn't really hurt, and his mother was smiling. She was happy, happier than she'd been in a long time. She always was when his father wasn't around, but never like this. He'd never seen her eyes shining so brightly or heard her gasp with such joy as the key grated in the lock.

The smell of fresh mint and crisp wood came out to meet them. Although the sky was still leaden and the wind was tugging at the apple trees, the cottage seemed full of sunlight. The walls were painted cream, yet they seemed yellow, almost as if someone had found a way to make paint from sunshine.

The children scampered into each of the downstairs rooms, and squealed with delight just as Blanche's children had done as they opened the pine panelled door beside the fireplace, and discovered the narrow spiral staircase.

Their footsteps rumbled across the ceiling as they explored the upstairs rooms.

'Like a herd of wild ponies,' laughed Blanche.

Edith threw her arms wide. 'This place has everything.'

Blanche nodded as she took in the familiar surroundings that were no longer hers to use, to hide in when she wanted to be alone with her thoughts.

It had been in her mind to drape blankets over grass picked from the overgrown garden. Once dried, the grass would have made temporary but comfortable beds for a time. But not today. The rain was unrelenting, and the grass was plastered flat to the ground. Instead she sent John to collect unwanted pieces of furniture from the attic of Somerset Parade. Once Horatia donated a few items, the cottage would be very well furnished.

Horatia's behaviour had surprised her. She'd always known that she was no simpering buttercup, but also ambitious, determined and downright ruthless at times, but she was also brave and that, she thought, is what will attract Tom to her. She shivered.

Edith noticed. 'Are you cold?'

Blanche shook her head and hugged herself. 'Just excited. Life is like that. You think everything is humdrum then suddenly it changes and things are exciting.'

Edith pursed her lips and sucked in her breath. 'I reckon I've had enough excitement for one day.' She giggled like a girl. 'Did you see the way Captain Tom whacked that little man into them two others.' Holding her sides, she rocked with laughter. 'I'll remember that to my dying day.' She turned suddenly serious. 'And I'll also remember it as the day I moved into Little Paradise – thanks to my best friend.'

Blanche smiled. 'Is there anything else you would wish for?'

Edith's face turned surprisingly sour. 'Yes, but it shouldn't be repeated.'

'What is it?' Blanche asked.

Edith was thoughtful for a moment, then sniffed and said, 'Wish I had a husband like yours. Or one like Captain Strong.'

Referring to Conrad in the same breath as Tom was oddly disconcerting. She was fond of both, but in different ways. Conrad was a man she could depend on. Tom was a man who left her breathless.

–

After leaving Blanche, Edith and her children, Tom ordered the Strongs' coachman, Garmston, to take him and Horatia to the offices of Septimus Monk.

The carriage swayed as it pulled away on a particularly adverse camber. Tom and Horatia were thrown together, their faces inches apart, her breasts pressing against his chest.

'How did you know I was going to see Septimus Monk?'

Afterwards she wouldn't recollect him raising his hand before she tingled at the feel of his thumb following the curve of her jaw. 'Such fine features,' he said, his finger lightly brushing her lips.

Anticipation, hope and passion overruled the self-control she'd fostered for years. She'd loved Tom since she was twelve years old. Passion that had intensified with age loosened her tongue.

'You know about the properties, don't you?' Her eyes were wide and her gaze stayed on his mouth.

Tom nodded, his fingers on her face continuing to make her nerve-ends tingle, disarming her.

She sighed with pleasure. 'It's very important I buy them. I'll make a lot of money.'

'Ah yes. Money.'

She heard the sarcasm in his voice. He dropped his hand.

'No, it's not about money. I've got plenty of that. It's about recognition. It's about achieving whatever I set out to do.' Her voice betrayed her disappointment.

Tom was unmoved. 'Why do you feel you have to do it? To whom do you have to prove that you can make money?'

'Men, of course,' she replied adamantly.

A gap opened up on the seat between them as the carriage came to a rolling halt outside the offices of Septimus Monk.

Garmston opened the door.

Horatia paused. 'Are you coming in with me?'

Tom shook his head. 'You're a hypocrite, Horatia.'

Her mouth dropped open. 'How dare you—'

Tom carried on. 'This morning you went into a dangerous part of the city in order to help fight dirt, poverty and ignorance. I admired you for it, even though I suspect you wouldn't have gone if I hadn't forced you to.' He nodded at her surprised expression. 'Yes, I came across the documents by accident and I read the letter from your solicitor.' He waved a hand in a gesture of regret. 'I shouldn't have and I apologize for doing so. But when you lied about your reason for going into Bristol, I just had to call your bluff. I couldn't resist. I must admit, you coped rather well, but let's face it, Horatia, you're not exactly the charitable kind.'

The comment stung. Horatia was livid. 'How do you know, Tom Strong? You've never attempted to get to know me that well. The trouble with you is that you have never washed the dirt and poverty from your own mind. You have continued to see me as someone who can be dallied with, but not taken seriously purely because I was born into wealth and you were born into poverty. What is it, Tom? Are you afraid to see me only as a woman? Are you afraid you might like me too much for being the way I am?'

She was still bristling by the time Septimus Monk had invited her to take a seat. Seeing her hot face and breathlessness, he sent his assistant for a glass of water.

Oddly enough, she'd enjoyed her morning. Childish memories regarding a dolls' house had come back to her. The house had been furnished with miniature copies of the furniture at Marstone Court and peopled with small dolls that she could move around as she pleased. That was what it had felt like at Cabot's Yard, though the people, unlike the dolls, were less easily moved around.

Cabot's Yard had had a definite impact. She was just about to take a sip of her water, when a thought struck her. Cholera! Although situated on higher ground than Lewins Mead, Septimus Monk's office was close to the city centre. What difference would there be between the supply here and that further down the hill?

'I think I've changed my mind,' she said, handing the glass back to Monk's assistant. 'Do you think I might have a sherry instead?'

Chapter Seventeen

Deke Beasley scratched at his bare belly and opened his trousers to check if the ointment the bosun had told him to smear on his genitals was working.

In the dim light amidships, the state of his crotch wasn't easily discernible, but he could still feel the crab lice crawling through his pubic hair and beneath his arms. He'd scratched himself raw before reporting it, his tardiness due to the fact that he'd thought it was something worse, caught from a dockside whore in Vigo. He'd got drunk and shared her with an able seaman from an East Indiaman that had also put in at the Spanish port waiting for the weather to improve in the Bay of Biscay. They had just left the port and were on their way back to Bristol.

He sighed as he did up his pants. Oh well, it'll be gone by the time we dock, he told himself, and tried to sleep before it was his turn to go back on watch.

Clutching the thin pallet that had lately been vacated by the present watch, a man whose hygiene was worse than most, Deke turned himself over, buried his head in his blanket and tried to sleep.

He was dreaming he was drowning in a vat of warm beer when he was disturbed by a sound like mud squelched underfoot on the banks of the Avon. Opening one eye he looked towards the line of latrine buckets braced against the bulkhead where a figure was hunkered down, pants around ankles and groaning in pain as the squelching continued.

'Christ,' Deke murmured, as the close confines filled with an obnoxious stink. 'Rat died up yer ass, 'ave it?'

'Can't 'elp it, Deke,' the man groaned, retching and holding his stomach as he attempted to pull up his trousers. 'I'm sick, I am. Terrible sick.'

Deke recognized the man as Chinky Charlie, not one usually given to being sick. He uttered a curse as he closed his eyes and attempted to recapture his dream of drowning in the beer vat. What a time to be interrupted with a case of Delhi belly.

The bunk bed immediately behind him creaked. Chinky Charlie moaned as he crawled back beneath his blanket.

Deke opened his eyes again, then punched at a particularly lumpy point in his palliasse and tried again to locate the vat of beer.

He dozed, his sleep continually interrupted by Charlie's groans and frequent visits to the latrine. He was thankful Charlie wasn't in the bunk above. God knows what might drop down.

Chinky Charlie rolled in his bed, groaning more and visiting the latrine far less than he had been. Deke glanced at him. His arms were wrapped around his stomach, his knees drawn up over them like a baby with colic.

He could stand it no more.

'Christ!'

He got up. What with the groaning, the stink and the disturbed sleep, he had a strong urge to use the bucket himself. By the time he had, Chinky Charlie was quiet.

'Thank God for that,' Deke muttered as he settled himself back into his bed, the smell of stale sweat and full latrines fading as he drifted into sleep.

By the time he was called for the first watch, all hell had broken loose and his plans to collect his pay and get into the nearest tavern the moment they docked were thrown into disarray.

Chinky Charlie was dead.

'Cholera,' said the bosun, a giant of a man with a bushy black beard and a tattoo of a naked negress on his chest. This was the man who had given Deke the ointment for his infection of crab lice. He knew a bit about medicine, but he was not a doctor.

Other crew members present – men who'd faced 20-foot waves and 60 mile an hour winds – blanched visibly. Calcutta, Alexandria,

Valletta and Marseilles – they'd seen people drop like flies within twenty-four hours of first becoming sick. In Calcutta and other ports in India, they'd seen people stepping over bodies as thick on the ground as pebbles on the beach.

Deke bit at his finger until it hurt. Inwardly he cursed Chinky Charlie for getting sick and dying. His plans for celebrating his homecoming were in serious jeopardy. Cholera meant quarantine. He decided to speak up.

'Only a doctor would know that for sure,' he exclaimed, determined to further his aims at the expense of upsetting the bosun.

Displeased at his judgement being questioned, the bosun scowled, 'I know cholera when I sees it. I've seen it before in India and weren't we berthed next to an East Indiaman in Vigo?'

Averting his eyes, Deke stared at the floor rather than meet the bosun's accusing glare. He left it to one of the other men to ask how long they would be in quarantine.

The bosun's heavy beard and hairy upper lip seemed to devour each other as he sucked in his lips and frowned.

'Until we stops getting sick and dying.'

By the time they were sailing up the Bristol Channel, four men had been buried at sea.

Deke fumed as he went about his tasks, regaling those who had been so thoughtless as to die and upset his plans. They were almost home. Ahead of them the River Avon yawned like an open mouth, expelling smoky breath through the thick mist of an English dawn. So near, and yet so far…

The steam tug that hauled them up the Avon puffed intermittent clouds of black smoke, as if indignant to be towing a vessel destined for quarantine. The line twice as long as normal, keeping plenty of space between her and the diseased ship.

The *Lizzie Brady* eventually anchored in the Floating Harbour, 60 feet of water between her and the surrounding quay. A yellow quarantine flag was run up the mast. Everyone on shore would know she had sickness aboard.

Deke Beasley gazed at the shore, his hands haltingly winding the last sheet around the last cleat. He jumped and almost twisted his windpipe, as a heavy hand suddenly landed on his shoulder.

The bosun was grim-faced with warning. 'Don't even think about it, Beasley. Wait till we gets the all-clear then we're all ashore. You'll answer to me personally if you disobey that order. Understand?'

Deke swallowed, his Adam's apple seeming twice the size it usually was, such was his fear of the bosun, a man with hands that could snap him in two if he cared to.

'Aye, aye, bosun,' he said and managed a weak smile.

The bosun patted his shoulder with a hand the size of a butter paddle, and said, 'Poor old Chinky. Luck of the draw, eh?'

Yes, luck of the draw, thought Deke. Trust bleedin' Chinky Charlie to upset his plans – and the others too. He scowled. It was their fault for getting sick. He was hale and hearty – except for the crabs that was.

He was still thinking that it was none of his concern when darkness fell, the lights of the city twinkling amid the dark shapes of houses, churches and quayside taverns.

Deke's pay was eating a hole in his pocket and his mouth was dry as a sawdust floor.

He licked his lips. The sky was warm with summer and the prevailing westerly had given way to a warm wind from the south. After ten months at sea, a man deserved a pint. He also deserved a woman. Hopefully Edith wouldn't have given birth this time. Babies distracted women from giving men their conjugal rights.

The night was still, the halyards hardly moving among the rigging. The only sound was from down below. The captain had issued extra rum in an effort to raise the men's spirits and keep them occupied until they could escape the confines of the ship and get ashore. There was singing, even a little laughter, though it sounded forced; no one could forget they had cholera aboard.

Those crewmembers on deck dozed in the warm air. They were lying up one end of the ship.

Deke made sure he was at the other end when he slipped over the side and swam ashore.

The cold water invigorated his aching joints and revived his spirits. Soon he would be partaking of his conjugal rights with his long-suffering wife, p'raps give her another offspring to keep her loyal when he left on his next voyage.

The fact that he might infect her with crab lice did not enter his head. Neither did the fact that he might also be carrying a far deadlier disease which could kill his whole family.

-

The last touches were being made to the first new steamship and Tom was filled with excitement. Although trained beneath sails, he was looking forward to voyaging with steam. He knew he was standing at the cusp of a new age and looked forward to all it promised.

At around four o'clock in the afternoon, the engineer putting the finishing touches made him an offer he couldn't refuse.

'I have to get the nameplate for the helm founded at the brass-works,' he said in a thick Scottish accent. 'But I need to know her name.'

They were standing beneath the propeller, a huge device with eight blades, proven to be more efficient than paddle wheels.

'Ah!' Tom eyed him thoughtfully. 'Are you a drinking man, sir?'

'Yes, sir. What else would you expect with a name like Donald McGregor?'

'And when do you need to know her name?'

'She's a number in the registration book at the moment, sir. She needs a name for launching and for her registration plate. I intended getting the plate founded tonight. It's a final touch and should be fixed on her helm minutes after she's launched. But launching takes no time at all. Brass founding takes skill and time and cooling and polishing.'

Tom nodded in understanding. 'I'll come with you to the foundry, Donald, and will tell you her name there, but I expect the strictest secrecy. After the job is done, we'll christen her in traditional style at a local tavern I know. How does that suit you?'

The Scotsman rubbed his orange beard and grinned. 'Suits me fine, sir. Sounds as though we won't be getting home till late though, not that I've far to go.'

Together they went to the brass foundry and stayed there till late watching the manufacturing process. The heat was as bad as a sugar refinery, though the smell was metallic rather than sweet.

It was late evening by the time the brass plate was formed. It would cool overnight before it was polished. After drinking more than he'd done for years, Tom decided to take a cab to the nearest inn rather than all the way to Marstone Court.

They bid each other goodnight, both warm with rum and pride in the new ship. Donald sang her praises – to a Scottish tune – all the way along the street.

'Take care,' Tom shouted after him before climbing into the cab.

The heart of the city was dark and empty, though shadowy forms loitered in dark doorways. Tom presumed most of them to be whores.

By the light of a wall-hung gas light, he saw very different people bundled amidst sticks of furniture outside an old building that had once been a sugarhouse. Intrigued and unsure of what he was seeing, he peered out. The sounds, smells and sight immediately appalled him. Children cried, small faces peered above blankets and worried-looking men and tired women looked on, seemingly helpless to do anything.

The cabbie cracked his whip in order to push past the mass of blanketed bodies spilling from the pavement and onto the road. The horse surged forward, but someone stopped it. A gaunt face with matted hair appeared at the carriage window.

'Spare a penny, sir?'

Tom looked past him. 'What are these people doing here?'

'It's their home, sir. Mine too.'

'I've never seen the homeless furnish the street before,' he said, his gaze fixed on the barley-twist spirals of an old-fashioned tester bed, propped against the wall, a sad and lonely statement to home-lessness.

'They used to live inside the building, but the landlord's thrown them out on the street 'cos he's selling the place. See? It's all boarded up.'

No light shone out or was reflected in glass panes. The building was a mass of darkness.

'Who owns it?' he asked.

'Cuthbert. Sydney Cuthbert,' the man grinned. 'At least that's what he calls 'imself now. But I knows 'im from way back. He used to be Cuthbert Stoke in the days before he turned into a gentleman. Biggest crook in the Pithay. Now he's got his fingers in anything that makes a profit. Even owns the abattoir some of us 'ere work in. Don't pay us much though. Seems to think we should reckon it a privilege, though now and again we gets a few innards given to us to make a stew.'

Tom frowned. 'Seems Mr Stoke has gone from bad to worse.'

He passed the man a handful of silver as the cab driver, impatient to get going, looked down at him.

''Ere,' said the man, 'ain't you Captain Tom Strong? I saw you fight at the Fourteen Stars. You'd have known Stoke, wouldn't you? He used to arrange them fights. I saw you there.'

'Yes,' Tom said grimly.

Tom's stomach churned as the cab rattled on and the homeless were left to the night and the pile of silver he'd given them. He'd always suspected that Cuthbert Stoke had no scruples. Now he knew it for sure.

The Greyhound was one of the most comfortable inns in the city and willingly let rooms to late-night arrivals. Tom slept in a feather-filled mattress that dipped beneath his weight and curved around his body. His room was situated above the broad arch that separated the inn from the Post Office next door. Each time a mail coach went through the arch, the sound rumbled up through the building, shaking the windows and rattling the doors.

Sleep eventually receded, as the sounds of the city filtered into the room from the street below. Sleds scudded over cobbles along with the clattering of hooves and cartwheels. Seagulls screamed above the harbour and the plaintive voice of a cockle seller soared into the air. 'Buy me cockles! Lovely live cockles, straight from the Severn. Buy me live cockles!'

Tom opened his eyes and took a deep breath. His mouth was as dry as the air that sneaked through gaps around the windows and doors, yet he felt refreshed.

He'd dreamed that he was back at Marstone Court beneath the elm trees and seeing the park deer eyeing him from a distance. He dreamed of watching Blanche chase a kite with Sir Emmanuel's other children, her half-brothers and half-sisters as it had turned out, or being alone with her at night, her eyes luminous in the light of a low hanging moon.

The cry of the cockle seller rose again and finally reminded him that he wasn't in the country, that he was in Bristol and he had to get to the shipyard by eleven. Today would see the launch of the very first steamship of the Strong Shipping Line. A fine future lay ahead and he looked forward to it.

Thoughts of the future and the present fused with the past. He remembered the homeless people he'd seen and the mention of Cuthbert Stoke. He blamed him for the taste in his mouth rather than the dirt of the city.

A servant brought warm water in a Wedgwood ewer. He felt better once he'd splashed his face and stripwashed his body. Throwing back his head, he closed his eyes and took more deep breaths. He thought of yesterday, of Blanche and the fact that she was handing the cottage over to Edith. He knew she'd been there on the last occasion he'd visited Little Paradise and understood why she had pretended she wasn't. It was foolish for them to be there alone. He would not compromise her reputation. He still loved her but their paths had divided. Their futures lay in different directions.

After buttoning his shirt and trousers, he shrugged himself into his waistcoat. He'd just settled himself on the side of the bed and reached for his boots, when shouts and heavy footsteps sounded from the street below. Boots thudded up the stairs, thundered along the landing. Without knowing why, he felt a tightening in his stomach in reaction to an instinctive fear that the footsteps were coming for him.

Stranger still, it came as no surprise when the door sprang open beneath the weight of heavy fists. Four strangers filtered into the room, their mouths grim and a hardness in their eyes.

'Captain Thomas Strong?'

The man who spoke had a thinner face than the others and, although he was tall, his shoulders were less broad and his arms moved freely in his sleeves as though his coat had been made for someone much bigger. A long chin rested on his cravat, and he spoke in a nasal tone, his lips hardly seeming to move.

Tom forced himself to be calm and began pulling on his boots. 'Who wants to know?'

The man with the thin face lifted his head higher. 'Sergeant Ezekiel Gibb, Her Majesty's police. I'm here to arrest you for the murder of one Reuben Trout.'

Trout! For a moment it was difficult to unscramble his thoughts, though one thing persisted. Nelson had told him the case was closed.

'Trout died years ago,' he managed eventually.

'A murder is a murder no matter when it was committed,' said Sergeant Gibb, 'and we have a witness who says he saw you do it.'

Tom's blood ran cold. He recalled the ugly face, the boil that seeped a sticky yellow fluid down the side of Reuben Trout's nose, the loose bottom lip that seemed perpetually drawn away from the yellowing teeth... the greasy clothes... and that night... that terrible night...

'I didn't murder him,' he said calmly. 'I was merely a witness.'

Gibb's gaze was unblinking. 'We have a witness who states that you murdered this man Trout. He's sworn a statement and says he saw everything.'

Tom shook his head. 'He's lying. A boy killed Reuben Trout because he'd killed his mother.'

Gibb raised one eyebrow disbelievingly. 'And the boy's name?'

Tom hesitated. He'd told Sally Ward's son, Clarence, to run away. The boy had deserved a chance and even though Tom had known that suspicion was likely to fall on his own shoulders, he had taken that chance. He now had no choice but to tell the truth. 'Clarence Ward. His name was Clarence Ward.'

'And where can we find this Clarence Ward?'

Tom shrugged. 'I don't know what happened to him. I left Bristol and so did he.'

'But you came back, and you're the one being accused of the murder.'

Tom shook his head. This was a nightmare. Surely he would wake up soon. 'But I didn't do it.'

'Every man is innocent – until proven guilty.' Gibb looked smug.

Tom was less than convinced of the authenticity of the words – would he be proved innocent despite the evidence of a witness he knew did not exist?

'What if I refuse to go with you?'

'Sir!' bellowed a constable with a ruddy complexion and bushy dark eyebrows. 'We will make you go with us, sir! We're policemen, sir!' With obvious relish, he dangled a set of manacles from his right hand.

Ezekiel Gibb threw him a thunderous expression, though his rebuke was delivered in surprisingly calm tones. 'Speak when you're spoken to, Higgins, there's a good fellow. I am the man in charge here,' he said, his bushy side-whiskers bristling.

Chastised like a schoolboy caught brandishing his catapult, Higgins swung the manacles behind his back and dropped his gaze to the ground.

'We'll trust you as a gentleman to come quietly,' Ezekiel Gibb said. 'Do you have a statement to make, sir?'

Gibb was awkwardly deferent, obviously preferring to arrest a known villain from the rougher quarters of town where a heavy hand was of more use than a kid glove. Tom found himself almost pitying the man, though his sympathy didn't prevent him from defending himself.

'Reuben Trout deserved to die. The man was a pig. I had *reason* to kill him – although I didn't. He'd killed Sally Ward, Clarence's mother, and Jimmy Palmer, master of the *Miriam Strong* training ship when he set it ablaze. After making enquiries, I discovered his whereabouts from a man named Cuthbert Stoke, an ostler, pimp, and fight fixer, who was also a font of local criminal information. I believe he calls himself Councillor Cuthbert nowadays.'

Gibb eyed him speculatively and sniffed. 'Be in no doubt, Captain Strong, the rope would have stretched this Reuben Trout's windpipe, but, as it is…'

'You aim for it to stretch mine!'

Gibb looked sheepish.

Tom was worried. After all this time, the death of a dockside ruffian should have been long forgotten. Nelson had assured him it was. But someone had remembered. Someone had *wanted* to remember, and that someone – for whatever reason – had wanted him arrested.

'Why did this man come forward now?' he asked as he reached into a cupboard set into an alcove beneath the eaves and brought out a well-cut navy blue overcoat with caped shoulders and velvet-edged sleeves. All four policemen scrutinized him as he put it on; best quality wool compared to their rough serge.

Gibb said, 'Apparently he had to join his regiment immediately. He assumed someone else would report it. In the meantime, he was posted to foreign parts.'

Tom racked his brain as he buttoned his coat. He couldn't think of any military man he'd known back then. Besides, there'd been no one in the stable when he'd found Reuben Trout except for Clarence.

'Am I allowed to know this man's name?'

'I don't see why not. His name is Osborne. Silas Osborne.'

The name meant nothing to him. The stable had been dark. He couldn't know for sure that someone had been watching, though if they had they would have known the truth, that Clarence had killed Reuben. It could only be that he was standing witness for money, but who would want to do that and why?

'If you'd like to come quietly, sir... We don't want any trouble.'

Gibb spoke as if he were straining his words through his teeth, leaving in his throat those that were not needed.

Tom reached for his gloves, soft leather ones made for him back in Boston and purchased by his wife. Looking at them instantly triggered happy memories. They'd had a good marriage. Had she lived, he thought grimly, he wouldn't be in this mess. In an odd way it made him angry with her for being dead, as if she had not loved him enough to live.

Once outside, he took a deep breath of air and promptly swallowed the sootiness that clung to the bridge of his mouth. His fear was far more difficult to swallow. Like a lump of lead, it sat on his tongue and tasted bitter.

This couldn't be happening to him. It was unreal, and he half wondered if he were still asleep and Blanche would come along flying a kite, the younger Strong children – Horatia, Rupert, Arthur and George – running along behind her.

The city was bustling with people going about their daily business, merging and re-emerging from the yellow mist that oozed from the quayside and glided along the street. They were forced to pause as a convoy of sleds carrying barrels of sugar skidded over the cobbles. Tom watched each one pass. More memories, this time of his old friend Conrad Heinkel and the times they'd spent together at the sugar refinery. Sometimes they'd smoke and sit silently, comfortable in the company of friends. Sometimes they'd dunk chunks of raw chocolate into cups of steaming, sweet coffee and talk about sugar, ships and the joys of travelling the world.

As they waited for the sleds to pass so they could cross the road, his eyes slid sidelong to the narrow alley that led to the quay where his ship, *Demerara Queen* lay at anchor. He considered running away, hoisting the sails and setting off.

What a foolish idea. If he headed for his ship, they'd be right behind him and *Demerara Queen* was a sailing ship. It would take an hour just to find a tug to get them out of the harbour – depending on whether the tide was in.

He considered losing himself among the traffic. There was plenty of it nowadays, more than he remembered. Carts laden with hay and straw, beer and bread, sacks of raw chocolate, cases of wine and carcasses, cleaned and gutted and ready for butchering. Pack-horses up from Cheddar, sacks of cheese and strawberries dangling from their backs, chaises, governess carts, growlers and landaus carrying ladies intent on shopping in Castle Street or Queen's Road.

They were all going somewhere and coming back again, he thought grimly, whereas he was going somewhere but quite possibly wouldn't be coming back.

Chapter Eighteen

Flags had been draped between the steamship's mighty masts and her huge funnel. The shipwrights who had built her attended the launch with their families. The faces of their wives and children were scrubbed and bright, their clothes freshly laundered for the occasion. The men stood with heads held high, proud of the iron-clad ship that would shortly sail the oceans once the final touches were made.

Prior to joining the VIPs who'd already arrived on the launch platform, Horatia stood with her father and half-brother, Rupert. Nelson had gone to fetch Tom from the Greyhound Inn after a Scottish engineer, his eyes still bleary from the night before, told them where he was.

Horatia tapped her foot impatiently. He should be here. Why did he have to go and get drunk last night of all nights?' As long as he's alone, she thought desperately, and not in the company of some common whore – he'd known enough of them in the past.

'If he's not here when the Lord Mayor's carriage appears, we launch without him,' said her father, his eyes suddenly straying from his watch to a dark-skinned young woman, the daughter of a shipwright judging by her clothes.

You're a slobbering lecher, Horatia thought, eyeing him disdainfully and wondering if Tom would end up the same. No. She couldn't contemplate it; she *wouldn't* allow it to happen.

The mayoral carriage, pulled by two magnificent Irish chestnuts, appeared on time. A brass band specially hired for the occasion struck up 'Trelawny' as the mayor stepped down.

Sober for once, Sir Emmanuel greeted the official dignitaries and their wives, oozing charm and conviviality. Rupert followed him. Horatia made an excuse and went looking for Tom.

She paced backwards and forwards, in and out of the wooden shed where the iron ship lay surrounded by admirers.

Where was he? Jealousy overrode her natural common sense. Another woman! That's what it was. And he was probably naming the ship after her. Blanche! He would name the ship for Blanche Heinkel, and he had no right to do that. What would her husband say? What would society say? But none of that really mattered to her. She didn't want the ship named after any other woman. She wanted it named after her and had hoped that was his intention. Now she wasn't so sure.

As she headed for the main gate, the Scotsman who had told them Tom was staying at the Greyhound barred her way. 'Excuse me, ma'am. It's the name, ma'am. That's why we were at the foundry so late last night, and seeing as it was hotter than hell in there, begging your pardon, ma'am, we wetted our whistles...'

'Yes, yes, you've already told us that. My brother has now gone to fetch him – presuming he's where he said he was going.'

'We went to the foundry for this...' He held out something wrapped in mutton cloth.

Before she had chance to take it, Rupert interrupted. 'Horatia. The dry dock's been filled with water. She's ready for launching. Do you know what you have to do? Do you know the ship's name?'

His sister's jaw dropped. 'No. I'm afraid I do not.' She couldn't help speaking sharply. Tom's presence at the launch meant so much to her, especially as she still hoped he was naming it after her. Not that she would ever admit such a thing – except to Tom.

Rupert looked astounded. His cheeks were like pink icing. 'Good God, woman. You're supposed to be throwing a bottle at its side shortly and you don't even know what to name it?'

Horatia was not going to take this lying down. 'Tom kept it to himself,' she said through gritted teeth.

'Begging your pardon, ma'am,' interrupted the Scotsman, 'but that was what I was trying to tell you. It's on here.' He handed her the bundle wrapped in mutton cloth. 'It's the brass nameplate for the bulkhead in front of the helm. That's the name Tom wanted.' Loud applause came from the direction of the ship as yet another speech ended.

Rupert cupped his sister's elbow. 'The speeches are over – thank God! Now for the *pièce de résistance*.'

She refused to let her half-brother carry the heavy brass plate. Holding it close to her body, she ran into the shed and up the steps to the launching platform. Smiling, she bobbed her head at every bewhiskered gentleman, including the mayor, and offered swift praise for a hat, a dress or good health to the ladies.

There was a table in front of her on which she rested the plaque, still swathed in its cloth. The suspense was unbearable, but she had resisted the urge to unwrap it. Slowly, her heart beating twenty to the dozen, she finally unfolded the cloth from around its precious cargo and saw the name Tom had chosen. Her heart skipped a beat. Her face burned and her throat was dry.

The lord mayor asked, 'Are you ready, my dear?'

She let the cloth fall back onto the plaque and nodded. 'Yes. I'm ready.'

Someone handed her the bottle of champagne. She gripped it firmly, ready to swing it towards its target as she fought the twin demons of anger and disappointment. Could she really do this? Yes, she said to herself. Tom Strong couldn't be bothered to attend the launch of this ship, so why should it matter to him? Yes, she decided. Of course you can.

'I name this ship...' She paused, reconsidered, then drew herself to her full height and swung the bottle with all her might. '*Horatia Strong!*'

A loud roar of approval exploded from the crowd, as the bottle smashed against the ship's side. Tugboat engines burst into life, and the iron ship with her four masts and huge funnel was pulled backwards. The band played and the cheers kept coming. Horatia shook hands with the mayor and other city dignitaries.

She didn't see Rupert uncover the plaque, or his expression harden. She didn't hear Donald McGregor complain to Rupert that a new plaque would have to be made.

Horatia was flushed with happiness and clapped along with everyone else. Once the applause had ended and the ship lay on the water, the VIPs filtered off to partake of the luscious spread laid out for important people in the shipbuilder's private house. The feast for lesser mortals was held in the building shed.

Horatia declined the arm of a city alderman and turned to take Rupert's instead. They were the last to leave. Rupert's expression was less than amiable.

'How could you!' he exclaimed angrily.

'Did I do something wrong?' she asked, her face flushed from the excitement of the occasion.

He eyed her accusingly, his jaw bristling with anger. 'That depends on one's point of view.'

Her smile faded when she saw what he was holding. The cloth the plaque had been wrapped in fell to the ground. The brass flashed with light as he turned it to face her. It said *Miriam Strong*.

Horatia couldn't stand criticism and turned instantly defensive. 'The plaque can be used again. He can name the next ship after her. I don't see that it matters.'

Rupert shook his head. 'Sometimes I can hardly believe I'm related to you. Don't you have any feelings at all? It mattered to him that *this* one was named after Aunt Miriam and the ship that was destroyed, where he trained.'

Much as she liked being regarded as a confident, powerful woman, Horatia hated anyone implying that she was insensitive. Pouting childishly, she said, 'She's already had a ship named after her.'

'It went up in flames. Tom chose that name for a reason. He feels he owes everything to Uncle Jeb and Aunt Miriam. They brought him up. He loved them and they loved him.'

'But I wanted this ship named after *me*, Rupert. I've waited for years for Tom to come back. Now he's here, and having him name a ship after me matters so much that it hurts.'

'But he didn't *want* it named after you,' said Rupert, his expression twisted with rage. 'It's up to you to tell him what you've done. I'm certainly not going to.' With that, he threw the plaque at her feet.

Horatia stared down at it. It was too late now to have second thoughts, but it didn't stop them coming. Her voice quivered nervously. 'You're right. I shouldn't have. What am I going to say to him?'

'Damned if I know. You made your bed, you lie on it,' Rupert said and stormed off.

Hoofbeats sounded just minutes later. Horatia turned her head and, despite what she'd done, her spirits soared. Nelson was returning with Tom. Then her heart seemed to rise to her throat. How could she possibly face him?

Hands tightly gripping the wooden balustrade, she was still there when Nelson ran in, swiftly followed by Rupert. His face was graver than she could ever remember.

'Where is he?' she asked, calmly having prepared her apology and fully expecting him to appear behind her brothers.

'I've not told Father yet,' Nelson began in a trembling voice. 'I thought I'd better tell you first.'

'What is it?' said Horatia, flattening her skirt at either side so she could ably descend the narrow steps, fear already making her neck and shoulders ache with tension.

Nelson said nothing until they were face to face.

'Tom's been arrested,' he said quietly.

Horatia remembered the days when Tom had drunk at dockside taverns and fought for prize money. 'For fighting?' she asked, thinking a fine would no doubt get him released.

Nelson shook his head. 'For murder.'

–

The gaoler doffed his cap and brushed a few scraps of pie crust from his exuberant moustache.

'Sorry, sir,' he said, his keys clanging against the iron lock. 'But it's people in and people out all day, lock this door, unlock that door, fill in this form and fill in that, so I grabbed a bite while it was quiet.'

Rupert wrinkled his nose. Bristol Gaol smelled of old food and unwashed chamber pots.

Nelson squinted as his pupils adjusted to their gloomy surroundings. The walls were brown and the floor was of grey flagstones.

Rupert swung his walking stick over his shoulder in a flamboyant manner he'd adopted of late. 'Now we are here and your hunger is satisfied, perhaps we can see the prisoner?'

The gaoler doffed his hat again. 'This way, sir.'

They followed him down a set of steps leading to a heavy wooden door set in a solid stone arch. The door was obviously made of oak, dried and cured over the centuries to a silvery hardness and studded with nails the size of mushrooms.

Two more doors followed. Flagstones rang with their footsteps, and echoed off the dark walls and barrel-vaulted ceiling. Both men shivered within their well-cut trousers and warm woollen coats.

'He's in there, sir,' said the gaoler, indicating a row of rusting bars set into the crumbling wall.

Nelson frowned. 'I see no door. How can I possibly talk to Captain Strong without seeing him face to face?'

The gaoler looked embarrassed, shuffling from one foot to the other. 'You're to speak to him through the bars, sir. That's the rules. You stand up there.'

He indicated two stone steps immediately below the barred opening. On the other side, something moved.

'Nelson? Is that you I can hear?'

Rupert got to the bars before his half-brother. 'Captain Tom! It's Rupert. Nelson's here with me.' His voice shook with emotion.

Tom smiled through the bars, forcing himself to look confident and sound as though his present circumstances were just a silly mistake. Being positive, he reasoned, would keep his head clear, and he needed to think clearly if he was to get out of this.

'How did the launch go? Is the new *Miriam Strong* as inspiring as her predecessor?'

Rupert had explained to Nelson what Horatia had done. And the two brothers exchanged swift glances. There was a time and a place for everything and this wasn't it. Besides, they both felt it was Horatia who should do the telling.

'It was a splendid day for the Strong Shipping Line. Everything went according to plan,' Rupert lied.

'Tom!' Nelson nudged Rupert slightly aside, his gloved hands gripping the rusting bars. 'I can't believe this is happening. Why is it that the man was killed by unknown assailants one minute and by you the next?'

Tom forced a chuckle. 'Because a witness came forward.'

The brothers fell to silence.

At last Nelson said, 'I swear if I had known, I would never have asked you to come back.'

Rupert polished the silver handle of his walking stick, too nervous to keep still. 'I don't like riddles, old chap.'

'And this is indeed a riddle,' said Nelson.

Tom laughed. The sound bounced coldly off the bare walls, its warmth swallowed up in the gloom. 'You always preferred poetry if I remember rightly.'

Nelson snorted. 'The man must be a liar. Do you know who he is?'

'Yes. A man named Silas Osborne.'

'Do you know him?'

Tom had already racked his brain. 'Ten years ago I knew some of the most unsavoury characters in Bristol, but not this one.'

Rupert looked worried suddenly. 'You didn't really kill Trout, did you, Tom?'

'No! I'm as flawed as anyone, Rupert, and God knows I've trod many places where angels fear to tread, seen many dark deeds and done some things that I'm not at all proud of. But not this. Much as I would have liked to, someone got there before me.'

Rupert looked contrite, though not entirely convinced.

It was left to Nelson to reassure him. 'Tom's no saint, Rupert, but he's no demon either. He's been totally honest, and I for one, believe him.'

Tom added, 'Reuben Trout himself was a murderer.'

'Good that he's dead then,' exclaimed Rupert. 'Saves the city the expense of a rope!'

Tom's smile turned grim. 'The city may well use it on me instead.'

Rupert's face fell.

'Who did he kill?' asked Nelson.

Tom paused before answering. 'Two people I cared for. One of them, Jimmy Palmer, died in the fire on the *Miriam Strong*, which Reuben Trout had begun. He also slit the throat of a woman, the mother of one of the boys apprenticed on the ship.'

Nelson puffed out his cheeks. 'I'd feel like killing if someone murdered a friend of mine.'

'I can understand it too,' said Tom in a sombre voice.

Rust flaked from the bars beneath his tense grip. More rust fluttered down as he leaned his head on the grating, his arms braced against the thick walls as if in an effort to prevent them closing in on him.

'Clarence Ward was eleven years old when Trout killed his mother. Yes, I did go looking for Trout myself after finding out that he'd killed Sally *and* set the *Miriam Strong* ablaze, murdering Jimmy Palmer. Luckily the boys training on the ship all got out – no thanks to Reuben Trout. Only one boy was missing. That was Clarence. I later found him standing over Trout's body in the stables next to the Fourteen Stars inn clutching a bloodstained hammer. Mindful of the boy's background, and in the hope of giving him the same chance at life that your Uncle Jeb gave me, I told the boy to run, though I knew that without any other suspect, suspicion might fall on me. The whole waterfront knew I'd been looking for him. But nothing could have been proved – not without a witness. And there hadn't been one, I thought. And even if there had been, he would have seen Clarence kill his mother's murderer. Therefore Silas Osborne has to be a liar.'

Rupert frowned. 'But why would he lie? What is there to gain by doing so?'

'It's obvious. Money!' said Nelson. 'He's been paid to lie.'

'By whom,' said Tom. 'And why?'

'And how do we find out?' said Rupert.

Tom frowned. Ten years had passed since Reuben Trout died. A lot of people who had known him might also have passed on. 'I think you'd better leave that side of the matter to me. The most beneficial thing you can do at present is to use your influence to get me out of here.'

'We'll do our damnedest, but it won't be easy,' said Nelson.

'I know you will.'

Tom thanked whomever it was in heaven that had sent the Reverend Jeb Strong out on that cold night many years ago when all he'd had to eat were the sugar-covered splinters of a sugar barrel. The Strongs were the only family he'd ever known and they were powerful.

'I've put your Red Indian into the orangery, by the way,' Rupert piped up suddenly. 'I was going to have her stored in the stables, but it didn't seem right.'

'Or warm enough,' Tom added with a laugh, 'bearing in mind her state of undress.'

Rupert made the first move to leave. 'I think we should go, Tom. We have to set about getting you out of here. Horatia is waiting outside, impatient to know how you are. She's terribly worried and wanted to see you, but they only let wives in. She tried telling them she was your sweetheart, but they didn't care.'

'Sweetheart!' Tom exclaimed. He laughed as if surprised, but the sound was hollow, because that, he realized, was exactly how Horatia saw herself.

After they'd gone, Tom stretched out on the meagre comfort of the iron-framed bed and straw-filled palliasse. His muscles ached as a result of inactivity and the damp that seeped through from the River Frome, which gurgled like laughter on the other side of the wall. It would cripple him before very long, he thought wryly – if the hangman didn't get him first.

He laughed at the absurd irony of it all. It had happened ten years ago. Even if he found Clarence, was he likely to confess and take his place on the gallows? Not very likely, thought Tom, and resigned himself to the fact that the power of the Strong family might at least save him from the noose. Even banishment to Australia was preferable to that. For now it was all he could hope for.

–

Outside, in the shadow of the high walls of the prison, Horatia paced up and down at the side of the carriage. On seeing her brothers emerge from a small door set into the massive main gate, she stopped abruptly and asked for their news. Her tone alone was sharp enough to cut steel.

'Patience,' said Nelson as he helped Horatia up into the carriage. Once inside, away from prying eyes and ears, he repeated everything that Tom had said. 'I thought I might hire a man to make enquiries in the right places.'

Rupert added, 'In the meantime I'm going to make enquiries of some of the judges that are well disposed towards our family. Tom insists – and I think he could have a point – that he is the best person to make enquiries in "the right places" as Nelson puts it. For that he needs his freedom, so we need to hire the best lawyer in the city to argue his case. I thought Father's old friend, Justice Augustus Todd-Winter would be just the ticket.'

'Don't be ridiculous!' said Horatia, taking a cigarillo from a silver case and snapping it shut.

The brothers were taken aback. Although they were used to their sister pulling them up short and turning their noses in the right direction when they strayed, her sharpness still made them shrivel from the head down.

Nelson recovered first. 'Now look here, Horatia—'

Horatia's frosty gaze froze him to silence. 'You will do none of these things. Yes, we do need a lawyer and an investigator, but we do not need one of the doddery old judges or lawyers of father's acquaintance. We need a lawyer who knows how to obtain information and no questions asked. Until this so-called witness is dealt with, Tom is in danger of getting his neck stretched. Money needs to grease the right palms and threats made to those who profess to uphold the law. They all have secrets their mothers and wives would not wish to know about. There are narks and grasses and spies and sleuths all over this city, and I know a man who knows them.'

'Good Lord! Where did you learn all those words?' Rupert exclaimed, blinking with surprise and the smoke from the cigarillo.

Nelson slumped back in his seat. 'Not from the sort of man I'd want to meet I'm sure.' A sudden terrifying thought took hold of him. 'He's not a lover of yours, is he?'

Smoke curled up in front of Horatia's open mouth as she burst into laughter. 'I think he'd be more likely to love you, my dear brother, than me.'

Nelson looked at his sister as though she were the ultimate cuckoo in the nest, a very different breed from himself. 'Genteel young ladies should know nothing of men like that,' he exclaimed.

The look in her eyes said it all. Horatia was not a genteel and thoroughly nice young lady. She made it her business to know what was going on in the world.

Rupert grimaced and shifted uncomfortably, sliding along the shiny leather upholstery each time the carriage turned a corner or hit a rut. Things were not working out the way he'd thought they would.

The two brothers had come out from the prison feeling honoured that Tom had asked them to help him. In one fell swoop Horatia had made them look fools.

'I'll spend any amount of money, I'll turn over every stone in this accursed city to get at the truth, and woe betide anyone who gets in my way,' she said. 'So if you feel afraid of allying yourself with the likes of a woman whose connections are not entirely nine tenths of the law, say so now.'

Nelson laid his head back against the leather upholstery, closed his eyes and shook his head. 'I'll leave it in your hands, dear sister.'

Horatia allowed herself a triumphant smile, even though the man she loved most in her life was in danger of hanging. Nelson would do whatever she said.

Now for Rupert.

'Well?' She fully expected him to agree, though perhaps more reluctantly than Nelson.

He smiled and his eyes sparkled mischievously, just like when he was a boy. Horatia knew he was going to say something that she wouldn't like.

'By the way,' said Rupert – and there was no doubting the cocky look in his eyes – 'Tom asked how the launch went. I said I would leave it to you to tell him all about it.'

–

She punished them with total silence all the way to the offices of Septimus Monk. On arrival they attempted to alight from the carriage.

'Stay there,' she snapped, and they did so.

'Good grief,' said Nelson, as she disappeared into the portico, 'I thought she was going to bite my head off.'

'She did,' grumbled Rupert. 'I feel distinctly chewed.'

Monk's assistant made a futile attempt to stop her entering the inner office. 'You do not have an appointment, madam,' said the dark-eyed youth who looked as though he might be Spanish.

'I don't need one,' she proclaimed and swept him aside.

'But he's already—'

She pushed the door to Monk's office open so hard that it banged against the wall leaving a crack in the plaster.

Septimus was sitting on a sofa without his jacket on. A plump-faced young man sat next to him. His face turned bright red and he leapt to his feet on her entering.

Septimus slowly buttoned his trousers.

Ignoring them, Horatia began pacing the room, her hands tightly clasped in front of her and a look of the most intense concentration on her face. 'This is a matter of the utmost urgency. I need to speak to you now, so get rid of your toy, if you please.'

The two men exchanged looks. They were a little slow in responding.

Horatia was in no mood to be kept waiting. She rounded on him, her fists on her hips and the glow of battle in her eyes. 'Mr Monk, I am not in the least shocked at what you do or who you do it with. I pay you to deal with my affairs, and so far have found you very fit to do so. Your personal life may disgust me, but your professional capabilities leave me very satisfied indeed. Now! Can we get down to business?'

Monk looked bemused. He turned to the boy. 'I'll see you again, darling.'

The young man's eyes flickered with embarrassment at the endearment, but he recovered on seeing that Horatia was not in the least bit interested.

'Goodbye, Septimus.'

'Goodbye, my dear.'

The young man nodded at her. She managed a smile.

Septimus Monk cleared his throat, pulled up a chair for her use and sat himself in the one behind his desk. 'I trust the emergency is worth the intrusion.'

'As much money as the task is worth.'

Monk raised his eyebrows and clasped his hands across his waist-coat, which gaped slightly. 'This sounds a very serious proposition indeed.'

'It is. I need you to be your most cunning, your most clever and your most ruthless.'

'Oh,' he said, his face bright with interest. 'My three favourite attributes. You are already forgiven.'

Chapter Nineteen

It was Edith who informed Blanche that Tom had been arrested. 'Jim Storm Cloud told me,' she said. 'I was walking along the quay and he stopped me. He looks very worried.'

Shaking her head in disbelief, Blanche sank into a chair by the window. 'Tom wouldn't murder anyone. I know he wouldn't.' Her voice was barely above a whisper.

'That's what I thought,' said Edith as she cleared away the tea things.

Blanche shivered in a sudden draught. She looked to see if the drawing-room windows had blown open without her noticing. They had not.

'Are you all right?' Edith asked.

'It's this corset,' lied Blanche, her hand resting on her ribs. 'It's much too tight.'

Her face burned. Edith looked at her knowingly. Judging it was time to change the subject, Blanche reached for her needlework basket.

Peering and picking at the multi-hued threads, she said, 'Are you certain this Jim Storm Cloud had his facts right? Are you sure he's not trying to frighten you and have you fall into his arms? I can see you quite like the man.'

It sounded trite to say such a thing, as if Tom being arrested was of no real importance to her when the opposite was true. But she had to play down her true feelings, even from Edith.

Simpering at the implication of her being sweet on Jim, Edith was adamant about the details. 'But I can't believe that Captain Tom would do such a thing, and neither does Jim Storm Cloud and he's been friends with the captain for a long time,' said Edith, opening the door, the tray of crockery balanced on her arm.

Blanche swept a hand out in front of her as if dismissing the problem. 'Tom's not a murderer. I won't believe it.'

'Did I hear correctly?' Conrad stood there, the width of his shoulders almost filling the door.

Blanche had always avoided mentioning Tom's name in Conrad's presence. Conrad had liked and spent time with him, but he'd be a fool indeed if he believed she hadn't cared for Tom. Something flickered briefly in his eyes then was gone.

'What exactly has happened?' he asked more congenially.

Again, Edith repeated everything that Jim Storm Cloud had told her.

Conrad agreed that it was awful and unbelievable.

'Perhaps those tea things could go downstairs now,' Blanche said finally. If she allowed Edith to ramble on, the fact that Blanche had already met Tom was bound to slip out. But Conrad mustn't know because then he would expect her to explain in greater detail, and if she had to do that he would see her guilt written large all over her face.

Edith and the tea tray finally departed and the drawing-room door was closed.

'My dear,' said Conrad, taking hold of her hands. 'Do you think I should do anything about this terrible affair?'

No one but Conrad could be so charitable, thought Blanche. It seemed a terrible imposition to ask him to do anything, but she couldn't help it. The words were out of her mouth before she could stop them. 'What can you do, my dear? We know nothing of the details, do we?'

Conrad massaged the backs of her hands with his thumbs, his eyes lowered as though he were considering whether he should mention something. At last he said, 'Yes, my dear. I do. The night before Tom sailed for America ten years ago, he came to call and told me of finding Clarence Ward, Sally's son with a hammer in his hand and this man, this Reuben Trout lying dead in the straw. He said he could not possibly turn the boy in and had told him to run. I don't think he really expected to be blamed. The dead man had many enemies, but perhaps Tom has enemies too.'

She didn't know how she knew, but Conrad had noticed her breathlessness. Perhaps he also knew she hadn't admitted to knowing that Tom was back in England. A few years of living together and habits, mannerisms, the blink of an eyelid, the barely imperceptible tightening of expression, were easily read. But Conrad is charitable, she told herself. Let bygones be bygones. Surely all that mattered was a mutual regard for an old friend?

'Can you do anything?' she asked.

For a moment she saw pain in his eyes and wished he hadn't heard, wished she hadn't asked him to help. He loved her deeply. She knew that. He also knew that there was still a soft spot in her heart for Tom Strong and if he asked her outright, she couldn't deny it.

'I will see what I can do,' he replied, and she found herself loving him for it.

—

At some time past midnight, Tom woke abruptly and stared into the darkness.

He'd been dreaming of the men he'd faced in the boxing ring, their faces bloated by punches, blood trickling from a split nostril or a cut lip. How many men had he fought? Fifteen? Twenty? He'd won most of those fights. Any one of his opponents, or even one of the men who'd served under him on board ship might bear a grudge for some trivial slight and want revenge.

Lying in the darkness, it seemed suddenly funny that he hadn't thought about it before. He'd pummelled some men and ordered others to do things they hadn't always wanted to do. What the hell did he expect?

He burst out laughing at the absurdity of it all.

'I don't see anything funny,' someone shouted from another cell.

P'raps he got a bit of belly and bum in there with 'im,' someone else shouted.

Tom's laughter diminished. Of course it wasn't funny. It was tragic. Sally Ward's life had been tragic, and so had that of her son. Where was Clarence now?

The rest of his sleep was fitful. He'd missed the launch of his beloved ship and if he didn't clear his name he wouldn't get to sail on her either.

–

At the insistence of Horatia Strong, Septimus Monk visited Tom in his cell. Although he'd accompanied Horatia to Monk's offices, Tom had never seen the lawyer in the flesh. His appearance came as something of a surprise.

Septimus Monk was extremely tall and wore a green striped waistcoat, a frock coat with braided collar and cuffs, and a large, yellow spotted cravat.

Just for once, Tom felt small, almost dowdy in the presence of such a large, colourful man.

Monk sniffed as he looked round. 'We can better this,' he said, raising a lace-trimmed handkerchief to his nose and keeping it there. He wore rings on three fingers of each hand and the smell of violets wafted around the bare walls with each graceful wave of his hand or tilt of his head.

Tom stood fairly and squarely in the middle of the cell, which seemed to have become much smaller since the arrival of Septimus Monk. He said nothing in response to the lawyer's initial comments.

'Your freedom is gained,' said Monk, unperturbed by his client's silence. 'Get your things together. Everything is arranged. You'll be back at Marstone Court in time for lunch.'

Tom buried his hostility and indicated the clothes he stood up in. 'This is all I have.'

'Good,' said Monk from behind the handkerchief, which he kept firmly held against his nose. 'Two hours. Be ready.'

Consternated and slightly angered by Monk's verbal frugality, the delivery of which was almost as sharp as the hooked nose above the handkerchief, Tom grabbed the man's arm as he turned to leave. 'You mean I'm a free man?'

Monk's eyes were like black beads. 'Of course not. A sympathetic judge has placed you in the custody of Sir Emmanuel Strong. Miss Horatia is collecting you in the carriage. You are to reside at Marstone Court until such time as you are brought to trial, which basically means that as long as you don't leave the county, you can do as you please.'

'My God,' said Tom, throwing back his head and closing his eyes.

'God had nothing to do with it,' said Monk. 'You were just lucky enough to employ the good services of Septimus Monk, barrister and solicitor at law.' The corners of a smile appeared at either side of his handkerchief. 'I am also a man who knows who does what to whom – on a very personal level – in this city.'

'I'm impressed.'

At that moment, it struck Tom just how dangerous a character Monk really was. Although his body shouted muscular masculinity, his clothes were too dandified for Tom's and many other men's tastes. And yet, thought Tom, his mind, his acquaintances and the way he carried out his work were deadly.

Monk sniffed the cologne-soaked handkerchief. 'Money talks and has told those who matter that a gentleman's word is his bond. I persuaded them that as a member of the Strong family you were an honourable man and did not deserve to be incarcerated with the less than salubrious characters one finds in these places. I also reminded the most powerful of these personages that I had seen him most becomingly dressed in a black lace corset and silk stockings. The blue garters with little bells and pink satin bows were particularly fetching, if I remember correctly.'

Tom was both amazed and amused by his candour. Septimus Monk knew everything about everyone. He was likely the most dangerous man in the city.

'So in effect I am under house arrest. Is that what you are saying?'

'Only if you want the best legal representation in the city,' stated Monk. Eyeing their surroundings with obvious disdain, he added, 'I do not conduct my business in pigsties.' He cocked an eyebrow. 'And I only work for very large fees. Very large fees indeed, Captain Strong.'

–

Tom was tempted to jump into the carriage, get to Marstone Court and soak away the damp stench of prison.

'*Tempus fugit*, Thomas Strong! Or do you prefer the accommodation provided by Her Majesty's prison?' Green feathers fixed to a dark red bonnet bobbed out of the carriage window. Horatia looked impatient.

He knew he should thank her cordially, then turn swiftly away and go to do what had to be done. But he owed her the courtesy of acknowledging his debt to her and his adopted family. Smiling, he took hold of her gloved hand, running his thumb over the soft chamois before holding it to his mouth, his eyes fixed on hers.

'How can I ever repay you?'

He fancied she held her breath, assuming he was going to kiss her mouth. Her disappointment was tangible when he only kissed her cheek, like a brother would his sister.

'You need a bath,' she said, wrinkling her nose and pushing him away with an air of repugnance. 'And your clothes stink. I only hope we have enough soap and water at Marstone Court.'

Smiling, he shook his head. 'I'm most grateful for everything you've done, Horatia, but I can't come with you just yet.'

'Why not?'

'There are questions that need answering. I need to find Clarence Ward.'

'No, you don't. Septimus Monk will find him. Please, Tom.' Her voice pleaded. Tom looked towards the far gate that opened on to the main thoroughfare running alongside the Floating Harbour. Tradesmen were setting up stalls and sweepers were shovelling horse droppings into the river. Within a black shadow thrown by a prison tower, someone watched him.

He released her hands. 'I have to go.'

Horatia almost fell out of the carriage window, her indignation ringing in his ears. 'You're supposed to come home with me! You can't just go wandering around the city as if you were a free man!'

He shook his head. 'I have to find Clarence Ward. Not that he's likely to rush to hang in my place, but my plight may tug at his conscience. It's a slim hope, but it's all I have.'

'Leave it to the lawyer. He's well paid and well connected,' Horatia pleaded.

Tom shook his head. 'I value my life. I will not risk its continuance to a pretty-smelling peacock with the airs of a lord and the habits of a—'

'I know what he is,' said Horatia. 'He has the Greek disease. I know that! I also know he has the shrewdest legal mind in Bristol.'

'As Jeb would have said, God helps those who help themselves. Now leave me to investigate. Go home. I promise I shall see you there. I promise!'

Tom couldn't find any words to explain how he felt. He couldn't sit around at Marstone Court waiting for someone else to turn a stone and study what crawled out. It was his life under threat, no one else's.

He waited until the coach had rumbled away, sparks flying as iron shoes struck the cobbles. It then occurred to him that he'd failed to ask her about the launching of *Miriam Strong* and she had not offered any details. It would keep. There were more pressing matters to attend to.

He made his way to where the prison tower threw a black shadow. Jim Storm Cloud stepped out from where he'd been hiding without comment and proceeded to walk beside him. They walked silently, each giving the other space to think and speak in their own good time.

Tom sensed Jim's concern, but did not meet his eyes. Instead he studied the narrow alleys that radiated away from the quay, upwards to Steep Street, Zed Alley and Christmas Steps. He remembered the smaller alleys didn't have names. Dirt, despair, debauchery and desolation; those were the words conjured up by the places in which he had spent his early childhood before his adoption by Jeb Strong.

When the thoughts became too big, he said, 'I know this city, Jim. Some call it a city of churches. You see the spires?'

Jim traced the line of spires from St Nicholas, to St John's to St Stephen's and beyond, in the far distance to St Mary Redcliffe, and back to the square turret of the cathedral. He nodded. 'I see them.'

A movement in an alley, perhaps an angry exchange between a quayside whore and her client, caught Tom's attention.

'In my boyhood I thought it was hell,' he said quietly.

'And in your manhood?'

Tom shrugged. 'I don't know. What do you think, Jim?'

Jim hesitated then said, 'I remember the missionaries coming to our village and telling us about hell and heaven. They said both were of our own making. I believe they are right.'

Tom went with him on board the *Demerara Queen*. He needed to think about where he should start his investigations.

Resting his hands upon the ship's rails, he hunched his shoulders and looked down into scummy water that clung like glue to the side of the ship. 'They didn't know this city.'

Jim shook his head resignedly and smiled. 'I will stay on the ship, Captain, while you find out whether you've returned to heaven or hell, though I would prefer to help.'

'I don't think you can. This is private business.'

'If that is how you want it.'

'That's how I want it,' said Tom and walked away.

He made his way alongside the Floating Harbour to where the River Frome met the Avon. The water around the opening where the smaller river tumbled out was the colour of liquid moss and looked solid enough to walk on. Steam rose with the warming day, whirling every so often each time someone emptied a pail of house filth to sink or swim upon the grim surface.

'Well, that hasn't changed much,' Tom muttered. Taking shallow breaths and burying his mouth into his collar helped him cope with the stink. Eventually, the worst was left behind as he headed towards the Fourteen Stars, the place at the heart of all his troubles.

The black-timbered tavern was unchanged. It still attracted an odd mix of customers – ruffians you'd prefer not to meet in a dark alley and men of means, smoking best Virginia, drinking port and wagering on the next fight, regardless of whether it was between cockerels, dogs or men.

A man smoking a stately meerschaum raised one black and querulous eyebrow. 'Are you looking for somebody in particular?'

'A familiar face,' Tom answered. His eyes searched the shadowy figures bent over pewter mugs, their faces ruddy from rough weather and too much drink.

'What name?' asked the man with the pipe.

The others bent to their tankards, uninterested in talking to strangers and hostile to questions being asked about anyone. The old man, Tom decided, was his best bet.

'Clarence Ward. He'd be about twenty years old now. I remember he had brown hair and blue eyes. Ordinary looking,' he added almost apologetically.

What a fool he must sound. How many twenty-year-olds were there in Bristol with brown hair and blue eyes? Hundreds? Thousands?

The old man's mouth widened in what could have been a smile or a sneer.

'You means Sally's boy, don't you?'

Tom was taken by surprise.

The old man nodded, his old eyes sparkling. 'I remembers you. You're Tom Strong. I also remembers you and 'er being friends – if you know what I mean.'

He winked lasciviously. Tom controlled a sharp denial. There'd been many people who'd assumed Clarence was his son. Few could understand that his interest in the boy and his mother was primarily because he had felt able to identify with them. Like the boy, he'd seen his own mother sell her body and steadily slide into despair.

'Do you know his whereabouts?' he asked.

The old man screwed up his right eye and fixed him with a hard stare from the other.

'Could be I do – though not direct, if you knows what I mean. Not where he actually is – more so's where 'e might be, if you knows what I mean.'

This was obviously a man who liked taking his time telling a tale, Tom thought. Resigned to the fact, he pulled up a stool and ordered a measure of rum for himself and a jug of cider for the old man, who thanked him before draining half the contents, his pipe remaining clenched in his teeth as he drank. After wiping his mouth with the back of his hand, he fixed his one eye back on Tom's face and resumed his tale.

'Did well for 'imself, so I 'ear. I heard he had some sort of accident. Knocked 'is head or sommut, was sick, then got adopted by a rich man – nowhere near as rich as the Strongs mind you, but plenty in 'is pocket and 'is fingers in many pies, if you knows what I mean.'

Tom resisted the urge to tell him that he didn't need to keep repeating himself. He knew exactly what he meant. Patience was not one of Tom's virtues, but he made the effort.

'Go on,' he said.

The old man poured the rest of the cider down his throat before he spoke. Not a drop was spilt despite the meershaum pipe jiggling at the corner of his mouth.

'Terrible dry in here,' he said, wiping his mouth with the back of his hand.

Tom ordered another. It was a small price to pay for his life.

He was almost trembling with amazement at the news that Clarence had been plucked from poverty by a wealthy man, exactly as he had been. He was glad for the boy, but also glad for himself. If it was true that a man of means had adopted Clarence, he should be easier to find than on the mean streets of the city.

'So who was it adopted him?'

The old man shrugged and wiped his mouth again before answering.

'Don't know, Cap'n. Terrible times it was then, a lot of toing and froing of people because the cholera had come again, and people were dying. Those with the wherewithal were locking their places up, or selling property for a song and leaving the city. 'Twas the making of some and the undoing of others, if you knows what I means.'

Tom eyed the old man suspiciously and wondered how much was true and how much the old man yearned for someone to talk to. 'It's not much to go on.'

'Though I did hear that the family went to Australia. Come to think of it, I'm pretty sure they did. Course, you could check it with Aggie, her that used to run her narrowboat up and down the Severn.'

Australia! It was the worse thing the old man could have said. Tom's hopes for finding Clarence in the bosom of his adoptive family disappeared.

His gaze wandered around the old inn he knew so well. It was next door, in Bennetts Carriers, that he'd fought the odd bare-knuckle fight. There was one in particular that he'd purposely lost in an act of revenge. Cuthbert Stoke, who had once frequented this place, arranged fights, owned run-down hovels and kept a stable of streetwalkers, had bet a lot of money on him winning. He smiled at the thought of Stoke's face when he'd lost. That was for Sally, he thought. Stoke had treated her shamefully. He blessed her memory before bidding farewell to the old man.

If he couldn't find Sally's son, he desperately needed to interview the witness who'd fingered him for killing Reuben Trout. Ah yes, he thought grimly, perhaps I should talk to him first.

Chapter Twenty

Horatia put her hand to the deed of transfer.

'I'm paying an exorbitant amount for this property. The man must be a crook.'

'Yes, you are, and the man is a crook. This is the man I told you about. He calls himself Sydney Cuthbert, started life as Cuthbert Stoke.'

'So you did.'

Horatia gritted her teeth. She didn't like anyone getting the better of her, worst of all a crook. But she had to pay. He had something she wanted. Monk encapsulated it in a nutshell.

'Money well spent, Miss Strong. You'll double your investment once the property is demolished in order for the new sewers to go through.'

For a moment she rested her chin on her hand and eyed him thoughtfully. Septimus Monk had his ear to the ground, was shrewd, quick-witted and secretive. He was everything she wanted in a lawyer, a business associate and a fixer. She couldn't fault his work, a fact she found hard to swallow. She actually *liked* finding fault in men's work and the wealthier and cleverer they professed to be, the more she liked it.

Her eyes fell back to the deed. 'I congratulate you on getting vacant possession. An odd property. This document describes it as a sugarhouse, and yet people were living there. Was this actually true?'

Monk nodded. 'It did indeed used to be a sugarhouse, but the present landlord Mr Cuthbert had divided it into rooms. There were people living there until fairly recently. He charged exorbitant rents, so I understand. He is something of an extortionist.'

'So I see,' said Horatia wryly. 'He's charging me far more than these properties are worth, but at least you got these people out very quickly,' she added with some surprise.

'Not me personally – an acquaintance skilled in the practicality of such matters. It was very well dealt with.' Monk looked thoroughly satisfied, like a cat that's just ate the rat, thought Horatia.

'And the *Mathilda*?'

'Off on her first voyage on your behalf. I think we can look forward to a very good return on capital. I believe you will be well satisfied with the results.'

Horatia rose to her feet in a rustle of dark blue silk. 'I trust I will be. I commend you, Mr Monk. You have so far lived up to your reputation.'

'And you to yours, ma'am.'

Horatia cocked her head. 'You do surprise me. I didn't think I had one.'

'A man's head on a woman's shoulders. Quite formidable.'

'Hmm,' she muttered thoughtfully, unwilling to be flattered by the admiration she saw in his eyes. 'Pity my father doesn't think of me the same way. You are an enigma, Mr Monk, in that you are not put off by my gender.'

He shrugged. 'Why should I be? My loins are unresponsive to your sex. You and I are of the same mind, Miss Strong,' he said tapping his forehead. 'We are aroused by challenge, the thrill of achieving and being different from the rest of our kind.'

Horatia wasn't entirely sure she agreed, but was pleased to count on Monk as one of her most trusted allies.

She swept through to the reception and Monk's assistant held open the door. Before she'd had half a chance to exit, a big man with a hard face and a shiny head pushed past her.

'Mr Osborne,' she heard the dark-eyed youth exclaim.

'Where's Septimus?' the newcomer demanded loudly. His fists were clenched and he smelled of old gin and raw fish.

'Where he always is.'

Horatia had glimpsed enough of the newcomer to know that he was part of the darker side of Monk's life. The boy was brave to tackle him.

Osborne! The name rang a bell and caused her to linger. Wasn't that the name of the man who claimed to be the witness of Reuben Trout's murder? The man who had put Tom in gaol. Could it be a coincidence?

Osborne barged into Monk's office. The sound of the door slamming back against the wall sent the windows rattling.

Horatia exchanged looks with the young man. 'Who is that man?'

'Silas Osborne.'

It was the same name. 'What is he?'

The boy spat into a brass spittoon. 'Something to be avoided.'

–

Tom frowned as he made his way down Steep Street. He'd enquired at a few of his old haunts. He'd bought a few drinks, slapped old friends on the back and mulled over old times. No one knew what had happened to Clarence Ward. He'd checked with Aggie Bennett as the old man had suggested. She confirmed the worst had happened. Clarence had indeed gone to Australia. The results had been disappointing, but he forced himself to be cheerful.

Steep Street swept down from Ashley Down Heights. At certain points he could have believed he was on top of the world. Spread out before him were the russet tiles and blue slates of roofs. Beyond sailing ship masts and steamship funnels pierced the skyline. People, horses, carts and cabs went about their business in the streets below. Where Steep Street spilled out into Stoke's Croft, he spotted the dark green carriage in which Horatia had come to pick him up from prison. It was stationary outside an imposing mock Roman edifice of the Queen Anne style building he recognized as being the offices of Horatia's solicitor, Septimus Monk.

The carriage horses rattled their harness as he approached. The coachman continued to snore into his coat collar.

Tom sighed. His day had proved fruitless. A ride back to Marstone Court with a good soak in a tub of hot water at the end of the journey seemed a grand idea.

–

Silas Osborne was a brute, though not particularly bright. The money Stoke had paid him to lie was gone. Most of it had been spent on drink, gambling and two whores at a time. Word had got to him that he could now make more by telling the truth.

In the privacy of the inner office, Silas proposed that he be paid £500 to change his story. Septimus offered him £100. Silas agreed. 'Once I'm paid, I'll be off. And no one better come after me, or it'll be the worse for them,' he growled as he waved a clenched fist.

Despite the fist, Septimus didn't even blink as he eyed Silas over his steepled fingers, a habit he always adopted when carefully considering a number of options. His voice was calm and collected. 'I cannot agree to what you ask without the express consent of the Strong family, though I will advise them to accept your offer.'

Silas's laugh was rough and ragged. 'Strikes me as they'd be stupid not to, unless they wants Tom Strong to hang.'

'Nevertheless,' said Septimus, rising slowly, almost menacingly from his chair, 'that decision rests with them.'

Finding himself faced with a larger man than himself, a man not known to be a coward, but one who held a grudge and had ugly acquaintances, Silas opened the door – and found himself face to face with Horatia Strong.

Horatia, who had heard nothing of the conversation, directed her anger at Monk. 'What business do you have with this despicable man?'

Monk appeared unfazed. 'If you want him to tell the truth and let Captain Strong off the hook, he wants money.' He regarded her with interest, as though her decision would make or break both her family and Monk's business.

She didn't give it a second thought. 'Give him it.'

Silas guffawed, his laughter exposing a set of uneven teeth, chipped and stained yellow. 'Now there's a lady who knows what she wants.'

Tom's shadow fell in the doorway. 'What is it she wants?'

Those in the room swivelled at the sound of his voice. Horatia looked surprised. Monk didn't. Silas Osborne looked as if he were about to give battle.

'P'raps you,' he said threateningly, his whole body tensing like a fighting cock suddenly scenting a fight. 'Silas Osborne', whispered Horatia.

Tom was instantly on his guard. He'd seen the likes of Silas before around the city taverns; loud-mouthed bullies who enjoyed inflicting injury – especially on those who couldn't fight back.

Preferring not to see Tom hurt, Horatia grabbed his arm and tried to guide him out. 'Come along, Tom. It's time we were off.'

Monk tried to help. 'In here, sir,' he said, indicating that Silas should re-enter his office. 'Perhaps we could have a drink before you go?'

Silas didn't move. 'What about my money? If you want me to tell the truth then I wants my money. Pay me or you hang, Tom Strong.' He thrust his face close to Tom's.

A split second before it happened, Tom sensed the other man's body readying to strike. Silas raised a fist. Tom warded it off. Silas fell against a chair before landing flat out on the floor. His eyes rolled in his head as he tried to focus.

Tom's shadow fell over him. 'You'll have nothing from me or my family! You are a liar, Silas Osborne. A liar, a bully and a cheat.'

'Sir,' said Monk, his grip firm on Tom's arm, 'go now. Leave the man to me.'

Tom faced him. 'No money is to be paid to this man. He was paid to say he saw something he didn't. Now he wants money to tell the truth. He'll not get it. Is that clear?'

Monk exchanged a look with Horatia.

Silas Osborne got up onto his elbows, his bloodshot eyes fixed defiantly on Tom. 'I'll have my money or you'll hang.'

But why?

For whatever reason, someone had wanted him dead. Before Silas could move, Tom reached down and grabbed him by the throat. 'Who paid you to lie, Silas? Who paid you?'

Silas spat a loose tooth from his mouth. A trickle of blood and spittle crept down his chin. 'No money, no information.'

The world swam before Tom's horrified gaze and in the mist and mayhem Silas Osborne sneered up at him, a taunting, mocking caricature of death.

Driven by an enormous surge of anger, Tom yelled, heaved Silas forward then slammed him back so his head cracked against the floor.

Horatia screamed.

Septimus Monk grabbed Tom's shoulders and pulled him back, before checking Silas Osborne's pulse. 'You'll get nothing more out of him for a few hours,' he said finally, his voice level. 'He's out cold.' Horatia held her hand to her mouth. 'He's not dead?'

Septimus shook his head. 'No. Just unconscious.'

Tom's chest heaved from the exertion. He stared down at Osborne as if in surprise. This was not what he'd wanted. He'd needed to know who so hated him that they were prepared to see him hang for something he hadn't done. He turned to Monk. 'I'm sorry to mess up your office.'

Monk waved a beefy hand as if it were a rose. 'Alexander will tidy up.'

The dark-eyed youth was already picking up folios and bundled deeds that had been knocked to the floor.

Horatia looked worried. 'Can we go home now, Tom?'

He nodded.

Septimus Monk saw them to their carriage.

'At least we know the truth,' said Horatia. She looked at Monk. 'This does mean Tom is free now?'

Monk's expression said otherwise. 'Someone has opened a can of worms,' he said ominously. 'No matter what that buffoon in there says, a case has been opened. It would be useful to know who put Osborne up to it, but that aside we have to prove beyond a shadow of a doubt that Captain Strong is innocent and that this Clarence Ward was the actual perpetrator. So far, I have not been able to find him.'

Tom sighed and felt for Horatia's hand in an effort to reassure her, though God knows, he was hardly reassured himself.

'I did hear he might be living in Australia,' he said to Monk.

'Ah!' said Monk. 'That's inconvenient.'

'And tomorrow Silas Osborne will tell us who opened that can of worms,' said Tom, his eyes dark with anger, his knuckles stinging from the impact on Osborne's chin.

'Useful, though a minor matter,' said Monk. 'Our prime objective must be to locate Clarence Ward, otherwise your only option is to leave the country. Perhaps you could visit the Strong plantation in Barbados?'

Tom shook his head. 'I'm no good at growing sugar, besides Rivermead is run by Otis Strong. He won't thank me for landing on his doorstep.'

'Think on it. The law is more lax in the colonies towards gentlemen.'

Horatia looked up at Tom. 'If you have to go then I'll go too.'

'Let's hope it won't come to that.' Not for the first time since coming back, he felt he was swimming against the tide and nothing he could do would stop fate having its way.

Chapter Twenty-One

Otis Strong surveyed the dark cane fields rolling towards the hills where a sickle moon shone as sharp as the blade of a knife. A beautiful sight, but he wasn't seeing it. His thoughts were elsewhere.

When Viola, Blanche's mother, had been alive, he had greatly loved Barbados, mostly because he had loved her, even though she had given birth to his brother Emmanuel's child. Things had been easier then, though not so easy as when the plantation was established by his grandfather. His word had been law and life had been easy for the family, though hard for those toiling in the fields. Planting sugar cane was back-breaking; harvesting it was worse, the sharp leaves cutting fingers, arms, bodies and faces, which easily became infected. Urine had been the most curative measure for healing cuts and hardening flesh. Even so, most workers only lasted seven years, hence the need for fresh supplies of slaves from Africa.

Since abolition, things had changed greatly, though for the most part, his own workers accepted their lot. The 'maroons' – people of mixed race, a little bit of African, a little bit of Indian, and a little bit of English blood all wrapped up into one – were the problem. Some years before they'd been given their freedom and plots of land in which to grow their own food. Now they were demanding more of a say in government, more land to farm, specifically a part of Rivermead, the largest plantation on the island. The leader of the particular group of maroons threatening him was named Samson Jones. He was coming tonight, had demanded to speak to him 'in view of past agreements and family ties,' he had said.

Otis had not known what he'd meant, but was willing to listen rather than risk the outbreak of violence. There had been too much of that in the past few years. Other landowners had been set upon, some killed. Retribution from the garrison at Bridgetown had been swift. Otis was not a man of violence and preferred compromise to confrontation. Tonight was not going to be easy.

A crocodile of torches like broken stars wound down the dusty road between the cane fields, broadening as those carrying them filtered through the gate and approached Rivermead House.

Samson Jones stood head and shoulders above everyone else. His skin shone like waxed wood in the light of the torches and he was well muscled beneath his rough cotton shirt and shin-length trousers. Barefoot and bareheaded, he came to a halt at the head of his band, his jaw firm as rock and his mouth sensually petulant as though he were about to kiss someone rather than demand what he regarded as his rights. He carried a sheath of paper in his left hand, which he waved face high. At the same time he nodded to those around him, his eyes not leaving the face of Otis Strong.

'It was agreed and signed that the land between Rock Ford and Cripple Beach was ceded to us on the death of the owner. We demand our rights. We demand our land.'

Otis had every intention of keeping his temper; in fact, he'd never been a man for losing it. He'd been given to understand by those in authority, those in Bridgetown who thought they knew everything about what went on in the island, that these people were usurpers, who would destroy property and steal land that wasn't theirs. The papers being waved looked legal but much as he wanted to compromise, he couldn't take them at face value. Rivermead was the font of his family's fortune, passed down from one generation to another. He could imagine what his brother, Emmanuel would say, that he'd always been weak and deserved to be the second son, a mere shadow of his older brother. For once in his life he had to stand up to these people just as his father and his brother would. Otis felt sick to his stomach. He pulled his waistcoat down more tightly, as if that might help hide his fear. Externally, he did his best to look and sound brave.

'The land you mention belongs to the Strong family. I cannot possibly believe that you have any legal documentation—'

Samson Jones moved faster than Otis could move. 'Read it!' he exclaimed, waving the papers underneath Otis's chin. 'Read it! You signed this paper.'

Otis blinked nervously. He wasn't as young as he was, but he wasn't yet that old that he'd lost his memory. He would have remembered if he'd signed any such undertaking, surely?

'Read it!' shouted Samson, unfurling the paper and pressing it into Otis's face with his big, brown hands.

Otis took the paper and eyed the torch flames and the sweating bodies stretched before him. The sight and smell were overpowering, but not so much as the fear that made him want to run into the house and lock and bolt his door against them all. But he couldn't run. During the exchange with their leader, the glossy-faced throng had fanned out around him, blocking his escape.

Although he already carried one torch, Samson Jones grabbed another and held both close to Otis's face, their light and sparks falling onto his coat sleeves and leaving scorch marks. 'Read it!' he repeated through gritted teeth, his eyes shining determinedly.

Shaking and afraid, Otis did as he said, his heart sinking as he read on, checked the signature and saw it was his own. As he read, he remembered.

'I, Otis Strong, bequeath the said section of land to...'

He read the name again and again, not because he wasn't sure he'd read it right, or because he didn't know it. On the contrary, he knew it very well.

'Viola Bianca,' he said softly.

Myriad memories came flooding back: her naked pride when he'd first seen her; the warmth of her body next to his on the many nights they'd slept together, her brazen flamboyance; the way she'd made him laugh; and her generosity to her relatives, some of whom she employed as servants.

Viola's half-brother, Merrill, he now recalled was one of those servants and had had a host of children. Samson Jones was his grandson.

He couldn't help but brush a tear from the corner of his eye. Viola had meant everything to him and thinking of her stopped him feeling afraid. If only she was here. She'd take care of the menacing crowd and send them packing with a rain of hard slaps and a flurry of shouted oaths. Suddenly he felt totally lost, totally alone.

'Now do you see?' said Samson, his eyes dark as he studied Otis Strong, off-shoot of a family that had ruled over a large part of Barbados for three generations.

Carefully, almost reverently, Otis folded the paper back into three sections. Why couldn't he remember signing this? The answer was obvious. He'd been drunk and Viola had persuaded him. Or perhaps she'd forged his signature?

Swiftly, aware of a rumbling resentment in the sweating bodies pressed around him, he undid the paper again, brought it close to his face, studied the signature again and realized the truth. A little drunk he might have been, but he'd signed willingly.

The question was, why now? 'You've taken a long time coming forward with this,' he said pointedly to Samson, drawing himself up as tall as he could and doing his best to seem brave.

Samson smiled. 'My grandfather died just two months ago. He'd hoped my cousin Blanche would come back and see that the land would pass over peacefully. But she ain't come back, so now we wants what's ours.'

Otis was too frightened to ask how the paper had come into the hands of a group of maroons. Some had been freed, owned land and had infiltrated certain lower echelons of officialdom on the island, and were not easily trifled with. They had a certain status, a little education and knew their rights.

'I wish to share my inheritance with people in need,' said Samson as though he had read Otis's mind.

Barbados had turned ugly for Otis Strong. Viola had died and left him lonely. His wife Emily – whom he'd learned to tolerate – had become susceptible to mood swings and was best left alone. God knows what she would have to say about this. Worst of all was the thought of facing his family – especially his brother Emmanuel – and telling him what he'd done in a moment of drunken debauchery. All his life he had swum in the wake of his ruthless father and equally ruthless brother. As the second son, he had always felt less than perfect. Although he had strived to be like them, he'd never quite made it. Sometimes he'd envied his younger brother Jeb. Third in line for everything, Jeb had been true to himself, never emulating anyone and mostly mocking of both his father and his eldest brother. If only he'd joined the church like Jeb.

Samson roused him from his thoughts. 'I want this sorted out, Mr Strong! I want this sorted out now!'

The crowd around him shouted in support. Otis felt his knees giving out as he eyed the ugliness in their faces. Suddenly he could not go on. He could not help but give into them because he feared them. Year by year the descendants of people who had once lived and died in the cane fields were becoming more powerful. Before long, he decided, they would rule the island and the British would go home — or die where they stood.

'I can do nothing tonight,' Otis began, his voice weak as his feelings of helplessness and his fear of facing Emmanuel intensified. 'Tomorrow. Tomorrow I will attend to this. I promise.'

A murmur of disapproval ran through the crowd like a low rumbling of thunder. For a moment Samson's big, brown eyes were wide with suspicion. His face was so shiny with sweat it seemed to be moulded from glass.

Otis held his breath, surrendering to his fate, his decision made about what he should do next once Samson had agreed – if he agreed. If not, they'd probably kill him here and now.

At last Samson's expression changed. 'Tomorrow. We will be back tomorrow.'

Feeling defeated and worn-out, Otis walked slowly back to the house. He'd shamed his family. He had to recognize the legal document. There was no doubt it would stand up in law. Emmanuel would be furious and he would be dragged home. Bristol was like a nightmare, a place he had no wish to remember. It was Barbados he loved. Here he could gaze at the sea and the stars and dream of the days that used to be when Viola was with him.

He'd been walking with his eyes fixed on the ground. When he looked up, his heart almost stopped beating. At first it seemed as if the house were on fire until he realized it was only the reflection of receding torchlight, ebbing like a fiery tide along the road back to Bridgetown.

Accompanied by a number of house servants, Emily stood waiting in the hall, her presence as cold as the black and white tiles that covered the floor. Her hair was tucked up under a lace-edged cap and although it was close to bedtime, she was still dressed, her demeanour as rigid as her whalebone corset and the frame of her skirt.

'The militia must be sent for or we'll be killed in our beds,' she said, her voice an odd monotone, bereft of emotion.

Otis was staring at the floor, wishing he wasn't here, wishing he could turn back the clock and sit sipping fruit juice with Viola, the love of his life, who had instinctively known when to stay silent and when to ask questions, when to make love, and when to stroke his ego, which, for the most part, had been dented all his life.

'Go to bed,' he said, his voice low and his head still bowed.

Emily ignored him and barked at a servant. 'Godfrey! Go for the militia. Tell them to come straight away.'

Godfrey, a thin-shouldered man with a large head that seemed too big for his body, leapt to obey.

'No!' Otis held up his hand, almost as though it were an axe about to come down on someone's head. 'No! Go to bed. All of you!'

Even the servants looked surprised, eyeing each other as if needing confirmation that this was the same Otis Strong they'd always known.

Oblivious to any change in him or any unease in their servants, Emily said, 'They should be—'

'Go to bed!'

Seeing that her husband had, for once, stood by his decision, Emily sighed in exasperation. 'Oh well, if you wish. What does it matter if we are dead tomorrow? Who's going to know? Who's going to care?'

She shooed the servants away, fetching the nearest, a small boy kept to shine shoes, a quick clip around the ear. 'You heard your master. Off with you!'

'You too,' Otis mumbled.

Emily frowned. It wasn't done for a family member to give orders to another member while the servants were still around. 'Not in front of the servants, Otis, I am your wife after all and it just isn't done—'

Otis raised his head suddenly and glared at her, all the pent-up detestation showing in his eyes and the grim way he spoke. 'Get out of my sight, woman! Leave me alone!'

Emily opened her mouth to protest at his treatment then thought better of it. She tossed her head, which might have been coquettish when she was young, but nowadays it made her jowls tremble and the veins stand out on her throat. 'Very well. We'll talk in the morning.' With that, she stalked up the stairs to her own bedroom, at the opposite end of the house to the one Otis occupied.

Otis slumped in a chair for a while, as the butler walked around softly, bolting and barring windows and doors, dousing candles and oil lamps, before retiring.

Emily was a difficult woman and he'd always had trouble conversing with her, but tonight she had said something very poignant indeed. Who would miss them if they were killed in their beds? The answer was no one. They had no children and didn't love each other. The only woman he'd ever loved was gone. There was only Rivermead, and such was his love for Viola that he'd inadvertently signed away a portion of it. Emmanuel would be furious, and quite rightly so. Otis was mortified. There was nothing left for him to love except memories.

The house creaking around him as it settled for the night finally roused him from memories of the past and thoughts of those he had loved.

After wiping his eyes on the backs of his hands, he looked towards the windows and the moonlit garden beyond. Was it his fancy, or did he see someone waving at him from around the frangipani tree? He thought he saw a flash of mauve, though it could have been mist. He chose to think otherwise, opened the door and went out.

The mauve mist seemed to hover briefly then disappear some way ahead of him. He didn't know how long he followed before it vanished into the whitewashed house with the green tin roof that looked out towards the cane fields and the hills in one direction, and the sea in the other.

When the mist reappeared, it seemed to be hanging like a veil beneath the moon. A gleaming path of light shone over the sea from the shore to the moon.

Tears streaming down his face, Otis ran to the beach – and then he saw her, he was sure it was her, standing at the end of the glowing path, just below the moon and above the sea.

'Viola!' Her name was no more than a breath in his mouth. The past and his memories were preferable to the present and even the future and he wanted them back – most of all, he wanted Viola.

Without undressing, he waded into the sea, the warm water drawing him like a lover's arms further and further towards the moon where it hovered above the distant horizon.

Chapter Twenty-Two

It came as a shock to hear that Silas Osborne had lost his mind.

'Damn!' shouted Tom, his hands on his waist, his jacket flying out behind him as he paced the room.

Horatia sat white as a sheet, staring at nothing in particular. 'What do we do?' she said.

Tom shook his head. 'It certainly puts everything in perspective.'

'It certainly does,' said Horatia, clasping and unclasping her hands.

Earlier that morning, Rupert had lied for her. He'd told Tom about the ship launch and said the reason it hadn't been named *Miriam Strong* was that the nameplate was late in coming so no one knew what to name her. It was suggested that the name be changed regardless of the launch. Tom pointed out that to change a ship's name once she was launched was unlucky.

The news about Silas Osborne overshadowed everything.

Tom sighed heavily. 'I suppose if I'm to escape the gallows, I have to go to Barbados, though I can't say I'm looking forward to the prospect.'

Horatia was sitting like a coiled spring, waiting for the opportunity. 'Not even if I come?'

Tom smiled at her. 'You've been good to me, Horatia. I can never thank you and your brothers enough for all you've done.'

Horatia wasn't happy at sharing his gratitude with her brothers, but she'd put up with it for now. His smile made her heart leap and she could never remember him being so warm towards her as he had been of late. She smiled back. What a joy it was to mean something to him. And all because of a boy named Clarence Ward. She hoped he was never found.

A thought seemed to cross his mind, causing the corners of his mouth to turn down. 'I was looking forward to running my own fleet out of Bristol.'

'We can start one in Barbados,' Horatia blurted. 'Or even Boston.' She'd been thinking about this ever since Monk had stated Tom's chances of being tried for murder.

Tom smiled sadly and shook his head. 'I have one ship. You have one ship. It's hardly enough.'

'I have money,' she said, a look of promise in her eyes.

'Surely not enough.'

She smiled. 'Oh yes, I do. It's just a case of realizing my assets – brick and stone assets in case you were thinking otherwise.'

He ran his eyes over her. 'The assets I see before me are quite outstanding.'

Horatia reached out and caressed his cheek. He caught her fingers, kissed her palm, then each of her knuckles.

Horatia felt as if her body was unravelling, trying to become liquid in order to get outside of her stays and the layers of petticoat that girded her loins.

'I'm going to buy you a fleet,' she said, her dress ballooning out around her as she sank to her knees and looked up into his face. 'I'm going to sell my properties and buy you a fleet of steamships.'

Tom stared at her in disbelief. Her offer amazed him. 'You'd do that for me?'

'Of course I would. You should know that.'

He smiled. 'You're a very clever woman, Horatia Strong.'

She smiled back. 'I know, but I've proved my point.'

He'd never seen her so soft and had never felt so vulnerable. Blanche had rejected him and rightly so. In the past he'd resisted Horatia's advances, but not any more.

The moment sang like a nightingale and still echoed in their ears when their lips met. He ran his hands up her neck, caressed her jaw.

She leaned forward, her breast filling his hand, rising and falling rapidly with her breathing.

The feel, the smell, the look of her aroused him. He couldn't deny that. So why shouldn't he let himself go? Why shouldn't he give her what she wanted? He knew how she felt. He'd always known.

Her hand was on his thigh when they parted, both breathless and flushed with promise.

Horatia rose to her feet. 'I'm going to sell my assets as quickly as possible.'

'And how will you do that?'

Slowly, she let his hands slip from her grasp and headed for the door. 'I'll take the quickest route of all,' she exclaimed, her eyes bright with excitement. 'I shall sell everything – except the *Mathilda* – to my father.'

The swiftness with which she thought things through left him breathless. He smiled and shook his head in amazement, finding himself admiring her once again.

She looked piqued. 'Trust me, Tom. All this talk of hanging will be left behind. We'll be happy,' she said before she left to see Sir Emmanuel. 'I promise you we'll be happy.'

It didn't occur to him until she'd gone that he might not have fully understood the meaning of what she was offering. Were they to leave the country as loosely related cousins, or did she have something more intimate and binding in mind?

Cross that bridge when you come to it, he decided. In the meantime, go along with her plans. After all, what choice do you have?

–

Emmanuel sat numbly in a chair, staring at nothing in particular and belching loudly on account of the brandy he'd consumed. Although it was barely mid-morning, he'd already polished off the entire contents of the decanter. Drinking too much had become a frequent habit, a form of escape from truths he didn't wish to face or memories too painful to remember.

When Horatia found him, he was still sitting, solid and unmoving, his face marbled with pink veins. As she entered, the mantel clock – an ornate affair of white Dresden with a bright brass face – struck eleven.

'I want to sell all my assets. In order to do this quickly, I think it will be best if you buy them.'

Emmanuel sat unmoving at first, then slid his eyes sidelong.

Presuming his lack of response was due to drink, she carried on.

'Septimus Monk has advised that Tom leave the country. Barbados would be safest, though Tom favours Boston, but neither of us is sure about his welcome from his former-in-laws. I prefer Barbados. The law is more forgiving of crimes committed by white men in the West Indies. Before I dispose of my assets, I would like you to write to Uncle Otis. Ask him if he could locate a decent house for us. I understand he may not want relatives living with him at Rivermead. Convince him that we have no intention of interfering in the running of the plantation. Explain if you like, the reasons for us coming and our determination to build up the Strong Shipping Line as an adjunct to sugar, not as a rival or a replacement.'

Horatia stopped pacing. She was used to her father being too drunk to take in what she was saying, but he usually gave some kind of response. Today there was none.

Horatia looked down at him and frowned. She sniffed. Yes, of course he was drunk. The smell of brandy was on his breath, on his clothes and seeping with the sweat from his pores. His mouth hung open. He turned to look at her. His eyes were utterly blank. Slowly he raised his hand and held out a piece of paper – a letter. Horatia took it and began to read. As the news hit her, she sank into a chair.

Her Uncle Otis was dead, and what was worse, it was hinted in the letter that he'd taken his own life. According to the solicitor, he had walked into the sea and his body had been found the next morning when a group of fishermen had hauled in their catch. He had been hanging in their net, dripping, dead and chilly white.

'Why?' she whispered.

She scanned the letter again. There had been an uprising in Barbados and many maroons – the peasant farmers, descendants of freed slaves – and plantation workers had been killed or injured. The plantation was being run by the estate manager who had also sent a letter. It was this letter that captured Horatia's attention:

> ... *I am running the plantation in fit manner, though Mrs Strong refuses to let me have sight of papers I deem necessary to the running of the estate. She insists the house is private property and that she will shoot me if I try to enter. In truth, I fear for her sanity. She has not been well for some years now, though Mr Strong would not have her put away...*

'Good God!' Horatia threw back her head and closed her eyes. Her uncle's wife was going mad.

On opening her eyes, the sight of her father's recumbent figure, his round belly rising and falling, made her angry.

'Well, Father,' she said, bending over the back of his chair, her chin almost resting on his head, 'what a wonderful family are we Strongs! Your brother has drowned himself, your sister-in-law is mad, one of your sons depends on opium to get him through the day and you yourself depend on drink. Could it be that the sins of the fathers are coming home to roost?'

Emmanuel's eyes flickered and his jaw moved as if he were masticating his worries to pulp.

Horatia straightened, stalked to the window and snapped back the curtain. 'Well, that settles it. Tom and I will *have* to go over there. We can move into Rivermead.' And get Emily locked up, she thought. Then it will be just Tom and I, two souls thrown together by fate. Having barely met her uncle, she felt no grief at his passing; on the contrary, her spirits soared. Poor Uncle Otis had done them a favour.

'Casey is a fit man to run the estate,' her father murmured, his words ill-formed and slurred with drink. 'Nelson or Rupert I think should go over there...'

'No!' Horatia spun round. 'You're not thinking straight. Of course someone has to go over there before that bloody woman burns the house down! But I think it best if I go – with Tom.'

His ruddy complexion and barrel gut, acquired through many years of over-indulgence, caused her to pause. Never in all her life had she seen weakness in him. Perhaps she hadn't been looking close enough to see that he was a mere shadow of his former self. Age and good living had laid him low. 'I'm too old to cope with it,' he said, shaking his head.

Horatia grew impatient. 'Did you hear a word I said, Father? Did you hear me say that Tom has to leave Bristol and that I am going with him?'

His eyes were still bleary, but he blinked as if the details had indeed sunk in. 'You and Tom?'

She nodded and prepared herself for him to disagree. His smile surprised her.

'I think that's the best thing that could happen. In fact, I have already allowed for it to happen. I altered my will the moment I heard he was coming back.'

He surprised her even more when he suddenly sat up and took hold of her hand. 'Horatia, you are truly my daughter. The spirit of Isaiah and Samson Strong shines through you more than it does your brothers. You deserve to inherit everything, but as a single woman?' He shook his head. 'No. I don't think that proper, but as a married one? Yes, my dear. Marry Tom Strong and control of the Strong fortune will pass to you. In the meantime, until my demise, why not start off with Rivermead? It seems a grand idea to me.'

He slumped back into his chair, the lucid moment seemingly passed, but then his eyes blinked open again and he popped forward. 'And best for you both if you get Mad Emily locked up unless you shoot her before she shoots you.'

Following his comment, a lesser woman would have needed smelling salts and someone to loosen her stays. Horatia glowed. It was everything she'd ever wanted. Her mind worked quickly. Marriage had formed part of her plan to escape to Barbados, though she hadn't mentioned it, believing that in time Tom would see it as a natural progression. The stakes had now increased. Initially her business and property assets would have been enough to finance their new venture. What her father was suggesting – eventual control of the Strong Sugar empire – could finance a whole navy!

As her father gazed into space, she eyed the broken veins that lined his cheeks and had turned his nose the colour of ripe plums. Judging by a painting hanging on a wall in the first-floor landing, he'd been a handsome man when younger. Now he was white-haired and bloated with brandy. He'd been too distant a parent to love, but she'd always respected him, though knew he could lie in order to impress.

The will. She had to be sure.

'Is this the brandy talking, or do you really mean it? Is there really a will that leaves everything to me?'

A smile slowly crossed his face, his red cheeks shining as he began gurgling with amusement. 'I know you well, Horatia. I know you as well as I know myself, because there's so much of me in you. I can see it in your eyes and in your actions. I know Septimus Monk fronts some of your little schemes... and don't ask how I know,' he said the moment she opened her mouth to do so. 'I also know how close you and Tom have been in the library. Suffice to say that I still have my faculties and my contacts. I'm not dead yet.'

Horatia bit her lip. It was an uncomfortable feeling to be told that someone had been spying on her, and not just with regard to business in the city, but also at home – here at Marstone Court.

The truth came in a flash. 'Duncan!' The footman.

'Clever girl! Follows you round like a spaniel,' chuckled her father.

His laughter died. Horatia guessed he was thinking of his brother. Refolding the letters, she said, 'I think I can live in Barbados. And Tom has no choice.'

Emmanuel's expression fell as he contemplated his brother's demise. 'When we were younger, Otis used to copy everything I did, as though by doing so he might become the eldest son instead of the second.' He sighed and clasped his hands across his belly. 'But it was no good. He was always weaker – always second best.'

Horatia straightened. She didn't really want to hear about Uncle Otis and her father's childhood. The present and the future were all that mattered, and her dreams looked as though they might come true. Things were happening so fast and she didn't mind if things progressed even faster. She was excited beyond belief but, at the same time, she would leave nothing to chance.

'I want to see the will.'

Smiling, he shook his head. 'My judgement was correct. You're a typical Strong – never believe anything unless you see it with your own eyes. I'll have a copy sent to your lawyer – that gaudy fellow, Monk. But I want it kept secret until my death. You must not divulge its contents to anyone. Is that clear?'

'It is.'

Of course she would keep it secret. Her brothers would be furious. It filled her with pride to know that she was favoured and they were not. And she would know and they would crow, confident in their ignorance they would inherit everything.

Emmanuel covered his eyes with his hand.

It was not the time to look excited, but Horatia couldn't help it. Turning from her father, she looked out over the rolling parkland where a stray dog chased sheep beneath the trees. A vast fortune and the man she loved. The future looked too wonderful to be true. Then she heard him chuckle. Was he playing with her, merely pretending she would be favoured in his will? She decided then that she could not trust what he'd said. She would have it confirmed.

'Poor Uncle Otis,' she said in as sad a voice she could manage. 'What a shame he didn't have children.'

'Hopefully you and Tom will have children.'

The comment startled her at first then her body tingled as she recalled the feel of Tom's hand on her breast.

'I want you to promise me something.'

For a man who had drunk so much and so early in the morning, he was incredibly lucid, though it came in spasms, his mind drifting in and out of an alcoholic mist.

'What is it?'

'If neither you nor your brothers have male issue, my wish is that Max Heinkel inherits.'

Horatia was shocked to silence. This was not something she'd considered.

Her father took advantage of her surprise. 'He's a Strong. You know it and I know it. You are the exception, Horatia, the only member of the Strong family capable of being head of the family. Nelson has a daughter, but it's his son I'm interested in. Max Heinkel is a Strong on both sides of his family.' He looked at her searchingly. 'Unless you know anything to the contrary.'

She shook her head. The matter of Nelson's liaison with his half-sister Blanche was something they never talked about.

Her father looked at her intently. 'Promise me you will carry out my wishes, Horatia. Promise me, and everything is yours.'

Horatia nodded. 'Of course I will, though I doubt Blanche Heinkel, or indeed her husband, will be very happy about it.'

'Ah, yes! Blanche Heinkel.' He sighed as a man does when he reaches a certain age and realizes that he is closer to his death than his birth. 'Her mother's skin was as soft as velvet, you know – and not black, not really even brown. Just creamy dark, like milky chocolate, and she had the most pert...'

Horatia was angered by the faraway look in his eyes and the way his hands followed imagined curves. 'Father! At least have the courtesy to remember that I am the daughter of your first wife, to whom you were married at the time.'

'My head aches. I need to sleep,' he said then, burying his head in his hands. Horatia watched as he struggled to his feet. Her emotions ranged from sadness to pity to anger and disgust, as her father belched and broke wind with each step he took to the door.

'My God,' Horatia muttered. She felt sick as she regarded his deteriorating body. Death conquered even the most powerful of men and would not be bought off with money, gems or parcels of land. Soon he would die.

After she'd left him, she went looking for Tom but was told he'd gone into Bristol to make last-minute arrangements before the new steamship left for Nova Scotia. She gave orders for black crêpe to be taken out of storage and draped over suitable ornaments and a painting of Otis that hung on the landing.

She felt no sorrow. On the contrary, Otis drowning couldn't have come at a better time. Tom would be told all about it – including the will – when he got back from Bristol. And she would be ready for him.

After taking a bath, she looked at her reflection in a full-length mirror. Her négligé was white. Tiers of lace decorated the neckline and sleeves and tumbled like frozen snow from her waist. Her hair fell loose over her shoulders.

I look like a bride on her wedding night waiting to be deflowered, she thought. Tom will be *my* husband. I will be *his* wife.

'My husband,' she said, the word rolling satisfyingly over her tongue. Married people were owned by each other. She would be owned by him, but more importantly, he would be owned by her.

She eased the garment from her shoulders and imagined it was Tom doing it. Finally, she let it fall to the floor. Now he was looking at her over her shoulder, seeing her creamy body, her rounded hips and full breasts.

'You can't resist,' she said to his imagined reflection, and smiled.

Chapter Twenty-Three

In the marble and gilt surroundings of the grand salon, where some of the best Dutch masters fought for dominance with the blue sky and pinkish clouds of a painted ceiling inhabited by gods, nymphs and pudding-faced cherubs, Duncan paced his way to the drawing room with a fresh bottle of brandy. His eyes brightened when he saw Horatia. He bowed respectfully.

Horatia had always enjoyed teasing the footman, throwing him soft smiles, stroking the side of his face after he'd done her some particular favour. Today there were more important things on her mind.

'Have you seen Sir Emmanuel?' she asked. It was some time after her speaking with her father about Uncle Otis and the matter of the will.

'He's asleep in the Egyptian room.'

Horatia arched her eyebrows. Her father's habit of sleeping in the stone sarcophagus prior to his death amazed her. 'If that lid should slip he'll be sleeping in there permanently,' she remarked.

'Would you like that?'

Duncan's question caught her off-guard. She felt herself reddening, her skirt swishing as she came to a standstill.

'What are you suggesting?' She sounded suitably angry.

Duncan's brown eyes looked at her as though seeing her soul. 'Sir Emmanuel is not quite the man he was.'

'No,' she said, shaking her head, her voice laced with guilt. 'No, he most certainly is not.'

'Shall I tell him you were asking after him when he wakes up?'

Horatia shook her head. It had occurred to her that before she told Tom anything about the will, it made sense to check that it really existed. She already knew the details but wanted to be sure that its contents were exactly as her father had outlined.

'If he asks after me, tell him that I'm gone into Bristol.'

Duncan nodded. His dark eyes looked at her as if inviting a telling word, a soft caress. But Horatia offered none of this. She was thinking of her father lying in a solid stone sarcophagus, the lid suspended on ropes threaded through iron pulleys. What if they should break? What if there should be an accident?

She stood there for a long while after Duncan disappeared, looking out at the parkland, her hands tightly clasped and the light from the window turning her eyes light grey and her skin milky white.

What if there should be an accident?

A moment in time, a sudden thought that stayed fixed in her head. She would never understand where it had come from, why such a deed could implant itself so deeply. Her father had done many wicked things in his time, though had remained likeable – just as she had.

But the thought took hold. Seemingly in the grip of a temporary madness, she drifted towards the newly constructed Egyptian room...

Her soft pink cheeks stiffened as if they'd become layered with frost. It was as if every drop of blood had drained from her head. As she floated along the corridor, she harboured an unreal feeling; it was as though her feet weren't touching the ground, like a dream where limbs hang heavy and propulsion seems to be independent of body or mind.

Hesitantly, she opened the door of the Egyptian room, her heart beating hard against her ribs, her mouth so dry that her tongue stuck to its roof. She'd rarely entered this sacred shrine of his. She took root in the centre of the room, her mouth open and her eyes round and searching.

The place was eerie and imparted a feeling of eternity. Painted gods posed on clay-coloured walls, their stance stylized and their kohl-edged eyes staring sidelong in mute surprise, almost as if they'd been discovered doing something they shouldn't be doing. Horatia's heart beat faster.

The room had no windows. Candles burned in tall, bronze sconces, a glassy-eyed cobra wound around each base, eyes flickering red in response to the candlelight.

The hem of her dress sounded like a broom sweeping the flagstone floor as she skirted the sarcophagus, all the time eyeing the hanging slab. The stout ropes holding it dropped from a central pulley, which in turn hung from a wooden gantry, the ends tied into iron hoops set into the floor.

She heard him snoring, but didn't look in. The whole thing seemed ridiculous. Why couldn't he lie down on his bed like any normal person?

He's mad, she thought, and suddenly detested him. If his eccentricities became known, the family would be a laughing stock. She cursed him for becoming the man he was.

Trailing her fingers along the edge of the coffin, she looked up at the ropes. It amazed her that he could lie asleep with the lid hanging over him like that. Surely he must know it was dangerous?

Her gaze wandered up and down the ropes, noting areas where the sisal had been rubbed thinner than in other places. She ran her finger down one of the thinner strands. Her breathing quickened. Her eyes shone brightly. An accident… Such a dreadful thought, but it could happen. What would it take for it to happen?

This was so wicked! Her heart beat so hard it made her ribs ache as she trailed her fingers over the cold. That damned will. She wished her father hadn't told her its content. Guilt and ambition were fighting for her soul.

She closed her eyes and reasoned with her conscience.

I can't.

Afterwards she would be appalled at what she'd done, but for now she was exhilarated. It was as if she were standing on a cliff about to dive off into icy water. She knew the danger, that she might drown or hit her head on a submerged rock, but she couldn't help herself. If nothing untoward happened, she might well be swimming in a pea-green sea, queen of her domain.

Quietly and carefully, she undid the first rope and let it slide through until the corner had lowered enough.

The gantry's shadow fell over the far wall where a winged Horus stood rigid guardian of the tomb, though the flickering candlelight made him seem more real. The gantry shivered like a great, black giraffe. On closer inspection, she could see it had a hammer-like mechanism held in the teeth of a toothed iron cog. At the side there was a wheel and a handle. This, she realized, would release the cog and the slab would come down. The ropes passed close to the iron teeth – too close. Some, as she had seen, were frayed and if another rope gave, the remaining two – there was one to each corner – might be too weak to hold the lid of her father's tomb.

The workmen had left some tools in a wooden box near the door. Prising open the lid, she found a saw. Although it was quite heavy, she managed to lift it and run it across one of the remaining ropes. They were incredibly tough. The sound of saw teeth grating filled the room and somehow – she would never know how – brought her to her senses. Her courage faltered. The saw fell from her hand. Her hands flew up to her cheeks.

'What am I doing here?' She shook her head. An earring was dislodged. She didn't see it fall to the floor.

Her father was hardly the most righteous of men, but he certainly didn't deserve to die, and certainly not by her hand.

The saw had made little impact on the ropes. Just a few strands had disentwined from the main twist. The ropes would hold. Her father would wake up and drink another day.

She paused at the door. Perhaps he wasn't in there and Duncan was mistaken. Perhaps she hadn't heard him snore.

For one guilty moment, she was tempted to look into the sarcophagus and wake him up just in case the ropes gave. Instead she retied the one she'd undone.

He was her father and at one time she'd loved him; that was before her mother had died, before he'd married Verity, his second wife, before he'd taken to drink. Just at the point when she was tempted to lean over the side of the sarcophagus, wake him up and tell him she loved him, a loud belch followed by an equally loud fart echoed around the room.

Her guilt and her love flew out of the window. 'Good grief! How much longer do I have to put up with this? You are disgusting, Emmanuel Strong. Why are you still here? Why do you still live?'

Her face burned with indignation and her hands itched to smack anyone who dared tell her that it was really guilt.

She flung open the door. Duncan was outside. He made her start. She regained her composure and shot him a sidelong look as if to say, *You haven't seen me here. Say nothing.*

'I have to go to Bristol,' she said sharply.

'Yes, miss,' he said with a slight bow, his eyes following her as she swept along the passage towards the marble-floored reception hall, the grand staircase and her own room.

—

After she'd gone, Duncan sniffed the air. Horatia had left a drift of her own, personal perfume. He had grown to know that perfume well over the years. In the privacy of his narrow bed he had fantasized that she was with him, her body tight to his and her scent upon his pillow. During the day he did as Sir Emmanuel had asked and kept an eye on her at Marstone Court, sometimes going into the city.

Following her and seeing what she did often made him jealous, and he wanted to strangle her. Her dalliances with Captain Strong were very hurtful, and he'd dearly like to tell her so, but deep down she must know. He told himself that she only consorted with Captain Strong to throw her father off the scent and that she loved him, her footman.

He'd always looked at her lovingly and had convinced himself that she looked at him in the same way. Of course she couldn't possibly admit that she was in love with him because she was afraid of being rejected. It was up to him to make his feelings clear.

He must prove to her that he loved her beyond any other woman, beyond life itself.

Shoulders back, arms held stiffly at his side, he entered the Egyptian room.

Pausing, he considered what he had heard her say. *Why do you still live?* When she had come out of the room, he had seen the look in her eyes. Over many years he had prided himself on interpreting exactly what Horatia wanted from those looks of hers. Others could not possibly see what he saw there. Despite their differences in race, colour and class, he knew she depended on him, perhaps even loved him. He certainly loved her and would do anything – anything at all – for her. He always had and he always would.

–

Conrad met Tom at the shipyard where he proceeded to tell him about the problems he was having with the sugar supply.

'There is plenty of sugar, but transferring it from ship to barge is expensive.'

'You need new premises.'

Conrad nodded. 'Which will cost much more money.'

Tom eyed the iron-clad side of his new steamship. 'Which is why you are here.'

He had always respected Conrad Heinkel and regarded him as a friend. They hadn't been in contact since his return from Boston. Deep down both men knew the reason but they kept their discourse on a business level.

Conrad looked very serious. 'I am looking for funding. There are various interested parties, but I am choosy as to those I do business with. You are one of those I trust.'

Tom shrugged. 'I have little money of my own, Conrad.'

'You have these ships,' said Conrad, nodding at the first of the Strong steamship fleet.

Tom found himself swelling with pride to see the admiration in Conrad's eyes, but he understood where the conversation was going. 'And in time I might like to use them as collateral for diversifying into related ventures. Yes. I can see the sense in that, but you have to bear in mind that I would have to refer to other members of the board, which is only now being set up.'

Conrad nodded and rested his big, red hands on his walking stick. 'I understand. I can hold out until then. I take it that Sir Emmanuel will have the last say on the matter.'

'As always.'

They both turned their heads at the sound of a carriage arriving. Horatia waved out of the window.

'One of the strongest of the Strongs,' said Conrad with an ironic humour that amused Tom.

Chips of stone sparked from the loose covering of the ground between the shipyard office and the yard as the coach came to a standstill.

The usual acknowledgements and introductions were made before Horatia said to Tom, 'May I talk to you in private?'

Tom apologized to Conrad. 'If you will excuse me...?'

'Of course. I will walk around your ship, if I may.'

Conrad left them.

Horatia pulled Tom into the carriage and told him about the will. 'Can you believe it?' she said, her eyes bright with excitement. 'He'd been in his cups, of course – hardly the first time, but this was different. He told me I'm to inherit the bulk of the Strong interests and that I'm the best business brain in the family. There are a few stipulations attached to my inheriting, but I'm sure they can be overcome.'

He wondered why she sighed so heavily and fluttered her eyelids like an untouched girl. He should have known then that something was afoot. He should have known that she was manipulating events to suit her own ends. When Horatia set her heart on something and thought there was a chance of obtaining it, nothing – absolutely nothing – could stand in her way.

He dragged his concentration back to what she was saying.

'And please, say nothing of this to my brothers. I'm on my way to see Septimus Monk and will instruct him to look into the matter.

He has spies everywhere, even in the office of the family solicitors. I have to have it confirmed. I have to know if my father's mind was so addled by drink that he was telling me a fantasy rather than the reality of the situation. His moods change so often nowadays. Indeed, I sometimes think he's going quite mad.'

She sighed heavily. 'Once I know for sure, I shall immediately capitalize on my investments, perhaps transfer money from my trust fund for buying ships. There's no point in selling what I've got if I'm in line for inheriting a lot more. Once Monk informs me that everything is in order, we can make plans to go to Barbados.'

Tom frowned. 'I still don't see that Barbados is a better place to go than Boston. And what will your Uncle Otis say?'

'Ah,' she said her expression changing. 'I think that is partly the reason why Father was so forthcoming in all this.'

'Well?'

'Uncle Otis is dead. Father received a letter this morning.'

'I'm sorry to hear that.' He took a deep breath as he considered the situation, then said, 'So it's Boston, I think.'

'No,' she said, shaking her head and frowning. 'Why do you say that?'

As he took hold of her hands, he remembered the feel of her breasts the day before and felt aroused. He forced himself to look away, to watch as the tugs prepared to push and pull the newly built ship off to a wharf where she'd be loaded with the goods she was destined to carry around the world.

'If your father should die, you have to be here to run everything, but I can't stay. As you said, I will be safer abroad.'

'No, no, no,' she said, and he could almost believe that it was genuine concern he could see in her eyes. 'You have to be with me. I have to be with you. That's one of the stipulations of the will, you see.'

It was an odd feeling, to know what was to come, to see the type and size of noose he was putting his head into. But there was no getting away from it. He had a clear premonition of what she might say next. When she did so, it came as no surprise.

She looked away, almost as if it didn't matter to her one way or the other – yet he knew it did. It mattered very deeply.

'We have to marry. Father insists.'

Tom tried to remember how tightly his valet had tied his cravat that morning, and whether it had felt as restrictive as it did now. He picked his words carefully, but they still sounded clumsy and ill chosen. 'A man can bequeath money and property in his will. He cannot bequeath a man's life. It is not his to do so.'

'He seemed to think there were very good reasons for us marrying.'

'What about reasons why we shouldn't marry?'

'Can you think of any?'

Tom thought about it. He'd known Emmanuel for most of his life and knew the way he considered things. Horatia, like everything else in his life, was a commodity. Sir Emmanuel would only think of the financial aspects of such a union.

'I should imagine that your father has many reasons for thinking that a marriage between us would work very well, but there are also reasons why it might not.'

Her chin stiffened. 'Because you still love Blanche?'

Until then, he'd admired the determined thrust of her chin. It reminded him of prizefighters determined to take a hit rather than appear to lack courage. The accusation *did* take him unawares.

'Blanche is not an option,' he said, shaking his head and wishing circumstances had been different. 'Though I admire her greatly,' he added. 'Although married to a wealthy man, she goes out of her way to make life easier for others.'

Horatia exploded. 'She's a marshmallow! An insipid creature who hardly seems to know that she's alive.'

Tom blinked. Horatia's vehemence surprised him. Her whole body seemed to heave with annoyance. Tom gathered his thoughts, determined not to placate her.

Finally he went out of his way to irritate her. 'She makes me feel warm. Perhaps if you were as generous of spirit I wouldn't balk so much at the thought of marrying you.'

Horatia's face dropped. He knew he'd disappointed her, but to his surprise, she swiftly gathered herself.

'You were really impressed that day you came across us in the city?'

He nodded. 'Lewins Mead is not a tea party. It was no surprise to see Edith there. I could also understand Blanche's presence. She's been married to Conrad for a very long time and has acquired his charity. But you? I must admit to some surprise.'

Horatia smiled. 'So there you are then. I'm not as heartless as you think. I felt genuinely sorry for those people and I truly believe the city should be cleansed of its bad airs and dirty waters.'

'I take my hat off to you,' he said, and did so.

He was being amusing, lightening their conversation so that neither of them had to back down.

Horatia held back her smile. 'Sometimes I think you might one day make a gentleman.'

'Sometimes I forget that you're a lady, but then I do know the real you.'

She eyed him quizzically. 'The real me?'

'The one I first met when I was about nine years old.'

'I wasn't a lady. I was a girl.'

'No,' he said, shaking his head. 'You were a bitch, a spoilt, selfish little bitch.'

At first she sucked in her breath and looked aghast.

Tom remained unfazed, his expression unchanged.

Slowly, she began to shake with mirth. 'You're right. I was. Remember when you sang that dirty little ditty you'd heard on the quayside?'

Tom nodded. 'Most certainly. About a lady that frequented such places, if I remember rightly.'

'About a whore! It was about a whore!'

It amused Tom that she spoke with such enthusiasm. There was warmth in the way she said it, a certain pride as though the knowledge he'd brought into the house from his dire beginnings had lightened her world, when in fact, it should have darkened it.

His beginnings had been dismal, yet his humour, his natural love and affection had attracted her.

'You should not even know such a word.'

'But I do, thanks to you.'

His expression softened. 'And thanks to you I'm out of prison. For the moment, at least.'

'So there,' she said, cocking her head to one side and eyeing him with as much sauce as a dockside tart, 'it's only sensible that you marry me. Neither of us is perfect, and the rough edges of each of us can soften those of the other.'

Her eyes were very blue. Sometimes they were grey, at least it seemed that way, but when she was in a warm mood and communicating cheerily with those around her, they always looked blue. God help anyone close by when they turned grey.

'Am I pretty enough?' he heard her ask.

He nodded slowly, but said nothing. He was too busy imagining her hair loose from its pins spread over the pillow. He could get lost in that hair. He imagined the quickening of her breathing, the warmth of her belly, the cool hardness of her breasts. She was hard to resist.

'I suppose so,' he said off-handedly, ashamed of the way he was feeling and not wanting to believe it.

'A fine ship,' said Conrad, who had returned.

Horatia took the opportunity to convey the bad news to him. 'My father's brother, Otis Strong of Bridgetown, Barbados, is dead.'

'God rest his soul,' said Conrad. 'Please convey my condolences to your father.'

'He drowned,' she added swiftly, as though she had more important matters to deal with and wanted to get it over with.

Tom sensed there was something more that she wasn't saying.

Conrad was suitably sympathetic. 'That's dreadful.'

Horatia dabbed dutifully at her nose.

'I will tell my wife of this sad occurrence,' said Conrad. 'She was fond of him during her time growing up in Barbados.'

Horatia's eyes flashed. 'She would be, under the circumstances.'

Tom threw her a warning look. It was neither the time nor the place to mention that Blanche's mother had been Otis's mistress. She sniffed, turned her face skywards as if to study the flock of marauding seagulls wheeling overhead.

'Please pass my regards to your wife,' Tom said to Conrad.

'I will indeed, if I see her.' Conrad chuckled and shook his head. 'A while ago when we lost our child I was worried about her sitting around and sinking deeper and deeper into despair. I could barely get her out of the house, and when she did go out, it was only to cross the river and sit in the window of that cottage she named Little Paradise. Now she is involved in improving people's living conditions and has started by letting one of our servants and her family move into the cottage.'

Tom swallowed the lump rising from his chest to his throat. Conrad was talking about the woman he loved most in the world. Loving was the most painful emotion he'd ever felt. He'd loved his mother, he'd loved Jeb, he'd loved Sally – in his own way – and he'd loved Blanche most of all.

Slapping Conrad in the brotherly manner men have, he said, 'You are a lucky man, Conrad, and your wife is a wonderful woman.' He looked tellingly at Horatia. 'Rich women are not usually so generous.'

Horatia's expression turned smug as though she knew something he didn't. 'I know all about the servant moving into the cottage. It's Edith! She used to work for us at Marstone Court. She used to help Blanche when she was nurse to my half-brothers and sister. She also used to have a nice sideline in reclaimed King Charles Spaniels. Edith needed help. The place she lived in was appalling and although Little Paradise is better, it has no furniture. I promised I would donate some. There's plenty in the attic at Marstone Court.'

'That is very good of you, Miss Strong,' said Conrad, tipping from the waist. 'I hope your goodness inspires the same in others. It sounds as though you are going to end up like my wife – not just giving gifts, but also giving of your time. Most commendable, my dear. We can only love you for it.'

Sensing Horatia was trying to impress, Tom made a point of saying, 'Knowing Blanche, I can easily imagine her helping Edith place the furniture and sew the curtains. Your wife has a generous heart. Any man would be proud of her.'

'I'm taking some furniture there tomorrow,' blurted Horatia.

Tom raised his eyebrows but maintained a serious expression.

'Very generous,' said Conrad. 'You too will make someone a very good wife one day, Miss Strong, eh, Tom?'

'Yes,' said Tom, and had the impression that Horatia would eat him then and there if he gave her the opportunity. 'I'm sure she will.'

She asked Tom if he would be accompanying her back to Marstone Court. He said he would not. 'I have further business to discuss with Mr Heinkel,' he told her. 'Perhaps you can call in here on your way back from the solicitors?'

She was happy when she left, her day mapped out before her. First, instruct Septimus Monk to check her father's will, then a coach ride home with Tom. She could easily excuse him for being busy.

Tom felt he had to make amends. Meeting Blanche in Little Paradise had been precious to him. At night he dreamed of her, smelled the apple blossom, heard the wind whispering through the trees just outside the window. Being alone with Conrad for a while and listening to his problems regarding transport costs seemed small recompense for being tempted to seduce his wife. He felt he owed it.

Conrad puffed on his pipe between bouts of explanation. 'The cost of sugar refining at the Counterslip has become prohibitive,' he said, the bowl of his pipe resting on his chest as he and Tom shared a drink at a local inn. 'I am thinking of building a new factory closer to the Floating Harbour. That way I won't need to use barges to transport raw sugar from ship to factory. I would also like to diversify, which is why I wanted to talk to you. When your shipping company finally goes public, I would like to buy shares.'

Tom took a sip of port. It was thick and red as blood and tasted creamy. 'You don't need to ask my permission to do that.'

Conrad smiled self-consciously and Tom fancied he saw a sudden flush on his features that had nothing to do with drink.

'I must confess that I was worried when I heard you had returned to Bristol. I thought you would come looking for Blanche. Please forgive me for not contacting you sooner. You were my friend in the past. I should not have been so foolish as to think either you or my wife would betray me in such a way.'

Tom was lost for words. He'd seen Blanche before he'd seen Conrad and felt guilty about it. He turned the conversation back to business.

'What will happen to your old factory if you move out?'

'There are a number of possibilities. Someone of a different trade may wish to buy it, or I could convert it into rooms for rent, just as Mr Cuthbert did the old sugar house in Lewins Mead, the one Miss Strong is about to buy.'

Tom remembered the deed he'd read. He was sure the address was the same, but he needed to make sure. 'Which building is this?'

Conrad explained. 'Miss Horatia Strong has bought herself into a very lucrative venture indeed. Not only has she acquired a number of properties at a very reasonable price, but their location is directly on the line of the new sewer. The city council will be anxious to buy. No doubt she will make a very handsome profit.'

From his description, Tom immediately recognized the place as the one surrounded by homeless people, which he had seen the night before his arrest.

'I see.'

He also realized then that there would be a part of Horatia she would never share with him. She had an astute mind and an incisive business sense. The will to achieve, to overcome all the odds in the pursuit of wealth and success, would always be with her. Much as he admired her, there were things about her – deeply hidden traits in her character – that were not entirely palatable. Delectable and deadly – those were the best words to describe Horatia Strong.

But why should you be surprised? he asked himself. Horatia is hard-headed. Stop thinking of her beauty; she is a younger version of Sir Emmanuel Strong. There is little to choose between them.

Chapter Twenty-Four

Edith leaned towards Blanche in her living room at Little Paradise. 'What the bloody hell's she brought me... madam?' she muttered and winked wickedly.

Blanche bit her bottom lip to stop herself from laughing out loud. Horatia was outside, overseeing the unloading of furniture from a country wagon with big wheels and pulled by a pair of plough horses. The horses were tossing their heads and snorting steam, petulant to be brought into stony streets rather than the soft mud they were used to.

Some of the items Horatia had brought were enough to set their eyes out on stalks.

'I don't think Edith is going to have much use for this,' said Blanche as tactfully as she could about the suit of armour one of the men had just unloaded. 'It's a little large for a cottage,' she added. It was the best excuse she could muster to avoid giving offence. Horatia had *tried* to be generous but was far from being practical. She didn't need to be. She had servants to do that.

'You could put it in the garden,' Horatia said helpfully.

Edith opened the visor on the helmet and peered in. 'I s'pose I could use it to force the rhubarb.'

The children were running in and out, all except Freddie who had other plans for the sword that had come with the armour. 'Is this real?' he asked.

'Yes,' said Edith, 'And you ain't 'aving it. You'll cut yer bloody 'ands off!'

Horatia was on her way back in, backwards this time and barking out orders to the two men carrying a rosewood settee with cabriole legs and honey-coloured upholstery.

Edith looked flabbergasted. 'Blimey!'

'In here... careful... mind you don't damage it.'

The men carefully manoeuvred the elegant piece through the door.

Blanche had already brought things round from her own house in Somerset Parade, items that she judged would suit the house without looking too grandly out of place. Horatia had done the opposite. The things she'd brought would have been perfect in a Clifton drawing room – or against the grey stone of Berkeley Castle. They were intimidating and opulent in the simple rooms of Little Paradise.

Horatia hovered. Blanche sensed she wanted to speak to her in private even before she asked her to walk with her to the carriage.

Blanche followed her down the garden path. It was only big enough to walk single file. From behind she studied Horatia's square shoulders and stiff back. Horatia obviously had something on her mind. Blanche felt an ominous churning in her stomach.

They stopped out in the lane. A chili wind whipped at their skirts, sending them billowing out like giant bells. Horatia held her hat and seemed disinclined to look Blanche in the eyes.

Blanche had heard that Tom was spending more time in Horatia's company. It pained her to think it, but she wondered how far it was likely to go. She decided to be forthright. 'Do you have something to tell me about Tom?'

The distractedness disappeared. 'No,' snapped Horatia, as if Blanche had stepped over some imaginary line. 'I wanted to ask you whether Conrad had told you about Uncle Otis. You haven't mentioned it.'

Blanche looked down at her hands. Her fingers were long, their nails dusky pink like rosebuds. 'Yes. He told me last night directly after leaving you and Tom.' She frowned so she wouldn't cry. Enough tears had been spent the night before. News of his death had resurrected thoughts of her beautiful, outrageous mother, mistress of one man and mother to the child of his brother. She remembered Barbados, running along a beach, the blue waters tumbling against blindingly white sand. It was all in the past, just like Otis was now. There was only one thing she still wanted to know. 'How did he die?'

Horatia hesitated and took a sharp intake of breath. 'He wasn't well. He had problems, worries...'

Blanche looked at her in a way that conveyed she wouldn't be satisfied until she knew the truth. She never uttered a word – she didn't need to.

Reeling beneath the intensity of Blanche's gaze, Horatia stumbled over her words. 'He... um... killed himself... Apparently he walked into the sea and drowned. He couldn't swim, you see.'

Blanche shook her head. Her look was just as intense, but tinged with a question. *Why?*

Horatia looked down at her purse, fiddling with the strings that she'd wound around her wrist. 'I think...' she began then raised her eyes to the apple trees as she fought to explain. 'The plantation manager said...' She stopped. An odd look crossed her face as though she'd just realized something. 'He was lonely! He killed himself because he was lonely.'

Blanche stood open-mouthed. 'Poor Otis.'

The two women looked at each other. Blanche didn't know what it was, but suddenly they had become closer.

'He was good to me – and to my mother,' she said.

Horatia fixed her eyes on her hands as she nodded in agreement. 'I suppose he was. I understand your mother was very special.'

'I think so.'

'It must be quite wonderful to have a mother who is special. I don't know whether mine was or not. I don't remember her very well. I was very young when she died.'

Until this moment, Blanche had never felt the slightest sympathy for Horatia, simply because there didn't seem to be any point. After all, Horatia had everything, yet suddenly she seemed more bereft than Blanche could ever have imagined. She also seemed smaller.

It occurred to her that she was the one who'd had the better life with a warm family on a tropical island. Horatia's childhood must have been cold. She'd been looked after by an army of nurses and governesses who'd been far more familiar than parents.

Eventually, when the silence had run its course, she said, 'Loneliness is a terrible thing.'

'Very terrible.'

'Don't be lonely, Horatia. And don't allow Tom to be lonely.'

Horatia's eyes flashed indignantly. 'I am not lonely!' With a swish of velvet-trimmed skirt, she turned to leave. 'I have to go now. The men will finish unloading the rest of the furniture.'

Blanche almost laughed. Horatia had sounded as if she'd been doing most of the shifting and lifting herself. But this was not the time for flippancy. She'd hit a raw nerve. She'd heard it in Horatia's voice.

Horatia climbed quickly into the coach. Once the door was closed and the coachman up in his box, she leaned out of the window and called, 'Please do as you wish with the furniture. If there is anything you do not want, please dispose of it as you see fit.'

'Remember to give my condolences to your father,' said Blanche. Who is also my father, she thought as she watched the carriage disappear from the end of the lane.

Although she knew beyond a shadow of doubt that Sir Emmanuel Strong was her father, she still thought of Otis Strong as the main man in her life before she'd left Barbados. His affection for her mother had been obvious. If only they'd been able to marry, if only they'd been allowed to...

All gone, she thought. Like the wind and the summer and the bodies beneath the tombstones in the churchyards, the people and the years had passed away.

The chilly wind made her rub at her arms. Summer was fading. The apple trees were heavy with fruit, the fallen harvest scattered in the grass, much to the delight of wasps, bees and birds.

The men unloading the farm wagon finally finished their task – they had been paid for their trouble by Horatia – and were soon heading home.

The lane fell to silence. The common was empty except for the sheep nibbling among the grass and gorse on the common. Blanche wasn't really seeing them. She was thinking about Tom. He was usually a taboo subject, but today she'd fancied there had been a triumphant look in Horatia's eyes. Blanche was convinced that something had developed between her and Tom. She tried not to feel jealous. She had no reason to. Mrs Conrad Heinkel was a respectable woman. Blanche Bianca, the girl from Barbados who had loved Tom Strong, was long gone.

Someone tugged at the wide skirt of the pale blue dress she was wearing.

'Look,' said Freddie, holding out his jersey in which he'd packed about three pounds of early windfalls. 'Enough for an apple pie, do you think?'

'Plenty,' laughed Blanche. She followed him back to the house.

Examining the curved ends of a bed fashioned in the French style, Blanche shook Horatia from her mind. 'What about if we take this upstairs?' she said to Edith.

Edith's eyes shone with pleasure. 'It's very grand. I've never 'ad a bed like this before.'

Blanche held one end of what seemed to be the headboard. 'Well, you're going to have one now. Help me get it upstairs.'

Edith laughed. 'I thought I was supposed to be working for you. It seems more like you're working for me, helping me get this place sorted.'

'I could hardly leave you and the children lying on bare boards. What sort of an employer would that make me?'

'And what would that make me?' Edith retorted, pulling in her chin and puffing out her cheeks. 'Useless,' she said, laughing as she hunched her shoulders and rubbed at her back.

They laughed and the sound of their laughter lifted Blanche's spirits. She and Edith were old friends and no matter that their lives had gone in different directions they couldn't stop being friends.

The bed pieces were finally all in place, complete with a mattress and clean white sheets, blankets and a cotton counterpane in the same pale mauve as the flowers on the wallpaper. _

Downstairs a fire was lit in the grate in an effort to dry things out, and a stew of mutton and vegetables was beginning to bubble in a cast-iron pot set on the hob.

Bit by bit, the cottage was becoming a home and although they'd all been up since early that morning, everyone worked hard, determined that furniture, curtains, carpets and cooking equipment would all be in its proper place by the end of the day.

'Well!' Blanche exclaimed finally, wiping her brow with the back of her hand. 'That's that done.' She looked around the first of the two bedrooms, certain that Edith and her family would be happy here, and far healthier than they'd been in Lewins Mead.

Freddie looked out of the front window and she stood with her hands on her hips, gazing at the shaft of sunlight that slanted through the back window, the pretty patchwork coverlet on the children's bed, the chairs, the chest of drawers and the picture of a group of dogs given by Horatia and already hanging from a nail on the wall. The latter had probably belonged to Lady Verity, Sir Emmanuel's second wife and Horatia's much-despised stepmother.

Blanche smiled to herself. No doubt Horatia had taken great pleasure in disposing of her stepmother's things.

And why shouldn't they like it here? she thought, listening to the children playing in the garden below.

Freddie's back suddenly arched with tension. The laughter from the garden ceased. The shaft of sunlight faded to grey as the sun hid behind a cloud and she thought she heard footsteps.

She looked over his head at the apple trees that were bending before a sudden gust. She rested her hands on his strained shoulders. 'What's the matter, Freddie?'

He twisted round, his eyes like saucers. 'He's back,' he said, his voice barely above a whisper.

Suddenly there was shouting, a man's voice raised in anger, then Edith shouting back and the sound of children scrambling up the stairs.

'You slut! You dirty slut, you bin living with a bloke behind me back.'

A piercing scream sounded from below, as the children spilled into the bedroom, throwing themselves at Blanche and hiding their faces in her skirt.

At the sound of a slap, Freddie clenched his fists and dashed off down the stairs.

'Stay here,' Blanche ordered the girls, and followed, wishing her skirt wasn't so wide, a distinct impediment in a stairwell only a few inches wider than her shoulders.

She guessed that Edith's husband was home.

Deke Beasley did not fit her ideal of a merchant seaman. At no more than five feet tall, the top of his head barely reached his wife's eyebrows. He was dressed in a blue Guernsey of well-oiled wool, patched corduroys and a black peaked cap. Judging by the redness of his face and his foul language, he made up for his lack of height with an over active temper.

Freddie launched himself at his father's legs, pummelling his groin with his fists just as he had the ruffians they'd met at St John's Arch. 'Leave her alone!'

'Get off, you little sod!' A stiff cuff of the ear, and Freddie went flying, but he sprang back up and resumed his defence of his mother.

Deke Beasley raised his hand again, his other gripping Edith's throat. Suddenly he saw Blanche. His arm remained raised. He looked shocked, unsure what to do next.

Blanche adopted her most superior stance. 'What are you doing in my house?'

His mouth dropped open. One flash of her eyes was enough to make the oldest hearts leap with desires they'd long thought dead, and when she looked angry they wished they were dead.

Deke Beasley was no exception. He let Edith go, pulled his cap from his head and wrung it as though he were strangling the neck of a chicken. In an effort to ingratiate himself, he tried smiling, but only served to look shifty.

'Beggin' yer pardon, ma'am. Didn't know we 'ad visitors. 'Er,' he said, pointing at Edith, 'should 'ave let me know. But there, that's the way she is. Didn't even wait till I got in on the *Lizzie Brady* to move 'ouse.'

'Really?' Blanche was angry. If she'd been a man like Tom Strong, she might have hit him. He was detestable, the way he apportioned blame to his wife and hit her and his son. Even the way he continued to wring his cap, class deference written all over his face, made her angry. No wonder Edith had moved with lightning speed out of Lewins Mead at the mention of the *Lizzie Brady* having docked. And now she knew why. Deke Beasley was hardly the best of husbands, but there was something more worrying about his return home.

He was presently pouring words as if they were tea. 'Well, imagine 'ow I felt, yur ladyship, 'ome from the sea and finding nobody at 'ome. No welcome. No food nor drink no howdy doo—'

'I'm not interested in your feelings,' Blanche snapped. 'I believe the *Lizzie Brady* docked three days ago and that she was quarantined.'

Deke looked shifty and immediately searched for an excuse. 'A man's throat's tarred with salt after all that time at sea... Couldn't stay aboard, could I?'

'So you went drinking,' Blanche interrupted sharply. 'You went drinking knowing that the ship was quarantined because of cholera. Have you any idea how many people you've put at risk? You stupid, stupid little man!'

Deke licked his lips and blinked nervously as he worked out how best to handle this uppity upper crust female. He could hardly deny it. The stink of cheap porter was on his clothes and his breath.

His face rumpled, a mass of lines from forehead to chin in a crude effort to elicit sympathy. 'I works 'ard, yur ladyship, an' a man's a man after all—'

His efforts were wasted. Blanche was livid. 'And a bully!'

Deke Beasley's big blue eyes and moon-shaped face gave him a deceptively innocent look. Poor Edith. Fingers of redness around her neck and a bruise rising beneath her left eye. Who could blame her for moving out before her husband got home?

Deke stopped wringing his cap and his face turned scarlet as he looked questioningly from one woman to the other. 'A man's got rights! Doesn't a man 'ave rights in 'is own 'ouse? Well, dun 'e? He don't expect to come to what 'e thought was 'is house and find people sick and dead there, does 'e?'

Blanche turned cold. 'What people? What are you talking about?'

Edith looked horrified. 'Molly? Do you mean Molly?'

Deke pulled his cap over his head, the peak lopsided over his eyes. 'The hunchback was dead as a dodo when I saw her. So was two of 'er kids, and t'other was on its way out.'

Blanche tried to swallow the sudden dryness of her mouth, but it wouldn't budge. When she managed to find her voice, her words seemed scratched and disjointed.

'What did you do about it?'

Even before the words were out of her mouth, she knew what answer Deke Beasley was going to give.

'Nothing. It weren't my concern.'

'You left a child with her dead family? What about her husband?' It was a slim hope. Edith had told her Molly's man was a shadowy figure who disappeared at regular intervals and only returned when he had nowhere else to go.

He shrugged. 'That's a bloke who ain't never been around very much.'

Blanche could hardly believe her ears. 'And you have, I suppose!'

Edith sank onto the settee with the cabriole legs, her face hidden in her hands. 'It's my fault! It's my fault!'

Blanche knelt down in front of her, grasped her shoulders and shook her. 'It was not your fault.' She turned an icy glare on Edith's husband then sprang to her feet. 'But you,' she cried, pointing her finger so close to his face that he took two steps back. 'You knew you had cholera aboard your ship, but you had to have a drink, never mind how many people you might have killed from your selfishness.'

Deke Beasley opened and shut his mouth like a fish gasping for air. He certainly couldn't speak in his defence, mostly because Blanche wouldn't let him.

Blanche thought through everything Dr Budd had said; that drains filled up and allowed sewage to seep into fresh water. Deke had no doubt used the privy in Cabot's Yard, but then, she thought, eyeing his dirty but healthily round face, he wasn't ill. It was Molly who was dead.

Blanche patted Edith's shoulders, but didn't take her eyes off Deke Beasley. 'I'm wrong. Molly probably picked it up on the day we went there when the storm water filled the drains and ran into the well.'

Deke Beasley guffawed, a loud, short noise. 'Well, there you are then.'

Blanche shot him an accusing look. 'But I'd still like to boil you in oil!' She turned to Freddie, who was glaring at his father, anger burning in his eyes. 'Freddie. Get someone from the harbourmaster's office. Tell them there's a man here who's jumped quarantine.'

'Hey, you little swine,' Deke shouted, and sprang to catch him, but Freddie was quick and bolted out of the door.

'You wouldn't turn me in, would you?' he said to Blanche.

Blanche ignored him.

'What about the one that's sick? Poor little mite. No one to look after it,' said Edith.

Deke patted his wife on the shoulder and murmured, 'Now then, old girl…'

Blanche looked at him incredulously. The man could turn as swiftly as a coin and she would have liked to have given him a piece of her mind, but there were more important matters to attend to. 'I'll see that she's taken to the hospital,' she said, tossing her coat over one arm, and grabbing her gloves and purse. 'You can come with me if you like, Edith.'

Deke attempted to reassert himself, strutting like a turkey, as though he were ten feet tall. 'No need for that. She'll be all right with me.'

'It is obvious she will not,' cried Blanche.

'Who do you think—'.

Blanche fetched him a sharp clout around the ear. Deke Beasley was stunned to silence.

'Get out of my house this minute. Return to your ship, or otherwise it's clink for you when Freddie gets back.'

Rubbing his reddening ear and looking astounded that someone – especially a woman – would have the guts to lay a hand on him, he began backing towards the door. Blanche kept pace with him, her hand pointing over his shoulder towards the door.

'Your ship or Bristol Gaol. Out!'

Deke Beasley's eyes flicked nervously to his wife and back to Blanche. He managed a nervous laugh. 'You wouldn't really turn me in, would you?'

'Absolutely!'

One look at her face and Deke's decision was swift, and his feet were even swifter.

Edith didn't bother to look up when he went but kept her face hidden in her hands. When she did emerge, her expression was anguished, and her ire was directed at Blanche.

'Now look what you've done. What are me and the kids going to live on now that he's gone? We need the wage. Without it, we're lost.'

Blanche threw back her head and closed her eyes. She had overlooked the practicalities of Edith's existence in her enthusiasm to do good.

'I'm sorry,' she murmured. 'You're right.' She fumbled in her purse. 'I'll make up the shortfall myself. Better keeping you poor and alive, than paying for you to be buried.'

'I know he ain't much good, but having him was better than starving.'

Blanche looked at her incredulously. 'Is it? How often did he beat you, Edith? How often did he spend most of his wages in the tavern?'

Edith hung her head and sank back onto her knees.

'Take this.' A sovereign, Blanche decided, would feed them for a while until she could persuade Conrad to use his influence at St Peter's hospital where the Board of Burgesses dispensed a weekly allowance to those without enough to live on. 'Go on. Take it.' Blanche prised Edith's fingers open and pressed the coin into her palm. 'Regard it as your wages for this week.'

Edith sighed. 'What about Molly and her kids?'

Blanche looked at her friend's lined face. She was thirty-two, and although she'd always look older than her years, in these last weeks Blanche fancied she'd seen an improvement. But at this moment she looked as worn-out as when they'd been reunited on St Augustine's Quay.

Edith was asking her to intervene. She could hardly do otherwise. 'I'll make sure the child is taken into the hospital. Doctor Budd will do his best for her. Do you want to come?'

Edith shook her head. 'I don't think I can bear it.'

When Blanche looked back at Little Paradise, Edith was standing in the doorway under the twisted wood of its canopy. Two daughters were standing on either side of her, their heads leaning into her skirt as though she were a big, soft pillow.

And she is, thought Blanche with a small smile. Molly McBean had known that very well.

'Cabot's Yard,' she said to John as he helped her into the carriage.

He looked surprised, even worried, not surprising given their last experience in the place. But he knew better than to question.

When they got to St Augustine's Quay, John insisted he find a boy to hold the horses so he could accompany her. His face was a picture of distaste as he followed her and observed once again the ramshackle surroundings, the dirty children and the stink of human waste.

'Goodness, Mrs Heinkel. What would the master say if he saw you frequenting a place like this?'

'He'd pray that God would protect me,' Blanche retorted.

John didn't argue with that. He knew it was true. Conrad Heinkel was a good man, incapable of thinking an uncharitable thought or carrying out an unrighteous action. He glanced nervously from side to side, jumping at the slightest noise and movement, and glad he'd had the time and foresight to slide a pistol into his belt.

The smell of filth worsened. John coughed. Blanche soldiered on, her heart pounding as she contemplated what she would find. She prayed she'd stay healthy.

The doorway of Edith's old house seemed even more crushed by the overhead beam than when she'd last seen it. It had also taken on a certain significance. Deke Beasley must have loved this house. The size of the doorway matched his height and diminished his inferiority.

However, the man who came out of what had been Edith's house today was tall and broad-shouldered, with skin that shone like copper.

Blanche recognized Jim Storm Cloud. He looked devastated.

'I came to see Edith,' he explained in response to her questioning expression. 'I was told a woman and her children was dead and thought it was her, but it wasn't.'

'I understand it's her neighbour and children. Are they all dead?'

'All except the youngest.' There was no joy in his eyes, just a flat, lifeless expression like a shutter brought down over a window. 'Cholera. Agents of the harbourmaster have been around. Apparently her husband's ship rides at anchor sporting a yellow flag.'

'So I hear.' Blanche's heart slid to her boots.

'Captain Tom is well,' he added, although she did not remember voicing a question.

'I'm glad,' she said, and suddenly Tom's image swam before her eyes. She blinked and he was gone. She gathered her thoughts. 'Have burial arrangements been made for Molly and her children?'

'I told Captain Tom what had happened. He has made arrangements.'

He would. His kindness made her smile. 'I should have known. And the youngest child? Where is she?'

'He took her to the hospital of the man who fights cholera. He told me to tell you so.'

She opened her mouth thinking to ask how Tom knew she would be coming. Jim pre-empted her.

'He did not know for sure you would come. He just felt you would.'

Chapter Twenty-Five

Septimus Monk modelled himself on Francis Walsingham, head of Elizabeth I's network of secret police and spies. And like Walsingham, he had a sexual preference for men – young men, the younger the better.

Although principally running a law practice from his home and office in Little Prussia Lane, a stone's throw from the square tower of St James's Barton, in Stoke's Croft he maintained a network of spies throughout the city; useful in the procurement both of information and young flesh.

Michael, the young lad who had recently become his favourite, entered the office carrying a silver tray, which held a ship's sherry decanter and two squat glasses.

Michael seemed the soul of humility, but Septimus wasn't fooled. His eyelids had slid sidelong in an attempt to study the young man sitting in the chair opposite Septimus. He was jealous, and Septimus loved it.

'Tell me,' he said, smiling across at Gilmour Cuthbert and resting his chin on one finger of his clenched right hand, 'the cut of your clothes is really quite impeccable, Mr Cuthbert. Do share the address of your tailor with me.'

The young man, who had called to see him with an important item of legal information, swallowed his aversion to the man sitting opposite him and said, 'Of course.'

'He's obviously very good with his tape measure – or he can assess your body with just a glance. Admirable. Quite admirable.'

Gilmour Cuthbert took a large gulp from his glass and flushed slightly.

Michael's eyelids flickered, but only Septimus noticed it.

'Now,' said Septimus once Michael had left the room. 'You say the information you have will completely exonerate Captain Thomas Strong in the matter of the murder of Reuben Trout?'

Gilmour nodded. 'Yes.'

'So tell me what you know.'

Luckily, Gilmour's need to get the matter off his chest was stronger than his dislike of Septimus Monk. He'd watched Tom Strong after hearing his name mentioned by his father and had been intrigued at his father's reaction. He also remembered someone else mentioning it a long time ago, someone who had turned out to be more than just a friend to a lonely boy. He'd never told his father of his meeting with Clarence Ward and what he'd found out about his father and himself. But he'd decided to tell Monk.

Taking a deep breath, he said, I've met the murderer. He unburdened to me everything that happened that night.'

Septimus raised his eyebrows. This was indeed an inspiring turn-up. Resting his elbows on the fine-tooled leather of his desk and lacing his fingers together in front of his face, he leaned closer.

'So tell me what happened that night.'

A trifle flustered, Gilmour looked down at the floor and licked his dry lips as he put his thoughts into order.

'Reuben Trout killed a woman named Sally Ward. She had a son named Clarence who was enrolled at the Merchant Seamen's apprenticeship school on board a ship called the *Miriam Strong*. It caught fire and the captain was killed. There was a rumour that Reuben Trout was responsible for that too. However, when Clarence found out that Reuben Trout had likely killed his mother, he went in search of him, found him and killed him. Tom Strong saw it and told him to run otherwise his life would be ruined. So he did, but in him running, the blame seemed to fall on Captain Strong. But he didn't do it. Clarence was the guilty one.'

Gilmour Cuthbert squirmed under the intense scrutiny of Septimus Monk and found it nigh-on impossible to look him straight in the eye.

'And where is this Clarence Ward now?' Septimus asked.

'Australia. A place called Botany Bay, but he's willing to give evidence. I know he will.'

Septimus slumped back in his chair. 'So you confirm the rumour already relayed to us, but why would he put his neck in a noose to save another? And why should I believe you?' Monk shot forward again, his eyes seeming to fill his face. 'Have you, by any chance, concocted a story on behalf of the Strong family in order to subvert the course of justice and let a guilty man free? Are you trying to take me for a fool?'

Gilmour sat bolt upright. 'No! Most certainly not!'

'Then tell me why I should believe he exists and, if indeed he does, why I should accept the word of a convict exiled to the colonies?'

'No! No! You misunderstand!' Gilmour flushed like a girl.

Septimus eyed him sceptically. What would Walsingham have done in his place? Stretch him on the rack in order to get to the truth? Apply thumbscrews? Whip him until his back ran bloody? Septimus shivered with pleasure. Unfortunately, there was nothing to do but to listen to whatever excuse was about to be given.

'He's not a convict,' Gilmour blurted. 'He's a parson. He was full of remorse following the murder and Captain Strong's intervention, so he turned to God. That's why he went to Australia. He thought it was where he deserved to be – out there with the convicts, preaching to the godless and sharing their privations in an effort to obtain forgiveness.'

Septimus frowned. Reformed characters who turned to religion worried him. He was suspicious that their reformation had more to do with currying favour with the lords of Lincoln's Inn rather than the Lord of Heaven.

'But how do you know that he was telling the truth?'

Septimus almost drooled when Gilmour Stoke sighed, tossed his tawny curls away from his face and closed his eyes.

'He was my brother,' Gilmour whispered as though the answer pained him. He sighed again. 'My father knew Sally Ward – in the full biblical sense of the word. I was born before Clarence. My father married my mother and left her in the village in which she was born. After my mother died, I was sent away to be brought up by my father's aunt. Later, I was enrolled in a boarding school because my father wanted me to be a gentleman. Apparently Sally came to the house with Clarence in her arms demanding money. I knew nothing of this at the time, only later on.'

Rubbing at his forehead with one long finger, Septimus settled back in his chair as he thought things through.

'And how did you find this out?' he asked solicitously.

'My aunt was dying. I went to see her and she told me everything, such as that my father had not always been a gentleman, that in fact he had once lived "by his wits" as she'd put it. She told me about Sally coming to the door with Clarence and how my poor mother had found out that her husband earned his money off women like Sally.' With a mortified expression, he looked away. 'If you know what I mean.'

Septimus made no comment. Gilmour's information about Stanley Cuthbert was a gold nugget he would ferret away for future use. He'd never liked the man. Learning that he'd once been little more than a pimp was not a big surprise, but to have his gut feeling confirmed, to have genuine information to build on… well, who knew when it might come in useful.

'Armed with the information from my aunt, I went searching for Clarence and found him. Eventually we both confronted our father and demanded Clarence be granted the education I was receiving. It was some time later that he headed for Australia.'

Deciding the meeting was at an end, Septimus Monk rose from his chair and came round from behind his desk.

'I'm very pleased you came to tell me this, Gilmour. Most enlightening. I'm sure the Strong family will be very grateful to you.' Panic registered in his eyes as Gilmour sprang to his feet. 'Please… you won't tell my father that I told you, will you? He'd be furious.'

Septimus frowned. 'What's there to tell? Quite frankly, without bona fide evidence, your story amounts to nothing towards the innocence of Captain Strong. I need something more convincing than second or third-hand statements. I can hardly ask the authorities to drop the matter purely because someone told me of someone who was there and actually did the dirty deed – what?'

Gilmour almost jumped out of his skin and went quite pale. Aware that he'd raised his voice, Septimus apologized. 'Please understand, dear sir, I either need a statement from you or a statement from him.'

'That's what I have,' said Gilmour, reaching excitedly into his coat pocket. He pulled out a piece of folded paper, the thicker sort used by solicitors for their never-ending folios – for which they were paid generously.

'Clarence wrote it out a few months after the murder and before he left for Australia. In case of need, he said. And here it is.'

Septimus Monk felt the blood surge in his veins as his fingers touched those of the handsome son of Sydney Cuthbert. Pulling himself together, he quickly perused the curled handwriting, then nodded thoughtfully. 'This will be very useful.'

'Will it clear Captain Strong's name?'

'Assuredly.'

'And this meeting will remain a secret? I wouldn't want my father to hear of it.'

Septimus covered the young man's hand with his own, his smile reminiscent of a giant cat about to eat its own young. 'Of course not.'

–

'Walsingham would have been proud of you,' he said to himself that night after turning the matter over in his head and realizing that he could make a good deal more than his standard fee per folio if he played his cards right. And Septimus Monk was *very* good at playing cards.

The sleeping Michael lying beside him mumbled a drowsy response, though he didn't appear to have really heard what was said.

Septimus smiled to himself. Information. The world turned on information. Walsingham had known that, and so did he. At sometime in the future, Sydney Cuthbert would rue the day his son had divulged a family secret to Septimus Monk.

'Wonderful,' Septimus murmured, blew out the candle and snuggled up to his latest companion.

Chapter Twenty-Six

Sir Emmanuel Strong went to bed in the stone sarcophagus one morning and was not discovered missing until the afternoon of the next day. It wasn't unusual for him to miss dinner and he sometimes stayed in bed until late morning. His personal valet, McDermid, had finally entered his bedroom and discovered his bed had not been slept in.

Questions were asked from one servant to another. Both Horatia and Tom had set off early that morning for Bristol, Horatia with more cast-offs for Edith and Tom making more enquiries about Clarence Ward in the more disreputable areas of the city.

Rupert was away on business in London, and Nelson had made an announcement that he was staying with friends in Portland Square. It was presumed by Horatia that Rupert was with a lady friend. In the case of Nelson she knew it to be true, the services of a professional woman paid for in an up-market house frequented by the city's élite.

The door to the Egyptian room had only been opened and the accident discovered when a maid with a feather duster and a sweeping brush had entered to do her weekly clean.

Messengers were despatched to find Horatia and Tom. By the time they returned, the house was in uproar.

No one questioned that the death of Sir Emmanuel Strong was anything other than an accident. The wooden crane used to hoist the lid off the sarcophagus had been used on St Augustine's Quay for many years before. The ropes had not been strong enough. Sea air was known to be corrosive, the wood had been rotten and Sir

Emmanuel should not have got drunk and put himself to bed in a 3,000-year-old sarcophagus.

–

Tousle-haired and dirty faced, Molly McBean's younger child, Gertrude, was dying.

Blanche mopped the child's brow with a piece of red, wet flannel, her heart breaking with every rasp of the little girl's feeble breath.

Dr Budd's shadow fell over her and she felt the pain in his drawn-out sigh. 'She'll come to shortly and be in pain again.'

'Can you do something for her?'

'I could give her more opium, should she need it.'

The heavy feeling in her stomach made Blanche almost retch, a mix of anger and pain. Should she need it… It came to her exactly what he meant.

She looked up at him. 'Is there nothing you can do?'

Sad-eyed, he shook his head.

Choking back the sobs, Blanche looked down on the grimy face, the scabbed lips and the crusted dirt around the turned-up nose. Poor little soul, like a skinny cherub beneath the dark grey blanket, a bag of bones held together by skin.

'There's a ship quarantined in the city docks,' said Dr Budd, rubbing at his eyes, which burned with tiredness. He'd been up half the night. 'I have to attend. I'll be back as soon as I can. Mrs Abbot will let you out.'

Blanche couldn't bring herself to say that the child's own father had absconded from that ship and likely spread the disease all over the city. The damage was already done.

Dr Budd went on his way to visit other patients. Blanche hardly noticed him leaving. Looking down at Gertrude McBean, she was reminded of Anne and the long wait through the night when she'd slept and found her child gone. This child too, she thought, will last through the night, almost as though accustoming herself to the darkness, then drift into death as the morning light chased the night away. It would happen just before dawn.

Mrs Abbot, one of Dr Budd's able ladies who nursed the bed-ridden, asked her if she'd like a cup of tea.

She shook her head. 'No... No. I have to go home to my own children soon.'

Blanche was sobered by the thought and very thankful. Anne had died, but she still had other children. Molly and her family had been wiped out for want of clean water. She sighed. It didn't seem right in this age of progress and ripening empire that it was possible to die just from drinking dirty water. Surely the priorities of the great and good were all wrong.

The shadows in the hospital lengthened as the sun set behind the grand portals of St Mary's on the quay. Blanche sat tremulously, her gaze fixed on Gertrude, watching as her face grimaced in pain and her little legs folded up into her chest.

Concentrating on the child, she did not at first notice the shadow that fell across both her and the bed. Until then, the shaft of sunlight that fell through the window had warmed her back. She gave an involuntary shiver before realizing that someone was there and presumed that Dr Budd had come back early.

'It won't be long,' she said sadly without turning, her voice quivering with heartfelt pain.

'Blanche.'

Her shoulders went rigid at the sound of his voice. At first she resolved not to look. Her resolve was short-lived. The moment she did look at him, she knew immediately that something had changed. He looked smaller as though he were being crushed beneath a great burden. His eyes were sad, but seemed like sapphires in their gloomy surroundings.

'How is the child?'

She shook her head. 'Not good, I'm afraid.'

'I'm sorry. I did everything I could as quickly as possible.'

She looked down at Gertrude, whose life appeared to be ebbing away before her eyes. 'Poor child. Poor Molly. None of them had much of a life. How sad it is to bring children into the world, only to have them snatched away again.'

'It must be. I have as yet had no experience of such a predicament, though I think it is time I took a step in that direction.'

A while back, Blanche might have blushed at such words. In the past she would have assumed he was asking her to marry him.

She smiled lamely instead. 'I'm afraid I have already taken that step so cannot oblige. You will have to find your wife elsewhere.'

He nodded and seemed as if he were having a battle within himself to say or not say something very important. At last he seemed to pull himself together and plunge straight in, just as if he were diving into an ice-cold river.

'I'm thinking about getting married.'

'Who to?'

'To Horatia.'

Blanche nodded. 'What can I say? You're a bachelor.'

He looked down at his hands. Her gaze followed his. She liked his hands. They were slightly rough, but honest and enticingly warm to the touch. She raised her gaze to his face. His lips were full and he had an odd way of lifting one eyebrow when he laughed. His face was not perfect, but it was strong and he had the respect of many.

'I know what I *want* to say,' he said in a voice not much more than a mumble. 'I wish you were free.'

The blood rushed to her cheeks. 'I'm not.' She looked away, not wanting to read his eyes and see that he really meant what he was saying.

'That's the problem, which is why I am going to ask Horatia.'

She looked down into her lap at the bowl of warm water and the soggy piece of flannel. She had no reason to rebuke him. She settled instead for, 'I hope you will be very happy.'

She looked back at the child, the sweating skin and pained expression. The smell of bowel movements was dreadful but couldn't be helped. The little she had eaten had gone right through her.

'I want children,' said Tom, his gaze fixed on the pale face of the child. 'I want to raise him or her with as much love as Jeb Strong gave to me. It's by way of payment, I think.'

There was a hauntingly beautiful smile on Blanche's face when she looked up at him. 'Very commendable, though not surprising. I'm not going to rant and rave about you marrying Horatia. I understand your reasons. Strangely enough, I think it will work – though I don't want it to, not if I was truly honest. But I can't be selfish. It wouldn't be fair.'

Her laugh was tired, emotional and perhaps even a little mad. Kneeling, he embraced her and she sobbed against his shoulder.

She looked into his eyes, and although she knew she had no right, the tears came and she knew they were for her and Tom as well as for Gertrude. 'I'm sorry... I can't bear it...'

The tears were like a spring flood. Once she started she couldn't stop.

His cheek was firm against her hair and he made soothing noises like a father to a child lately woken from a nightmare.

'I'm so sorry,' he said, and was ashamed to find he was more sorry for himself, for their lost love, for fitting in so neatly with Horatia's plans, than he was for the dying child.

Blanche breathed in the smell of him, the mix of tobacco, maleness and strength. 'I want the child to live,' she whispered.

Tom sighed. 'We can't always have what we truly want.'

–

Conrad Heinkel slammed the desk with clenched fists as he rose to his feet, his face red with anger.

'Your demands are exorbitant!'

Sydney Cuthbert, formally Cuthbert Stoke, pimp, ostler and bare-knuckle fight fixer, now gentleman by dint of owning the most rundown properties in Bristol and bringing livestock for butchering to Bristol from Ireland, laced his thin fingers together and narrowed his eyes. He was not afraid of loud voices. Since becoming a respectable, though not entirely honest businessman, he had quickly learned that the upper classes used words freely in order to get what they wanted.

Conrad Heinkel and his cronies on the city council wanted him to allow the planned new sewer to cross his land, which meant a number of his properties would be blighted and have to come down – if they didn't fall down before then; none of them was in very good repair and most dated from before the Reformation of Charles II.

His properties were at the lowest point of the city and close to the river, the best place to site a main sewer. Smaller sewers would flow into this from the hillier parts of the city, out to a pumping station and beyond that, the sea.

'I am in business to make a profit,' Stoke said, spreading his arms in a helpless manner and shrugging.

'We all are, Mr Cuthbert,' exclaimed Josiah Benson, a man lucky enough to have married into the Strong sugar family through his wife Caroline, Horatia's younger half-sister. 'We are all in business to make a profit, but with wealth comes responsibility. Our city is at risk from disease caused by bad water, according to our friend Doctor Budd. It is in our power, as elders of this city, to do something.'

Stoke shook his head and shoved the written offer they'd put to him back across the table. 'I'm afraid this is not enough to inspire my conscience. I want double.'

The council chamber erupted in outrage, but Stoke stayed calm. Eyeing the well-fed faces of people born into status and money only made him more determined to milk as much out of them as possible. Most of them could afford to be patronizing about the health and conditions of the city, though few had ever visited the dark alleys and sordid courtyards that he knew so well.

Sydney Cuthbert, as Cuthbert Stoke, had been born into that squalor. It had made him the man he was today. He understood that the strong prey on weaker men in order to rise out of the gutter. What did the likes of them born on country estates and living in Clifton know about sickness and poverty? Nothing! He knew it made you hard. It made you look out for yourself and yourself alone.

He narrowed his eyes in a contemptuous manner. Conrad Heinkel might be a rich man, the biggest sugar refiner in the city, but he was foreign. It was this that made Stoke feel superior because *he* was a born and bred Englishman – though without the benefit of good birth and connections. He had clawed his way up from the gutter and would do all in his power to climb further. He couldn't expect to be the richest man in the city; that particular slot fell to the Strong family. However, he aimed to go far and when he was gone, his son Gilmour, product of a wife he'd abandoned years ago, would reap the benefits. Yes, he thought with a self-satisfied smile, a man should have a son. He was glad he'd taken the boy on when his mother had died.

The meeting broke up, the council of landed gentry and merchants muttering among themselves that his demands could not possibly be met, and Stoke convinced that they would go some way to satisfying the sum he required. If they offered him 50 per cent of what he'd asked for, then he would take it, but in his experience it was always better to ask for more than was really required.

Conrad was bursting with anger, but he'd get the better of that upstart Sydney Cuthbert, by God if he wouldn't.

He waved his carriage away. 'I will walk back to the office,' he said to John, his face red and his head aching.

Having walked most of the anger out of his system, he reached his office at the refinery. The smoke from the tall chimneys tinged the air with warmth and sweetness and stained the sky yellow. In the privacy of his office, he got down on his knees and prayed to God.

'Help me sway this man, oh Lord. Help me achieve this both for the people of this city and the peace of mind of my wife. Let my participation in this venture be a memorial to my daughter Anne's memory – if it please you,' he added before rising.

His knees made a cracking sound as he got to his feet. The fact that he was a big man – hale and hearty as the old English used to say – put a heavy load on his joints and they were becoming painful.

He dabbed at the sweat on his cheeks with a clean handkerchief. The starched cotton smelled fresh and sweet and reminded him of his wife. It had always been his habit to leave the premises at the same time as his factory manager and the foreman, a tough Irishman named James Flanagan, but tonight he had a yearning to get home early.

He checked with Flanagan that everything was in order, reminding him to damp down the furnaces before leaving, so they simmered during the hours between eight in the evening and five in the morning when the stokers came in to fire them up to full temperature.

On his way out, the gritty taste of charcoal came out to greet him from the char room. The usual bevy of beer fetchers were hunkered down outside, rubbing at eyes made red by the dust-laden air. Edith's son, Freddie, smiled up at him and tugged his forelock.

'I thought we'd seen the last of you since your move to Little Paradise,' Conrad said.

'Me father's 'ome,' said the boy.

Conrad raised his eyebrows questioningly. 'And that makes a difference?'

A look of resignation crossed Freddie's freckled face. 'Best not to be 'ome when he is.' His face brightened suddenly. 'Though we ain't seen much of 'im lately since Mrs Heinkel had words with 'im.'

Conrad chuckled to himself at the thought of Blanche giving Freddie's father his marching orders. He remembered Blanche telling him that Edith's husband had escaped the quarantined *Lizzie Brady* and that cholera had broken out in the area where Edith used to live. That would make her very mad indeed, he thought, still chuckling.

Today she had gone to the hospital, and although he feared her going there, Conrad trusted she'd be sensible and adhere strictly to Dr Budd's instructions on disease hygiene. Conrad would be travelling home alone.

Summer heat rose in waves off the shiny black coachwork and the glistening backs of the matching bays who were dozing, haloes of flies buzzing around their heads.

John was fast asleep inside the carriage, his jacket folded into an impromptu cushion beneath his head.

Conrad raised his walking cane and tapped him gently. John started.

'We are going to collect my wife from St Peter's,' he said, and waited patiently as the surprised coachman gathered his coat and hat and scrambled out.

The high ceilings of the hospital echoed with the everyday sounds of occupation. Nurses in white aprons and white caps flitted along narrow corridors where the only light fell in bright oblongs from open doors.

Conrad made his way to the children's ward, the oldest part of the building yet surprisingly in the best condition. Dark oak panelling covered the walls and divided larger rooms into smaller ones. The floors were of bare stone and the fluttering of wall-mounted oil lamps did little to alleviate the gloom.

He didn't quite know why he ached to see his wife so much. It wasn't just because of the fresh-smelling handkerchief or the fact that the council meeting had not gone to plan, thanks to Stanley Cuthbert. The truth of the matter was he'd wanted to hit the man's weasel-like face. He was furious with his intransigence over selling his land for the sewerage project. It was an affront to good citizenship, to himself, his wife and their dead child.

Conrad found himself walking on tiptoe, mindful that he was in a place where the sick deserved respect.

Later, he wished he had been heavier footed. Perhaps then he wouldn't have seen his wife in the arms of another man.

It felt as though a knife had been plunged into his heart. He loved her so well, thought to give her everything she wanted, even to making her happy again after the death of their child. Following Anne's death, he had pretended to be asleep in those hours just before dawn when Blanche had left the warmth of the bed and gone to Anne's room with only her grief for company. He had hoped that beating the disease would heal her hurt.

Not for the first time, he felt unworthy of her love despite everything. He was not a handsome man. He was big, bluff and red-faced, and his corn-coloured hair was turning grey.

Tom had always been the presence in the background, the shadow that passed across her features when they were alone. He was jealous of his good looks, his brave heart and his adventurous image. He could never be any of those things. He was just a hard-working man who praised God and enjoyed the technicalities of turning raw cane and beet into sugar.

Not wishing to lose his wife, he decided to avoid confrontation. Slowly, he retraced his steps then walked forward again, his footsteps echoing along the corridor and heavy upon the stone-flagged floors.

Blanche was bending over the bed on which lay a clearly ill child. It would have made sense for Tom to be looking on, but he wasn't. He was looking straight at Conrad, as though he'd fully expected to see him there.

'Conrad,' he said, extending his hand.

Conrad took it and smiled too and couldn't help suspecting that Tom had seen him before he retraced his steps.

'Not the best of times,' Tom added.

At first Conrad wasn't quite sure what he meant, until he looked at his wife, her shoulders convulsing with sobs as she brought the sheet up over the child's pale face.

–

Losing a friend and losing a lover were inextricably bound together in this instance, Tom thought as he rode back to Marstone Court.

The sooty, sulphurous air of the city, its glassworks, sugar works, rope works and new gas works, all contributed to making him feel more dirty and degraded than he'd ever felt in his life. He had meant to explain more fully about his reasons for marrying Horatia, but Conrad had arrived unexpectedly early.

As he'd held Blanche in his arms – perhaps for the last time – he had noticed a shadow falling across the floor, thought he'd heard something but hadn't been able to let her go. Only minutes after that, Conrad had entered. There was something about his expression that had not been there before, something colder. That was when it came to Tom that he had somehow lost a very good friend.

He called at the shipyard on the way back to Marstone Court. The second of his steamships was nearing completion. He dismounted, passed the reins to a boy and stood admiring the great iron structure presently filling the construction shed.

'She's looking fine,' said the engineer, a bundle of drawings beneath one arm and something wrapped in a cloth beneath the other.

'She is indeed,' said Tom, his hands on his hips. 'I'm sorry I won't be here to see her launch.'

'Well, at least there won't be any confusion over her name this time. We can use the plaque we should have used the first time,' said the man, 'though I don't really understand why the little lady got the name wrong.'

'Don't give me your excuses, man. She couldn't be named without you saying her name or handing over the plaque to Miss Strong,' said Tom.

'Well, I don't know why not. I gave Miss Strong the plaque, which was wrapped up so no one else could see. I'm not calling her a liar, mark you...'

Tom slapped the palm of his hand against his head. He should have known! Horatia had been devious all her life, always wanting her own way.

The building that housed the offices of Charles Hillman Shipbuilders was constructed of grey pennant stone and a Welsh slate roof. The door was painted green and squealed like a scalded cat each time it opened – as it did now.

'Captain Strong!'

Tom recognized Charles Hillman himself, his pale hair streaming out behind him from beneath a blue silk topper.

'There's bad news, I'm afraid,' he said, coming to Tom's side. He turned to the architect. 'Have you told him, McGregor?'

'Ah, no. I'm sorry. I was so wrapped up in this ship,' he said slapping the plans with one hand and looking embarrassed. 'Remiss of me... sorry,' he said again.

'One of the stable lads was sent on a fast horse to find you in the city,' Charles Hillman explained. 'Sir Emmanuel is dead.'

Tom was still for a moment. 'Do you know any details?' he asked eventually.

Charles Hillman shook his head. 'He seemed too flustered and in too much of a hurry to say much, just that he had to find you, Mr Nelson and Mr Rupert as soon as possible.'

If Tom hadn't been given the news of Sir Emmanuel's death, he might have seethed with anger all the way back to Marstone Court. Horatia naming the ship after herself now seemed so trivial compared with the passing of a man he'd known most of his life. Emmanuel had been a selfish man, but also a big man, and he had left a large gap that someone had to fill.

Evening was crisping the air and sending birds roosting in the trees. The last plough and pair were turning for home, leaving row upon row of sharply turned furrows behind them. He remembered this as being his favourite time of day. He used to wave to the ploughman and the cowherd turning the herd out into the field after milking. Tonight he hardly noticed their presence.

Nelson was already there when he got back to Marstone Court and gave him the details of his father's death.

'I can't believe it,' he kept saying over and over again, shaking his head, his fingers splayed across his face and leaving red marks on his cheeks.

Tom patted his shoulder and poured them both drinks. Nelson drank back glass after glass without bothering to add anything.

Tom frowned. 'I can hardly believe it myself.'

He left Nelson blubbering in a chair, too drunk to get to his feet.

There was no one in the Egyptian room when he got there. The lid of the sarcophagus lay in pieces on the floor. It had broken after being manhandled from the coffin. Apparently Sir Emmanuel's coat tail had been caught beneath the lid. The maid saw the lid was closed and recognized the coat the master had been wearing the day before. McDermid, Sir Emmanuel's valet, had been looking for him all that morning. The maid's screams had brought the whole household to the room and the truth was discovered.

He heard footsteps behind him, but did not look round.

'It's so cold in here,' said Rupert.

Tom peered into the sarcophagus, noting its hand-hewn interior and the pillow at the bottom.

'Where is he now?' he asked, remembering his pledge to see that Sir Emmanuel was interred where he wished.

'He's been taken by the funeral directors. Arrangements have been made for him to lie in the nave of Bristol Cathedral for a few days. Horatia insisted. She says there will be many who will want to pay their last respects to him before he is finally interred in the family tomb.'

'He wanted to be buried in this,' said Tom, knowing it was useless to try to change the family's mind, but feeling duty-bound to make the old man's wishes known. 'He didn't want to be interred with the rest of the family, not with two wives already there,' he added with a wry smile.

Unlike Nelson, Rupert was dry-eyed and empathized with Tom's humour. 'I can well understand that,' he said. 'And no doubt my brother and sister will regret flouting his request when they see some of the other females in his life traipsing down the aisle of Bristol Cathedral.'

Circumstances being as they were, Tom had no intention of talking to Horatia about Barbados or matrimony. She would be too upset over her father's death, he told himself, and was grateful that Sir Emmanuel had given him time to ponder the problem.

There were so many reasons why he should marry her. Love had nothing to do with it. Perhaps lust did. Horatia was attractive. Many men had sought to marry her. He never had, which had only made her more determined. There was also the prospect of a successful steamship line tied in with the sugar trade. There was also the fact, though he hated to admit it, that he had no other option. He needed to live abroad, it was time he settled down and there was nothing to be gained by being in love with Blanche. She was unattainable. Horatia was readily available and came complete with a fortune. Added to which, Horatia as a woman scorned, could be dangerous. Blanche would be blamed and Horatia would seek revenge. Blanche, perhaps even her son, could get hurt in the process.

Needing to calm his soul and raise his spirits, he made his way into the rose garden. At the end of the pebble path, which ran through rose-covered arches, was an ornate arbour constructed from decorative iron and painted green. Here and there patches of paint had fallen off, revealing the rust beneath.

Making himself comfortable on the iron bench, he lit a cigarillo and inhaled deeply. He would have preferred to sit there alone for an hour or so, admiring the salmon brightness of sunset slowly turning to purple. Before the shadow of her voluminous skirt fell over his feet, he heard its swish, swish, swish, as Horatia walked along the path.

The first thing he noticed about her was the absence of redness around her eyes. Horatia had not been crying over the death of her father.

'Where have you been?' Her voice was strident, almost hostile as he made room for her to sit down beside him.

A few more petals fell from the rose bush, fluttering to the ground like broken wings.

He sensed Horatia stiffening beside him, her perfumed aura, meant to attract, now permeated with the stench of long-harboured jealousy.

'I was thinking of your father,' he lied, though it seemed only reasonable given the current circumstances. 'He wanted to be interred in his Egyptian room.'

'A tomb! In the middle of the house!' She shook her head. 'Unthinkable. It was the drink. A few years and I really would have had to think of putting him away. 'No,' she said, shaking her head with greater emphasis than before, 'he'll be interred in the family vault with everyone else.'

Tom drew more deeply on his cigarillo. She took it from his fingers and drew on it too. They were silent, both thinking their own thoughts and not necessarily about Sir Emmanuel's passing.

Tom looked at Horatia; the pearl-like skin, the classically beautiful features, the ripe lips and the blue eyes presently gazing into the distance. He wasn't sure, but he thought she was smiling.

After a while, she said, 'I take back some of what I have said about my father in the past. At times I thought him ruthless, at other times a fool, a man who used women for his own pleasure, but never admitted that occasionally they could be as clever, or cleverer than he was. In these latter days I discovered a new respect for him.' She turned abruptly to Tom. 'That's why I chose Bristol Cathedral. He'll be lying there for two days before being taken to the family vault.'

There was a shine in her eyes that Tom couldn't quite comprehend, a luminescent glow as if for the first time ever, Horatia had what she'd always wanted and was where she'd always wanted to be. The look unnerved him and he decided to change the subject.

'Nelson is very unhappy. I wonder if he might return to Barbados. He was always happier there.'

'Pah!' Horatia spat. 'Nelson is like a child with a toy that's lost its wheels.'

Tom grinned at her analogy. 'Is that what his wife is? A toy without wheels?'

Horatia's sigh was full of exasperation. 'Don't be facetious. You know very well what I mean.'

Tom's face was hard, his lips seeming to split over his teeth. 'You're sounding like a shrew even before you've become a wife.'

Aware of his threatening tone, Horatia forced a smile. 'We can't worry about Nelson, or Rupert or Caroline. It's you we have to worry about,' she said, her finger stroking his cheek. 'Once father is buried and the will is read, we have to go to Barbados – or would you prefer to hang?'

Checkmate, he thought, and did not respond but drew the last flavour from the cigarillo and, as the final rose petals fell to earth, flicked the burnt stub into their midst.

Later he went back to the Egyptian room. He didn't often pray, but on this occasion he felt a great urge to beg forgiveness that he had failed to carry out Emmanuel's wishes. Resting his clasped hands on the side of the stone coffin, he bent his head. Out of the corner of his eye, something glittered close to his right foot. He picked it up. A pearl drop earring set in gold entangled within the frayed rope. He'd seen Horatia wearing a pair just like it. Thoughtfully he tossed it from palm to palm. The ropes had been hanging directly above the coffin. The hook of the earring had been embedded directly into the twist, which could not have happened unless she'd been leaning very close, directly below the crane and above the sarcophagus.

Too many questions rose in his mind and for now he had no answers. Best to sleep on it, he decided, tipped the earring into his pocket and left the room.

Chapter Twenty-Seven

Death, where is thy sting? Tom thought. He was gazing out of one of the library windows across the sweeping parkland of Marstone Court and contemplating the unfairness of life – and death.

There was less of a sting to the death of Emmanuel Strong than that of Gertrude McBean. Emmanuel had lived in a grand house with plenty of servants, money and mistresses. Gertrude McBean had not even lived long enough to be a mother worn down with the burden of too many mouths to feed.

The man sitting behind the mahogany desk coughed before raising his voice and calling to order those attending the reading of the last will and testament of Sir Emmanuel Strong.

Horatia's dress rustled like dry leaves as she took her seat. She looked triumphant, mistress of all she surveyed. Tom sat next to her and had the most urgent need to prick her bubble, to see a look of dismay on those proud features. More in keeping with the occasion, he reasoned.

He felt in his pocket then smiled as he took hold of her hand. She smiled back, misinterpreting his reason for doing so.

'I think this is yours,' he said, and passed the pearl earring into her hand.

Still smiling, Horatia opened her palm. Her features froze. Dots of colour sullied her high cheekbones.

He noted her breasts rising and falling more rapidly, and, as though she had suddenly remembered where she was, she began to dab at her eyes with a lace-edged handkerchief – just as she was expected to.

Tom adopted a bemused expression. 'I went to pay my last respects to your father at the cathedral. The funeral directors did a very good job. I presume he died in his sleep and did not wake up to find himself in a coffin – at least I hope so. I saw no blood beneath his fingernails,' he added so only she could hear.

'Are you insinuating…?' Her voice was hushed. Her face was white. 'No,' she said, shaking her head.

Tom let his gaze wander around the great library at Marstone Court where first editions of all the great books of the nineteenth, eighteenth and even the seventeenth century, sat behind glass doors, their gilded spines gleaming. Above the fireplace hung a painting of a pair of red and white setters, three brace of pheasant and partridge arranged around their paws.

This, he thought to himself, would all be Horatia's. But although she deserved to inherit, he could not disregard his suspicions. Neither could he marry her now. It wasn't until Joseph Compton-Morgan, a relative of their notary in Barbados, began to read the will that he looked at her profile and knew he was wrong. Her bottom lip was trembling and her eyes were filled with tears. She was angry, but she was also upset. The two never mixed in Horatia unless she was feeling beaten and wrongly so. He studied the other family members.

Nelson looked contained, no doubt because he had taken a little opium to calm his nerves, which needed a lot of calming nowadays. He blamed his wife, of course. She didn't understand him, besides which she was getting fatter and older. He didn't see himself that way. When he looked at her he saw only flaws. When he looked at his reflection in a mirror, he still saw the golden-haired Adonis he used to be. He failed to notice the dark shadows beneath his eyes, the nervous tic fluttering at the side of his mouth or the beginnings of a tremor in his hands.

Rupert was daydreaming, his thoughts elsewhere judging by the expression on his face. He still wanted to go to sea. Now his father was gone, there was nothing to stop him doing that.

Caroline, who was now Lady Josiah Benson, sat next to him. She had greeted Tom with all the old warmth of her youth, then had taken her seat as far away from her half-sister, Horatia, as possible.

Everyone had presumed that the reading of the will was a formality; trust funds and varied properties in Bristol, London, Scotland and Ireland would be apportioned with generous allowances to each of the children. The bulk of the inheritance, including Marstone Court, the sugar plantations on which the family wealth had been founded, the refineries, the shipping and banking interests, would go to Nelson, the eldest son. Regardless of whether he was capable of running such vast interests, it was surely his by right of birth.

The old Tom would have felt he had no right to be there. The new Tom, fired up with dreams of a shipping fleet, had resigned himself to the fact that he belonged. It had taken a long time in coming, but he knew he would always be part of them. He frowned as he attempted to reconcile his suspicions about Emmanuel's death and Horatia's reaction to his veiled accusation that he now regretted. It wouldn't be easy, but he had to make amends. He touched her hand. She looked at him. He mouthed, 'I'm sorry.' She blinked then looked away, but did not move her hand from beneath his.

Once coughs and clearing of throats and rustling of dresses had fallen away, the solicitor cleared his own throat and began.

'I, Emmanuel Gordon Ludovic Strong, being of sound mind...'

There were the usual legacies to long-term servants. Compton-Morgan reddened with embarrassment as he read out a larger one to a lady named Dolores Delaney of Park Row, Clifton.

Tom smiled.

'A man reaps as he sows,' said Rupert, who wouldn't have said a word if he hadn't been drinking.

'And Father certainly did a lot of sowing,' Nelson added, which resulted in disapproving titters from the older relatives gathered.

As Joseph Compton-Morgan repeated the most important paragraph of the last will and testament of Sir Emmanuel Gordon Ludovic Strong, mouths dropped open and eyes almost popped out of heads.

'…Over the years I have seen fortunes made by one generation only to be squandered by the next. The Strong family have so far bred sons that have increased its wealth. It is my dearest wish that this tradition of the new generation outperforming the last is continued. In my opinion, neither of my two surviving sons is capable of this. However, it has come to my notice that my daughter's business acumen far outshines that of my sons. Therefore, the management and overall responsibility for the varied business interests, including that of the sugar industry on which the family fortune is based, I bequeath to my daughter, Horatia Georgiana Adelaide Strong, but *only* on the proviso that she marries my nephew by adoption, Thomas Jebediah Strong. After much serious thought, I deem such partnership to be advantageous to everyone in the family. I know the family fortune will be safe in her hands. However, I do realize that her shrewd business sense needs to be tempered by integrity. Regretfully, she has less of this precious commodity, which is why I stipulate her marriage to Thomas Strong, a man of the greatest integrity, thanks in part to my brother, the Reverend Jebediah Strong.'

There was a united gasp from those assembled, like a noisy draught rushing down a chimney.

The lawyer looked up at those gathered. 'I am instructed by the deceased that the next part of the will is for close family members only – including Mr Thomas Strong. I have to ask everyone else to leave the room.'

Horatia did not move a muscle as less close relatives – including aunts and uncles by marriage, cousins and even Caroline's husband, left the room. Only Tom, Horatia, Rupert, Nelson and Caroline were left.

'You are all sworn to secrecy on this next part of the will. Do I have your word?'

Everyone nodded in agreement and uttered muffled affirmation.

'Then I will continue,' said the lawyer.

He cleared his throat again and bent to his task.

'Should this match not occur, I bequeath said inheritance to Maximillian Conrad Heinkel, a boy I believe to be my grandson and likely to be influenced both by his adoptive father, Conrad Heinkel and his mother, my daughter Blanche...'

Horatia wasn't listening. Her heart danced. The Strong fortune was hers... so long as... She eyed Tom sidelong. The Strong fortune and Tom was all she'd ever wanted.

But Tom was frowning, his hands clenched between his knees. She hadn't expected him to look happy exactly, but she had expected him to say something. His thoughts seemed to be elsewhere. She hardly noticed the lawyer, Caroline, Nelson and Rupert leave the room.

Now it was her turn to clasp his hand. As she did so, the earring fell to the floor. 'The beginning of a new era,' she said. 'You and I.'

He didn't answer at first, when he did his words surprised her. 'You really loved your father.'

At first she was speechless, then she said, 'Of course I did. How could you ever have doubted me?'

He shrugged. 'I found the earring entangled in one of the ropes. I knew how much you wanted to inherit and I feared...'

She touched his face. 'At any other time I might be angry with you, but not today.'

His eyes locked with hers. 'Then I won't be angry at you about naming the ship after yourself.'

Her smile lit up her face. She looked young again, as fresh and full of herself as she'd been when he'd first been taken to Marstone Court all those years ago.

A cloud seemed to fall on both of them at the same time. Tom voiced what they were both thinking. 'Your brothers are not going to be very happy at this.'

Their fears were well founded. As those attending helped themselves to refreshments and grumbled their resentments, Nelson nudged his sister's elbow. 'You've got what you wanted, old girl. You're the one giving the orders.' His mouth curled with sarcasm as he looked at Tom. 'You came at a high price, Tom, and it was me who persuaded you to come back from Boston. You've done well. Congratulations.'

Despite the insult, Tom remained calm. He could understand how Nelson was feeling.

Nelson turned back to his sister. 'I trust you'll have the good grace to give me what *I* want.'

She'd not expected him to hate her for stealing his birthright, but there it was, burning like black coals in his eyes. 'You hate being in business. You've always said so.'

He shrugged. 'I'll live with it – so long as you allow me to run the plantation now Otis is gone. My wife and child will have to stay here, of course.'

Horatia exchanged looks with Tom. 'I can't do that, Nelson. Tom and I are going to Barbados, at least for the time being until things calm down.'

Nelson sighed and ran his fingers through his hair, plastering it back from his forehead. Tom sensed his exasperation. He was trapped in a loveless marriage.

As he turned to leave, Tom stepped into his path. 'A board of directors will be properly set up in this country to manage things. You'll serve on the board, Nelson. Both you and Rupert.'

He felt Horatia's eyes on him and guessed she was surprised that he was already taking control.

'Yes. That's right,' said Horatia, instantly recognizing Tom's attempt to placate her brother.

As a result of his addiction, Nelson's moods were far from stable. His calm countenance receded as his face reddened. His eyes grew round and angry, and he slurred, 'You don't understand! None of you understand!'

'Then tell us,' said Tom, placing himself between brother and sister, unsure what form Nelson's anger might take, but determined that Horatia would not be hurt. 'What do you really want to go to Barbados for? And don't tell me it's to grow sugar cane.'

Nelson seemed incapable of understanding what Tom was saying. His whole body was shivering. 'You don't understand,' he shouted again, then stalked off without a backward glance at his sister or a sideways glance at Tom.

'He'll come round,' said Horatia with a confidence Tom sensed she didn't really feel. 'He'll understand. I'll talk to him.'

–

Gilmour Cuthbert was grim-faced as he gained entry to a house in Park Row. It described itself as a gentlemen's club. Like most such clubs, women were banned – except those who lived in the rooms above and provided services of a sexual nature to the members.

A well-dressed woman, her prim looks and dark dress setting her apart from those selling their services, greeted him.

'As we haven't had the pleasure of seeing you here before, sir, perhaps you would like to sit awhile and talk to our young ladies before making a selection?'

Pretty young women, their clothes as fine as any debutante, their eyes bright with interest and gems twinkling from their ears, wrists and necks, smiled at him.

It was not what he'd been led to believe. The room was not red and filled with plush velvet furniture; the lighting was subtle, and swathes of cream and white lace were swathed romantically with bolts of green and blue at windows and doors.

He was led to a chair and offered cigars and brandy. He declined both. A blond man opposite him was indulging freely. Before swigging back a second or third brandy, he brought out a pouch and proceeded to sprinkle what looked like brown sugar into his drink. Gilmour thought he'd seen him somewhere before.

'Are you staring at me, sir?' asked the man.

'I'm sorry. I thought I knew you from somewhere.'

Nelson Strong raised his eyes disdainfully. 'Do you indeed?'

Gilmour frowned. 'Ah, yes. I do know you. You're Nelson Strong.'

'Indeed I am. Nelson Strong – gentleman of Bristol who much prefers to be in Barbados. But my sister's going there in my stead,' he said, his eyes fixed glassily on the granules floating on top of his drink. 'And all because of the threat of hanging to my dearly beloved prospective brother-in-law, Captain Thomas Jebediah Strong.'

Gilmour frowned. 'But surely that is no longer necessary? Surely your sister has passed on the information I gave to Septimus Monk that exonerates him from any suspicion of murder? Which means, of course, that he has no need to flee to Barbados.'

Nelson blinked. Suddenly the floating granules were no longer so interesting. 'What did you say?'

Gilmour repeated what he'd said, though omitted the reference to Barbados, the part that interested Nelson the most. Not that it was needed. Even Nelson's foggy mind reached the right conclusion.

The brandy slopped over as Nelson set his glass down on a table with a heavy thud. 'Come with me,' he said, pulling Gilmour to his feet.

'Wait! I have not completed my mission,' shouted Gilmour as he rummaged for something in the inner pocket of his coat. 'I've come here to save these women from sin.'

To Nelson's and the young women's amusement, he pulled out a Bible. 'And all shall be saved from thy wrath with the words of this book...' he began, but didn't get the chance to say any more.

'So long as he saves one for me,' muttered Nelson, bundling Gilmour out of the door. Outside he turned to the fresh-faced young man and straightened the shoulders of his beautifully tailored jacket. 'Do you realize what danger you are in attempting to save the sinners in establishments such as these? One huge pimp and you're a pile of horse manure – or at least rolling in it with a bloody nose and broken ribs for your trouble.'

Gilmour shook his head. 'No.'

His feet hardly touched the ground, as Nelson frog-marched him along the street.

'Where are we going?' he asked in a timorous voice.

'To save another soul,' Nelson replied.

'Whose soul is that, pray?'

'Mine,' said Nelson. 'Now tell me again about this evidence you gave to Septimus Monk.'

Chapter Twenty-Eight

No one was surprised that Horatia made a lovely bride and that the most elevated citizens were invited to the wedding, with the exception of Mr and Mrs Conrad Heinkel.

'I'm surprised that the family are included in your guest list,' said Tom.

'Why not? The cathedral has enough room.'

'That isn't what I meant. I was wondering if they'd forgiven you for inheriting the bulk of the estate.'

'I don't really care,' she said, and he could tell by her expression that she meant it.

Her dress was of cream silk. Rows of seed pearls ran down her bodice and the silk was of such a fine quality that the slightest breeze lifted the hem so it almost seemed as though she were floating. The veil was long and held in place with a circlet of white roses and purple violets. Her bouquet filled the air with the scent of lilac, roses, violets and apple blossom.

Tom tried not to think of funerals, to persuade himself that he could be happy, that Horatia had always determined to make him her own. Well, now he was hers, and once it was all over and they'd signed the register, he asked himself why he had done it, then answered his own question: there was no one else he could marry.

They spent a few days in a hotel in the city of Bath after that. Tom decided he liked the place, even though it was past its Regency glory days.

Horatia hated it, especially the invalids who crowded the pavements in their bath chairs and cupped their ears in the reception area, shouting their wants to their carers.

He hadn't quite known what to expect on their wedding night. She told him to turn off the light and he thought she was feigning shyness. He didn't doubt she was a virgin, but he found the idea of her being bashful hard to believe.

Then she pulled back the curtains and opened the window. Her naked body gleamed in the moonlight. Dressed in brocades and silks she was beautiful; naked she was more so, her breasts round and ripe, her body a long curve from shoulder to hip. Her hair hung to her waist.

'What do you think?' she asked him.

'That I will take you to bed,' he said.

Her body was warm beneath his and he explored it at his leisure. He caressed her neck, her bosom and her belly with his lips, heard her suck in her breath and sigh. She caressed his back and shoulders, but throughout the whole process, she lay unmoving beneath him. When he finally reached his peak, she rolled out from under him, disappeared into her dressing room, and came out smelling of soap and rosewater.

Later, he lay listening to her breathing. He didn't know whether she had enjoyed the experience, and he couldn't tell whether she was a virgin. Somehow, it didn't seem to matter. Whatever she said, whatever anyone said, theirs was a marriage of convenience. Horatia was capable of jealousy and affection, perhaps even love of a kind, but he wasn't sure she was capable of passion.

One week later, they were to leave the country.

'And not before time,' Horatia grumbled.

–

Tom was surprised to hear he had a visitor on the very day he was to depart to Barbados with his new bride. When he got down into the palatial reception hall of Marstone Court, an area big enough for a full-scale orchestra, Nelson, his brother-in-law, was being helped into a balloon-backed hall chair by two footmen, his face shiny with sweat and dark crescents beneath his eyes. 'Get off. Leave me alone,' he shouted as they tried to sit him upright. He slid forward once again, his legs buckling as he tried to dig his heels against the slippery floor.

A young man Tom did not recognize was with him.

'Tom, my dear fellow,' Nelson shouted on seeing him. 'You don't need to go to Barbados. Gilmour here will tell you all about it. You're free to go where you will, Tom. Free to set aside my sister if you wish to. She's had you by false pretences, Tom. *False pretences*!'

After straightening his jacket, the young man offered his hand. 'Gilmour Cuthbert. You may have known my father. He calls himself Sydney Cuthbert, although he was born by the name of Cuthbert Stoke.'

Tom was speechless. It was like being hit over the head suddenly, a numbness spreading from the brain throughout the body.

He immediately wanted to ask questions, but Nelson was presently his first priority.

'I take it Mr Nelson has not had an accident,' said Tom after swiftly weighing up his brother-in-law's appearance.

'He insisted I come here. We would have arrived earlier, but...' Gilmour spread his hands helplessly then went on to explain. 'I met him in a place of very ill repute, a place where...' The young man paused, afraid to mention that the place was a den of opium dealers, prostitution and debauchery, with a speciality in women from many nations.

Tom finished his sentence for him. 'A place where a gentleman should not be.'

'You are correct, sir,' said Gilmour Cuthbert with a curt nod of his head. 'I myself was there on the Lord's business. I save sinners, you see, ladies of the night. It is small recompense for my father's past dealings, but I do my best. He is ignorant of my mission, of course.'

'Of course,' echoed Tom, amazed by all this.

Gilmour went on. 'He seemed annoyed that you were leaving for the West Indies because of an accusation of murder. I informed him that I couldn't understand why that should be now that I had handed over certain information to Septimus Monk. Mr Monk assured me that he would pass the information on to you or a member of your family. It would mean you were a free man with no threat of the gallows hanging over you.'

Tom looked at him grim-faced. 'I take it that my cousin's mind was infused with opium.'

The young man nodded. 'Almost, though he threw his pipe down when I told him what I knew and frog-marched me out of the club and along to his carriage.'

Tom ordered the servants to take Nelson to his room. His mind reeled from the realization that the threat of hanging was lifted. But why hadn't this news been passed to him sooner? And just how did Stoke's son fit in?

'Will you take a drink with me?' he asked Gilmour.

'Indeed, thank you, sir,' said Gilmour Cuthbert and followed Tom to the drawing room.

'May I enquire as to the content of the information you have regarding the murder of Reuben Trout?' Tom asked, pouring a measure of claret for them both.

Gilmour nodded amiably. 'Of course, sir. I heard my father talk of you disparagingly, and knew from his tone that he hated you. I know what my father is like. You see, Clarence Ward was my brother.'

Tom was dumbfounded. Gilmour went on to recount the same story he'd told Septimus Monk.

'I told Mr Monk about the letter I received from Clarence Ward before he left for Australia confessing to the murder of Reuben Trout. He assured me the information would be passed on, and I know he was true to his word. A while later, after leaving a Bible class I'd attended at St Bartholomew's, I saw Miss Horatia Strong – now your wife – enter the offices of said lawyer some time later. I presumed he had told her that the true murderer had confessed and that you did not need to leave for Barbados, but I thought it best to check. I entered his offices and asked him. He assured me that it was so.'

Tom stood stunned. His mouth was dry as stale biscuits. His heart pounded and there was a sickness in his stomach.

'My wife went to see Septimus Monk?'

Gilmour Cuthbert's youthful confidence seemed to retreat as he answered, 'Well... yes... according to a friend of mine who lives with...'

Tom fancied he saw a blush on the stubble-free face; the boy had not started shaving yet.

Tom nodded in understanding. 'Please. Continue.'

Gilmour, his face reddening more, nodded. 'He heard him talking about it, saying that he'd told her and thinking she was a woman of outstanding cunning and that she aroused mixed feelings.'

Tom gritted his teeth. 'She certainly does.' He was oddly proud at hearing Horatia referred to as cunning. He was also angry that she had known he was cleared of the murder charge and had not told him, everything arranged, no doubt, by Septimus Monk.

He calmed himself as he saw Gilmour out. Before he left, the young man paused by the door, his expression betraying some inner struggle preventing him from stating something else. At last he blurted it out. 'I think my father may have a lot to do with you being arrested and the truth being withheld. My father is a rich man but is not always charitable. He tells me that men never get rich by being charitable, and that I should bear this in mind when I come to inherit his wealth.'

His eyes shone as he looked up into Tom's face. 'I hate to tell him that when I come to inherit, I will immerse myself in charitable works. I think it only right to return something of what you have earned on the backs of others to those more unfortunate than yourself, don't you?'

Tom was taken aback by the fresh-faced enthusiasm of Gilmour Cuthbert, though inside he burned with anger. He managed a warm smile as he shook the young man's hand and thanked him for bringing Nelson home.

'I apologize for his behaviour. I'm afraid he's rather obnoxious when he is under the influence of poppy juice.'

Gilmour laughed in a courteously inoffensive way. 'On the contrary, he was very amusing. He talked a lot but didn't appear to understand a word I was saying. He told me about being disinherited and half suspecting that his father's death hadn't been an accident. He told me it again and again. The exertion of talking and forcing me to come here caused him to pass out. It was late by then so I took him to where I live before coming here. Luckily, my father was out on business in Hereford. He'll be back shortly. He's booked a passage on your new steamship.'

'To Barbados?' Tom raised his eyebrows.

'To Ireland. My father owns a number of abattoirs. He visits the markets around Queenstown and brings livestock over for butchering.'

'And my ship calls in there first,' said Tom thoughtfully. Stoke was the last person he wanted as a companion on his ship even though he was getting off in Ireland.

He was still deep in thought when Gilmour said, 'I trust I haven't inconvenienced you too much.'

'Of course not.'

No, it wasn't Gilmour that had inconvenienced him. It was Horatia. She'd left him worrying about whether the hangman would get him before he could find Clarence Ward. All the wrongs she'd ever done him served to stoke his anger.

He saw Gilmour Cuthbert to the door and although he smiled, inside he seethed with anger.

Once the chaise had clattered off down the drive, he turned back into the house, his face like thunder and his fists clenched in tight knots at his side.

Horatia had known he was innocent, but had not told him and he knew damn well why. Then this about the will... The suspicion returned that she might have had something to do with her father's death. Nelson had obviously had the same suspicion. Although he wasn't always in his right mind, the fact that he'd voiced his misgivings – and to a stranger – was doubly disconcerting. He remembered the pearl earring. He remembered her expression at the reading of the will. The two didn't really marry up, but he had to be sure.

When he entered her room, she flung her arms around him, her head thrown back, her long neck exposed.

Arms rigid at his side and fists clenched, Tom did not move.

Sensing something was wrong, Horatia stepped back and he saw confusion in her eyes. She tried to smile, even laughing in a light girlish way – as if that would be enough to lift the surliness of his countenance.

'What's the matter? Is Nelson all right? I heard a carriage,' she went on. 'Who was it Tom?' Her voice wavered.

She reached for him. He stepped back. 'You have some very admirable attributes, Horatia, but you are also seriously flawed. All my life I observed two sides to your character, that which craves for love and that which craves for power. The latter has always tempered the former; frequently I asked myself how far you might go to achieve your desires. Until this moment, I never had an answer. Now I do. You, my dear, will stop at nothing to get what you want.'

Horatia was dumbfounded. 'I don't know what you mean.'

'Then let me enlighten you. You wanted a ship named after you, and achieved it by devious means. You wanted the power vested in your father. You got that too. You also wanted me. I must admit I was flattered and also lured by the prospect of running my own shipping company – belonging to just my wife and me.' He shook his head, his eyes dark and his hair flying out of control.

Horatia looked frightened. 'What are you saying?'

'That you are capable of anything, including murder. I find myself questioning your father's death yet again. The ropes were thick and strong, but frayed cleanly in one place as though someone had cut them.'

She shook her head, her eyes and expression full of denial. 'No! Her voice was broken. 'I... didn't... do... it. How could...

317

could... you... how could you... think I would kill... kill... my own father?'

Tom found himself wanting to believe her. She was beautiful and clever. Any man would be proud to be married to her. To some extent, Tom still was, but he was also wary.

Horatia's face burned, and not just with anger. She was terrified of losing him. 'Don't hate me, Tom. Please don't hate me.'

Her fingers dug into his arms. He tensed and much as he was disposed to respond, he didn't. He was punishing her for what she'd done and for what she was and realized he'd be doing that for the rest of their married life. 'I don't hate you, but I sometimes dislike you.'

'I saw my father asleep in there and saw the lid and the ropes, but I didn't do anything. I couldn't and I wouldn't. He was my father.'

Her eyes moistened with tears. Tom remembered her crying like that at the reading of the will. He'd believed them genuine. He wasn't sure now.

Horatia was surprised at the depth of her feelings. Tom mustn't hate her. 'I didn't do it. I went in there, I came out again, and when I came out...'

The truth came like a bolt from the blue. Her tears stopped and her mouth hung open. The thought was too terrible, but she couldn't deny it. Looks had always passed between her and the footman. It had amused her to see the desire in his eyes and the total dedication of a man in love with something he could never have. That look of his, she recalled it clearly. It was as if he had read her mind.

'Duncan,' she said, her voice hardly above a whisper.

Tom smiled sardonically and shook his head. 'How very like you to blame a servant.'

'But it's true!'

'More lies? Let me know when you wish to tell the truth.' He stopped by the door. What hurts most of all is you not telling me about the letter from Clarence Ward. Would you have let me hang if I hadn't agreed to marry you and go to Barbados?'

'Of course not!'

He eyed her coldly. 'I wish I could believe that.'

'You can't go!' He was her husband, bound to her for life in a proper ceremony in a church. There was no Blanche to stand in her way, no one at all to stop her from having what she wanted most. Why oh why hadn't she been straight with him? Why hadn't she told him that they didn't need to go to Barbados?

'I didn't think you would obey the terms of my father's will unless it was your only hope of escaping the gallows,' she blurted.

Suddenly he knew she was telling the truth, but somehow it seemed irrelevant. His anger ran too deep. 'Didn't you trust me to be innocent?'

'It wasn't that...' Her voice trailed away. In his youth she'd thought Tom capable of anything, after all, he had been born into the direst circumstances. Her heart felt as though it would burst. 'You're not leaving?'

He turned back. His eyes were dark with anger – and something else. Hatred, she thought, and instantly clutched at her bosom. He couldn't hate her. He said he couldn't yet she could see it there in his eyes.

'I find it hard to countenance living with a murderess.'

'But I didn't kill him. Duncan! It must have been Duncan. He was obsessed with me...'

Tom raised his eyebrows. 'Do you mean that a man actually loves you enough to kill for you?'

Horatia froze, her mouth wide open. Tom's words had sliced into the heart. What he was actually saying was that he didn't love her. She had convinced herself that her father's will was not the only reason for him agreeing to marry her and that he did harbour some affection for her, perhaps not exactly love, but something close to it. Now he was flinging the truth into her face. Well, he could only push her so far...

Her heart turned to ice and her words were bitter. 'So you only married me for my money.' She forced herself to laugh mockingly. 'You've sold yourself to a woman – just like your mother sold herself to men!'

It was the worse thing she could possibly say.

He hit her, the flat of his hand stinging her face. She fell. The portraits, the rich drapes, the velvet-covered furniture seemed to blur into a mass of colour, like paints on a canvas running into each other. She was on the floor, the room still spinning; one side of her face stung from the force of the blow.

Tom was instantly regretful. 'I'm sorry... I shouldn't have done that...'

He reached down to help her up. Horatia slapped his hand away, her face stiff with anger.

'Get out of this house! I never want to see you again. Get out! Do you hear me? Get out! Get out! Get out!'

Tom's moment of regret evaporated. This was the old Horatia, the haughty woman who became angry when she didn't get her own way, who didn't get involved in charitable works and treated her servants like dancing dogs. He reminded himself that she'd lied to him, that he'd suffered agonies wondering whether they'd get away in time before he was re-arrested, his mind torn between a fleet of ships and self-preservation.

His mouth closed in a grim line, and his eyes seemed to sink deeper into his head. 'I'll go, and I won't be back.'

Horatia staggered to her feet with the help of a side table on which balanced a Chinese vase, brilliant in the shine of its glaze and the blue of its pattern.

'Go! Go!' she shouted.

Tom opened the door and closed it behind him swiftly as the Chinese vase flew through the air and against the door where it shattered and showered to the floor.

He made his way to see Nelson, who was now quite lucid, though the ravages of his addiction had left his skin stretched tightly over his skull, and his eyes sunken deep into their sockets.

'Is it true?' he asked.

Nelson didn't seem to know what he was talking about. Tom found himself telling him everything. Nelson listened silently. At last he said, 'You should have married Blanche. You love her. You've always loved her.'

Tom was on the verge of saying that Nelson had loved her too, when he remembered that they were half-brother and sister and that Nelson should have loved her as such and not as a woman. Instead he said, 'At least there is one good thing to come out of this. Horatia won't go to Barbados by herself, and I won't go with her, which means you'll have to go.'

Nelson raised himself up on his elbows, his eyes regaining some of their old sparkle. 'Well, Tom my old friend, that at least means that one of us is going to have a happy marriage. Distance, as they say, makes the heart grow fonder, and my wife is indeed going to be at a great distance. I shall be in Barbados and she shall remain in Bristol.'

Tom grinned, the corners of his mouth quivering with amusement. 'I think the correct saying is that *absence* makes the heart grow fonder.'

Nelson laughed. 'Whatever the word, the saying is certainly going to work for me.'

Tom shook his head and smiled, but still felt a need to apologize. 'I'm sorry for springing this on you.'

'Tom, I think it's a wonderful suggestion.' Nelson smiled dreamily. 'Dusky maidens, a moonlit beach and pounding surf – and my wife on the other side of the Atlantic. I couldn't think of anything more wonderful!'

Chapter Twenty-Nine

Deke Beasley sneaked back to Little Paradise when no one was there but he never went back to his ship. Not only did Edith not get any money from him, but she also found that he'd taken the little bit she'd saved, which she kept in a jug in the cupboard.

Lack of money forced her to go looking for him in the taverns and doss-houses along the waterfront, and she sent Freddie out looking too. There was no sign. Edith knew she'd be better off without him and, wicked as it was, she'd often prayed for a storm and a mishap at sea.

Money being tight, Blanche helped out as much as she could with leftover food and fresh vegetables from the garden. She also gave her a little money, 'for all the little extras you do,' she said.

None of the servants in the Heinkel household complained about her getting preferential treatment, though Cook, who'd taken pity on Edith and her offspring, did say that her presence attracted Jim Storm Cloud to the house, which distracted the servants from their work. They were fascinated — aroused might have been a better word — by the bulging biceps and the silky black hair that hung to his waist.

'Now that's what I call a man,' said a scullery maid and got a thick ear.

Coping alone began to show. Edith looked tired and Blanche ordered her to have an extra day off.

'I can manage,' Edith protested. In order to emphasize the point, she went hell for leather at the dining table, until her tiredness caught up with her and she fell flat on her face.

On her extra day off, she slept in until eight-thirty, a luxury to someone who usually got up at five-thirty in order to get to Somerset Parade by six. As on other days, the children had taken care of themselves, warming up the porridge she'd made the day before, Freddie scooping it out into pale green porcelain bowls that were see-through if held up to the light. These had been one of Horatia's donations to Edith's household, too fine a quality for a humble cottage, but all that remained of a larger set at Marstone Court.

'One for you, Ma,' said Freddie proudly as he set her a bowl on the table. 'And I've made you tea.'

Edith sighed at the four little faces watching her from the other side of the table. She was blessed indeed. Her children were the most valuable gifts Deke Beasley had ever given her, in fact the only ones.

The porridge was thick but thinned after adding a little milk.

'Very nice,' she said when she'd finished, then thought of last night's supper and frowned. 'Do we have any of that mutton stew left for dinner and supper?'

Freddie peered into the iron pot hanging from a trivet above the fire. 'Enough. Though I'm not hungry, mind you.'

Edith shook her head. 'I can tell from your expression, Freddie Beasley, that we ain't got much left. I also know that you're bound to be hungry. It's only natural. You're a growing lad. There's nothing for it, but we have to see what we can get to throw into the pot and make it go further.'

But I'm not spending too much, she thought. The money Blanche had given her would go back into her tea caddy, which she'd hide much more efficiently this time. Without Blanche, they would all have starved, but Edith was proud. She preferred to stand on her own feet and make money for herself.

As they were about to leave, someone knocked at the door. She didn't recognize the man who stood there when she opened it, but he looked like a shabby crow. His clothes were black and shiny with age and grease. There was mud on his shoes and on his trousers.

Around his neck, which stuck forward like that of an angry chicken, was the most ragged and dirty scarf she had ever seen.

He bowed slightly as he lifted his hat from his head. 'Mrs Beasley?'

'Yes.'

'Oscar Odcombe's me name and I've come to collect me money.' His hand shot out so fast, Edith took a step back.

'Money? Money for what?'

He looked surprised, but not at all embarrassed by what he said next. 'The money for burying the recently deceased, yer husband, one named Deacon John Beasley.'

Edith was shocked. Mouth hanging open, she looked down into the begrimed hand of Oscar Odcombe, noting the black lines crossing his palm like the veins in an autumn leaf.

It took a moment for what he'd said to sink in. Once it did, she lashed out.

'Get away from yur! Me husband's not dead. No one's told me he's dead. Yur just one of them people who takes advantage of other's misfortunes.'

Oscar Odcombe used both arms to protect his head from Edith's blows and began his retreat.

'It's true, Mrs Beasley, it's true! I knows I should have told you two days ago, but we've been busy, and I did explain to Doctor Budd that I'd get round 'ere when I could.'

At the mention of the doctor, Edith's arms dropped to her side. 'Doctor Budd told you to come here?'

The frightened gravedigger nodded, though left his arms folded over his head. 'He ain't stopped, poor bugger. Didn't realize you ain't been told. Wouldn't 'ave been so blunt if I'd known.' Slowly, he let his arms drop from his head.

Edith thought about the few shillings left from her wages in her tea caddy. 'How much do I owe you?'

'Half a crown,' he said, and cautiously held out his hand.

Edith closed the door in his face and went to fetch the money. As she was counting it out, she thought of something that was both awful and funny. She hadn't asked how her husband had died.

Adopting as mournful a face as possible, she went back to the front door, slipped the man his money and asked him.

'Cholera,' he said.

'Cholera,' she repeated, as though saying it helped it to sink in. She let the money fall into his palm. Deke Beasley died from cholera, the disease he had thought left behind on his ship. It seemed a fitting end in one way, yet on the other hand, it did not. Deke Beasley had received a decent Christian burial, unjust for a man who had never been to church in his life except to be christened and married. It seemed ironic that his burial had been swift, compared to Molly McBean's little one.

Edith sighed. Her coffers and her food larder were less full than they had been. Despite still feeling tired, she had to go out to buy food.

Freddie insisted on accompanying her to the market in St Nicholas Street. Together they trawled behind the ramshackle counters behind which the merchants and farmers in from the country sold their produce. Edith was trying to save her money to buy meat, which would flavour another stew once the mutton was gone. Discarded vegetables were preferable to discarded meat.

What meat there was left proved too expensive. Edith bit her lip and wondered whether she could get a bit of fish down on the quay, or perhaps even a brace of pigeons from the street seller who hung around there until mid-morning. Their search for him took them along St Augustine's Quay until they were level with Tom Strong's ship. Jim Storm Cloud was hanging over the rail and his gaze never left them as they approached. There was no sign of the street seller.

Edith nodded a quick greeting. Jim Storm Cloud liked her a lot, judging by the times he came calling at Somerset Parade. So far, he had not visited her at Little Paradise, perhaps because he knew Deke would be there. Whatever customs they might have in North America, she was sure they still held marriage to be sacrosanct.

But you're not married any longer, she thought, and a thrill of excitement shot through her.

She stopped the moment they came level with the ship. 'I'm out doing a bit of shopping,' she said brightly. 'Thought I might buy a brace of pigeons from a bloke that hangs around here sometimes. Haven't seen him, have you?'

Jim nodded. 'Yes, but he sold all his game.'

'Oh.' Edith couldn't help sounding disappointed, and thought she must look it too. 'Could have done with that. He charges a fair price, and I certainly don't want to pay too much. I've just paid half a crown for me husband to be buried. He died of cholera, you know.' She jerked her head at Freddie and ruffled his hair. 'I'm the only breadwinner they got now. Got to do what I can and can't afford to waste money.'

Jim seemed to think, then moved. He disappeared without saying a word, and Edith found herself feeling disappointed. But he wasn't gone for long. He came back up on deck and walked down the gangplank onto the quay.

Normally, Edith would have lapped up the look of him, the long stride, the gleaming hair and the hawk-like features. Today, the rabbits he held in one hand and the red plumed birds he held in the other attracted her attention.

'For you,' he said.

He towered over her, his warmth gently soothing. Suddenly, she felt very small in his presence. Deke had told her he would always look after her, but never had. This man did not need to say anything. He was there, a barrier between her and harm.

'I don't know what to say,' she said, and couldn't stop the tears running down her face. 'It's so good of you.'

'You have no husband now. Someone has to take care of you.'

Smiling through her tears, she said, 'I thought it was Tom you took care of.'

'Yes. I am like his shadow, I am there in the background but unseen by most.'

'You're very kind,' she said, touching his hand as she took the gifts he offered.

'I think you are too,' he said, and Edith blushed.

Silly me, she said to herself, and all because of a couple of rabbits and a brace of pheasant.

But it wasn't just that, and she hoped Jim felt the same way.

-

There were only half a dozen passengers on the maiden voyage of the *Horatia Strong* to Barbados. One of them was Nelson. Another was Stoke – addressed as Mr Cuthbert by the crew – who was only going as far as Queenstown, Ireland in order to negotiate pig prices and shipping arrangements.

A ribbon of blue sky stretched above the Avon Gorge as they made their way out to sea and a prevailing westerly blew up the Bristol Channel.

By the time they'd left the mouth of the river, a bank of cloud was covering the blue and the wind was piling the sea into white-capped waves. The tide was running in the opposite direction to the wind, so the sails were hauled in, the two funnels chuffing up huge clouds of steam.

Nelson leaned over the rail, his nostrils dilating as he sniffed in the salty air and eyed the sleek-backed gulls wheeling and diving above the moving ship. He'd travelled across the Atlantic many times and had never got sick. His head was unusually clear and he was as excited as a schoolboy on a special adventure. When he got to Barbados he'd have Rivermead House to himself. The estate manager had written to say that Otis's in-laws had committed Emily to an asylum for her own safety. He'd already decided to have a house full of nubile servants to wait on his every need. The cane fields would be left to the manager. Nelson was not interested in growing sugar, only in spending the money it generated.

Going to sea was not a first-time event for Stoke, but he only did it when it was really necessary. He'd been offered a big contract to supply the army at Taunton Barracks with pork products and the best place to buy pigs was Ireland, the market at Queenstown in particular. Normally he would have left the negotiations to Sean Casey, a man he employed to run that side of his business, but Sean was sick and getting sicker. He'd caught syphilis from a woman who called herself an actress. It was rumoured that the only performance she'd ever given was to a whole battalion of dragoon guards at the barracks in Old Market. It was too short notice to send anyone else, so Stoke had to go himself.

Much to Nelson's great delight, Stoke was puking over the side rail before they'd left the Bristol Channel.

Nelson sidled up alongside him against the rail. 'Bring it up, man. The gulls won't waste it,' he cried, and fetched Stoke a hefty slap on the back.

Unfortunately, the ship rolled at the same time as Nelson delivered the blow. Stoke was winded and not at all amused. He spun round on Nelson, pure venom plastered all over his face along with a dribble of sick at the side of his mouth.

'Have a care, Nelson Strong. You're like that bastard cousin of yours that should have hung by the neck a while back, except that your weakness is opium whereas his is the coloured wife of a German – foreigners both, bastards all!'

Nelson was furious. Grabbing the man's coat lapels, he thrust his own haggard face into that of Stoke. He didn't know where his strength came from, but he knew he had the courage to use it. Cuthbert, or Stoke as he used to be called, had done the Strongs much harm.

'How dare you insult my family! How dare you insult Mrs Heinkel and her husband!' He tightened his grip, glad to see the man's face turning slightly purple.

Stoke scowled. 'When I get back to Bristol, everyone shall know that the Strong family has an incestuous secret involving a coloured girl, her half-brother and a deceased knight of the realm. See how that does it for the Strong family reputation. I'll destroy you! I'll destroy you all!'

'I'll kill you!' Nelson's hands closed tightly around Stoke's neck. His shout brought the first mate and a crewmember running along the deck.

Brawny arms and calloused hands dragged them apart. 'Come, come, gentlemen,' shouted the first mate as he and the other man held them back from each other.

'I'll see you before I disembark, Nelson Strong.'

'Be sure that you do,' Nelson responded.

They returned to their cabins accompanied by a merchant seaman instructed to keep an eye on them both.

Down in his cabin, Stoke gloated over what he knew and decided that at some time in the future, he would destroy Tom Strong by different means. He'd get to his heart if he hurt Blanche Heinkel. Yes, he decided, that's what I'll do.

Nelson lay on his berth, nursing his anger like a wounded puppy. He could not forget what the man had said and instinctively knew that he'd use it against his family. That night he barely contained the anger he felt on seeing Stoke sitting opposite him at the dining table. The only time he didn't feel that anger was when he was under the influence of opium, which he smoked through an ebony hookah he'd acquired on the waterfront at Bristol.

Slowly but surely, he drifted into a continuous state of dreamlike absurdity where he took revenge on all those who had ever upset him. Top of the list was his father who had passed him over with regard to inheriting the Strong fortune in favour of his sister.

Being passed over in favour of a younger brother was bad enough, but a sister? A woman?

Then there was Blanche. Why hadn't he been told that she might be his sister? The boy would never have been born – or would he? What did he look like?

The face he'd seen superimposed on that of the boy drifted away on a sea of opium, and when he dreamed it was of Stoke. His grin was as wide as that of a snake, toothless because his teeth were so small and hidden by the hairs around his mouth. The closer they got to Ireland, the more he wanted to stamp on his head, to send him curling and writhing into the sea.

The Irish Sea had a terrible reputation and showed its temper on a regular basis. Clouds swirled low, merging like molten metal into the heaving sea and the wind turned fierce. The ship should have got to Queenstown in two, three days at the most. The weather, the winds and the tide all contrived to hold them back. A boiler broke down so they were forced to fall back on the sails.

Nelson shivered as the icy wind tore at his hair and sprayed icy water over his face. On spotting Captain Walker, he raised a hand in greeting. Walker barely acknowledged him. He was too busy overseeing the safety of his ship, staggering from port to starboard, his thick legs braced.

Wave upon wave tossed the ship's prow skywards so at times it felt as if they were flying. Sliding into the following trough was like diving into the blackness of hell, stomach churning at the prospect of not rising up again.

As the ship yawed for the twentieth time, Nelson grabbed a rope and held onto a rail. Once the wave had crashed on the deck and they had again tilted skywards, Nelson saw Stoke staggering up onto the deck, having no doubt discovered that to stay below was worse on the stomach. Stoke lunged to the ship's side, hung his head over and retched.

A wave drenched him, and for a moment he was hidden from sight. The ship twisted as her master tried to stay slightly off the wind. Nelson balked at the possibilities of what could go wrong; if the wind and a wave caught her beam on at the same time, the ship would roll. Full to the Plimsoll Line with a shallow keel and heavy rigged masts, she wasn't likely to right herself.

And Stoke would be gone, he thought. The fact that he would be gone too didn't worry him. He hadn't made the best of his life. He hadn't always been a good man. Perhaps his own child might do better being brought up by his wife's family rather than inherit the less than respectable past of the Strong family.

His own past weighed heavily on his mind, though he was not so selfish as to want the crew to die. They all had wives and families of their own, no doubt. He watched them struggling to reef down the heavy canvas sails, their bare feet slipping on wet spars and blood seeping from recent rope burns.

Gritting his teeth, he eased forward, his eyes fixed on Stoke, the hate coiled up inside him like a clock spring, tighter and tighter, tensed beyond breaking point.

Uncaring that the wind stung his face and the sea dripped from tendrils of hair that clung to his cheeks, he crossed the deck and, progressing slowly, hand over hand, he made for Stoke.

The sea, the wind and the heaving ship no longer mattered. The hatred he felt for this man, coupled with his own guilt, made him more determined than he'd ever been in his life. This man had to be stopped, not because he would squeeze him for every penny he had, but because he must not be allowed to ruin the lives of the people he loved. Max must never know who his real father was; that was *his* shame, *his* guilt. And Blanche deserved to be happy.

The fault, he'd decided, was his, and it was up to him to do something about it. Stoke was the man who sought to gain from it.

Screaming through the sails, the wind hid all sound of his approach. Stoke suspected nothing. The ship's rail was high, and although Stoke's torso was half over Nelson knew that his destruction was dependent on lifting the man off his legs.

Bracing his legs, he timed his moment, lunging on Stoke at the same time as the ship dived into yet another trough. Soaked in spray, hidden by an avalanche of sea, Nelson found strength he never knew he had. Wrapping his arms around him, he heaved him off his feet, up onto the rail and left the surge of the waves to provide the momentum.

Soaked to the skin, Captain Walker chose to turn round just as the wave hit the starboard quarter. At first he saw two figures struggling amongst a green wall of sea.

Once the ship had righted itself and the wave had drained from the deck, there was nothing. Both men had gone.

Chapter Thirty

Before dinner, Tom escaped into the garden where the wet scent of September helped clear his mind. He'd always liked the garden at Marstone Court. He went to his favourite seat at the end of the rose-covered promenade, hidden by red-berried honeysuckle. Although a little damp, he sat down and lit a cigarillo, a habit he'd taken to one night in Hispaniola when a hurricane was lashing the ships to the shore and there was a fair likelihood of them all being blown to kingdom come.

He heard the rustling of her dress and smelled Horatia's presence before he actually saw her. Unlike the half-naked women of the tropics, she had that musty, slightly sweaty smell, due of course to her tight bodice and voluminous skirt. Once a week it was sprayed beneath the arms with rose water, but was seldom laundered. Poor laundresses, he thought. What a job they had.

She smiled down at him, though looked a little drawn. The news of Nelson's death had come as a shock. Rupert would go to Barbados in Nelson's place and was glad to do so.

Tom moved sideways so she'd have room to sit. Close to, she smelled of violets, dabbed around her neck and enough to override the smell of her dress.

She sat very close; as if that would bridge the gap that had sprung up between them following her admission that she'd known he was proved innocent of murder before they'd married. He kept his eyes fixed on a large cabbage rose whose golden petals were falling to earth one by one. He heard her sigh as she took a deep breath.

'Have you decided what to do?' she asked.

He carried on smoking and stared straight ahead.

Horatia tried again. 'I mean, about the ships. Are you going to run them from here?'

'I think so.'

He was aware of her body relaxing and heard her sigh of relief.

'But I'm not sure whether I will be here.'

He heard her intake of breath. 'But who will run the shipping line?'

'You will.'

'What will you do? Where will you go?'

He shrugged. 'Wherever fate takes me.'

Her relief turned to anger. 'You can't do that. You can't leave. It's desertion!'

He looked at her. Her lips were pink, her flesh was white and her eyes were blue enough to drown in. She was a piece of best quality Dresden, chillingly white and wonderful to look at, but hollow inside.

'I don't care what it is. There are some trips I need to make in order to win cargoes. I shall concentrate on them while I think things through.'

'But you can hire an agent to do that,' Horatia protested.

'I could, but I won't.'

'Tom, you have to believe me when I say I didn't know that Duncan was going to do what he did, if he did it, but it may just have easily been an accident. The ropes were...'

'Have they found him yet?'

Unwilling to chance his luck, Duncan had run away, presumably to sea though no one could be sure. An under footman returning from an assignation with a housemaid, had seen him leave the room. He was the last man to enter the room that night before the maid entered in the morning. The police had asked a few questions. Duncan had bluffed it out but had gone by the next morning.

'Not that I am aware.'

'Are you sure?'

'Of course I am! Don't you trust me?'

He looked at her again. 'Can you blame me? You're my wife. I must accept that, but trust? I can never trust you again, Horatia, certainly not if my life depended on it.'

'Tom, I knew it couldn't be you that killed Reuben Trout. The man hired his brutality to anyone who would pay.'

'Including you?'

She flustered. 'I was looking after our interests.'

'The Strong family, you mean?'

'And yours, Tom.' She tried to touch his hand, but he pulled away.

He blew a circle of smoke. 'I never wanted to come back here,' he said, eyeing the birds flocking overhead prior to flying off to warmer climes.

'But surely it was worthwhile,' said Horatia.

He didn't need to look at her to know she had an intense expression on her face and was desperate for him to reply that yes, it had been worthwhile.

'I was trapped.'

'You were only in prison for a while.'

He looked at her. She paled, half expecting what he was about to say. 'I didn't mean Bristol Gaol. I mean you and your father dangling the prospect of a shipping line in front of me, and steamships at that. My own fault too, I suppose. I blame my own ambition and willingness to rise to a challenge. But the damage is done. You're my wife in name, but don't expect it to be so in practice.'

Horatia gasped. 'What do you mean?'

'You know what I mean. Your behaviour leaves me cold.'

'But if we don't have children, if we don't have sons...' Her breasts rose more quickly in time with her breathing.

'I know. The money goes...' He paused. 'Elsewhere.'

'You could try,' she said.

He knew it embarrassed her to speak of the lack of intimacies between them. Every night was the same; she lay in bed waiting for him to pull her into his arms. Only when the urging of his loins and the vision of Blanche became too much to bear did he finally surrender, though without preliminary caresses and kisses.

'I want a child,' Horatia blurted. 'We have to have a child.'

Tom shook his head.

Horatia sat bolt upright, hands clasped in her lap and gazed straight ahead. 'I have consulted a solicitor. As Max is Nelson's son, he is entitled to inherit and I'm not afraid to make it public. There! Is that enough to persuade you?'

The implication was clear and a cold hand seemed to squeeze Tom's heart. He studied her chiselled features, as perfect and cold as marble.

'You were sworn to secrecy. You cannot make it public that Max is Nelson's son. Blanche would be devastated, and the boy's life would be affected for ever. Even when he becomes a man, the finger of public morality would be pointed in his direction.'

'I don't care about that. I want you to love me – properly. I'm not like one of the trollops you knew so well from St Augustine's Quay.' Years ago he would have slapped her face, but the years had tempered his reactions. He thought of the years ahead, married to a woman he'd once respected but did not love. He'd thought their marriage would be tolerable, not infused with the passion he felt for Blanche, but happy enough. But Horatia had fallen back to type and would have dragged him off to Barbados. He would not have known he was innocent until they got there or perhaps not at all. He knew her well enough to think she would have held the threat of hanging over him for ever. Horatia liked being in control.

The only thing he could do was go back to sea. He'd made up his mind but was not going to tell her, not until he'd made final arrangements at least. The *Demerara Queen* was getting ready to depart under the captaincy of Jim Storm Cloud. He would go with it and not tell her. But first, he had to see Blanche. He had to see her one last time and warn her.

–

Horatia watched the sun glowing in the west. She'd wiped the tears from her eyes, and the evening air cooled her cheeks.

The sky was clear, and a plume of smoke from a bonfire was curling up from the direction of the kitchen garden where some pieces from her father's collection of Egyptian antiquities were being burned. No one could stand entering her father's personal retreat as it was. Soon she would have it decorated in a modern style with richly coloured wallpaper and heavy drapes of green brocade and furniture with turned legs and sprung cushions.

Two servants were manhandling the wooden carving that Tom had rescued from a dockside inn and were heading towards the smoke. At first, Horatia raised her hand, meaning to tell them that the carving belonged to her husband and shouldn't be burned, but she changed her mind. She was his wife but he wasn't treating her as such, not in bed where it truly mattered. All the perceived hurts she'd suffered at his hands came back to haunt her and made her clench her teeth so hard that her jaw ached. Well, let them take his precious carving and burn it to cinders. It would serve him right.

Wood smoke had a delicious smell, one she'd always appreciated, but the thought that the smell might be coming from something Tom loved, suddenly made her change her mind again. She called for the men not to burn it, but they didn't hear her.

The grass was damp under foot, and even though she kept to the path, the hem of her dress became sodden with dew.

There was a doorway set in the wall surrounding the kitchen garden. Horatia went through. The bonfire was directly ahead of her, but there was no sign of the Indian or the two men who'd been carrying the carving.

She called out. At first there was nothing except the call of nightjars, and the hoot of an owl from across the meadow.

She stepped further towards the fire, aware that shadows were getting longer and that soon the sun would set and the garden and the world would be in darkness. Horatia stared at the fire, the sparks rising from the crackling wood like burning butterflies. Just when she least expected it, the shadows lengthened and stepped out from the woods.

Startled, Horatia's hand flew to her throat.

'Sorry to frighten you, ma'am,' said one of the gardeners, his hat immediately snatched from his head. 'We're just burning up the rubbish – as ordered.'

'The wooden statue – where is it?'

The two men looked at the bonfire, then at each other, until one of them said, 'Well, it were there a couple of minutes ago.'

'Well, where is it now?'

They both shrugged and exchanged puzzled looks.

Horatia sighed impatiently. 'So what did it do? Walk off by itself?'

One of the gardeners shifted from one foot to the other. 'Maybe it's off with the fairies, it being such a heathen thing an' that.'

The man wished he were mouse-high as Horatia glared at him in utter disbelief.

'Fairies indeed,' she exclaimed, stamped her foot and stalked off.

—

Autumn leaves rattled as they blew against the front door of Little Paradise.

'I'm going to sweep them away once and for all,' Edith muttered, putting the darning to one side and reaching for her broom.

On opening the door, she came face to face with Jim Storm Cloud, or at least with his chest. The doorway was low and he had to duck to come in.

'What are you doing here?' she asked, as he stood, the top of his head brushing the ceiling.

'I am going away. I am ship's captain now.'

Edith's face dropped. 'Oh!'

'But I will be back.'

Edith made a face. 'Now where have I heard that one before?'

Jim looked hurt. 'I am not like your husband. I will be back when I say I will be back, and I will not go to tavern first.'

'Oh,' Edith said again, more lightly this time.

'And I have brought you a present.'

Things were definitely improving, thought Edith. The tall American, who was at least twice the size of the late Deke Beasley, led her back outside, though this time he forgot to duck and banged his head.

After making suitably sympathetic noises, Edith found herself face to face with a Red Indian effigy that had more than a fleeting similarity to the flesh and blood example standing next to her, except that it looked as if it were female.

'Oh!' she said, unable to think of a single world to say, or at least one that conveyed appreciation she didn't really feel. What in the world would she do with it?

Sensing her confusion, Jim came up with the answer.

'I brought her here to remind you of me when I am away.' He pointed at the blackened backside where the wood had started to burn. 'She had been badly treated. She needs a good home. Will you look after her for me?'

Edith sighed happily. 'Of course I will, and like you say, she'll remind me of you.'

Jim beamed. 'Good.'

Memories of Deke Beasley were hard to shift. Although Jim had told her he would be returning, the old doubt returned. She couldn't help wanting to make sure.

'Are you sure you're coming back?' she asked, and immediately found herself assessing how many logs the wooden effigy would make if she ran short of fuel during the winter.

Jim's big hands grasped her shoulders and took her breath away.

'I have told you I will be back, and I mean it.' He nodded at the wooden statue. 'We have nowhere else to go, so we both belong here. What do you think?'

Edith smiled. 'I suppose we do.'

–

Sweeping inland from the Atlantic, the prevailing westerly funnelled into the close confines of the Avon Gorge, then spilled upwards around the brick towers of a new bridge designed by Mr Brunel.

The towers were presently lying abandoned, the instigators of the project having run out of money.

Following the departure of the construction gangs, Clifton Down had reacquired its rural character, sheep grazing amid the long grass and wispy strands of 'grandfather's beard' flying on the wind along with the last of the dandelion clocks.

'Not too close to the edge, Max,' Blanche shouted, her anxious gaze following her eldest son as he ran backwards. Like her younger children, his head was thrown back, his attention fixed on the paper kite that whirled and dived above their heads.

'Be careful,' she shouted again, one hand pressed on her bonnet, which seemed in danger of joining the kite.

The brisk breeze caught at her skirt and sent strands of hair flying across her face. The kite soared high on the breeze, then suddenly dived into a windless pocket, tumbled through the air and tangled in the branches of a tree. His hat thrown to one side and his blond hair flying, Max ran towards the tree, half of which hung over the cliff edge, its roots pulled from the ground.

'Max! No!'

Anxious to get to him, but blinded by the breeze, Blanche caught her foot in tangled grass and fell to the ground, her skirt billowing in the air.

There were other people enjoying the last of the fine weather on Clifton Down. It was only to be expected that someone would offer to help her up.

Flustered and winded, she took the hand that was offered her.

'Are you all right?' he asked.

She was too surprised to say anything. The last person she'd expected to see was Tom.

'I thought you were in Barbados with your new bride?'

'Well, I'm not. Don't worry,' he said with a swift smile. 'I'll get it down.'

Before she had a chance to thank him, he'd bounded off. Like a boy, she thought, and it made her feel warm.

The children stood aside as he said something to them before climbing the tree. She remembered the children at Marstone

Court being as attentive to Tom when she'd first come to England. There'd always been something different about him, his presence enhanced by the tales he told of sea monsters, distant lands and exciting adventures.

Used to climbing masts, Tom scrambled up onto the lower branches, pulling himself up by his arms and pushing up with his legs. He made short work of it, retrieving the kite far more quickly than Max would have done.

The kite was flying again by the time Tom got back to Blanche, who was still brushing grass seeds and sticky brown burrs from her dress.

'They almost match,' he said with amusement as he plucked a single burr from the chocolate-coloured dress she was wearing. 'Like movable spots.'

She laughed lightly, almost as if they were strangers, and avoided returning his gaze. Instead she kept her attention fixed on her children. They were the only barrier she had between Tom, passion and ruin.

'How did you know I was here?' she asked.

'I went to Little Paradise. Edith told me you were up here.'

Blanche laughed. The lovely sound drew him to look at her.

'Edith knows me well, too well I think sometimes,' she said.

'She's like a sister to you.'

'She makes me laugh, even though at times she's quite outrageous.'

Tom smiled. 'Nelson was like that.'

'Yes. I suppose he was.'

They both fell to silence as they considered his passing. Blanche spoke first.

'I take it they have not found his body.'

'No. Thank you for coming to the memorial service.'

'It was the least I could do.'

She paused as one of her daughters tumbled into the grass, then got up, brushed herself off and waved to her mother to confirm she was all right.

'Horatia wants a child,' Tom said.

The suddenness of the statement took her by surprise. A strand of dark hair blew across her face as she looked at him – then wished she hadn't. One look into those clear, blue eyes, and she wanted to fall in to his arms. She brushed the thought away, but not too far because she liked the way it made her feel.

'Isn't that a matter you should be discussing with her, not me?'

Tom took a deep breath. 'She wants your child.'

Blanche was taken aback. 'Max? I was afraid she might now that Nelson is gone. She probably feels that he should inherit Nelson's wealth, and will disclose my... indiscretion with Nelson should I refuse. Is that her intention?'

Tom frowned. 'You do not seem overly concerned.'

Blanche felt her face reddening.

He touched her hand. 'You're blushing. I didn't mean to embarrass you by resurrecting the implications of your son's birth.'

She shook her head. 'You're not embarrassing me because of what you *believe* to be the truth. I'm blushing because it seems I have to tell you the real truth. I'd hoped to avoid it, for Conrad's sake as much as for Max.'

Tom looked at the people promenading, riding, and playing amongst the rich grass of Clifton Down. He wasn't quite sure of what he was about to hear, but intuitively, he knew it had something to do with him.

Blanche waited until a couple mounted on matching dapple-greys sauntered past, the dark green of the woman's riding habit like a jewel against the gold and grey-green of the grass.

'I gave birth to Max six months after Conrad married me. Do you understand what I'm saying, Tom?'

At first a mix of conflicting emotions crossed his face. In a way it amused her. Men were not entirely aware of the cycles of women, the map of their being.

'It takes nine months from conception to birth, Tom. Conrad and I married straight after you left, a mere week or so after leaving Marstone Court following my... lying with Nelson in the woods near the church. But I was already carrying, Tom.'

She had no choice but to look into his face then. This was such an important confession. She had to know how he felt about it. She saw him swallow. He couldn't take his eyes off her as the truth dawned and he became as wise as she.

Much to her surprise, he shook his head. 'If what you are saying is true, why is it that Max looks so much like Nelson?'

Blanche looked at him intently. 'Why shouldn't he? My father was Sir Emmanuel Strong. I'm Nelson and Horatia's sister. Why shouldn't he look like a Strong?'

Tom didn't protest. But it wasn't every day that a man acquires a son he didn't know he had.

There was just one question that needed answering; Blanche could see it there in his eyes and decided to explain before he could ask.

'Conrad could cope with adopting a child who would be much disadvantaged if the truth got out, but he couldn't possibly cope with Max being yours. Despite his kindly and sometimes sanctimonious exterior, Conrad is a jealous man. I thought it better for all concerned that he never knew the truth. I told him the child had been born prematurely. Being a man he accepted that.'

Tom found it hard to drag his eyes away from the strong-limbed boy who bolted ahead of his sisters dragging the kite behind him. It was Blanche who reminded him that the daylight was dying and it was time to go.

Before she left, she touched his arm. Her eyes glistened. 'Marriages are not always made in heaven, Tom. Horatia loves you. Give her what she asks. Make the most of what you've got.'

'Just as you do with Conrad?' There was a bitter edge to his voice that he immediately regretted. 'I'm sorry. I didn't mean to say that.'

'Yes, you did. It was the truth. You always spoke the truth.'

He lifted one eyebrow in the familiar way as he smiled. 'So compromise is the truth to a happy marriage.'

She nodded. 'Compromise and be happy... well... as happy as you can be.' She squeezed his arm. 'I wish I could kiss you,' she said softly, 'but the children might see me.'

'Then do it anyway.'

A loud cheer went up as the kite soared into a cloudless sky that was crisp with the promise of frost. The children ran after it, Blanche and Tom totally forgotten.

He knew before turning round that she was looking at him. A moment, and the warmth of her lips were on his. The world, the present and the past all faded beyond his closed eyes. This was bliss, a moment to savour for ever.

Afterwards, he watched her from a distance and wondered what to do next. Everything had seemed cut and dried before she'd told him the truth about Max. The *Demerara Queen* was ready to sail, but leaving Bristol was no longer an option. Max being his son had changed all that. He had to stay, at least to keep Horatia from upsetting the delicate lie that Blanche had woven around her son. Like her he would compromise and do his best to be happy. He wasn't sure he'd be good at living with Horatia, but he had a lifetime to try. Practice makes perfect, he thought and smiled at the fact that neither he nor Horatia were perfect. Perhaps their imperfection would be their strength.

Also by Erica Brown

The Strong Family Trilogy

Daughter of Destiny
The Sugar Merchant's Wife
Return to Paradise